A gem of an island almost undiscovered by tourists, with brilliant white sand beaches and bluegreen lagoons complemented by the friendliness of the people.

People, Annette found, did not want any hint of danger in the kind of articles it was her business to write. Even the ones who would never go to the places she described, who could not afford it, did not want to hear about danger or even unpleasantness; it was as if they wanted to believe that there was somewhere left in the world where all was well, where unpleasant things did not happen. An unspoiled Eden; that had been a useful phrase. Once, staying home meant safety, though tedium as well, and going to the places that were her specialty—the Caribbean, the northern half of South America, Mexico—meant adventure, threat, pirates, brigands, lawlessness. Now it was the reverse, home was the dangerous place and people went on vacation to snatch a few weeks of uneventfulness.

—from Margaret Atwood's *A Travel Piece*

Bantam-Seal Books edited by John Stevens

BEST CANADIAN SHORT STORIES
MODERN CANADIAN STORIES

Best
Canadian Short Stories

Edited by John Stevens

SEAL BOOKS
McClelland-Bantam, Inc.
Toronto

BEST CANADIAN SHORT STORIES

A Seal Book / October 1981

5 printings through August 1989

Cover photograph courtesy of Photo Media

All Rights Reserved.
Copyright © 1981 by Bantam Books.

"The Murderer" by Yvette Naubert from *Tales of Solitude*. Originally published in French by Le Cercle du livre de France under the title *Contes de la Solitude*. Translation copyright © 1978 by Margaret Rose.

"Some of His Best Friends" from *Only the Gods Speak* by Harold Horwood; copyright © 1979 by Harold Horwood. Reprinted by permission of Breakwater Books.

"The Iron Men" from *The Snow Walker* by Farley Mowat. Reprinted by permission of The Canadian Publishers, McClelland and Stewart Limited, Toronto.

"A Field of Wheat" from *The Lamp at Noon and Other Stories* by Sinclair Ross. Reprinted by permission of The Canadian Publishers, McClelland and Stewart Limited, Toronto.

"Penny in the Dust" from *The Rebellion of Young David* by Ernest Buckler. Reprinted by permission of The Canadian Publishers, McClelland and Stewart Limited, Toronto.

"Benny" from *The Street* by Mordecai Richler. Reprinted by permission of The Canadian Publishers, McClelland and Stewart Limited, Toronto.

"Gingerbread Boy" by Phyllis Gotlieb. Reprinted by permission of Phyllis Gotlieb and Virginia Kidd.

"The Dead Child" from *Enchanted Summer* by Gabrielle Roy. Reprinted by permission of The Canadian Publishers, McClelland and Stewart Limited, Toronto.

"The Lost Salt Gift of Blood" from *The Lost Salt Gift of Blood* by Alistair McLeod. Reprinted by permission of The Canadian Publishers, McClelland and Stewart Limited, Toronto.

"The Sorcerer" from *The Hockey Sweater and Other Stories* by Roch Carrier. Reprinted by permission of House of Anansi Press Limited, Toronto.

"The End of the World" by Mavis Gallant; copyright © 1967 by Mavis Gallant. By permission of Georges Borchardt, Inc.

"The Grecian Urn" from *Shoeless Joe Jackson Comes to Iowa* by W.P. Kinsella. By permission of Oberon Press.

"Bloodflowers" from *Bloodflowers* by W.D. Valgardson. By permission of Oberon Press.

"The Loons" from *A Bird in the House* by Margaret Laurence. Reprinted by permission of The Canadian Publishers, McClelland and Stewart Limited, Toronto.

"Travel Piece" from *Dancing Girls* by Margaret Atwood. Reprinted by permission of The Canadian Publishers, McClelland and Stewart Limited, Toronto.

ISBN 0-7704-2174-1

Seal Books are published by McClelland-Bantam, Inc. Its trademark, consisting of the words "Seal Books" and the portrayal of a seal, is the property of McClelland-Bantam, Inc., 105 Bond Street, Toronto, Ontario M5B 1Y3, Canada. This trademark has been duly registered in the Trademark Office of Canada. The trademark consisting of the words "Bantam Books" and the portrayal of a rooster is the property of and is used with the consent of Bantam Books, 666 Fifth Avenue, New York, New York 10103. This trademark has been duly registered in the Trademark Office of Canada and elsewhere.

PRINTED IN CANADA

U   13 12 11 10 9 8 7 6 5

CONTENTS

The Trouble with Families . . .

Magic, Symbols and Fantasies

INTRODUCTION

Before reading *Best Canadian Short Stories* you may find it helpful to glance through these introductory remarks. "The" has been left out of the title deliberately, since the twenty-six selections in this book are not, definitively, *the* best Canadian stories ever written. However, they are certainly among the best such stories published between the 1850s and 1980s. Most of them date from after 1930 because, proportionately, few really good stories were written in Canada before that time. By 1930 Mazo de la Roche and Morley Callaghan had made reputations in Canada and beyond its borders, but except for a few other writers like Charles G. D. Roberts, Stephen Leacock and Duncan Campbell Scott, they stood out in lonely eminence. Fortunately for readers, the next fifty years saw the ranks of Canadian writers augmented by such first-rate storytellers as those included in the pages that follow this preface. Some, like Sinclair Ross and Ernest Buckler, have been admired almost as long as Callaghan. Others, like Mavis Gallant and Alice Munro, whose stories first appeared in the 1950s and 60s, form a sort of middle generation. Both Gallant and Munro now have a readership abroad that extends from Europe to Australia, and in North America are frequent contributors to magazines like *The New Yorker, The Atlantic Monthly* and *Saturday Night*. Many other names in this anthology have also gained international recognition. More recent arrivals on the writing scene, Margaret Atwood, Alistair McLeod and W. D. Valgardson, have all had work chosen for publication in the annual *Best American Short Stories*.

Obviously Canadian short fiction of the last half century, as it is represented in *Best Canadian Short Stories*, qualifies as world class, but even the four stories culled from the relatively barren ground of the period before 1930 command the reader's attention with their narrative energy and the light they cast on the strange workings of the human mind. "Labrie's Wife" is a masterly depiction of a Scottish fur trader's failure to recognize the havoc he is causing in the heart of a French woman much his superior in passion and intelligence; "The Mariposa Bank Mystery" still dazzles with its flamboyant and loving mockery of small-town pretensions at the turn of the century; the development of suspense in a nightmare wilderness in "The Cabin Door" holds readers in its grip as successfully as when it was first published; and the tersely realistic treatment of a crude 1850s marriage custom in "The Charivari" is proof that not all writing of that early period in our literature was floridly sentimental.

The earliest of the four stories, "The Charivari," was not written as a separate piece. It is part of a chapter in Susanna Moodie's autobiographical tale of life in Ontario, *Roughing It in the Bush*. It is not, of course, unusual for such stories to be read independently of the larger works to which they belong and, as a self-contained narrative embedded in a longer work to which it is related by plot or theme, the short story has been around for two thousand years and more.

The short story can be found in books as diverse as the Holy Bible and the unholy *Satyricon*, a Roman novel written during the reign of Nero. From those respective works, I am going to discuss two ancient tales, "Joseph and His Brothers" and "The Matron of Ephesus," because they can help us read all the stories in the present collection with greater insight.

These two stories present opposing views of human nature, thus providing opposite magnetic poles to orient us in narrative's moral range. For undeniably, any story with genuine imaginative power contains a strong moral element. That is, its writer tells the reader, indirectly through his events and characters, "Whether you like it or not, the brief repast I set before you here is flavored with an essential truth concerning man." In "The Charivari" that flavor is tart, the view of humanity unflattering, but in "The Matron of Ephesus," also a story about marriage, the taste is utterly acid, the view of humanity sardonic. Here is a summary to illustrate the point.

A married woman of Ephesus is so renowned for her virtue that people travel from neighboring lands to gaze on her. When her husband dies suddenly, she follows his body into the tomb, vowing to stay there until she starves to death. For five days she remains in the tomb, loudly lamenting. About this time several thieves are crucified next to the tomb and a soldier is stationed to guard the bodies from relatives who might take them down for burial. As he is eating his supper one night, the young soldier hears the sound of the woman's mourning from the adjacent sepulchre. He enters and, struck by the woman's beauty, urges her to share his food and wine. Gradually she submits to his allurements, and after the repast makes love with him in the presence of her husband's corpse. While they are enjoying life, the parents of one of the thieves steal their son's body off the cross for burial. In the morning the soldier discovers the loss and determines to forestall punishment by falling on his sword; but the woman cries, "I would rather see a dead man hung up than a live one struck down," and to conceal her lover's dereliction of duty she helps him nail her husband's body to the cross.

The tale, told by a degenerate poet and greeted by guffaws from his audience, proclaims a world devoid of moral order, a tragically absurd world in which all of man's protestations and desperate efforts to endow his life with significance have no meaning beyond the satisfaction of the moment. And even that flicker of pleasure is usually followed by some disastrous consequence.

Few of the stories arranged in the various thematic groupings of this book create worlds as bleak as the extreme represented by the cynicism of "The Matron of Ephesus," although the five in the section entitled "Men and Women: Tragic and Ironic Views" all tend in that direction. Perhaps closest in ironic chill is Alice Munro's "The Beggar Maid," followed by Mazo de la Roche's "Quartet." Both stories concern marriages that began as apparent love matches but culminate in revelations of hatred. Glimpsing her former husband briefly in an airport, Munro's protagonist half expects to see his face take on the habitual expression that used to preface their reconciliations. Instead, she sees him make a savagely hateful grimace "—infantile, self-indulgent yet calculated; it was like an explosion of disgust and loathing." In "Quartet" an aggrieved wife tells her former sweetheart of her elegant husband's vices ("He's sly and he can be violent") as the despised husband, an Italian who speaks no English, looks on uncomprehendingly.

Of all the stories in this collection that cast human existence into a pessimistic and ironic perspective, "The Charivari" is probably the mildest: although settlers in upper Canada abuse marriage

with their mischievous charivaris, married love itself is still considered to be part of a grand moral design. The garrulous neighbour whom Mrs. Moodie uses as narrator even ends on an upbeat
note, exclaiming, "I assure you Mrs. M—, that the charivari
often deters old people from making disgraceful marriages, so
that it is not wholly without its use." But the scenes of murder-
ous violence that she has recited earlier invite us to realize that
her crude approval floats just above the author's undertow of
irony, a current that moves the story more than halfway toward
the tragic-ironic world of "The Matron of Ephesus."

Morley Callaghan's "The Snob" is another teaser in which
gall is mingled with honey so that the story leaves a bittersweet
aftertaste. The main character, an impoverished student, quarrels
with his upper-class girlfriend because he is embarrassed when
he unexpectedly comes across his working-class father in a local
bookstore. The youth manages to regain the girl's affection, but
only after slighting his father, whose quiet dignity suffuses the
climax and dénouement of the story. Although Callaghan permits
us to see the father only through the eyes of the student, it is the
older man's deep hurt that haunts both the protagonist and the
reader at the end of the story. ". . . yet he kept thinking, as he
would ever think, of his father walking away quietly with his
head never turning." The reader yearns to add a scene of forgiveness and reconciliation, but there is little evidence in the
story to support that hope.

In the section "Violent Encounters," you will find the story
whose perspective is closest of all to the nihilistic world of "The
Matron of Ephesus." Yvette Naubert's young French-Canadian
police lieutenant, the central character of "The Murderer," lives
in a nightmare city where meaningless crises are terminated by
pointless deaths. After what looks like his accidental killing of a
bystander in a bank-robbery shootout, the policeman gradually
becomes convinced that he committed the act intentionally. Even
intimate moments with his fiancée are tainted by his obsession
until finally their lovemaking is akin to the incident in the tomb
at Ephesus: "She too had become a different person to Gilbert.
Her soft skin took on a greenish hue, like decomposing flesh."
This study of neurotic violence with its bizarre conclusion evokes
an urban world that is weirdly surreal, yet disturbingly familiar
to us.

The other ancient narrative that I shall ask you to keep in mind
as an archteype when you read the stories in this anthology is

"Joseph and His Brothers," for it presents a positive contrast to the vision of life found in *Satyricon*'s "The Matron of Ephesus." Young Joseph, favorite son of the Hebrew patriarch, Jacob, is so envied by his half-brothers that they conspire to sell him into slavery. Some foreign merchants journeying through Canaan take Joseph from a pit into which his brothers have thrown him and transport him to Egypt, where he is sold to one of Pharaoh's officers. After many ordeals, Joseph's God-given ability to interpret dreams and his shrewd intelligence enable him to rise to the position of Pharaoh's trusted viceroy. Years later, during a period of persistent drought, his brothers travel from Canaan to Egypt to beg the viceroy to sell them supplies from Egypt's ample granaries. His brothers fail to recognize him when Joseph faces the supplicants. He toys with them awhile, but finally, in a scene of great emotion, reveals his kinship. Joseph then embraces his brothers in forgiveness and brings them under the shelter of his great power.

"Joseph and His Brothers" has become familiar to readers of the literature of the western world as an archetype of the theme of love triumphant over wrongdoing. Its conclusion proclaims that the moral world is essentially just and is regulated by the hand of Providence. Despite its sombre events, "Joseph and His Brothers" is both a romance and a comedy. It is a romance because of the hero's perilous adventures and the striking coincidences that lead to his triumph. And it is a comedy, not because it is filled with humor, but because it ends happily, with reconciliation in a world that is patterned to defeat the wicked and reward the good.

In the section "Magic, Symbols and Fantasies," Roch Carrier's "The Sorcerer" and W. P. Kinsella's "The Grecian Urn" play interesting modern variations on this theme. Carrier's black sorcerer is a tattered version of Joseph whom Carrier's narrator accosts one day in Montreal, years after the occasion when he and other Quebec villagers had cast the black man into a pit of humiliation with their mockery. This twentieth-century viceroy presides over ample granaries of clairvoyance and when his erstwhile oppressor pleads, "Monsieur! Monsieur! . . . Will you read my hand?" the sorcerer replies, after a moment of absorbed silence, "I can read that there's something you're sorry about." Does his enigmatic statement convey forgiveness, or is it a vengeful attempt to square accounts for the wrong suffered long ago? To answer the question the reader must scan Carrier's sparsely planted signposts.

"The Grecian Urn" is richer in detail but also requires reflection before it yields up its fabular message. This time the special power is not wielded by the Joseph figure in the story but by a character whom the reader is tempted to see in the role of villain. Once again, though, the protagonist has been wronged and once again the perpetrator of that wrong returns to him to appeal for aid. Giving aid this time involves hiding in a museum after hours in order to rescue the wrongdoer from the world pictured on the antique urn that inspired Keats' famous ode. Kinsella's wildly inventive story shows that an astute comment on human values need not be solemn. Exactly what that comment is I am still pondering. I think it has something to do with the magic underlying humdrum daily life and the possibility that even the most ordinary person may break through to it.

A third, more serious variation on the theme is provided by Mavis Gallant's "The End of the World" in the section "The Trouble with Families. . . ." An errant father who, years before the story begins, had delivered his children into the captivity of poverty by abandoning them, is dying in a French hospital. The narrator, one of the abandoned children who is now an adult, travels to France to attend the father in his last days and there achieves a muted forgiveness and reconciliation with him. Despite manifold ironies, the story affirms the essential goodness of life and the rightness of love.

Of course, all five stories in the first section, "Men and Women: Romantic and Comic Views," adhere strongly to the optimism of the archetypal Joseph story, even though their plots bear little or no resemblance to it. In each of them the reader is sure almost from the outset that no matter what pitfalls may threaten to entrap the heroes and heroines, things are going to turn out happily for them in the end. Well, there might be just a little uncertainty about whether the ending of Alden Nowlan's "The Girl Who Went to Mexico" is indeed a happy one. Sam Baxter's amorous letters to a widow in distant Ontario result in her invasion of his New Brunswick farm for face-to-face contact. Since an unwanted marriage seems in the offing, "tragic and ironic" might more aptly describe the fate Sam has brought on himself, were it not for the reader's strong suspicion that this shy man really needs the resolute Amelia whom, as the story ends, he is about to meet.

There are no question marks hovering over the conclusions of the other four stories in this section, least of all in Leacock's "The Mariposa Bank Mystery." Unlike Yvette Naubert's luckless police lieutenant, Leacock's hero is triumphant. He has foiled an attempted bank robbery and is now settled happily ever after with his beloved Zena "in one of the enchanted homes on the hillside in the newer part of town where you may find them today."

But whether they conjure up visions of a savage dark or of the sunlit fields of day like those around Mariposa, the twenty-six writers included here will hold you fast during the time that it takes to read their stories. And some will hold you longer than that. By the way, consider it incidental that they are all Canadian stories. Read them not because they are Canadian, but because they are too good to miss.

John Stevens

Best
Canadian Short Stories

Men and Women:

Romantic and Comic Views

THE CABIN DOOR
by Charles G. D. Roberts

What was known as the County Line Road, though in winter a highway of some importance for the sleds and sleighs of the lumbermen, was in summer little more than a broad, straight trail, with grass and wild flowers growing undisturbed between the ruts. Just now, in the late and sodden northern spring, it was a disheartening stretch of hummocks and bog-holes, the bog-holes emphasized by a leg-breaking array of half rotten poles laid crossways. It was beautiful, however, in its lonesome, pallid, wistful fashion, for its hummocks, where dry enough, were already bluing tenderly with the first violets, its fringes were sparsely adorned with the shy blooms of wind-flower, dog-tooth, and hepatica, and scattered through the dark ranks of the fir trees on either side were little colonies of white birch or silver poplar, just filming with the first ineffable green.

To the slim girl who, bundle in hand and with skirts tucked up half-way to the knee, was picking her steps along this exasperating path, the wildness of the scene—its mingled harshness and delicacy—brought a pang which she could but dimly understand. The pale purpling of the violets, the aerial greening of the birch tops against the misty sky, the solemnity of the dark, massed fir trees—it was all beautiful in her eyes beyond anything words could suggest, but it made her heart ache with something like an intolerable homesickness. This was incomprehensible to her, since she was already, in a sense, at home. This was her native wilderness, this was the kind of chill, ethereal, lonesome spring which thrilled through the memories of her childhood. And she was nearing—she could not now be more than twelve miles from—the actual home of her childhood, that grey cabin on the outskirts of the remote and windswept settlement of Stony Brook.

3

For the past three years—going on for four now, indeed—
Sissy Bembridge had been away from this wild home, working
hard, and saving her wages, in the big shoe factory at K——,
down by the sea. Called home suddenly by word that her mother
was ill, she had come by train to the end of the branch, and tried to
get a rig to take her around by the main road to Stony Brook.
There was no rig to be had for love or money. Too anxious to
wait, and confident in her young vigour, she had left her luggage,
tied up a few necessaries and eatables in a handy bundle, and set
out by the short cut of the old Line Road. Deaf to all dissuasions,
she had counted on making Stony Brook before nightfall. Moreover—though she would never have acknowledged to herself that
such a consideration could count for anything when all her thoughts
were on her mother's illness—she was aware of the fact that
Connor's gang was stream-driving on the Ottanoonsis, and would
be by now just about the point where the Line Road touches the
river. Mike Farrell would be on the drive, and if she should
chance to pass the time o' day with him, and let him know she
was at home—why, there'd be no harm done to anybody.

For hours the girl trudged on, picking her way laboriously
from side to side of the trail, and often compelled to stop and
mend a bit of the corduroy roadway before she could get across
some particularly bad stretch of bog. Her stout shoes and heavy
woollen stockings were drenched with the icy water, but she was
strong and full of abounding health, and she felt neither cold nor
fatigue. In spite of her anxiety about her mother, her attention
was absorbed by the old familiar atmosphere of the wilderness,
the haunting colours, the chill, elusive, poignant smells. It was
not till fairly well along in the afternoon, therefore, that she
awoke to the fact that she had not covered more than half the
distance which she had to travel. The heavy going, the abomina-
ble state of the road, had utterly upset her calculations. The
knowledge came to her with such a shock that she stopped short
in consternation, almost dropping her bundle. At this rate she
would be in the forest all night, for it would be impossible to
traverse the bog-holes in the dark. Child of the backwoods
though she was, she had never slept out alone with the great
trees and the mysterious night stillness. For the first time she cast
a look of dread into the vistaed shadows of the fir trees. Forgetting the violets, the greening birches, the delicate spring smells,
she hurried on at a reckless pace which soon forced her to stop
and recover her breath. The best she could hope was to reach the

river shore before dark, and perhaps find the camp of the stream-drivers. She felt cold, and tired, and small, and terribly alone.

Yet, as a matter of fact, she was by no means so alone as she imagined. For the past half hour or more she had been strangely companioned.

Keeping parallel with the road, but at a distance, and hidden in the shadows, went an immense and gaunt black bear. For all his bulk, he went as noiselessly as a wild-cat, skirting the open spaces, and stopping from time to time to sit up, motionless as a stump, and listen intently, and sniff the air with sensitive nostrils. But his little, red-rimmed, savage eyes never lost sight of the figure of the girl for more than a few seconds at a time.

For bears this was the hungry season, the season of few roots and no fruits, few grubs and little honey. The black bear loves sweets and berries far better than any flesh food, however dainty. And human flesh he either fears or dislikes so heartily that only under special stress can he bring himself to contemplate it as a possible article of diet. But this bear considered himself under special stress. His lean flanks were fairly clinging together from emptiness. To his eyes, thus prejudiced, the fresh young form of Sissy Bembridge, picking its way down the trail, looked appetizing. Girl was something he had never tried, and it *might* be edible. At the same time, this inoffensive and defenceless-looking creature undoubtedly belonged to the species Man, as his nostrils well assured him. Therefore, small as she was, she was apt to be very dangerous, even to go off at times with flame and a terrifying noise. He was afraid to show himself to her, but his hunger, coupled with curiosity, led him to track her, perhaps in hope that she might fall dead in the trail and so make it safe for him to approach and taste.

The girl, meanwhile, under the influence of her uncertainty and fatigue, was growing more and more apprehensive. She assured herself that there was nothing to fear, that none of the wild inhabitants of these New Brunswick woods would dare to interfere with a human being. At the same time she found herself glancing nervously over her shoulder, as the shadows lengthened and deepened, and all the wilderness turned to dusky violet. From the wet pools began the cold and melancholy fluting of the frogs, the voice of solitude, and under the plangency of it she found the tears running down her cheeks. At this she shook herself indignantly, squared her shoulders, stamped her foot, and plunged ahead with a firm resolution that the approach of dark should *not* make her a fool. And away in the shadows of the firs the bear drew a little nearer, encouraged by the fading of daylight.

Just as it was growing so dark that she found it hard to choose her path between the pools and the bog-holes, to her infinite relief she caught sight of a cabin roof crowning a little rise of ground by the roadside. She broke into a run in her eagerness, reached the door, and pounded upon it breathlessly. But there was no light in the window. With a sinking heart she realized that it was empty—that it was nothing more than a deserted lumber-camp. Then, as if in answer to her vehement knocking, the door swung slowly open, showing the black darkness within. It had been merely closed, not latched. With a startled cry she sprang back, her skin creeping at the emptiness. Her first impulse was to turn and run. But she recovered herself, remembering that, after all, here was shelter and security for the night, infinitely preferable to a wet bivouac beneath some dripping fir tree.

She could not bring herself, however, to grope her way into the thick darkness of the interior. Stepping some paces back from the threshold, she nervously untied her bundle and got out a box of matches. Lighting one, she shaded it with her hand, crept forward, and cautiously peered inside. In the spurt of light the place looked warm and snug. She returned for her bundle, went in and shut the door. Then she drew a long breath and felt better. The camp was small, but dry and in good repair. It was quite empty, except for the tier of bunks along one wall, a rough-hewn log bench, a broken stove before the rude chimney, and several lengths of rust-eaten stove-pipe scattered on the floor. Lighting match after match, she hunted about for something to serve as fuel, for she craved the comfort, as well as the warmth of a fire.

There was nothing, however, but a few handfuls of dry, fine spruce tips, left in one of the bunks. This stuff, she knew, would flare up at once and die in a couple of minutes. She made up her mind to go out and grope about in the wet gloom for a supply of dead branches, though she was now conscious of a childish reluctance to face again the outer solitude. Almost furtively she lifted the heavy latch and opened the door half-way. Instantly, with a gasp, she slammed it to again and leaned against it with quaking knees. Straight in front of her, not twenty feet away, black and huge against the grey glimmer of the open, she had seen the prowling bear.

Recovering herself after a few seconds, she felt her way

stealthily to the bench and sat down upon it so as to face the two windows. The windows were small—so small that she was sure no monster such as the one which had just confronted her could by any possibility force its way through them. But she waited in a sort of horror, expecting momently that a dreadful shadowy face would darken one or the other of them and glare in upon her. She felt that the eyes of it would be visible by their own light, and she summoned up all her resolution that she might not scream when it appeared. For the time, however, nothing of the sort took place, and the two little squares continued to glimmer palely.

After what seemed to her an hour of breathless waiting, she heard a sound as of something rubbing softly along the logs of the back wall. She swung around on her seat to stare with straining eyes at the spot where the sound came from. But, of course, all was blackness there. And she could not keep her eyes for more than a few seconds from the baleful fascination of the window-squares.

The door of the camp was a heavy one and sturdily put together, but along its bottom was a crack some half an inch in width. Presently there came a loud sniffing at this crack, and then the door creaked, as if a heavy body were leaning against it. She shuddered and gathered herself together for a desperate spring, expecting the latch or the hinges to give way. But the honest New Brunswick workmanship held, and she took breath again with a sob.

After this respite, a thousand fantastic schemes of defence began to chase themselves through her brain. Out of them all she clung to just one, as possibly offering some hope in the last emergency. Noiselessly she gathered those few handfuls of withered spruce twigs and heaped them upon the top of the stove. If the bear should succeed in squeezing through the window or breaking down the door, she would light the dry stuff, and perhaps the sudden blaze and smoke might frighten him away. That it would daunt him for a moment, she felt sure, but she was equally sure that its efficacy would not last very long.

As she was working up the details of this scheme—more for the sake of keeping her terror in check than for any great faith she had in it—the thing she had been expecting happened. One of the glimmering grey-blue squares grew suddenly dark. She gave a burst of shrill, hysterical laughter and ran at it, as a trapped rat will jump at a hand approaching the wires. As she did so, she scratched a bunch of four or five matches and threw them, spluttering and hissing, in the face of the apparition. She had a glimpse of small, savage eyes and an open, white-fanged mouth. Then the great face withdrew itself.

Somewhat reassured to find that the monster could be disconcerted by the spurt of a match, she groped back to her seat, and fell to counting, by touch, the number of these feeble weapons still left in the box. She had only six more, and she began to repent of having used the others so recklessly. After all, as she told herself, *that* bear could not possibly squeeze himself through the window, so why should he not amuse himself by looking in at her if he wanted to? It might keep him occupied. It occurred to her that she ought to be glad that the bear was such a big one. His face alone had fairly filled the window. She would save the remaining matches.

For a good ten minutes nothing more happened, though from time to time her intent ears caught the sound of cautious sniffing on the other side of the log walls, as if the enemy were reconnoitring to find a weak point in her fortress. She smiled scornfully there in the dark, knowing well the strength of those log walls. Then, all at once her face stiffened and she sat rigid, clutching the edge of the bench with both hands. The door had once more begun to creak and groan under the weight of a heavy body surging against it.

There was a sound of scratching, a rattle of iron claws, which told her that the beast was rearing itself upright against the door. The massive paws seemed to fumble inquisitively. Then her blood froze. She heard the heavy latch lift with a click.

The door swung open.

She felt as if she were struggling in a nightmare. With a choked scream she leaped straight at the door. She had a mad impulse to slam it in the monster's face and brace herself, however impotently, against it. As she sprang, however, her foot caught in one of the pieces of stove-pipe. She fell headlong, and the pipe flew half-way across the floor, clattering over its fellows as it went, and raising a prodigious noise.

Through a long, long moment of horror she lay flat on her face, expecting a gigantic paw to fall upon her neck as a cat's paw falls upon a mouse. Nothing happened. She ventured to raise her head. The door was wide open and the doorway quite clear. A dozen feet away from it, at the edge of the road, stood the bear, staring irresolutely. He had been rather taken aback by the suddenness with which the door had flown open, and had hesitated to enter, fearing a trap. The wild clatter of the stove-pipes had further disturbed him, and he had withdrawn to consider the situation. In one bound the girl was at the door and had shut it with a bang.

The problem was now to fix the latch so that it could not again be lifted from the outside. She lit one more precious match, examined the mechanism, and hunted frantically for a splinter of wood with which to jam it down. There was nothing in sight that would serve. She tried to tear off a strip of her petticoat to bind it down with, but all her underwear was of a most serviceable sturdiness, and would not tear. She heard his breathing close to the door. Desperately she thrust a couple of fingers into the space above the latch, so that it would not lift. Then with the other hand she whipped off one shoe and stocking. The stocking was just the thing, and in a minute she had the latch secure.

It was no more than secure, however, before the weight of the bear once more came against the door. From the heavy, scratchy fumblings the girl could perceive that her enemy was trying to repeat his former manoeuvre. On this point, at least, she had no anxiety. She knew the door could not now be unlatched from the outside. She could almost afford to laugh in her satisfaction as she groped her way back to her seat.

But her satisfaction was of brief life. The door began to creak more and more violently. It was evident that the bear, having once learned that this was a possible way in, was determined to test it to the utmost. The girl sprang up. She heard the screws of a hinge begin to draw with an ominous grating sound. Now at last the crisis was truly and inevitably upon her. And, to her amazement, she was less terrified than before. The panic horror had all gone. She had small hope of escape, but her brain worked calmly and clearly. She moved over beside the broken stove, and stood, match in hand, ready to set fire to the pile of dry spruce tips.

The door groaned and creaked. Then the upper hinge gave way, and the door leaned inward, admitting a wide streak of glimmer. For some moments thereafter all sounds ceased, as if the bear had drawn back cautiously to consider the result of his efforts. Then he came on again with more confidence. Under his weight the door came crashing down, but slowly, with the noise of yielding latch and snapping iron. As it fell, the girl scratched the match and set it to the dry stuff.

In the doorway the bear paused, eyeing suspiciously the tiny
blue spurt of the struggling match. After a second or two,
however, he came forward with a savage rush, furious at having
been so long balked. The girl slipped around the stove. And just
as the bear reached the place where she had been standing, the
spruce tips sparked sharply and flared up in his face. With a loud
woo-oof of indignation and alarm, he recoiled, turned tail, scurried out into the road, and disappeared.

In a couple of minutes the cabin was full of sparks and smoky
light. The girl ran to the door and peered out. Her heart sank
once more. There was the bear, a few paces up the road, calmly
sitting on his haunches, waiting. He had seen camp fires before,
and he was waiting for this one to die down.

Sissy Bembridge knew that it would die down at once, and
then—well, her last card would have been played. She wrung
her hands, but in the new self-possession which had come to her,
she could not believe that the end had really arrived. It was
unbelievable that within some half a dozen minutes she could
become a lifeless, hideous, shapeless thing beneath those mangling
claws. No, there must be—there was—something to do, if she
could only think of it.

And then it came to her.

At first thought the idea was so audacious, so startling, so
fantastic, that she shrank from it as absurd. But on second
thought she convinced herself not only that it was the one thing
to be done, but also that it was practical and would almost
certainly prove effective. But there was not a moment to be lost.

Snatching up one of the fragments of stove-pipe, she used the
edge as a shovel, and carried a portion of the blazing stuff to the
open doorway. Here she deliberately set fire to the dry wood-
work, nursing with hand and breath the tiny uplicking flames.
She fed them with a few more scraps of spruce scraped up from
another bunk, till she saw that they would surely catch. Then,
with her stove-pipe shovel, she started another fire in the further
corner of the camp, and yet another in the uppermost bunk.
When satisfied that all were fairly going, she retrieved her
stocking from the broken latch, reclothed her naked foot and set
her bundle safely outside. Then she looked at the bear, still
sitting on his haunches a little way up the road, and she laughed
at him. At last she had him worsted. She darted in through the
doorway—now blazing cheerfully all up one side—and dragged
forth the heavy bench, that she might have something dry

to sit on while she watched the approaching conflagration.

Her calculation—and she knew it was a sound one—was that the cabin, a solid structure of logs, would burn vigorously the whole night through, and terrify the bear to final flight. If it should by any chance die down before full daylight, she would be able to build a circle of small fires with the burning remnants. And she felt sure that in daylight her enemy would not dare to renew the attack.

In another ten minutes the roof was ablaze, and soon the flames were shooting up riotously. The woods were lighted redly for hundreds of yards around, the pools in the road were like polished copper, and the bear was nowhere to be seen. Sissy dragged her bench and bundle still further away, and sat philosophically warming her wet feet. The reaction from her terror, and her sense of triumph, made her so excited that fatigue and anxiety were all forgotten. She grew warm and comfortable, and finally, opening her bundle, she got out a package of neglected sandwiches and made a contented meal.

As she was shaking the crumbs from her lap, she heard voices and pounding, splashing hoofs from up the trail. She sprang to her feet. Three lumbermen came riding into the circle of light and drew rein before her in astonishment. "Sissy—Bembridge—*you!*" cried the foremost, springing from his saddleless mount.

The girl ran to him. "Oh, Mike," she exclaimed, crying and laughing at the same time, and clutching him by the arm, "I *had* to do it! The bear nigh got me! Take me to mother, quick. I'm *that* tired."

THE MARIPOSA BANK MYSTERY
by Stephen Leacock

Suicide is a thing that ought not to be committed without very careful thought. It often involves serious consequences, and in some cases brings pain to others than oneself.

I don't say that there is no justification for it. There often is. Anybody who has listened to certain kinds of music, or read certain kinds of poetry, or heard certain kinds of performances upon the concertina, will admit that there are some lives which ought not to be continued, and that even suicide has its brighter aspects.

But to commit suicide on grounds of love is at the best a very dubious experiment. I know that in this I am expressing an opinion contrary to that of most true lovers who embrace suicide on the slightest provocation as the only honourable termination of an existence that never ought to have begun.

I quite admit that there is a glamour and a sensation about the thing which has its charm, and that there is nothing like it for causing a girl to realize the value of the heart that she has broken and which breathed forgiveness upon her at the very moment when it held in its hand the half-pint of prussic acid that was to terminate its beating for ever.

But apart from the general merits of the question, I suppose there are few people, outside of lovers, who know what it is to commit suicide four times in five weeks.

Yet this was what happened to Mr. Pupkin, of the Exchange Bank of Mariposa.

Ever since he had known Zena Pepperleigh he had realized that his love for her was hopeless. She was too beautiful for him and too good for him; her father hated him and her mother despised him; his salary was too small and his own people were too rich.

If you add to all that that he came up tò the judge's house one night and found a poet reciting verses to Zena, you will understand the suicide at once. It was one of those regular poets with a solemn jackass face, and lank parted hair and eyes like puddles of molasses. I don't know how he came there—up from the city, probably—but there he was on the Pepperleighs' verandah that August evening. He was reciting poetry—either Tennyson's or Shelley's, or his own, you couldn't tell—and about him sat Zena with her hands clasped, and Nora Gallagher looking at the sky, and Jocelyn Drone gazing into infinity, and a little tubby woman looking at the poet with her head falling over sideways—in fact, there was a whole group of them.

I don't know what it is about poets that draws women to them in this way. But everybody knows that a poet has only to sit and saw the air with his hands and recite verses in a deep stupid voice, and all the women are crazy over him. Men despise him and would kick him off the verandah if they dared, but the women simply rave over him.

So Pupkin sat there in the gloom and listened to this poet reciting Browning and he realized that everybody understood it but him. He could see Zena with her eyes fixed on the poet as if she were hanging on to every syllable (she was; she needed to), and he stood it just about fifteen minutes and then slid off the side of the verandah and disappeared without even saying goodnight.

He walked straight down Oneida Street and along the Main Street just as hard as he could go. There was only one purpose in his mind—suicide. He was heading straight for Jim Eliot's drug store on the main corner and his idea was to buy a drink of chloroform and drink it and die right there on the spot.

As Pupkin walked down the street, the whole thing was so vivid in his mind that he could picture it to the remotest detail. He could even see it all in type, in big headlines in the newspapers of the following day:

APPALLING SUICIDE
PETER PUPKIN POISONED

He perhaps hoped that the thing might lead to some kind of public enquiry and that the question of Browning's poetry and

whether it is altogether fair to allow of its general circulation
would be fully ventilated in the newspapers.

Thinking all that, Pupkin came to the main corner.

On a warm August evening the drug store of Mariposa, as you
know, is all a blaze of lights. You can hear the hissing of the
soda-water fountain half a block away, and inside the store there
are ever so many people—boys and girls and old people too—all
drinking sarsaparilla and chocolate sundaes and lemon sours and
foaming drinks that you take out of long straws. There is such a
laughing and a talking as you never heard, and the girls are all in
white and pink and cambridge blue, and the soda fountain is of
white marble with silver taps, and it hisses and sputters, and Jim
Eliot and his assistant wear white coats with red geraniums in
them, and it's all just as gay as gay.

The foyer of the opera in Paris may be a fine sight, but I doubt
if it can compare with the inside of Eliot's drug store in Mariposa—
for real gaiety and joy of living.

This night the store was especially crowded because it was a
Saturday and that meant early closing for all the hotels, except, of
course, Smith's. So as the hotels were shut, the people were all
in the drug store, drinking like fishes. It just shows the folly of
Local Option and the Temperance Movement and all that. Why,
if you shut the hotels you simply drive the people to the soda
fountains and there's more drinking than ever, and not only of
the men, too, but the girls and young boys and children. I've
seen little things of eight and nine that had to be lifted up on the
high stools at Eliot's drug store, drinking great goblets of lemon
soda, enough to burst them—brought there by their own fathers,
and why? Simply because the hotel bars were shut.

What's the use of thinking you can stop people drinking
merely by cutting off whiskey and brandy? The only effect is to
drive them to taking lemon sour and sarsaparilla and cherry
pectoral and caroka cordial and things they wouldn't have touched
before. So in the long run they drink more than ever. The point
is that you can't prevent people having a good time, no matter
how hard you try. If they can't have it with lager beer and
brandy, they'll have it with plain soda and lemon pop, and so the
whole gloomy scheme of the temperance people breaks down,
anyway.

But I was only saying that Eliot's drug store in Mariposa on a
Saturday night is the gayest and brightest spot in the world.

And just imagine what a fool of a place to commit suicide in!

Just imagine going up to the soda-water fountain and asking for five cents' worth of chloroform and soda! Well, you simply can't, that's all.

That's the way Pupkin found it. You see, as soon as he came in, somebody called out: "Hello, Pete!" and one or two others called "Hullo, Pup!" and some said: "How goes it?" and others: "How are you toughing it?" and so on, because you see they had all been drinking more or less and naturally they felt jolly and glad-hearted.

So the upshot of it was that instead of taking chloroform, Pupkin stepped up to the counter of the fountain and he had a bromo-seltzer with cherry soda, and after that he had one of those aerated seltzers, and then a couple of lemon seltzers and a bromophizzer.

I don't know if you know the mental effect of a bromo-seltzer.

But it's a hard thing to commit suicide on.

You can't.

You feel so buoyant.

Anyway, what with the phizzing of the seltzer and the lights and the girls, Pupkin began to feel so fine that he didn't care a cuss for all the Browning in the world, and as for the poet—oh, to blazes with him! What's poetry, anyway?—only rhymes.

So, would you believe it, in about ten minutes Peter Pupkin was off again and heading straight for the Pepperleighs' house, poet or no poet, and, what was more to the point, he carried with him three great bricks of Eliot's ice cream—in green, pink and brown layers. He struck the verandah just at the moment when Browning was getting too stale and dreary for words. His brain was all sizzling and jolly with the bromo-seltzer, and when he fetched out the ice cream bricks and Zena ran to get plates and spoons to eat it with, and Pupkin went with her to help fetch them and they picked out the spoons together, they were so laughing and happy that it was a marvel. Girls, you know, need no bromo-seltzer. They're full of it all the time.

And as for the poet—well, can you imagine how Pupkin felt when Zena told him that the poet was married, and that the tubby little woman with her head on sideways was his wife?

So they had the ice cream, and the poet ate it in bucketsful. Poets always do. They need it. And after it the poet recited some stanzas of his own and Pupkin saw that he had misjudged the man, because it was dandy poetry, the very best. That night Pupkin walked home on air and there was no thought of chloroform, and it turned out that he hadn't committed suicide, but like all lovers he had commuted it.

I don't need to describe in full the later suicides of Mr. Pupkin, because they were all conducted on the same plan and rested on something the same reasons as above.

Sometimes he would go down at night to the offices of the bank below his bedroom and bring up his bank revolver in order to make an end of himself with it. This, too, he could see headed up in the newspapers as:

BRILLIANT BOY BANKER BLOWS OUT
BRAINS

But blowing your brains out is a noisy, rackety performance, and Pupkin soon found that only special kinds of brains are suited for it. So he always sneaked back again later in the night and put the revolver in its place, deciding to drown himself instead. Yet every time that he walked down to the Trestle Bridge over the Ossawippi he found it was quite unsuitable for drowning—too high, and the water too swift and black, and the rushes too gruesome—in fact, not at all the kind of place for a drowning.

Far better, he realized, to wait there on the railroad track and throw himself under the wheels of the express and be done with it. Yet, though Pupkin often waited in this way for the train, he was never able to pick out a pair of wheels that suited him. Anyhow, it's awfully hard to tell an express from a fast freight.

I wouldn't mention these attempts at suicide if one of them hadn't finally culminated in making Peter Pupkin a hero and solving for him the whole perplexed entanglement of his love affair with Zena Pepperleigh. Incidentally it threw him into the very centre of one of the most impenetrable bank mysteries that ever baffled the ingenuity of some of the finest legal talent that ever adorned one of the most enterprising communities in the country.

It happened one night, as I say, that Pupkin decided to go down into the office of the bank and get his revolver and see if it would blow his brains out. It was the night of the Firemen's Ball and Zena had danced four times with a visitor from the city, a man who was in the fourth year at the University and who knew everything. It was more than Peter Pupkin could bear. Mallory

Tompkins was away that night, and when Pupkin came home he was all alone in the building, except for Gillis, the caretaker, who lived in the extension at the back.

He sat in his room for hours brooding. Two or three times he picked up a book—he remembered afterwards distinctly that it was Kant's *Critique of Pure Reason*—and tried to read it, but it seemed meaningless and trivial. Then with a sudden access of resolution he started from his chair and made his way down the stairs and into the office room of the bank, meaning to get a revolver and kill himself on the spot and let them find his body lying on the floor.

It was then far on in the night and the empty building of the bank was as still as death. Pupkin could hear the stairs creak under his feet, and as he went he thought he heard another sound like the opening or closing of a door. But it sounded not like the sharp ordinary noise of a closing door but with a dull muffled noise as if someone had shut the iron door of a safe in a room under the ground. For a moment Pupkin stood and listened with his heart thumping against his ribs. Then he kicked his slippers from his feet and without a sound stole into the office on the ground floor and took the revolver from his teller's desk. As he gripped it, he listened to the sounds on the back-stairway and in the vaults below.

I should explain that in the Exchange Bank of Mariposa the offices are on the ground floor level with the street. Below this is another floor with low dark rooms paved with flagstones, with unused office desks and with piles of papers stored in boxes. On this floor are the vaults of the bank, and lying in them in the autumn—the grain season—there is anything from fifty to a hundred thousand dollars in currency tied in bundles. There is no other light down there than the dim reflection from the lights out on the street, that lies in patches on the stone floor.

I think, as Peter Pupkin stood, revolver in hand, in the office of the bank, he had forgotten all about the maudlin purpose of his first coming. He had forgotten for the moment all about heroes and love affairs, and his whole mind was focused, sharp and alert, with the intensity of the nighttime, on the sounds that he heard in the vault and on the back-stairway of the bank.

Straight away, Pupkin knew what it meant as plainly as if it were written in print. He had forgotten, I say, about being a hero and he only knew that there were sixty thousand dollars in the vault of the bank below, and that he was paid eight hundred dollars a year to look after it.

As Peter Pupkin stood there listening to the sounds in his stockinged feet, his face showed grey as ashes in the light that fell through the window from the street. His heart beat like a hammer against his ribs. But behind its beatings was the blood of four generations of Loyalists and the robber who would take that sixty thousand dollars from the Mariposa bank must take it over the dead body of Peter Pupkin, teller.

Pupkin walked down the stairs to the lower room, the one below the ground with the bank vault in it, with as fine a step as any of his ancestors showed on parade. And if he had known it, as he came down the stairway in the front of the vault room, there was a man crouched in the shadow of the passage way by the stairs at the back. This man, too, held a revolver in his hand, and, criminal or not, his face was as resolute as Pupkin's own. As he heard the teller's step on the stair, he turned and waited in the shadow of the doorway without a sound.

There is no need really to mention all these details. They are only of interest as showing how sometimes a bank teller in a corded smoking jacket and stockinged feet may be turned into such a hero as even the Mariposa girls might dream about.

All of this must have happened at about three o'clock in the night. This much was established afterwards from the evidence of Gillis, the caretaker. When he first heard the sounds he had looked at his watch and noticed that it was half-past two; the watch he knew was three-quarters of an hour slow three days before and had been gaining since. The exact time at which Gillis heard footsteps in the bank and started downstairs, pistol in hand, became a nice point afterwards in the cross-examination.

But one must not anticipate. Pupkin reached the iron door of the bank safe, and knelt in front of it, feeling the dark to find the fracture of the lock. As he knelt, he heard a sound behind him, and swung around on his knees and saw the bank robber in the half light of the passage way and the glitter of a pistol in his hand. The rest was over in an instant. Pupkin heard a voice that was his own, but that sounded strange and hollow, call out: "Drop that, or I'll fire!" and then just as he raised his revolver, there came a blinding flash of light before his eyes, and Peter Pupkin, junior teller of the bank, fell forward on the floor and knew no more.

* * *

At that point, of course, I ought to close down a chapter, or volume, or, at least, strike the reader over the head with a sandbag to force him to stop and think. In common fairness one ought to stop here and count a hundred or get up and walk around a block, or, at any rate, picture to oneself Peter Pupkin lying on the floor of the bank, motionless, his arms distended, the revolver still grasped in his hands. But I must go on.

By half-past seven on the following morning it was known all over Mariposa that Peter Pupkin the junior teller of the Exchange had been shot dead by a robber in the vault of the building. It was known also that Gillis, the caretaker, had been shot and killed at the foot of the stairs, and that the robber had made off with fifty thousand dollars in currency; that he had left a trail of blood on the sidewalk and that the men were out tracking him with bloodhounds in the great swamps to the north of the town.

This, I say, and it is important to note it, was what they knew at half-past seven. Of course as each hour went past they learned more and more. At eight o'clock it was known that Pupkin was not dead, but dangerously wounded in the lungs. At eight-thirty it was known that he was not shot in the lungs, but that the ball had traversed the pit of his stomach.

At nine o'clock it was learned that the pit of Pupkin's stomach was all right, but that the bullet had struck his right ear and carried it away. Finally it was learned that his ear had not exactly been carried away, that is, not precisely removed by the bullet, but that it had grazed Pupkin's head in such a way that it had stunned him, and if it had been an inch or two more to the left it might have reached his brain. This, of course, was just as good as being killed from the point of view of public interest.

Indeed, by nine o'clock Pupkin could be himself seen on the Main Street with a great bandage sideways on his head, pointing out the traces of the robber. Gillis, the caretaker, too, it was known by eight, had not been killed. He had been shot through the brain, but whether the injury was serious or not was only a matter of conjecture. In fact, by ten o'clock it was understood that the bullet from the robber's second shot had grazed the side of the caretaker's head, but as far as could be known his brain was just as before. I should add that the first report about the bloodstains and the swamp and the bloodhounds turned out to be inaccurate. The stains may have been blood, but as they led to the cellar way of Netley's store they may have also been molasses, though it was argued, to be sure, that the robber might well have poured molasses over the bloodstains from sheer cunning.

It was remembered, too, that there were no bloodhounds in Mariposa, although, mind you, there are any amount of dogs there.

So you see that by ten o'clock in the morning the whole affair was settling into the impenetrable mystery which it ever since remained.

Not that there wasn't evidence enough. There was Pupkin's own story and Gillis's story, and the stories of all the people who had heard the shots and seen the robber (some said, the bunch of robbers) go running past (others said, walking past) in the night. Apparently the robber ran up and down half tei streets of Mariposa before he vanished.

But the stories of Pupkin and Gillis were plain enough. Pupkin related that he heard sounds in the bank and came downstairs just in time to see the robber crouching in the passage-way, and that the robber was a large, hulking, villainous looking man, wearing a heavy coat. Gillis told exactly the same story, having heard the voices at the same time, except that he first described the robber as a small thin fellow (peculiarly villainous looking, however, even in the dark), wearing a short jacket; but on thinking it over, Gillis realized that he had been wrong about the size of the criminal, and that he was even bigger, if anything, than what Mr. Pupkin thought. Gillis had fired at the robber; just at the same moment had Mr. Pupkin.

Beyond that, all was mystery, absolute and impenetrable.

By eleven o'clock the detectives had come up from the city under orders from the head of the bank.

I wish you could have seen the two detectives as they moved to and fro in Mariposa—fine looking, stern, impenetrable men that they were. They seemed to take in the whole town by instinct and so quietly. They found their way to Mr. Smith's Hotel just as quietly as if it wasn't design at all and stood there at the bar, picking up scraps of conversation—you know the way detectives do it. Occasionally they allowed one or two bystanders—confederates, perhaps—to buy a drink for them, and you could see from the way they drank it that they were still listening for a clue. If there had been the faintest clue in Smith's hotel or in the Mariposa House or in the Continental, those fellows would have been at it like a flash.

To see them moving round the town that day—silent, massive, imperturbable—gave one a great idea of their strange, dangerous calling. They went about the town all day and yet in such a quiet peculiar way that you couldn't have realized that they were working at all. They ate their dinner together at Smith's Café and took an hour and a half over it to throw people off the scent. Then when they got them off it, they sat and talked with Josh Smith in the back bar to keep them off. Mr. Smith seemed to take to them right away. They were men of his own size, or near it, and anyway hotel men and detectives have a general affinity and share in the same impenetrable silence and in their confidential knowledge of the weaknesses of the public.

Mr. Smith, too, was of great use to the detectives. "Boys," he said, "I wouldn't ask too close as to what folks was out late at night: in this town it don't do."

When those two great brains finally left for the city on the five-thirty, it was hard to realize that behind each grand, impassable face a perfect vortex of clues was seething.

But if the detectives were heroes, what was Pupkin? Imagine him with his bandage on his head standing in front of the bank and talking of the midnight robbery with that peculiar false modesty that only heroes are entitled to use.

I don't know whether you have ever been a hero, but for sheer exhilaration there is nothing like it. And for Mr. Pupkin, who had gone through life thinking himself no good, to be suddenly exalted into the class of Napoleon Bonaparte and John Maynard and the Charge of the Light Brigade—oh, it was wonderful. Because Pupkin was a brave man now and he knew it and acquired with it all the brave man's modesty. In fact, I believe he was heard to say that he had only done his duty, and that what he did was what any other man would have done: though when somebody else said: "That's so, when you come to think of it," Pupkin turned on him that quiet look of the wounded hero, bitterer than words.

And if Pupkin had known that all of the afternoon papers in the city reported him dead, he would have felt more luxurious still.

That afternoon the Mariposa court sat in enquiry—technically it was summoned in inquest on the dead robber—though they hadn't found the body—and it was wonderful to see them lining up the witnesses and holding cross-examinations. There is something in the cross-examination of great criminal lawyers like Nivens, of Mariposa, and in the counter examinations of presiding judges like Pepperleigh that thrills you to the core with the astuteness of it.

They had Henry Mullins, the manager, on the stand for an hour and a half, and the excitement was so breathless that you would have heard a pin drop. Nivens took him first.

"What is you name?" he said.

"Henry Augustus Mullins."

"What position do you hold?"

"I am manager of the Exchange Bank."

"When were you born?"

"December 30, 1869."

After that, Nivens stood looking quietly at Mullins. You could feel that he was thinking pretty deeply before he shot the next question at him.

"Where did you go to school?"

Mullins answered straight off: The high school down home," and Nivens thought again for a while and then asked:

"How many boys were at the school?"

"About sixty."

"How many masters?"

"About three."

After that Nivens paused a long while and seemed to be digesting the evidence, but at last an idea seemed to strike him and he said:

"I understand you were not on the bank premises last night. Where were you?"

"Down the lake duck shooting."

You should have seen the excitement in the court when Mullins said this. The judge leaned forward in his chair and broke in at once.

"Did you get any, Harry?" he asked.

"Yes," Mullins said, "about six."

"Where did you get them? What? In the wild rice marsh past the river? You don't say so! Did you get them on the sit or how?"

All of these questions were fired off at the witness from the court in a single breath. In fact, it was the knowledge that the first ducks of the season had been seen in the Ossawippi marsh that led to the termination of the proceedings before the afternoon was a quarter over. Mullins and George Duff and half the witnesses were off with shotguns as soon as court was cleared.

I may as well state at once that the full story of the robbery of the bank at Mariposa never came to the light. A number of arrests—mostly of vagrants and suspicious characters—were made, but the guilt of the robbery was never brought home to them. One man was arrested twenty miles away, at the other end of Missinaba county, who not only corresponded exactly with the description of the robber, but, in addition to this, had a wooden leg. Vagrants with one leg are always regarded with suspicion in places like Mariposa, and whenever a robbery or a murder happens they are arrested in patches.

It was never even known just how much money was stolen from the bank. Some people said ten thousand dollars, others more. The bank, no doubt for business motives, claimed that the contents of the safe were intact and that the robber had been foiled in his design.

But none of this matters to the exaltation of Mr. Pupkin. Good fortune, like bad, never comes in small instalments. On that wonderful day, every good thing happened to Peter Pupkin at once. The morning saw him a hero. At the sitting of the court, the judge publicly told him that his conduct was fit to rank among the annals of the pioneers of Tecumseh Township, and asked him to his house for supper. At five o'clock he received the telegram of promotion from the head office that raised his salary to a thousand dollars, and made him not only a hero but a marriageable man. At six o'clock he started up to the judge's house with his resolution nerved to the most momentous step of his life.

His mind was made up.

He would do a thing seldom if ever done in Mariposa. He would propose to Zena Pepperleigh. In Mariposa this kind of step, I say, is seldom taken. The course of love runs on and on through all its stages of tennis playing and dancing and sleigh riding, till by sheer notoriety of circumstances an understanding is reached. To propose straight out would be thought priggish and affected and is supposed to belong only to people in books.

But Pupkin felt that what ordinary people dare not do, heroes are allowed to attempt. He would propose to Zena, and more than that, he would tell her in a straight, manly way that he was rich and take the consequences.

And he did it.

That night on the piazza, where the hammock hangs in the shadow of the Virginia creeper, he did it. By sheer good luck the judge had gone indoors to the library, and by a piece of rare good fortune Mrs. Pepperleigh had gone indoors to the sewing

room, and by a happy trick of coincidence the servant was out
and the dog was tied up—in fact, no such chain of circumstances
was ever offered in favour of mortal man before.

What Zena said—beyond saying yes—I do not know. I am
sure that when Pupkin told her of the money, she bore up as
bravely as so fine a girl as Zena would, and when he spoke of
diamonds she said she would wear them for his sake.

They were saying these things and other things—ever so many
other things—when there was such a roar and a clatter up
Oneida Street as you never heard, and there came bounding up to
the house one of the most marvellous Limousine touring cars that
ever drew up at the home of a judge on a modest salary of three
thousand dollars. When it stopped there sprang from it an excited
man in a long sealskin coat—worn not for the luxury of it all but
from the sheer chilliness of the autumn evening. And it was, as
of course you know, Pupkin's father. He had seen the news of
his son's death in the evening paper in the city. They drove the
car through, so the chauffeur said, in two hours and a quarter,
and behind them there was to follow a special trainload of
detectives and emergency men, but Pupkin senior had cancelled
all that by telegram halfway up when he heard that Peter was still
living.

For a moment as his eyes rested on young Pupkin you would
almost have imagined, had you not known that he came from the
Maritime Provinces, that there were tears in them and that he
was about to hug his son to his heart. But if he didn't hug Peter
to his heart, he certainly did within a few moments clasp Zena to
it, in that fine fatherly way in which they clasp pretty girls in the
Maritime Provinces. The strangest thing is that Pupkin senior
seemed to understand the whole situation without any explana-
tions at all.

Judge Pepperleigh, I think, would have shaken both of Pupkin
senior's arms off when he saw him; and when you heard them
call one another "Ned" and "Phillip" it made you feel that they
were boys again attending classes together at the old law school
in the city.

If Pupkin thought that his father wouldn't make a hit in
Mariposa, it only showed his ignorance. Pupkin senior sat there
on the judge's verandah smoking a corn cob pipe as if he had
never heard of Havana cigars in his life. In the three days that he
spent in Mariposa that autumn, he went in and out of Jeff
Thorpe's barber shop and Eliot's drug store, shot black ducks in

the marsh and played poker every evening at a hundred matches for a cent as if he had never lived any other life in all his days. They had to send him telegrams enough to fill a satchel to make him come away.

So Pupkin and Zena in due course of time were married, and went to live in one of the enchanted houses on the hillside in the newer part of the town, where you may find them to this day.

You may see Pupkin there at any time cutting enchanted grass on a little lawn in as gaudy a blazer as ever.

But if you step up to speak to him or walk with him into the enchanted house, pray modulate your voice a little—musical though it is—for there is said to be an enchanted baby on the premises whose sleep must not lightly be disturbed.

THE GIRL WHO WENT TO MEXICO
by Alden Nowlan

Ordinarily Sam Baxter heard a car stopping in front of his house in time to take a look out the kitchen window to see who was coming. He liked to be prepared for visitors. Not that he had anything to fear, but he was a shy man and surprises, including pleasant surprises, made him uncomfortable.

But that day he was cooking his supper, something he had had to do since his mother's death the previous year. He was frying steak with plenty of onions, steeping tea, warming up biscuits he had made a couple of days earlier, setting the table, listening to Don Messer and his Islanders on the radio, and rather enjoying all this noise and rushing about—when, happening to look up, he saw a girl standing in the doorway.

"Good afternoon, sir," said the girl, whom Sam had never seen before. "Could you tell me your name, please? If I get just ten more names on my list, I'll win a free trip to Mexico."

"My name?" stammered Sam. "Why, my name's Bam Saxter. I mean Sam Baxter. I mean what you want to know for? I mean what you up to, anyway, scaring a man pretty near to death that way?"

"Oh, you poor darling!" the girl wailed. " Did I really frighten you? I'm awfully sorry. I really am. I knocked, but you couldn't have heard me. I feel so silly I could just die!"

She was a pretty little blonde, about twenty years old, wearing what Sam remembered afterwards as a very pretty and rather daring dress, although actually Sam never quite dared look at a woman closely enough to notice the style and texture, or even the colour, of her clothes.

"Don't worry about it," Sam said. "You didn't really scare me. Now what did olu say you were selling?"

26

"Oh, no! I'm not selling anything. All I want is your name. You see—"

The girl talked, very rapidly and charmingly, while Charlie Chamberlain sang "McNamara's Band" and "An Irish Lullaby" and "Beyond the Sunset," and Sam's steak went from medium-rare, which he preferred, to well done. In the end, as the result of a process that still baffled him when he tried next day to reassemble it in his mind, Sam found himself paying three dollars for a year's subscription to a weekly magazine called *The Canadian Yeoman*.

The only other periodical to which Sam subscribed was *The Connaught County and Environs World Intelligencer* which most of its readers referred to, not without affection, as *The Blat*. So the arrival of his first copy of *The Canadian Yeoman* was a bit of an event in his life. As an Orangeman and a Royal Black Knight of Ireland, sworn to uphold the British connection, he was pleased that the cover carried a handsome colour portrait of the Queen and Prince Philip in the regalia of the Order of the Garter. In fact, he liked the portrait so much that he tacked it on the kitchen wall and, once or twice, even considered putting it in the gilt frame in the living room that now contained a sampler in purple and gold needlework reading: *What Is Home Without a Mother?*

Being a farmer who raised purebred Lacombe hogs, Shorthorn cattle and twenty-five acres of potatoes, he read most of the articles on agriculture. Since he had to prepare his own meals he occasionally clipped out a recipe. And, often, he felt a little electric tingle of nostalgia when he glanced at the page devoted to republishing old songs; when, for instance, he read:

> *My name is Peter Emberley*
> *As you must understand,*
> *I was born on Prince Edward Island,*
> *Nearby the ocean's strand. . . .*

Soon, as he went to bed on Tuesday nights, Sam was thinking, well, tomorrow's the day my paper comes. And he stayed up later than usual on Wednesdays, sometimes until ten-thirty or eleven, enjoying his magazine, smoking his pipe of Old Virginia tobacco, and listening to country and western music from Wheeling, West Virginia, and Nashville, Tennessee. This became his private little weekly festival. In time he got into the habit of finishing the evening with a little toddy of rum, hot water and sugar.

New covers were tacked up: Bobby Hull working in a hay-field, Prince Philip at the Royal Winter Fair, Brahma bull riding at the Calgary Stampede, wheat ripening in Saskatchewan, the RCMP musical ride. One week the cover pictured a group of Israeli farm girls in very tight shirts and shorts, but after a few days Sam took this one down and slid it under the radio.

Then, one Wednesday, the magazine didn't arrive.

"Oh, well, it will be here tomorrow, I guess," Sam said to himself when he found his mailbox empty. But that night he had nothing to read and he felt very lonely, just sitting there, smoking and listening to the radio.

At last he resentfully picked up the previous week's issue and, since he had already read everything else, found himself perusing the classified advertisements that occupied several of the back pages.

Farms For Sale, New and Used Clothing, Agents Wanted, Missing Persons, In Memoriam, Personal.

It was the column headed "Personal" that changed Sam Baxter's way of life.

Next day, when the current issue arrived, he hardly glanced at the cover, which showed a Scottish shepherd, his dog and a flock of sheep, before turning to the classified columns.

"Elijah coming before Christ," he read aloud. "Wonderful book free."

And there was an address, just as there were addresses in all the other advertisements in the "Personal" column.

There were notices inserted by the Millennial Dawn movement, the Christadelphians, the Rosicrucians, the Theosophists, the Socialist Labour Party, the Christian Nationalist Crusade, the Commonwealth Association for the Restoration of the House of Stuart, the Church of Jesus Christ of Latter Day Saints, the Unitarians, the Universalists, the Anti-Vivisectionists, the Baha'i World Faith, the Society for Herbal Medicine, the Knights of Columbus—each of them offering books, pamphlets, magazines or correspondence courses in exchange for a postcard.

Sam drove his half-ton truck into Hainesville and bought six postcards.

"Looks as though you're planning on catching up on your correspondence," said Albion Greeley, the postmaster, eyeing him curiously through his rimless glasses.

"Thought maybe I would," Sam answered.

"Suppose you're going to write to that brother of yours out in Detroit. Haven't seen any letters from him in a coon's age. And maybe you'll drop a line to your Uncle Bythie down Boston-way? You write him you tell him Albion Greeley was asking about him—hey?"

"Don't know as I'll be writing to either of them," Sam said.

"Well, I'd sooner be bit by a dog than poke my snout into somebody else's business," said Albion, turning away.

It took Sam most of an evening to write his messages and address his cards. The actual writing didn't take long, but he spent hours deciding which advertisements looked most interesting. After the cards were mailed, he walked to his mailbox every day with the same eagerness he had felt as a boy visiting his rabbit snares.

The replies came—first a trickle, then a flood. Before long he was receiving literature even from organizations to which he had not written.

He read it all, every word of it. He read the books of Charles Taze Russell, who maintained that the Great Pyramid was not an Egyptian tomb but a Hebrew prophecy. He read Helena Petrovna Blavatsky and learned about the transmigration of souls and the secret doctrines of the ascended masters. He read Gerald L. K. Smith, Daniel DeLeon, Baha'u'llah and the Book of Mormon. He read that sunflower seeds cured constipation and that his rightful sovereign was a Bavarian duke named Albrecht Von Wittlesbach.

"That Sam Baxter's got himself mixed up with one of them screwball religions," Albion Greeley reported. "Don't know which one of them it is for sure. Jehovah Witness, maybe. He may even be a Communist. Some of the stuff that fellow gets in the mail would scare you. The stuff I could tell about some people around here if I wasn't a civil servant sworn to secrecy! Wouldn't surprise me none, though, if the Mounties was around asking about Sam one of these days. No, sir, wouldn't surprise me one bit."

On the infrequent occasions when Sam went to town to buy livestock feed or replace worn-out parts on his tractor or potato digger, those who knew him pointed him out to those who didn't and whispered, "There goes the Mormon," or "That there's Sam Baxter, he's some kind of a Communist."

As for Sam, he was hardly aware that each of the books and

pamphlets he devoured was designed to convert him to a Cause. He was a Tory, because his parents had been Tories, and his grandparents, too, for all he knew, and because he suspected the Grits of being sympathetic to the Church of Rome. If he had been asked his religion he would have hesitated for an instant and then answered "Baptist," because while his mother had attended the United Church of Canada, the only church within walking distance of the Baxter farm for close to forty years, both she and his father had been raised as Baptists and, to the end of their lives, had believed that God had delivered a greater measure of His truth to the Baptists than He had chosen to entrust to Methodists, Presbyterians or anybody else.

He was neither baffled nor confused when in the same evening he dipped into *Isis Unveiled* and *The Secret Doctrine* and thumbed through the latest issues of *The Weekly People* and *The Cross and the Flag*. Astral bodies, Devachan, the Four Noble Truths of the Compassionate Buddha, the international bankers' conspiracy, industrial democracy through worker control of the means of production, the secret return of Jesus in 1914, the martyrdom of The Bab and of the Prophet Joseph Smith—these were not things he tried to understand or relate in any way to his own life. His reading was a kind of dreaming. He was not a convert or a student, but an adventurer.

Eventually, he wearied of this adventure and embarked on a more daring one.

The personal column of *The Canadian Yeoman* contained advertisements of another kind.

Middle-aged Ukrainian farmer, well-to-do, Catholic, wishes to correspond with Catholic widow, with view to matrimony. No objection to one or two children.

Woman, 46, considered attractive, good cook, wishes to hear from lonely bachelor or widower with means. Enclose photo in first letter. No triflers, please.

Man, 50, owner of successful small business, non-drinker, non-smoker, invites letters from middle-aged woman, Protestant church-goer with some private means preferred. Enclose snapshot, please.

Childless widow, 41, with small bank account, blue eyes, natural blonde, wants to hear from white Protestant between 40 and 60, preferably with means. No objection to one child. Object: matrimony, if suited.

The old Sam Baxter would never have dreamed of answering

such an advertisement. But the new Sam Baxter thought of himself as a rather reckless man.

At Steadman's 5¢ to $1.00 Store in Hainesville, he bought a nineteen-cent ballpoint pen, a tablet of pale blue paper and a package of white, blue-lined envelopes. Furtively he slipped in and out of a curtained booth in which he sat in semi-darkness, looking at himself in a mirror, while a coin-operated camera, its light flashing off and on, took his picture. When the machine coughed out a strip of four photographs, not much bigger than postage stamps, he put them in his wallet very quickly and did not take them out until he got home, where he examined them through his mother's old-fashioned reading glass and decided, finally, that, well, he must have been behind the door when good looks were handed out but at least he'd never scare a cat into having a miscarriage.

Then, slowly, almost painfully, he composed his letter:

Dear Madam,

Having seen your ad in The Canadian Yeoman my favourite paper I am dropping you a line to tell you I am a farmer here in New Brunswick a very beautiful place to live and guess I am an old bachelor (ha ha) because I had to look after Mother after Father died and don't see many women here my age that are not married although am not as old as all that either, will be 46 next Sept. 26 if God lets me live, and am lucky enough to have my health, which I think you will agree is the most important thing there is, and they say life begins at 40 (ha ha). Am sending you snap which you can use to scare the mice away (ha ha again). Own 260 acres of land here in Connaught County which I think is God's Country although that does not mean I have anything against Ontario where you live but when you are born somewhere that makes it different. Have 25 acres in potatoes which this year are $5 a barrel so am doing pretty good (knock on wood) although not rich or anything. Also have Lacombe hogs best breed there is and Shorthorn cattle. Hope I am not talking too much about farming but think farmer most important man there is in a way because if it wasn't for the farmer, everybody would starve, if you know what I mean. Am Protestant, Orangeman and great admirer of Mr. Diefenbaker. Read a lot because reading is a great pastime and also you learn a lot that way. I am well and trust you are the same. Drop me a line when you have time.

Yours Truly, Sam Baxter

* * *

When the reply came, he was afraid to open it, so afraid that he tore the unopened letter into four sections, intending to destroy it, and later had to put it back together like a jigsaw puzzle.

This is what it said:

Dear Sam,

I can see by your picture that you are a very kind man and by reading between the lines I can tell you are a very lonely one. I have been very lonely myself these last five years since my husband passed away. He was a conductor on the CPR so I get a small pension and don't have to worry about where the next meal is coming from, which is a blessing. And I like to play Bingo and watch wrestling on the television, which helps pass the time away. But to tell the truth I can't seem to get used to living alone.

From your letter, you sound a lot like Harry (my husband) and your picture even looks something like him. You have the same shy, gentle look he did. Something tells me that you and I have a lot in common and would like one another very much if we had a chance to get to know each other better.

Please don't think I write to every strange man like this, or make a habit of writing to strange men. Most of the letters I got after The Canadian Yeoman came out with my ad in it I didn't even bother answering. Some of them were enough to scare a woman to death. But I can tell that you are a gentleman.

I am sending you a picture of myself. In case you are interested, I am five feet four inches tall and weigh 135 pounds. Have brown hair and dark brown eyes. Before I was married I was a stenographer in Oshawa.

Harry and I never had any children, which is too bad in a way, because they sure would of been a great comfort to me this last few years. But it was God's will, I guess, so it must have been for the best.

Write soon and tell me more about yourself.

> *Yours Sincerely,*
> *Mrs. Amelia Brady*

Here is how Sam began his three-page reply:

Dear Amelia,

Maybe I should be writing dear Mrs. Brady instead of dear Amelia never having met you but after I read your letter I felt I knew you better than some people I've known all my life which may sound like a strange thing to say to a stranger but it is the way I feel and I can't help telling you so because Mother when she was alive used to say the time to give people roses is when they're alive and kicking and not wait until they're dead and gone. . . .

And here is how he ended it:

. . . so be sure and drop me a line as soon as you have time and feel like it and I'll be watching the mailbox every day just like a little kid waiting for a letter from Santa Claus (ha ha) except of course you're a lot prettier than Santa Claus (ha ha again) not that I judge people by their looks because beauty is only skin deep and handsome is as handsome does but I liked your letter so much I can hardly wait to hear from you again

Her answer came by return mail, and this time he did not tear it apart. They exchanged a letter a week, then two letters a week, and then three. Baha'u'llah and his Letters to the Kings, the Prophet Joseph and his Pearl of Great Price, the ravings of Billy James Hargis and the papal bulls of Marxism were all but forgotten. When new leaflets arrived they were tossed in the woodbox and, the following morning, used to kindle the fire. When Sam's subscription to *The Canadian Yeoman* expired, he almost decided not to renew it. Nowadays the only articles he ever read were those on potatoes, hogs and cattle, and most of the time he skipped even those. A second and much larger photograph of Amelia sat on the table beside his bed.

When she wrote that she wished to meet him, he shut himself in the barn and sat there for a long time with his hands over his eyes.

His letters had been truthful enough, yet he felt like a man who has told a very long and complicated lie and discovers that he has been found out.

It was not so much fear he felt, as guilt. "She'll despise me," he thought irrationally, "and I deserve to be despised."

He thought of suicide, but like most people who think of suicide he did not want to be dead, but only to die.

He considered running away, of hiding in the woods and living on trout and venison.

"What a fool I am," he thought. "I wish somebody would shoot me."

Then he realized that if he did not write to her again she would not dare invade his privacy—for that is how he regarded her now, as an intruder.

"Why can't the silly bitch leave things the way they are?" he wondered. "Why do women always have to come barging in where they're not wanted!"

So her letter went unanswered and when she wrote again he threw the unopened envelope in the stove. Weeks passed. Then one night, his telephone rang.

"Long distance calling Mr. Samuel Baxter."

"Huh?"

"Is Mr. Baxter there, please?"

"Who's calling?"

"May we speak with Mr. Baxter, please?" The tone of the operator's voice did not change from one of boredom to one of impatience; it simply became more bored.

"This is Sam Baxter speaking," Sam Baxter said.

"Sam! Is that you, Sam? This is Amelia."

What was there for him to say?

"Are you still there, Sam? It's Amelia Brady. I haven't heard from you for so long that I got worried. How are you, Sam? Sam? Operator, I think I've been disconnected. Operator!"

"Hello," said Sam, weakly.

"Sam, there's nothing wrong, is there? You haven't been answering my letters. I've been worrying myself sick."

"Well, I been feeling kind of poorly lately if you want to know the truth."

"You poor man! I'm coming right down there to look after you. Don't worry about a thing, you hear me! Let me see, what day is this? Tuesday. I'll be coming in on the train Thursday. What time does the train from Montreal get in there?"

"Six o'clock. Six o'clock in the evening, there's a CPR dayliner stops at Hainesville."

"Good enough. Well, you be waiting for that train, Sam Baxter!"

"Yes," said Sam, "I'll be there."

And he *was* there—standing on the station platform in his blue suit with the white pin-stripe, his red and green-striped necktie and tweed cap.

"Taking a little trip, are you, Sam?" asked Albion Greeley, who was there to pick up the Montreal mail bags.

"No," Sam answered. "Waiting for somebody."

"You're brother, I bet? Can't be your Uncle Bythie for this train don't bring no passengers from down Boston-way. Your brother Benjy's coming home, is he? Well, sir, everybody will be some glad to see Benjy again."

"Not my brother," said Sam. "Not my uncle neither."

"Well, now, I'd be the last man to nose into another man's business. If people took care of their own affairs the way they should they wouldn't have time to poke into other people's affairs is what I always say."

"Don't mind telling you," Sam said. "Everybody will know soon enough. I'm going to get myself married."

"You're going to get married! Did you say you were going to get married?"

"Yep," said Sam, rather proudly. "You see there was this girl that wanted to go to Mexico and—"

THE BRIDE'S CROSSING
by Howard O'Hagan

I, Felix Lemprière, beat my fist upon my chest.

Of course, Sergeant Tatlow—Sergeant Tatlow of the Royal Canadian Mounted Police—does not see me do so, nor does he hear the sound, although this is deep and, to me, like the rolling of a distant drum.

The sergeant does not see nor hear me because he is still a mile away, riding up the valley to my cabin. From the cabin door, a few moments ago, I saw his scarlet jacket spotted against the light green leaves of a grove of poplar trees. For the moment I did not see the horse beneath him—the tall bay with the blazed face—because the sergeant, following the trail, dropped from the poplars into the thick-growing willows of the valley bottom. The willows reached to his waist so that he seemed to be wading through them on legs longer than a man's legs or to be upheld and borne along by an invisible and mighty hand. His approach, armed with the law, fills the narrow valley with threat, throws a gloom upon it, like that of the dark cloud which goes before the storm. Yet Sergeant Tatlow—and that it is the sergeant from Brulé on the railroad fifteen miles away, I have no doubt, for his is the only scarlet jacket for miles around—the sergeant and I are old friends. Twice we have hunted together the mountain sheep. He is a patient hunter, a deadly shot. Still, for all that, always behind him is the law—the law which, like a wide-flowing river with hidden fords, bears some men up, casts others down.

I have now walked around behind the cabin and stand between the cabin and the corrals. Marie has walked with me—Marie Sangré, the daughter of old Pierre. As I am about to beat my chest again, she puts a finger to her lip. My fist unclenches. My hand falls to my side.

Then I commence to tell her what I have told her before. The

36

words, repeated, give me the courage I need. And I speak quickly as it appears that we have little time. Already it is late afternoon, an afternoon in early June when the mountains rise blue and the waters run lusty and at timberline the golden-crowned sparrow calls to his mate. This evening, this very evening, before the sun goes down, Marie and I are to be married. The priest has come and in the clearing before the cabin walks forth and back, head down, lips moving, as he reads his breviary. Also in the clearing several tepees have been set up and their smoke floats grey above the spruce forest, for many friends and relatives have arrived to witness the wedding. This, as the saying goes, is a day of days, a day of great gathering of people from near and far, from Solomon creek and the Grande Cache and the Athabaska valley. They number twenty, possibly even twenty-five. Never before on the Calling river have so many come together for such an occasion.

So I tell Marie again that, whatever happens, we will be married. Not all the constables, corporals, sergeants, inspectors and superintendents in western Canada, with their horses, will prevent our marriage. I am about to add, "not even God Himself," when I remember the priest and am silent. The priest has ridden in from the railroad on an old plough-horse, cassock kilted about his knees, because no church is nearer than Edson, one hundred miles out in the foothills.

But I am silent not only on account of the priest who paces on the far side of the cabin. I am silent most of all for lack of words. I think to myself, "Sure, we will be married, maybe, and then on this, our wedding night, when we were to ride up the new trail to the meadow by the stream where the caribou come down to drink, by which I would make camp and spread balsam boughs for our bed—tonight, instead of that, Marie will be alone and I will ride down to the railroad with the sergeant." This is what is in my mind for I know the law is not for me and mine. No, the law is for the red-headed man on the buck-skin mare who has sent the sergeant riding towards my cabin. So, at least, it seems to me.

Suddenly, in anger, I turn to Marie to speak this that is in me. Marie, who is only to my shoulder, takes my arm, squeezes it for me to be quiet and we walk side by side, to and fro, on the hard ground behind the cabin. After a few steps, I speak again, slowly now, almost with caution. Who is the sergeant, I ask, and what have I done that he should come between us? Is the man with the buck-skin mare a good man and worth the trouble he is causing? And I—what have I done that is wrong, that another man in my place would not have done?

It is true that the sergeant, with whom I have travelled in the hills, is a good man. Still, he has his duty. He is a big man, too, with a big chest, but not a chest so big as mine. True, instead of my purple silken shirt, he wears his jacket with gleaming buttons, breeches with yellow stripes instead of mackinaw trousers and boots with spurs instead of soft moccasins.

For all that, I am Felix Lemprière, I tell Marie, as she is Marie Sangré, whose great-great-grandfathers, French and Iroquois, long before the railroad or the Mounted Police were dreamed of, came by canoe and dog-team with the early traders and stayed to live here below the mountains, to marry the native Cree women, to hunt and fish and trap and guide, to ride proudly on horses and, later, to learn English from the priests and white settlers. We are a small people, a few hundred, but no man commands us. Each of us has his horses, his snowshoes, his trap-line, his rifle. Our life is a shadow that passes in sunlight, without hurt to what is around it. Yet the sergeant, my friend, with the law in his hand, is already close to my cabin.

What is it that I have done? I turn Marie's face gently so that she looks up the Calling river flowing by my cabin. Up there for three miles, hemmed in by river, walled by mountain, the hunting trail plows through muskeg where pack-horses sink and flounder and lose their shoes between sunken, grasping roots. During the hunting season, it has long been a horror of mud and pot-holes, of wearied horses and cursing men.

So, what have I done? I have done what no one else has done, though many others from down the river use the north-going trail by my cabin. I have, as they say, studied the situation, considered it from many angles and, during the two months of April and May just past, with the help of Marie's father, old man Pierre and his brother, Samuel, have thrown a log bridge across the river below my cabin and cut a trail up the other bank where, because it is a west-facing slope, the ground is drier. By this means, the trail avoids the muskeg entirely. Certainly, the bridge is narrow. It leans upstream and then downstream. It bends in the middle where old Pierre, a man wise in building, persuaded us to buttress it on a mid-stream rock. The bridge has no rails, no planking and the chinks between the three logs—three logs laid lengthwise, a set on each side of the mid-stream rock—are packed with moss. But it is a bridge, and it spans the white teeth of rapids where no horse could ford or swim. No man on horseback has yet crossed the bridge—this new bridge which, though half a mile below my cabin and on Crown land, I regard as my own because I and my people have built it.

I admit, without further words, that the idea of the bridge was not mine at the beginning. No, it was the idea of an English lord, a stranger, a man from over the seas. Him, last year in September, I took hunting into the sheep country beyond the head of Calling river. A very rich man, his family had made their money by collecting bird dung on the west coast of South America and selling it at high profit. This I have from Fred Brewster, a neighbour, himself a very great hunter, who recommended me to the English lord. No matter—the English lord was one given to thought and when, sheep, moose and caribou heads tied upon our packs, we returned down river from our hunt and for two hours wallowed through the muskeg just above my cabin, on reaching the corrals where we unpacked, he drew me aside. Like the horses, we were mud-spattered, sweating, and tired. More than that, the English lord was angry. "Felix," he said to me, "there should be a law against it—against a piece of trail such as that. Since there is no law, you might build a bridge." Then, standing on the little knoll in front of my cabin door, pointing downstream, he showed me where to build the bridge.

All that winter, that is to say, last winter, I reflected upon what the English lord had said to me. In the spring I rode north to the Grande Cache on the Smokey and talked to Pierre Sangré. So, in early April he and his brother, Samuel, came down to help me. Marie came with them to tend the fire and cook in the tepee. Between Marie and me, nothing had been arranged, but everything was understood. I had known her when she was but a girl, playing by the river with a doll made of feathers and rabbit skin stuffed with grass. Now that she was a young woman it was assumed, even without the words being spoken, that when her father returned north, she would remain with me. We would be married when the bridge had been completed. Life is not always gay and this would be a celebration, a double celebration, and one of note in the foothills.

Across that bridge, although yesterday its building was finished, no one so far has gone on horseback—as I have already stated. I do not deny that two mornings ago, a man tried to cross with his horse. His name is Cal Stubbins, a newcomer, a poacher

who takes fur from the traps of others, the red-headed man from
five miles down the river. While we worked on the bridge in
May, several times he rode up, watched us, spat and rode away.
Though he, too, travels the northern trail, he made no offer to
help. A lazy man, I thought, one who probably can sleep with
his boots on, upright in a chair. But his skin is light and
freckled, his eyes pale blue. My people's skin is brown and their
eyes are dark.

Two mornings ago early, when I happened to be alone on the
bridge, shaving bark from the logs with my axe, he came again,
this time with a friend from the city, a pack-horse following
between them. They were on their way up the river to fish. As
Stubbins spurred his buck-skin mare forward towards the bridge,
she snorted, shied at the smell of fresh-cut timber. There, the
river surging below, I braced my legs and faced him. I would not
let him pass. The bridge, so to speak, was not yet officially
open. First there was a ceremony, an important ceremony to be
performed—of which, naturally, I said nothing to Stubbins.

He dismounted, dropped his lines, came to me, shoved his
chest against me. Again, it was a big chest. Still, not so big as
mine. I noticed whiskey on his breath and dropped the head of
my double-bitted axe to the log on which I stood. Had he asked
me, I would have explained to him why, in the circumstances,
he would have to wait another day or two before taking horses
across the bridge. He asked nothing. He said to me, "Out of the
way. We're going across."

Then, before I had had time to reply, he turned his head back
over his shoulder. There on the rise of land, outlined against a
white cloud, was Marie standing on the trail leading down to the
bridge. She wore moccasins, fringed, moose-hide leggings, a
blue woollen shirt open at the throat and had her black, glossy
hair tied back with a blue ribbon. She was as beautiful, it seemed
to me, as a young birch tree which, by a stream, sheds light by
the dark forest. Stubbins' blue eyes turned from her to me.

'So," he said to me, "tough guy, eh?" He put his hand out to
shove me aside, repeating as he did so, "Tough, eh? Showing
off for your half-breed squaw . . ."

After that, after those words, I remember little. I remember
nothing at all until, lying flat on the bridge, I looked down and
saw the red head of Stubbins bobbing in the green swirl of a
backwater and farther away his black hat bouncing on the river
current. I wondered, how did Cal Stubbins get away down

there—Cal Stubbins who had wanted to use a bridge he had not helped to build so that he and his friend would not become bogged in muskeg on their fishing expedition? Then on my shoulder I felt a touch. "Come," said Marie. "Let him be—see, he is climbing up the clay bank." Marie hid her face behind her hand. She was laughing.

I inquired why she was laughing. "It is because," she said, "when you threw him off the bridge, I saw the soles of his riding gaiters and they were new and still very white and as he fell, his arms reached out for the water as though he were thirsty."

It appeared to me that all of this was hardly a cause for laughter. I was sure of it when Stubbins, shaking and dripping wet, climbed on his buck-skin mare and, his head raised arrogantly above me, exclaimed hoarsely, "You'll hear more about this, Mr. Felix Lemprière. Oh, I know your name all right. So will Sergeant Tatlow down at Brulé."

Stubbins and his friend from the city, before whom he had been humbled, did not go fishing—they might still have taken the old trail by my cabin through the muskeg. Instead, they turned back down the river the way they had come.

Now, two days later, on this day that was to be our wedding day, with Sergeant Tatlow only a few hundred yards away, facing Marie behind my cabin, holding her by the shoulders, I ask her, "Why did I turn Stubbins back from the bridge?" She smiles. She looks away. She knows well why I turned him back. I turned him back, I tell her, because it had been decided that she would be the first to cross the new bridge on the white two-year-old which this spring I have broken. She will cross the bridge this evening of our wedding. Her father and her Uncle Samuel will follow. After them will come myself and the priest, then the other people, and we will be married by the pool fringed with quivering poplars on the far side of the river. The bridge in days to come will be a mark upon the land, a sign to men who travel. It will be known as "The Bride's Crossing" and the day, our wedding day, that Marie on the white two-year-old rode across it, will be remembered. A small thing, you think, and unnecessary that there should be such occasion in the opening of a log bridge at the foot of the mountains? Then do not forget the cold, the snow, the wail of the winter's blizzard and long nights by lonely campfires on the trap-line and you will understand, perhaps, that at times an event, a festival even, is required to give light and push back the darkness of the year.

Such, at any rate, is our plan for the wedding, but as I speak to Marie and hold her closer to me, I hear the thud of hooves, the tinkle of spurs, the heavy breathing of a horse. Sergeant Tatlow, because Cal Stubbins has gone down to see him, has arrived at the cabin. It is not a trifling matter, I think, to have thrown a man from a bridge into a river. But what else, at the time, was there to do? The law—I know nothing of the law, except that it is made far away by men whose eyes are blue like those of Stubbins and whose way of life is not my own.

Marie lifts one foot in its pliant moccasin, puts it behind the other knee. She touches a finger to my throat. Then she grasps my shirt, pulls herself tightly to me. "Sergeant Tatlow," she says, "has come because he has heard we are to be married. See, he wears his dress uniform. That is why he has come. He is your friend and you are to be married." She nods.

She tells me that I should now go around to the front of the cabin and meet the sergeant. I reply that the sergeant may come to where I am. Marie leaves me. I walk over to the corrals.

Four horses are there behind the bars: two pintos, my clean-legged roan saddle-horse and the white two-year-old which is Marie's to take over the bridge. I speak, hold out my hand. The white horse, with his pink nostrils, nuzzles it. I could mount my roan, ride away, but that would mean that I would leave Marie.

In a few minutes the sergeant is beside me—an older man than I am, and not so tall and with a brown moustache. Because he is not so tall as I am, his eyes do not meet my own. They look above my head as though, when he spoke, he spoke to another who is behind and over-tops me. Then he looks away—at the white horse, up the valley, at the mountains. His moustache twitches, as if he were about to smile. Of that I am not sure for, under the moustache, I cannot see the corners of his mouth. He comes at once to the point.

He says, "Felix, I hear you have been obstructing the Queen's highway. More than that. I am told you used violence."

I do not comprehend. There is no highway nearer than that beyond the railroad and across the Athabaska valley, almost twenty miles away. The sergeant continues to speak. A trail through the foothills or the mountains, he tells me, is like a highway. All men are free to use it. By building the bridge, I improved the highway but I did not, therefore, make it my own.

Nor is the bridge my own for it rests on Crown land and is made of Crown timber.

"Suppose," the sergeant says, "a tree had fallen across the trail or across a road. You cut through the tree, cleared the way and then stood, axe in hand, defying any one to pass? An offence, Felix. A fine, at least, possibly imprisonment if you threatened with your axe."

I bow my head. I listen. "But I did not raise my axe," I reply. "I dropped its head to the deck of the bridge."

"Oh?" Sergeant Tatlow jerks his head sideways. Apparently he had heard it differently.

"And provocation," he asks me. "Did Stubbins threaten you?"

"No, but Marie, she was there . . ." For an instant, I am tempted to describe to the sergeant how she looked, uplifted against the white cloud, as though she were not on the earth at all but floating above it. The effort is beyond me. I repeat, "Marie—and he called her, he said . . ."

The sergeant raises his hand. "Never mind," he says, "I think I can guess the rest . . . and then you threw him into the water?"

There is no purpose in denying what I had done and what I would probably do again. The sergeant, my friend of the hunting trail, has a heavy hand. It claps me on the shoulder. "Good man," he says. "I might have done the same myself. It may be a lesson for him—and for others like him who forget that . . . well, that men are men."

Then his tone changes. "I might have done the same," he adds, "in your position. I do not know. I know only that you, Felix Lemprière, must come with me to stand before the magistrate at Brulé, charged with doing bodily harm and with obstructing by violence the Queen's highway."

I gasp, although what he has said is only what I feared he would say. "Brulé?" I ask. "And now, at once?"

From beyond the cabin we hear laughter, a phrase of song. Already the celebration of the wedding is beginning. The sergeant listens. He is not deaf, nor has he been blind to the tepees pitched before the cabin, nor to the priest walking in the clearing.

He turns to me. "Well, maybe not tonight. Maybe a week from now. I will arrange a postponement if you promise, on your word, to come down a week today."

I promise.

He takes my arm. "And do not worry too much," he tells me. "The magistrate, Mr. Falder, knows Cal Stubbins, knows him too well on his record as a poacher. Your word about the axe should stand against his. There may be a fine, a small fine . . ."

I smile. I am ready, I am able, even eager, to pay a fine. It is worth it to have seen Marie's face as Cal Stubbins pulled himself from the river.

"But the bridge, Felix," the sergeant is saying, "it is for any who wish to use it. It must be open tonight, by midnight, at the latest." He pulls his moustache with gloved fingers and his teeth show beneath it.

Tonight . . . Midnight . . . I wonder if the sergeant, before coming out to the corrals to speak to me, has had a word with the priest or with Marie and learned about the wedding because it is accepted by me, by all of us, that the bridge and the new trail are to be open this evening as soon as Marie had ridden on her white horse across the river.

Passing around the cabin I say to the sergeant, "The law . . . it is beyond me. I do not understand it." I am thinking of the business of the Queen's highway.

"The law," he replies, "is what men make it."

Now from in front of the cabin we see the priest and all the people going towards the bridge where they will wait. They are a group of many colours, of buck-skins, mackinaws, red and purple sashes and shawls flowing in the breeze so that there in the sunset they are like a garden of tall growing flowers which mysteriously moves down to the river.

From her tepee, beside her father, Marie steps freshly dressed in white—in a white, beaded suit of bleached caribou hide, with white moccasins on her little feet and with a white scarf tossed carelessly over her black head of hair, and framing her brown oval face.

She runs towards us, her scarf trailing behind, and the sergeant, studying the priest and all the people, turns to me and asks, "The best man—who is the best man?"

I bridle. My fist rises to beat my chest for I look around and I see no man in all the valley who is a better man than myself unless, indeed, it be the sergeant and, naturally, the priest. But Marie has overheard. She beckons to me. I go. Standing on tiptoe, leaning against me, she speaks softly, her breath warm on my ear. Listening, I realize I had not quite understood the sergeant's question about "the best man."

I leave Marie and return to his side. I say, "Perhaps . . ."

He answers, "Of course, Felix, for me—for a friend it is a high honour to be the 'best man' at your wedding."

So it is that, the sun low in the mountains and the shadows long about us, I wait with Marie and her father and her Uncle Samuel and the priest and the great congregation of people, at least twenty-five in number, and many more, counting the children, while the sergeant, as my best man, goes to the corral to saddle the white two-year-old on which my bride is to ride over the bridge to the pool on the far side of the river where, in the whispering shade of the poplar trees, we will be married.

EVERY DAY OF HIS LIFE
by Jack Hodgins

"If that Big Glad Littlestone ever gets married," some people said, "there won't be a church aisle on the Island wide enough for her to walk down."

"Poor girl," the more sensitive said of her. "The size of a logging truck and almost as loud. Thirty-six years old already and still no sign of a father for that boy of hers."

But Big Glad didn't waste time on people's opinions. Because here it was June again, which was her lucky month. It seemed to her that in all the years she had lived in this old house (measured by the life of that heavy lilac bush, covering half the yard) there had never been a June that felt so lucky. In the woods, all tangled up beneath the fallen hemlock slash, and hidden in the copper grass behind her place, the wild blackberries were ripening early and every day she found a brand-new patch to pick and fill her pail to make her wine. And the honeysuckle flowers all over the side of her house had never smelled so sweet.

But the early evening was the best time, the luckiest time. Every day that month, as soon as she had finished washing up her supper dishes and got Roger started at his piano practice, she came out onto the porch, stood breathing deep with her hands on her hips to take in all the scents the sun had stirred up during the afternoon, then walked out into her yard to water the tomato plants. And every day, too, she wore the same clothes: those little red sneakers, that same white bulging T-shirt, those striped knee-length shorts. And, of course, that was the way Mr. Swingler first saw her, in those clothes, in that garden, bending over her precious tomato plants, a sprinkling can in one hand.

What *she* saw first was a little round head that rode the top of the picket fence to the gate, then stopped and turned and looked at her, unblinking, perhaps trying to believe she was real. For a long time she stared right back. Then the gate swung open and a small bow-legged body carried that head down her path.

"Hey mister," she said. "Get your feet off of my gardeshias."

The little man hopped one step to the side and looked down at the flowers he had crushed. "Them ain't gardeshias, missus, they're geraniums."

"It's Miss," she said and stepped back, for she was spraying water on her own foot. "Miss Littlestone. And I don't know one flower from the other. When the logging camp closed down and they hauled all the other houses away I just went from yard to yard and pulled up what I liked."

The man lowered his eyes again but they popped back up to stare at her. She waited for him to speak but he just went on chewing and staring. Those eyes looked like two painted rubber balls controlled from behind by elastic strings.

Well, she couldn't stare back all day. She went up on the front verandah and picked a large red apple out of a box. "Have an apple," she said, and held it out for him.

"No thank you," he said. "The name's Swingler. This time of year I wouldn't say thank you to no man for an apple dried up and wrinkled as a old prune."

"Not store-bought ones," she said, and took a bite to prove it. "These are store-bought ones I got last Saturday in town. Must be grown in California or somewhere down there."

"No thank you," he said again, though she had half eaten it by now. For some time she stood there on that verandah, eating the apple, trying not to stare back at those rubber-ball eyes, and trying even harder to think of something to say. Her teeth started working around the core and she spat three seeds over the railing.

"That," she said at last, with a slight nod towards the mountain off behind her house, "is the prettiest sight on this island." She said this as if the mountain were fenced right into her own back yard and her name tacked on it.

The little man turned and put both hands on his hips to study the mountain, head cocked. "Not bad," he said.

"Not bad?" she said. "You won't see prettier."

"But you don't own it," he said. "Nobody owns a mountain."

This sounded like criticism to Big Glad, a reflection on her character. In a voice hard enough to show that no one walks uninvited into her yard and insults her, she said, "Where are you headed for anyway?"

"Paper mill," he said, eyes still on that mountain. "Looking for a job."

"Then you're a little off course, mister." She threw the core across the fence right from where she stood. "Took the wrong turn twelve miles back. Paper mill is on the coast; you're headed straight into mountains. Are you walking?"

"Don't see no taxi parked, do you?"

He said this without expression, certainly without sarcasm, yet it was too much for her. She drew back against the wall and folded her arms. "Well, I'm the only one lives in here, me and my son, and I got a car all right but I ain't driving you all the way back to the highway. You got a long walk ahead of you."

For answer he swung to look at her again and said, "Lady, you got the daintiest feet I ever seen."

Now Big Glad knew this was the luckiest month ever. She crossed her ankles and stood with the toe of one red sneaker pointed like a ballet dancer. "Thank you, kind sir," she said, and did a mock curtsey. Then she did a complete turn, on one foot, for him to see every side.

"Don't mention it, I'm sure," he said and jammed a cigarette into his mouth.

That he had a mouth she hadn't noticed before. Now she realized that there was more to his face, to his body, than two painted rubber-ball eyes. The top half of his head came forward—forehead, eyes, nose—as if something behind were pushing on it. The bottom half, his mouth, his chin, slid away from her—sucked back as if he had swallowed his own teeth and half his jaw. In fact, she thought, if he'd just turn his head he'd probably have no chin at all.

Because he wore a pair of loose overalls and a plaid shirt so big the sleeves had to be rolled up to meet his wrists, she couldn't tell what his body was really like. She guessed his age at fifty-five.

"Forty-seven," he said. He lighted the cigarette and ground the match into the gravel of her path. "Born forty-seven years ago on my old man's farm down near Victoria, lived every place on this island you could name since then. Never been in here before, though."

"Me, I was born in this old shack. There's been a new coat of paint on those shakes every year of my life. Only time I ever leave the place is to go to town, or when I go off for a month or two to cook in a logging camp up the coast."

Mr. Swingler looked around the clearing, at the bare spots in the grass, the piles of old brick and overgrown lilac. "How come they all moved?" he said. "Why didn't they stay right here like you?"

"Oh, as soon as the camp shut down they fell all over themselves to buy the same house they'd been crabbing about for years while they rented them. Then they hauled them out to the highway so they could watch the traffic go by. Front lawns the size of aprons. And for Saturday-night entertainment they sit at the front window and hope for an accident."

"Why didn't you move too?"

"Mister Swingler, that is a silly question. I like it here, it's much better with all them people gone. Sounds of trucks and cars and brakes squealing can't measure up to a squirrel's chattering or a deer in the underbrush."

Mr. Swingler did not say anything to that; he looked right past her. His chewing stopped. "What's that?" he said, and the chewing started again.

"Where?"

"Behind you. In the doorway."

Big Glad looked and there was Roger standing with his nose pressed flat against the screen door. "That's my boy," she said to the man, and, "Get your face away from that filthy screen," to the boy. Then she said to Mr. Swingler, who had moved up to stand at the foot of the verandah steps below her, "He's got plenty of talent, everyone says. Just ten years old, too."

Mr. Swingler glowered at the boy as if talent was the one thing this world could do without. He scratched behind one ear for a full minute. "Talent's all right," he said. "But you got to have guts as well."

At this the child's face faded into the shadow of the room behind. Big Glad moved in front of the door as if to protect her son. The boards creaked beneath her.

"Roger's all right," she said.

"Sure," he said. His gaze tried to penetrate the screen.

"They all say he'll go far."

"Sure," Mr. Swingler said. He walked over to one side of the lawn. He came back with both hands in his pockets. "Where's the best place for looking at that mountain?" he said, while inside the house the boy started finger exercises on the piano.

Big Glad came down off the verandah and took another look at the mountain. Maybe he had seen something she'd missed. "What do you mean?" she said. "That looks good from anyplace."

He took the time to look at her as if she were a simple child. Then, lowering his eyes, he shrugged and turned his back to her. "I'm going to paint it."

"Well, why didn't you *say* you were an artist? The best view anywhere is right from the top of my roof. But where do you keep you paints and stuff?"

Mr. Swingler looked at the steep gable roof like an engineer estimating its strength. Satisfied with what he saw (Lord, he'd need to be, she'd had it all re-done just three years ago, before Momma died) he nodded, said, "Show me where your ladder is and get me a few pieces of paper and your kid's water colours," and turned again to the view.

Big Glad had her thoughts on *that* kind of talk but this time she kept them to herself. Instead she asked, "Don't you carry nothing with you? Artists are supposed to carry a knapsack at least, but you just rely on people having kids with water colours?"

"A toothbrush," he said and without even turning to face her pulled a blue worn brush from one pocket. "And a razor." And he pulled that out too, from the other pocket, and held them both up high in case there was somehting wrong with her eyes. Then he faced her. "Now if you'll just show me where you keep your ladder."

She did. She pointed to where it was lying in the long grass down one side of the house. Then, because she had never met an artist before—an eccentric one at that—she hurried into the house, excited, to get him his paper and paints.

He went up the roof first, holding the pad of paper and Roger's Donald Duck paint set, and sat on the peak. She followed him on her hands and knees, carrying a glass of water and a pencil, cursing the tiny stones that cut into her skin and broke her fingernails. Then, puffing (Oh Lord, if Momma were alive she'd have another heart attack just at the thought of her daring), she sat beside him on the ridge facing the mountain and tried to make herself comfortable. "My goodness," she said, "this *is* nice up here. A little hard on the rear end, though."

Mr. Swingler braced himself by putting his feet wide apart. "You'll have to be quiet," he said.

She held her breath to please him and saw that he held the pad of paper on his lap, ready for action. The tin of paints was on the roof between his feet, one end propped up on a rock to keep it level. She heaved a great sigh and offered her face up to the sun as if here she was, ready for whatever was ahead. Let it happen, she thought, and planted her feet wide apart for balance, like him.

When she looked down again he had sketched in the scene with his pencil and was putting a light blue wash over the whole paper. She sniffed hard, said, "Just smell that lilac," and folded her arms under her great breasts.

But Mr. Swingler wasn't smelling flowers. Without even slowing the motion of his brush on that paper he said, "Can't you get that racket to stop?"

"What racket?"

"That kid of yours. That piano racket right below us."

She hadn't even noticed. Roger practised so much his noise had become part of the natural background for her. She had always thought there was nothing like music to calm the nerves. But apparently Mr. Swingler didn't agree, so she stomped one foot hard three times on the roof and listened to make sure the message was understood.

It was. The sounds from the piano became so soft they might have been coming with the sun from across the woods.

"That was Rachmaninoff," she said.

For a long time, for perhaps five minutes, she remained silent and watched him work. When the sun had dried the wash (he held the paper up as if to catch the rays that came at them horizontally across the tops of the firs), he began to work at filling in the colours of the lower slopes of that mountain. She couldn't see how a paint brush would be able to put in all those black snags that stood like rigid hairs down the burned-off side, but that was his problem.

"What we need is a drink," she said.

He didn't say anything to that, so she repeated. "What we need in this sun is a nice cold drink of my homemade dandelion wine."

This time she took his silence for agreement and backed on her hands and knees down the slope of the roof. At the edge she hovered for a moment, swinging her foot around over the eavestrough in search of the ladder. Then she went down and told Roger to play softly from now on if he didn't want a cuff on the ear, because Mr. Swingler was an artist and artists need real quiet if they're going to get inspired.

From a cupboard she took down two of her best glasses (Momma had never let her use them, preferring to do without rather than take a chance on breaking one) and put them on a tray to carry them into the back bedroom, which had become her storage room. There was no furniture in the room except the shelves she hammered together the same day she threw out Momma's bed at last (smelling of medicine and anger and death) and these shelves were filled with her homemade liquor. The one papered wall was lined with bottles of blackberry wine and down along the window wall there were twenty-five gallons of saki. The other two walls displayed her specialty—dandelion wine.

She stepped over the empty bottles on the floor and took down a half-gallon of dandelion wine to fill the glasses. With the bottle held tight against her breasts she listened for a minute to the music and hummed a few bars.

What was going to happen to her she wasn't sure, but whatever it was she was ready. Her heart pounded so hard she found it difficult to breathe. She hummed three more bars of the music to quiet herself and said, "Glad old girl, you got a real artist sitting up on your roof right now, good as trapped, and all you have to do is play it right to have him begging." She drank both glasses fast and filled them again. She put the bottle back on the shelf, picked up the tray, then changed her mind and put the bottle on the tray too, beside those full glasses. With the tray held out in front of her like an offering she marched out past the piano (saying,"Play on, Roger, play on" to her son, who would play all night if that was what she wanted) and through the living room, right outside to the front of the ladder.

"Coming up," she said, and waited with one foot on the bottom rung for him to come to her aid.

But she might have waited all day and night too for all the response she got. So she balanced that tray in one hand and went up the ladder slowly and carefully. When she had the tray balanced with one end on the top rung and the other on the eavestrough she called out again, this time a little louder: "Even a genius can take time out to be a gentleman. Give me a hand."

He did, too. He came down front ways, a way she'd never

dare, just as calm as he might if the roof were flat, and bent to pick up the tray. For perhaps a full minute she stared into his eyes and he stared back. They were brown eyes, those rubber balls, and each one had its own road map stamped in red on the white parts.

Maybe that's the sign of a traveller, she thought. Like spaced teeth. Well, traveller or not, he'd just walked down a one-way dead-end street. And unless he were a lot smarter than she thought, his travelling days were over.

He picked up the tray and she followed him on her hands and knees up that slope to the peak. Roger was starting in on something by Grieg. She didn't know the name of it and never did like it much. She stomped her foot again and it softened a little.

She sipped from her glass and let the wine slide down her throat slowly and quietly. No matter what she drank she always drank it like a lady. "My, that is good," she said. "I'd think this is the best batch I ever made." And she sipped again, pursing her lips while she thought it over, then nodded as she swallowed, as if to say Yes she was right the first time. She rolled her eyes to the sky when the warmth started to spread itself inside her. "You ought to have a wife," she said.

"I *had* one," he said, as if what she had asked about was a case of measles.

"What'd you do? Walk off and leave her high and dry?"

Mr. Swingler pushed one hand back through his hair and dug all his fingers into his scalp for a good scratch. "No, not that," he said, and flicked the dandruff out from his fingernails one at a time. "She stepped out onto the road to flag down a bus and was too slow at stepping back. That bus flung her through the air and left her draped over a barbed-wire fence like an empty gunny sack."

Big Glad raised her eyes to the mountain to compare it with his. He wasn't granting it enough power. She coughed daintily into her hand to show she was discreet, then said, "She buried near here?" as if she didn't really care but if he wanted to tell her she'd be willing to listen.

"She's not buried anywhere. She wanted one of these here cremations."

Big Glad never quite approved of cremations; there was something a little bit primitive about the whole idea. She cleared her throat again. "Well, even ashes have to have something done with them."

He swung his head to look at her, perhaps to see if she could take it. "I swallowed them," he said, and picked up his brush again to go on with his work.

Big Glad gulped at that, and swallowed too, and made a face. "Then you must be crazy," she said, and took another, longer drink from her glass.

"I read it in a history book," he said, and with one more stroke the peak of that mountain stood up, hard and true against the sky. "Some old queen did it way back when. Mixed the ashes in a glass of wine and drank the whole lot down."

She wondered when he ever stayed still in one spot long enough to read a book but said nothing about that. Instead she asked, "Why?"

He lifted his head at that as if here was one question he had never expected. He thought for a while. "Why? It seemed kind of romantic to me to keep my wife inside of me."

"Did you ever think of what happened to what didn't stay inside you?"

Evidently he hadn't considered that and wasn't going to now. He went on with his painting.

Still she wished she had thought of that. It made her mad that she had never thought of anything as smart as that. Not that she had ever had anyone to do it to. Her father had fallen down a well thirty-two years ago. And Momma died so mean a person would have choked on her ashes. There had never been anyone she'd cared that much about. She wondered if anyone would ever drink her ashes.

And speaking of queer people, she had known a few too in her time. "That reminds me of my mechanic," she said, "the one who works on my car."

"That car," he said.

"What's the matter *that* car?"

"I've been here more than an hour, most of the time sitting right up here on this roof, and I still haven't seen that car you keep on talking about."

"A car is not something you set up on a post like a flag for all to see. If you'll just lower your eyes a little you'll see a garage with door *closed* and *locked*. And if you'll just squint a little you might be able to pick out the orange colour of it through the window."

He looked, lowered his gaze and squinted against the sun, peered at the little roof-sagging building she meant. "Orange," he said, and picked up his brush again. He painted a tint of orange on the sky behind the mountain.

"That's not the colour of the sky," she said. "You're putting things there that you can't see."

"That's what I want to see," he said. "That's what the picture needed."

Big Glad refilled both the glasses from the bottle, though his was not empty. "I guess a man could set up here every day of his life painting that mountain and never paint it the same way twice."

"I guess," he said.

"I guess a place like this one here of mine is just exactly the right kind of place for an artist. He could paint his whole life long."

"Lady," he said, "you're right," and plopped that picture right into her lap so she had to close her knees fast to keep it from slipping right through.

It took a full minute for his words to sink in. When she realized what he meant she gulped another mouthful of her drink and said, "You mean you *like* it here?"

He turned to her and carefully lifted his painting from her lap. "I knew as soon as I came in sight of your house that this would be the kind of place I'd like to live in the rest of my life. Just look at that mountain! I never painted so good."

But Big Glad wasn't wasting breath on pictures. "Mister Swingler," she said. "Are you telling me that you want to move in, to live downstairs with me and Roger, to be a part of this family?"

He stopped admiring his own work long enough to look at her. "Well, I think that's what I been saying."

Big Glad sighed and sat back and folded her arms. "No man has ever slept under my roof without taking out a marriage licence first."

Mr. Swingler did some deep thinking about this. His eyes swung up to take in that mountain again, and then down to the sagging garage below. "I guess that makes sense," he said.

"It's only fair to my boy."

At the mention of her son they both listened to the sounds of Rachmaninoff again, sifting soft as sunlight up through the rafters of the house. Mr. Swingler said, "Now if there is nothing else, you get down off this roof and make yourself decent so we can go to town and celebrate."

Big Glad hadn't worn her hat since Momma's funeral. It was a flat-brimmed straw thing, with a cluster of plastic berries at the front. She set it on top of her head and looked in her bedroom mirror, pinching her cheeks to bring back a little colour to them. Then she slipped off her shorts and pulled on a black wool skirt. Again she admired herself in the mirror. Somehow she didn't feel like a bride yet, but that was because it all happened so fast. Who would have thought this morning that before dark she would have been proposed to?

She tiptoed past Roger (let him find out when they had that piece of paper to show) and went out onto the verandah. Because Mr. Swingler hadn't come down off the roof yet, probably putting some finishing touches on that picture of his, she sat down on the top step to wait and soon she began to shake through her whole body. She put her head down to try and stop the trembling.

When Mr. Swingler came around the corner of the house and saw her he said, "What's the matter with you?"

"We can't," she said.

He put his painted mountain on her verandah railing. "What do you mean can't? What else you been working on ever since I arrived?"

Big Glad was afraid to look up. All she could see was a wood bug working its way across the step. "But we hardly know each other."

Mr. Swingler laughed. "Lady," he said. "You made up your mind to catch me the minute I walked inside your gate. I could've been a murderer for all you cared."

She looked up at him. She hadn't thought of that. "You could still be a murderer. Or a thief or escaped convict. I don't know a single thing about you."

He winked at her and slid closer, one arm laid out like a broken wing on her railing. "If we get the licence we'll have three days to wait before we can make use of it. I guess by that time you'll know me pretty well."

"And if I die," she said, and swallowed. "And if I die, will you drink my ashes?"

He looked hard at her and thought a moment. Then he said, "Miss Littlestone, after the first time there's nothing to it."

At that Big Glad began to cry. She bowed down her hat, put her face in her hands, and sobbed. After a while she felt better, because after all she was a bride and brides do sometimes cry, and looked at Mr. Swingler, who was holding out one hand like a porter waiting for a tip. "*Now* what do you want?" she said.

He moved closer and bent down over her so that she could see those road maps of his again. "If you'll just give me the keys to the garage," he said, "we'll be on our way."

Men and Women:
Tragic and Ironic Views

THE CHARIVARI
by Susanna Moodie

It was towards the close of the summer of 1833, which had been unusually cold and wet for Canada, while Moodie was absent at D——, inspecting a portion of his government grant of land, that I was startled one night, just before retiring to rest, by the sudden firing of guns in our near vicinity, accompanied by shouts and yells, the braying of horns, the beating of drums, and the barking of all the dogs in the neighbourhood. I never heard a more stunning uproar of discordant and hideous sounds.

What could it all mean? The maid-servant, as much alarmed as myself, opened the door and listened.

"The goodness defend us!" she exclaimed, quickly closing it, and drawing a bolt seldom used. "We shall be murdered. The Yankees must have taken Canada, and are marching hither."

"Nonsense! that cannot be. Besides, they would never leave the main road to attack a poor place like this. Yet the noise is very near. Hark! they are firing again. Bring me the hammer and some nails, and let us secure the windows."

The next moment I laughed at my folly in attempting to secure a log hut, when the application of a match to its rotten walls would consume it in a few minutes. Still, as the noise increased, I was really frightened. My servant, who was Irish (for my Scotch girl, Bell, had taken to herself a husband, and I had been obliged to hire another in her place, who had been only a few days in the country), began to cry and wring her hands, and lament her hard fate in coming to Canada.

Just at this critical moment, when we were both self-convicted of an arrant cowardice, which would have shamed a Canadian girl of six years old, Mrs. O—— tapped at the door, and although generally a most unwelcome visitor, from her gossiping, mischievous propensities, I gladly let her in

"Do tell me," I cried, "the meaning of this strange uproar?"

"Oh, 'tis nothing," she replied, laughing. "You and Mary look as white as a sheet; but you need not be alarmed. A set of wild fellows have met to charivari Old Satan, who has married his fourth wife tonight, a young girl of sixteen. I should not wonder if some mischief happens among them, for they are a bad set, made up of all the idle loafers about Port H—— and C——."

"What is a charivari?" said I. "Do, pray, enlighten me."

"Have you been nine months in Canada, and ask that question? Why, I thought you knew everything! Well, I will tell you what it is. The charivari is a custom that the Canadians got from the French, in the Lower Province, and a queer custom it is. When an old man marries a young wife, or an old woman a young husband, or two old people, who ought to be thinking of their graves, enter for the second or third time into the holy estate of wedlock, as the priest calls it, all the idle young fellows in the neighbourhood meet together to charivari them. For this purpose they disguise themselves, blackening their faces, putting their clothes on hind part before, and wearing horrible masks, with grotesque caps on their heads, adorned with cocks' feathers and bells. They then form in a regular body, and proceed to the bridegroom's house, to the sound of tin kettles, horns and drums, cracked fiddles, and all the discordant instruments they can collect together. Thus equipped, they surround the house where the wedding is held, just at the hour when the happy couple are supposed to be about to retire to rest—beating upon the door with clubs and staves, and demanding of the bridegroom admittance to drink the bride's health, or in lieu thereof to receive a certain sum of money to treat the band at the nearest tavern.

"If the bridegroom refuses to appear and grant their request, they commence the horrible din you heard, firing guns charged with peas against the doors and windows, rattling old pots and kettles, and abusing him for his stinginess in no measured terms. Sometimes they break open the doors, and seize upon the bridegroom; and he may esteem himself a very fortunate man, under such circumstances, if he escapes being ridden upon a rail, tarred and feathered, and otherwise maltreated. I have known many fatal accidents arise out of an imprudent refusal to satisfy the demands of the assailants. People have even lost their lives in the fray; and I think the Government should interfere, and put down these riotous meetings. Surely it is very hard that an old man cannot marry a young gal, if she is willing to take him, without asking the leave of such a rabble as that. What right have they to interfere with his private affairs?"

"What, indeed?" said I, feeling a truly British indignation at such a lawless infringement upon the natural rights of man.

"I remember," continued Mrs. O——, who had got fairly started upon a favourite subject, "a scene of this kind, that was acted two years ago, at——, when old Mr. P—— took his third wife. He was a very rich storekeeper, and had made during the war a great deal of money. He felt lonely in his old age, and married a young, handsome widow, to enliven his house. The lads in the village were determined to make him pay for his frolic. This got wind, and Mr. P—— was advised to spend the honeymoon in Toronto; but he only laughed, and said that 'he was not going to be frightened from his comfortable home by the threats of a few wild boys.' In the morning, he was married at the church, and spent the day at home, where he entertained a large party of his own and the bride's friends. During the evening all the idle chaps in the town collected round the house, headed by a mad young bookseller, who had offered himself for their captain, and, in the usual forms, demanded a sight of the bride, and liquor to drink her health. They were very good-naturedly received by Mr. P——, who sent a friend down to them to bid them welcome, and to inquire on what terms they would consent to let him off, and disperse.

"The captain of the band demanded sixty dollars, as he, Mr. P——, could well afford to pay it.

"'That's too much, my fine fellows!' cried Mr. P—— from the open window. 'Say twenty-five, and I will send you down a cheque upon the Bank of Montreal for the money.'

"'Thirty! thirty! thirty! old boy!' roared a hundred voices. 'Your wife's worth that. Down with the cash, and we will give you three cheers, and three times three for the bride, and leave you to sleep in peace. If you hang back, we will raise such a 'larum about your ears that you shan't know that your wife's your own for a month to come!'

"'I'll give you twenty-five,' remonstrated the bridegroom, not the least alarmed at their threats, and laughing all the time in his sleeve.

"'Thirty; not one copper less!' Here they gave him such a salute of diabolical sounds that he ran from the window with his hands to his ears, and his friend came down to the verandah, and gave them the sum they required. They did not expect that the old man would have been so liberal, and they gave him the 'Hip, hip, hip, hurrah!' in fine style, and marched off to finish the night and spend the money at the tavern.''

"And do people allow themselves to be bullied out of their property by such ruffians?''

"Ah, my dear! 'tis the custom of the country, and 'tis not so easy to put it down. But I can tell you that a charivari is not always a joke.

"There was another affair that happened just before you came to the place, that occasioned no small talk in the neighbourhood; and well it might, for it was a most disgraceful piece of business, and attended with very serious consequences. Some of the charivari party had to fly, or they might have ended their days in the penitentiary.

"There was a runaway nigger from the States came to the village, and set up a barber's poll, and settled among us. I am no friend to the blacks; but really Tom Smith was such a quiet, good-natured fellow, and so civil and obliging, that he soon got a good business. He was clever, too, and cleaned old clothes until they looked almost as good as new. Well, after a time he persuaded a white girl to marry him. She was not a bad-looking Irishwoman, and I can't think what bewitched the creature to take him.

"Her marriage with the black man created a great sensation in the town. All the young fellows were indignant at his presumption and her folly, and they determined to give them the charivari in fine style, and punish them both for the insult they had put upon the place.

"Some of the young gentlemen in the town joined in the frolic. They went so far as to enter the house, drag the poor nigger from his bed, and in spite of his shrieks for mercy, they hurried him out into the cold air—for it was winter—and almost naked as he was, rode him upon a rail, and so ill-treated him that he died under their hands.

"They left the body, when they found what had happened, and fled. The ringleaders escaped across the lake to the other side; and those who remained could not be sufficiently identified to bring them to trial. The affair was hushed up; but it gave great uneasiness to several respectable families whose sons were in the scrape.''

"But scenes like these must be of rare occurrence?''

"They are more common than you imagine. A man was killed up at W—— the other day, and two others dangerously wounded, at a charivari. The bridegroom was a man in middle life, a desperately resolute and passionate man, and he swore that if such riff-raff dared to interfere with him, he would shoot at them with as little compunction as he would at so many crows. His threats only increased the mischievous determination of the mob to torment him; and when he refused to admit their deputation, or even to give them a portion of the wedding cheer, they determined to frighten him into compliance by firing several guns, loaded with peas, at his door. Their salute was returned, from the chamber window, by the discharge of a double-barrelled gun, loaded with buckshot. The crowd gave back with a tremendous yell. Their leader was shot through the heart, and two of the foremost of the scuffle dangerously wounded. They vowed they would set fire to the house, but the bridegroom boldly stepped to the window, and told them to try it, and before they could light a torch he would fire among them again, as his gun was reloaded, and he would discharge it at them as long as one of them dared to remain on his premises.

"They cleared off; but though Mr. A—— was not punished for the *accident*, as it was called, he became a marked man, and lately left the colony to settle in the United States.

"Why, Mrs. Moodie, you look quite serious. I can, however, tell you a less dismal tale. A charivari would seldom be attended with bad consequences if people would take it as a joke, and join in the spree."

"A very dignified proceeding, for a bride and bridegroom to make themselves the laughing-stock of such people!"

"Oh, but custom reconciles us to everything; and 'tis better to give up a little of our pride than endanger the lives of our fellow-creatures. I have been told a story of a lady in the Lower Province, who took for her second husband a young fellow, who, as far as his age was concerned, might have been her son. The mob surrounded her house at night, carrying her effigy in an open coffin, supported by six young lads, with white favours in their hats; and they buried the poor bride, amid shouts of laughter, and the usual accompaniments, just opposite her drawing-room windows. The widow was highly amused by the whole of their proceedings, but she wisely let them have their own way. She lived in a strong stone house, and she barred the doors, and closed the iron shutters, and set them at defiance.

" 'As long as she enjoyed her health,' she said, 'they were welcome to bury her in effigy as often as they pleased; she was really glad to be able to afford amusement to so many people.'

"Night after night, during the whole of that winter, the same party beset her house with their diabolical music; but she only laughed at them.

"The leader of the mob was a young lawyer from these parts, a sad mischievous fellow; the widow became aware of this, and she invited him one evening to take tea with a small party at her house. He accepted the invitation, was charmed with her hearty and hospitable welcome, and soon found himself quite at home; but only think how ashamed he must have felt, when the same 'larum commenced, at the usual hour, in front of the lady's house!

" 'Oh,' said Mrs. R——, smiling to her husband, 'here come our friends. Really, Mr. K——, they amuse us so much of an evening that I should feel quite dull without them.'

"From that hour the charivari ceased, and the old lady was left to enjoy the society of her young husband in quiet.

"I assure you, Mrs. M——, that the charivari often deters old people from making disgraceful marriages, so that it is not wholly without its use."

LABRIE'S WIFE
Duncan Campbell Scott

[Being an excerpt from the manuscript journal of Archibald Muir, Clerk of The Honourable The Hudson's Bay Company at Nipigon House in the year of our Lord, 1815.]

May Twenty-second, 1815

Today something happened which is bound to be of consequence in this outlandish place, and that I will set down here and make of record. Alec, who is getting more gumption now, although as unsteady in all his performances as he was ever, returned from his trip to the Flat Rock, and arrived safe with his two canoes and Ogemah-ga-bow, little Needic and his two sons. It appears that they had, by reason of the rough weather, to lay by at Dry Beaver Islands and had like to have starved if the wind had not gone down, for these fools of Indians will never learn not to devour half their rations in the first day out from the Post. They came in looking like wasps, their belts girt so tightly about their middles.

I could tell the moment I clapped eyes upon Alec that he had some bee in his bonnet, for he can no more control his countenance than an otter can help fishing. His face was all of a jump, and he spoke as if he had no spittle under his tongue. I have a plan to let the youngster speak when he is ready, and by this means I have the enjoyment of witnessing him cast about to get me to question him and assist him out with his story. When we were having a bit of dinner he fairly simmered, but he did not boil until I lit my pipe. Then he could stand my coolness no longer.

"We're to have an opposition!" he blurted out. I did not want to show any astonishment, but I nearly dropped my pipe, such a matter never having been thought of in Nipigon before. "You see," he went on, "I determined when I was at that part of the lake to go over to Keg Island and see if the cache was all right, and on St. Paul's Island, when we went ashore to roast some fish, we found two canoes loaded, and a Frenchman and three Indians.

"He asked me if I was with the English, and I lied to him straight enough, and said No! I was trading alone. Then he wanted to know where our Post was, and I said it was beyond the large island to the west. He said his name was Labrie, and that he was for the North West Company, and was sent in opposition to the English on the lake. So I decided to camp where I was, and not to go to Keg Island, but to come on here. I told him to keep due west, and not to land until he struck the big island, which was Cariboo Island, and not for any reason to camp on a little flat island half way there, which was full of snakes."

The youngster was mighty proud of himself at outwitting the Frenchman, but to take down his pride a bit, I provoked him by saying, "Well, poor Donald used to call you a clavering idiot, but if he had lived to this day he'd have had to invent a new kind of word for you. If your Labrie is anything of a trader he watched you away in the morning, and he will treat us in good Hudson's Bay Company rum when we first meet, having visited your little flat island full of snakes." Off went Alec trying to bite his beard, aping Donald's manner, poor lad; but he had yet a beard no longer than a pinfeather.

May Twenty-third, 1815

I was up before sun this day, as I had a restless night, thinking what I should do now we were to have opposition on the lake, a thing new to me who have scant experience. I determined to be smooth with them and observe them closely, and spoil them if I might with a fair face, and in all events to fight them with what weapons they may choose. I had wakened from a light doze with a sudden thought that I should possess myself of the point of land below the Post where I have always said the buildings should have been placed, which commands and oversees our present position. If it were seized by these pirates of Frenchmen, what then would become of our trade? They would eat it like a bear eats honey-comb. Alec could not see that, and provoked me with much grumbling that it was a useless work and a weary waste of muscle. It is curious how block-headed he is about all matters connected with trade; he has some acuteness belike but of what sort God alone knows. In the end I was mightily satisfied to see a stout staff with the ensign flying, and a small boat-landing, with one of the boats moored. We had the work done before midday, and for the rest of the time I had pleasure in looking down at the point which had an inhabited and secure look, under the Hudson's Bay Company's flag. If the Frenchmen have any idea of the shore about here there will be some *sacré*ing when they find the point taken up, for northwards there is no place for a foothold, and only in a cove, half a mile to the south, can they find level land enough for building upon. So when our Indians come down, and they should be here in a matter of four weeks, they are bound to reach the Post first, and I can keep my eye upon the rascals, who would, if they could, trade with the newcomers and forget old kindnesses and obligations.

May Twenty-fourth, 1815

Ogemah-ga-bow came up to say that one of Needic's boys had died last night, having over-eaten himself after his fast on the Dry Beaver Islands. Rain today.

May Twenty-sixth, 1815

Sundown yesterday on my bench before the door, whereby Needic had made a smudge to keep off the flies, which are now very bad, when I saw a canoe that was none of ours land at the point, and a man step out onto the new boat-landing. He looked all about him as if he was making an inventory of the place, and then he came slowly up the hill. He was a stout-shouldered, low-set fellow, with a black beard and small, bad eyes. Said I to myself as I saw him approach, "There is something mainly dishonest in your make-up, my man, and whatever one may have to do to keep trade from you it won't be very savoury in the doing if your methods are to be used."

"My name's Labrie," he said, running his hand through his hair.

I got upon my legs and said politely, "I heard of your being in the Lake from my man. Will you be seated?"

He said, "No" and looked over his shoulders at the Point.

"You have the Point under your flag," he remarked.

"Aye," I said, as dry as I could.

"The work has marks of newness."

"You are right, it was only finished yesterday."

The blood came into his face in an ugly way.

"Well, there can be no great objection to my trading a little."

"Not there," said I bluntly. "Under my company's flag what we take we claim and keep."

He breathed rather heavily, but held his tongue, and was going to walk away.

"Hold on," said I, "strangers are not treated so here, you must have a dram."

I called Alec, who brought the rum and the glasses. We drank healths courteously, then were ready to cut one another's throats.

"Did you ever taste better than that?" said I.

"I have as good," said he, "though it is the best, I can match it."

"Match it!" said I in a tone of surprise, winking at Alec, who flew as red as a bubble jock. We parted then but just as he was getting away he said over his shoulder, "Your man there has a damned queer idea of direction."

May Twenty-seventh, 1815

Sent Needic and his live boy and Ogemah-ga-bow's brother to Poplar Lodge, to have news of the hunters. The Osnaburgh packs from the north should now be two weeks out, unless the ice is later this year than last. Tomorrow I will put Alec and Ogemah-ga-bow to work clearing out the storehouse and setting things to rights. I am much exercised in mind over my responsibilities. It was bad enough last year, but now I have the whole management, and this opposition to contend with upon the back of it. I begin to be worn with it, what with loss of sleep at night, and thinking about nought else in the day. No sign of Labrie or any of his party.

May Thirtieth, 1815

This morning Labrie came up to borrow an adze, which I lent to him without any question. He seemed to want to be civil enough. When I asked him, however, if Madame Labrie had arrived, he seemed quite put about and mumbled something in his beard, which sounded nearly like "What affair is that of yours?" I paid no attention to him, not wishing to quarrel yet awhile, and without any further parley off he went with the adze, which I am fortunate if I ever see again.

Heat intense today, bring on a great storm of thunder and much rain. Had a great debate with Alec, when we were indoors, as to when the Osnaburgh packs will be in. I calculate in three weeks, as the water is like to be high, they will take the route through Mud Lakes to Negodina, as I wrote Godfrey. The old route to Wabinosh would take them much longer and, what with broken water and two desperate, long carries, there is a great risk of loss by that way. Alec thinks they will be down sooner. There is no doubt they have had a fine winter and if the pack can be safely landed it will be a great matter, and no doubt I shall hear good of it from the partners.

May Thirty-first, 1815

This morning when I was cleaning my pistols I heard a clear sound of laughter. Now laughter is an uncommon thing in this country, visiting us very infrequently. To be sure the Indians laugh, but that to me always has an unmeaning sound, and sometimes a bestial. Moreover, this laughter was different in kind, and one must have listened to it however absorbed he might have been. It was high-pitched and very clear and had something merry and withal innocent about it. It was contagious also and the mere sound of it made my very muscles twitch. There was no one visible, but after I had gazed awhile I saw Alec come up the steps from the warehouse. Not to appear interested before the lad I went back to my work. After a little he came in. I noticed his face was flushed and his manner excited. I paid no attention to him until he had knocked a dish off the table. It broke into three pieces. I was angry with him, good crockery not being by any means very plentiful in this country.

"Good God, man!" I cried. "If you're in such a state that you cannot avoid breaking the dishes, will you lie upon your bed for a while." He glared at me terribly, but had not a word to say. Then I kept quiet for as much as a quarter of an hour, and I could see it was fretting him; he fidgeted about greatly. Then he got up and went to the door.

"It seems to me you take mighty small interest in things."

I said never a word.

"Are you deaf this morning?"

I made no sound. He made no move for a minute, then he said, just as he was going out of the door, in an exasperated way, "That was Labrie's wife."

I could have laughed to myself, but when I had thought upon it for a time I began to perceive something bitter in his tone, and I reflected that of late I had treated him much as poor Donald used unthinkingly to treat me, and that he must be occupying my old position of complaint, and my heart was softened a bit, and I resolved to be more kind to him in the future, who is in much a good boy and canny in a sort about many things.

June First, 1815

I saw Labrie's wife for the first time this morning. An uncommon looking wench, with black hair and eyes and a mouthful of white teeth. I discussed her thoroughly with Alec, who sticks up for it that she is a handsome one. So she is, after her manner, though that I do not acknowledge to Alec. She looked me all over as if I were for sale, and when I coolly turned my back on her, that she might have a good look at that, she went off in a mighty huff.

Alex reports that there are two other women in Labrie's party, rather old and haggish. I have not clapped eyes upon them, not having visited the Cove. Although she went off in a huff, the young wench is a merry one, and it amuses her to hear Alec so aboundingly polite to her with his "Madame Labrie." "Madame Labrie" this and "Madame Labrie" that, whereupon she giggles or breaks out into wild laughter.

June Third, 1815

Needic back from Poplar Lodge, where everything is all right. Had an amusing conversation with the lad Alec anent Labrie's wife. The hussy comes about the house constantly, even when we are not here.

"Now what is she after?" said I.

"You have no understanding of women," he replied. "Of course she will come back when you treat her in that way."

"Now in what way?" said I. "Never do I look at her or pass the time of day with her."

"That is it," he retorts. "You are fairly insulting her, and she comes back."

"Do you try and be sweet to her and mayhap she would stay away."

"It is different with me," he says, biting his whiskers and

shrugging up his shoulders, just as the wench does herself. He has taken on a sort of mincing, balancing, half-Frenchified accent, and shrugs his shoulders.

"Are you afraid she would fall into the love weez you, Alec?" I remarked, trying hard to imitate the accent.

"It is not me she will be in love with."

"No, who then? Needic?"

"Needic!" he cried, going off with a great French shrug.

June Fourth, 1815

No word from Godfrey about the packs. I am getting a trifle anxious. Alec says there are more guns than yardsticks in Labrie's quarters, and makes out they are on for a fight. Labrie's wife came up at noon and made us an omelette with gull's eggs and fresh onion-tops. She is a clever wench and sat looking at me as I devoured it. I talked a bit to her. After she left, Alec sat frowning.

"You were very free with her."

"I merely spoke to her, but then she made a good omelette."

"You said too much to her. You nearly told her we expected the packs at Negodina by the Mud Lake route this year instead of Wabinosh."

"Well, and if I did?"

"It is all she wanted to know."

"Well, you seem to be always ready to stand up for the spy, if she be one," said I, turning the French accent upon him. This made him wroth, as it always does.

"You never seem to understand that a woman's not like a man. The best of them you have to watch, and more particularly when one of them is in love with you."

"That does not apply here," I said, "unless you have her assurances yourself."

"I would not make love to a married woman," he said hotly.

"That's why you guard yourself so carefully, is it? You are mighty pious. It is a pity you are not like me. Now for me Mr. Labrie's wife has no attraction whatever, commandments or no commandments."

This set him off again.

"Be careful you, Archibald Muir, that is what I have to say to you."

We could hear the lady herself laughing down at the landing, and it sounded so innocent that I could not refrain from smiling at the boy.

June Fifth, 1815

We had a scene last night with Labrie's wife, for which Alec has to be thanked, and in which I think he had a small revenge for my baiting of him. I will set down the occurrence here although it be against myself, and our national instrument. She had been hardly before the house, and it was in the dusk of the evening, when she asked me to play upon the pipes.

"Will you play upon the bag-pipes, Mr. Muir?" she said in a very civil voice. "I have never heard the bag-pipes."

Now I am always at pains to oblige a lady, if it be possible, so I went in and got the pipes, hearing Alec urge me also, so I had two willing to be pleased.

Well, scarcely had I begun to get the skin filled with wind when Labrie's wife began to laugh. Now I am willing to admit that the foreword to a performance on the pipes may be dispiriting, but I charge that what follows after when the instrument is well controlled, and when the melody pours forth in full cry, would serve to obliterate a greatly more dispiriting prelude. But in this case I did not get beyond that stage, for Labrie's wife laughed with so little judgment that I was put about. I saw something in Alec's face which led me to think that the whole matter was preconceived by him, and with that I laid down my pipes on the bench beside me. Not another note would I play. I am not much versed in women's ways, and what Labrie's wife did puzzled me. But of that I shall give Alec's explanation. At first she kept on laughing, and then she stopped suddenly and came forward looking sober enough, but with the wrinkles of the laughter not yet gone out of her face. There she stood about four feet from me with a bit of her dress in her hand, as I have seen school girls stand abashed having been found at fault.

"You are angry because I laughed?" she said.

I did not answer.

Then she came close to me and made as if to put her hands upon my shoulders, and when I looked straight upon her eyes she dropped her hands, made a sound in her throat, and turned and went away.

Then young Alec began to strut about like a bantam cock.

"I have to thank you for that performance," I said.

"Why would you prevent a woman from laughing?" says he, in a rage. "Don't you know enough of women to let them laugh and let them talk?"

"I can lay no claim to such a knowledge as yourself," said I, in a mighty sneering voice. "In truth I know naught about them."

"You have proved that this night," retorted Alec.

"Expound that, you young oracle," said I.

"Expound? You have sent her away with a sore heart, and she was minded to be playful with you, and that cuts sore on a heart such as hers. Don't you see it, man?" he cried, sort of dashing his hands down.

"I see nothing of the sort. She was angry simply because I wouldn't speak back to her."

"You might have spoken to her or not spoken, and she would never have minded if you hadn't looked at her in the way you did."

I saw it was no use my trying to fathom the young donkey, so I would speak no more to him.

June Sixth, 1815

Labrie's wife was up last night but I would not go out to see her, being tired of the body and her endless chatter. Alec and she talked for an hour; the boy would be contented to go on vapouring forever, I believe. I pretended to be busy with my papers, and in the end she went away. She came to the window just before she went, and I heard her fingers on the sash, but I did not look up, and I heard her low gurgling laugh as she ran away from Alec, who would go down to the landing with her.

He is as polite to her and as formal as if he were living by a code of court etiquette. I twitted him with that.

"Well," he says, mighty stiff, and pulling a solemn face, "she is a woman, and she is another man's wife."

"The last is her great virtue," said I, with a tone of sarcasm, at which he looked scornful and exceeding pious.

June Seventeenth, 1815

Good news yesterday. Toma came in with a message from Godfrey. The Osnaburgh packs are safe at Cache point on the Mud Lake route. The water is high and they have not had a mishap. In three days they should reach Negodina at the end of the lake. It is, as I have always said, a route more clean and handy than the Wabinosh route, and it will be adopted now from this out.

Woke up with a mighty sore head this morning and had words with Alec. It is inconceivable how domineering that lad has become.

"You were drinking with Madame Labrie last night," he said.

"And my lord is jealous," I replied, sneering at him.

"Ye have made a fool of yourself. What did you tell her?"

"Nothing that I rightly remember. Since when were you ordained my catechist?"

"Now I have told you many times," he said in a parsoning way, "that you did not understand the nature of women, and that you would let slip something that Labrie wanted to know. Now you have done so, I believe, between a glass too much of whisky and a pretty woman."

"Do you call yon a pretty woman?" I said, mocking his accent.

"I pity you!" he said, with great contempt.

He went away swinging his shoulders, much more the master than the man.

To set down the truth, although it be against myself, Labrie's wife came up in the evening of yesterday. I was more decent with the bitch, having had good news, and I treated her to some whisky, and drank with her. Alec was off watching Toma, as he thought Labrie might try to get hold of him. I do not just remember when she went away. God forgive me, I do not rightly remember anything about it.

Hardly had Alec dismissed himself when he came back very greatly excited, but in anger this time.

"They have gone," said he.

"Who?" said I, not thinking for a moment.

"Who! My God! Who? Why Labrie."

"Well what of that?" I said. "It is a good riddance of a vile lot of thieves out of God's country."

"That is all you see to it?" he said.

"Well, what more?" I replied.

"I seem to see that last night you told Madame Labrie the packs were coming by the Mud Lake route to Negodina, and that they have gone to stop them. I have my doubt they will not

barter with them. I seem to see that they will capture the furs and
that by no very gentle means.''

"You have said it before," I cried out, wroth with him and
with myself. "So yon slut is what I have always supposed her to
be.''

A dark look came into his face. "Choose your words!" he
cried, taking a step towards me.

"I'll neither pick nor choose my words," I said. "What do
you call her then that would take our hospitality and then do us
wrong?''

"Madaline would do no such thing," he cried, strutting about
in a way that looked comical to me. I laughed at him.

"Madaline! Madaline! We shall see what Madaline will have
done when we lose our furs. Why, man, you said out of your
own mouth that she had done it.''

"You lie," he cried, but it was here not impudence, so I paid
no attention to him.

After some parley and conversation, I sent him with three
canoes and all the able men, except Needic, to Negodina to
see what had fallen out. He is to send me back a letter, as
soon as he can, with the word. I am here now quite alone,
and in mind very much put about. I have been striving to
recall what passed between Labrie's wife and myself, but without any clear recollection. Ah, those women! I well remember
my father used to say, "At the bottom of every trouble, there
you will find a woman," and my mother used to retort, "And
likewise at the bottom of every happiness." Whereupon he
would kiss her.

June Tenth, 1815

Last night—waiting for word from Alec. This morning I went
down to Labrie's camp with Needic. They had left two tents and
some rubbish, and a little green box marked "M.L." Turning
the lot over I found two empty kegs marked "H.B. Co.," once
full of rum, which they had stolen from the cache on Keg Island.
So we heaped all together and set fire to it. It burned merrily,
and they are at least by that much poorer.

June Eleventh, 1815

I am in great spirits today. Last night I was awakened by
Needic, who had his boy with him. Everything had reached

Negodina safely, and there was no sign anywhere of Labrie's party. They will push on at once.

June Twelfth, 1815

This morning Labrie came back. Needic came up and told me, so about noon I took my pistols and went down with him to the cove. They had one tent up and the women were making the fire. The men went off and none of them would speak to us. I stood smiling in a taunting way, and just as I was about to leave, Labrie's wife came over to me. I perceived she had her arm wound in a cloth.

"Well, Madame Labrie, how did you hurt your arm?"

"Why do you call me Madame Labrie?"

"One must call you something. My boy, Alec, calls you Madaline."

Her face grew a darker red.

"You have been away for a while?"

"Yes," she said, "we were at Wabinosh, and I see you burned my box when I was gone.

"Were you ever in love?" she asked suddenly.

"Never," said I, "praise be to God."

"When you are I pray heaven you may be tortured in it."

"I am thankful of your good wishes."

"The other night you told me your packs were coming by Negodina. You understand? It was Labrie who shot me through the arm. He wanted to kill me for taking them to Wabinosh, but the others would not let him."

"The low rascal," I said, "to shoot a woman."

"And *you* have nothing to say about *me*?" She looked at me curiously, and put an odd emphasis on the *you* and the *me*.

"It is fortunate you made a mistake."

"A mistake!" she said. "Your boy Alec is twice the man that you are."

The hussy said that with a fluff of pride.

"Goodbye," said I from my canoe.

"Is that all, Archibald Muir, is that all?"

"Goodbye," said I, "and I hope your husband won't shoot at you again."

I looked back when we had gone a bit, and she still stood there. She did not make any sign towards me, though I waved to her in courtesy. Then she covered up her face in her hands.

No word of Godfrey and Alec. I sent Needic to Labrie's wife with two gold guineas for the box I had burned, probably the only gold she ever clapped her eyes on, as it is unknown in this trade almost.

June Thirteenth, 1815

The packs came in yesterday evening. Godfrey and the men all well. I mixed a keg of spirits for them and they made a hideous night of it. Too busy to write much now, but can do nothing more tonight. Looking back in the store ledgers I can see no such winter's catch. Great good luck. Labrie's party still hanging around. Alec went down as soon as he got back, and stayed longer than he ought, so I berated him soundly. Tonight at supper he said:

"Labrie shot her through the arm because she had taken them to Wabinosh and had misled them."

I paid no attention to him. By and by he said:

"You will be glad to know that she says you told her nothing about the packs."

"Did she?" said I, puzzled, as she had told me the contrary.

"I don't believe her," he added.

"You're complimentary to the ladies," I remarked.

"Here is something she asked me to give you."

It was the money I had sent her for that box of hers I burnt.

June Fourteenth, 1815

Busy all day between the storehouse and the fur press. Half the Indians are drunk yet. Alec says Labrie and his party have gone. May the devil's luck go with them. I thought Alec looked a trifle white in the face, and as if he was impatient to make me talk, but I had no time to be spending with him.

A wonderfully warm day, and the flies very bad, enough to madden one. Have pressed all the packs and now everything is in order for a move. What a grand night for the partners it will be when they see our canoes full of the finest come to land at Fort William. It should be of profit to me, and I expect to come back here or go somewhere a factor, if I comprehend the rules properly. About an hour ago I had just finished writing the last words when Alec's shadow came over the window. He seemed to stand there over long, and I was just on the point of crying out to him when he moved off. In a moment he came in to me. I did not

look up from my writing when he flung a scrap of paper down
before me.

"There!" he said, in an odd voice. "I found it under the sash.
It fell face down, so I saw printing on the back, I thought it was
but a scrap torn off a fur bill.

"Read it," said he.

I turned it over and observed that there were some words in
writing on the other side. I made them out to be: "Why do you
call me Labrie's wife? She is my aunt. Do you think I would
marry an ugly fellow like Labrie? They brought me up here to
help their plans. We shall see. If you want to know my name it's
Madaline Lesage. I learned to write from the Sister St. Theresa
at Wikwemikong. Is it not pretty? M.L."

Then I recalled how she had come to the window, one night
not very long ago, when, I opine, she had left the paper there.

"Well!" I said coolly, "and what is it now that you have to
say about Madaline Lesage?"

His face had a tortured look upon it. He tried to speak. "She
was—she was the bravest, the dearest"—he stopped there and
hung down his head. "Oh, my God, you cannot understand.
You can never understand!"

He moved away and stood by the door. I thought upon what
he had said. No, I did not understand. Then I tried once more to
go on with my page. But I was detained by the sound which is as
uncommon as that of laughter in these outlandish parts. The
sound of sobbing. Just for a moment it brought back to me the
sound of my sister's voice as she sobbed for her lover when they
brought him back dead and dripping out of the sea. I had a vision
of it as if it were snapped upon my eye in a flash of lightning, she
leaning her forehead upon her wrists against the wall. I looked
up at Alec and there he was leaning at the door-post, his shoulders all moving with his sobs. I understood in a flash. I pray God
to forgive me for the sin of blindness, and for always being so
dead to others in my own affairs. I went towards him knowing
that I could not give him any comfort. So he went out from the
house and walked alone through the gloaming. I perceived that a
change had come over him. I had always considered him a bit of
a boy to be ordered about, but there was a man walking away
from me, resolute in his steps, big in his bulk, and weighed
down as if he was carrying a load, bearing it as if he was proud
of it, with energy and trust in himself.

QUARTET
by Mazo de la Roche

Behrens hesitated at the corner of the Via Parthenope and the Via Santa Lucia, wondering whether or not he should take a carriage to his destination. The moment his hesitation was noticed by the drivers who stood laughing and talking together on the seaward side of the street, the group broke up and the members of it hurried toward him, beseeching and commanding him to ride in the particular carriage of each.

He looked from one healthy, sunburned face to another, not understanding a word they said. He wished he had not hesitated, for it was a fine January morning, exhilarating for a long walk. He shook his head doubtfully, and half turned away, but two of the drivers followed him, one on either side, inviting him to take various expeditions.

He found himself beside the carriage of one of them, who, with a wide gesture, implored him to enter, shook out and displayed proudly a ragged, woolly rug for covering his knees.

Behrens had just put a foot on the step when his eye fell on the horse, its drooping head, its wretched side through which the bones seemed ready to protrude. Seeing his expression, the other driver caught him by the arm and pointed triumphantly to his own horse farther along the street.

"Very fine horse!" he exclaimed, unexpectedly in English. "Very fine. Fat. Round. Go very fast. The very best horse in Napoli!" He drew Behrens toward his carriage. "Very fine carriage, too. Very beautiful. *Molto bello!*"

There was no doubt about it, this horse, of a bright chestnut, was sleek and well cared for, able to work; while the other poor beast had little endurance left in him. Behrens chose the chestnut.

When Behrens had seated himself, a bitter altercation began between the two drivers. The first seemed to have half a mind to

81

carry Behrens by force to his carriage. The second sought to climb to his seat, but the other pressed his body between, waving his whip and letting loose all his Neapolitan vitality in curses.

Behrens, rather anxiously, awaited an exchange of blows. Seeing the flash of their eyes and teeth, he felt that even a thrust from a knife would not be surprising. He had a mind to alight from the other side of the carriage, but miraculously, the dispute ended, the second driver gave the first a halfhearted push on the chest, got onto the seat, and cracked his whip. The first strolled back to his companions, his rage apparently subsiding into tolerance. A moment later he was again laughing and talking in the sunshine.

Above the blueness of the bay was the blue arch of the sky. From Vesuvius rose a golden feather that spread and hung plumelike against the sky. Capri lifted a bronze shoulder from the sea. From behind the Castello dell'Ovo a racing skiff rowed by eight youths darted into the open, their bare arms shining in the sun. They uttered a rhythmic musical singsong as they pulled. It was all delightful, Behrens thought.

He planted his stick between his feet, clasped his hands on it, his eyes obediently following the pointed whip of the driver, but his mind not taking in the descriptions in broken English of the buildings. He was thinking: "All of this is perfectly natural to Alice. By now none of these things looks strange to her. This is her home, and she's absolutely used to it. Loves it, I suppose."

Everything he saw he tried to see not as a tourist, a stranger, but as Alice, who was now accustomed to its foreignness. A little band of blind musicians was playing by the roadside. Extraordinarily sweet, wistful music, Behrens thought. He fished out a coin and threw it on the small tin plate one of them held out. The blind man bowed, smiled, but at that instant a bicyclist, passing between, knocked the dish from his hand and the coin to the road. Behrens gave a "Tck!" of compassion and craned his neck as the carriage rolled on to see whether the man had recovered the coin. He could see him on hands and knees groping for it. His comrades had begun a fresh tune. Behrens sighed.

His eye was now caught by a friar of some sort, whose bare red heels showed at every step beneath his rough habit. His tonsured head gleamed; his face had an expression of inscrutable patience. Meeting him were two tiny children in white fur coats unbelievably short above slender bare legs. Their nurse, wheeling a perambulator, wore a black velvet skirt, a yellow lace-trimmed apron, and a fringed scarlet shawl. Her gleaming black hair was massed beneath a tortoise-shell comb. The friar passed them without seeming to see them. "And all this strangeness," thought Behrens, "is as natural to Alice now as Massachusetts once was."

They turned into the shadowed intricacies of the side streets. The driver continued to point out objects of interest, and Behrens suddenly remembered that he had never told the man where he wanted to go. He leaned forward and touched him on the arm.

"Please drive," he said in his slow, rather heavy voice, "to the villa of Count Rombarra."

Even as he heard his own voice saying the name, it seemed unbelievable that he should be going to see Alice. Six years since he had seen her, and that on the day of her marriage to Rombarra. How exquisite she had looked that day! Beautiful, with the pride and happiness of a freshly opened flower. And it was Rombarra who had brought that happiness, not he! He had never been able to stir her to anything warmer than a feeling of placid friendship for him. He was an old story. A great disadvantage it was to be neighbors and all that, if you suddenly fell in love with a girl and wanted to impress her. He had been able to make no impression in that way; it had taken Rombarra with his Latin fire to do that. Well, he was going to see her now, after six years, and, thank goodness, he had got over it and would be able to make a friendly call without any humiliating embarrassment on his side.

A young woman was letting down a basket by a rope from a balcony, and a man was waiting with silvery little fish to put into it. In a doorway an old woman was cooking apples over a charcoal fire. The air was full of unfamiliar sounds. It was all strange and exhilarating to Behrens. After all these years of hard work and colorless surroundings, he felt as though he were experiencing a new birth. In this ancient place he felt his own newness as ludicrous, even pathetic.

If only he had someone, as naïvely impressed as himself, as companion! Supposing that he and Alice were making this trip together for the first time. On the voyage over and in the hotel he had met several couples abroad for the first time, laughing together, getting mixed over the foreign money together, experiencing this new birth together. But, he remembered, it would not have been new to Alice, after all, for she had been to Europe twice as a young girl. Strange that he should have forgotten, when it had been on one of those trips that she had met Rombarra.

A street rose on his right, ascending in a flight of sunswept stone steps. One above another were the stands of the flower sellers, mingling the colors of carnations, roses, violets, and heliotrope. A small boy ran from the nearest stand, holding a bunch of violets toward Behrens.

Behrens shook his head. No, he could not take violets to Alice. Rombarra might not like it. He felt sure that Rombarra of the sloe eyes and chiseled features would not like it. But the boy thrust the nosegay onto Behrens' knees, running alongside and holding up his little brown paw for money. Behrens could not resist him. He found a five-lire piece and put it into the hand.

They were on the heights, the old city spread out below. It looked immense, crowding about that blue bay. A great, rather frightening foreign city for a young girl like Alice to have come to. The driver had alighted and was awaiting his fare. Behrens paid him and entered the gate, glancing curiously about the terraced garden with its urns, its statues and trickling fountain. Apparently without reason his heart began to pound heavily; his lips became dry; and he found no moisture on his tongue to moisten them. He rang the bell, wishing very much that he was not carrying the little nosegay of flowers. Still, if Alice were alone, if, perhaps, Rombarra were busy with his own affairs somewhere, it would be all right. Alice might like to have the flowers, for the sake of old times, her old life.

He was shown into a vast, high-ceilinged room, furnished with quite wonderful antique pieces, Behrens supposed. But he thought, standing there, his heart still thumping, that he should have hated to live with them. One would have the feeling always that they would look exactly the same five hundred years hence, when one's bones were only a handful of dust.

And the penetrating chill of the room! He shivered in his handsome gray tweed coat. He heard steps, voices. Alice and her husband and her little girl of four (Behrens had forgotten about the child) came into the room. They shook hands. Rombarra's long, cool finger touched Behrens' without enthusiasm. Alice's hand was hot and dry, Behrens noticed, and her fingers seemed to curl almost feverishly about his. Her eyes smiled up at him beautiful as ever, more beautiful—or perhaps he had forgotten just how lovely she was.

Behrens thought, with a sudden pang, that Rombarra was a much more suitable mate for her physically than he would have been. Rombarra was wearing the romantically dashing uniform of an officer of the cavalry. Alice explained, in her voice that had exactly the same soft, precise quality as of old, that they had just returned from the Horse Show, where her husband had been riding. He was very fond of horses and had gone remarkably well in the show. Behrens congratulated him, and the Italian smiled, showing a rim of perfect teeth.

Behrens wondered, with sudden misgiving, if Rombarra understood English. But, surely, after six years of marriage with Alice, he would have learned to speak her native tongue. Behrens knew that he himself, slow though he was, would have learned to speak Arabic, had it been the language of Alice. He said, in halting French, to Rombarra:

"I was congratulating you on your success in the Horse Show."

It was as though he had touched an electric button. Rombarra's face became brilliant. He began to talk swiftly and eagerly in French. Behrens could not understand a word, and murmured so, apologetically, to Alice.

"Oh, it does not matter," she said. "I want you to come and sit down by me. It's so wonderful seeing you again after all these years."

Behrens sat down near her. He felt intensely embarrassed, for Rombarra's intelligent eyes were fixed on his face, not with the look of suspicion that Behrens had half anticipated, but with a look which seemed to say: "Come, now! Let us talk about horses. I can see that you are fond of them and so am I. Let us talk about them."

Behrens said to Alice:

"Please explain to your husband how stupid I am. I knew my French was very bad, but I didn't realize how little I have of it."

"It does not matter," she repeated. "And he understood quite well that you were congratulating him."

"But what was he saying to me?"

"Really, I did not notice. I was thinking only of you—how strange and wonderful to see you here." She was sitting on the edge of the sofa, poised in an attitude that suggested recklessness— Behrens thought that she looked like a bird just about to fly upward. Behind her stood a tall bureau, inlaid with ivory, on the top of which was a nude female figure in alabaster in an attitude of gentle resignation. The contrast between this figure and Alice was so great that Behrens' eyes and mind were held by it for a space and he missed what Alice next said.

She had drawn her little girl beside her, and he now heard her say:

"You knew I had a child? Her name is Félicité. She was born in the first year of our marriage or, you may be sure, I should never have called her that."

Behrens was startled and bewildered. Why had Alice spoken so? And in front of her husband, even though he understood little English? Was it possible that Alice was not happy?

He covered his discomfort by picking up the little girl and putting her on his knee. He placed the nosegay of violets in her hands, glad to be rid of it.

"Flowers," he said emphatically, hoping that in this case he would be understood. "I brought them for you."

The child took them, laughed, and held them to her face. She jigged her little body happily on his knee.

"Children always loved you," Alice said; then spoke to the child in Italian.

"*Grazie, signor,*" murmured Félicité. She threw herself back against Behrens, laughing roguishly. She had never lain against such an enormous, comfortable body before, and was delighted by its proportions.

Behrens, looking down at her, felt a deep and tender thrill pass through him. Alice's child! And he had once hoped that Alice's child would be his also. He bent his head and pressed his lips against her hair.

"You little darling!" he murmured. He had never known anything so delicious as the feel of this supple, exquisite little body in his arms. He wondered if Rombarra loved her as he would have done.

When he raised his eyes, they looked straight into those of Rombarra, who was leaning forward, an expression of gratification on his handsome face. They smiled across the child.

"*Bellissima bambina!*" cried Behrens, reckless of what a few words of Italian might bring forth.

Again the Neopolitan's face was illuminated, but this time there was added to its brightness a tender pride that touched Behrens. Rombarra broke into a flood of musical Italian which ended in a pointed question.

Behrens turned ruefully to Alice. "Whatever does he say?" he implored.

"He is asking you if you have any children of your own."

Behrens shook his head. *"Non, non,"* he said. *"Je n'en ai pas."*

At once Rombarra obligingly turned to French.

"But," exclaimed Behrens desperately, "how can I talk to him? The moment I say a word or two in Italian or French, he says so much that he frightens me! Doesn't he know any English at all, after—after all these years?"

"No," returned Alice in a cool, clear voice. "He is far too narrow-minded, too stupid, to learn English."

Behrens could scarcely credit his senses. Alice, sitting there poised on that sofa, with the reckless air of a bird about to fly straight upward, calling her husband narrow-minded and stupid before his face, to Behrens, whom she had not seen for six years!

"For God's sake, be careful!" he said.

"Oh, there's no danger. He doesn't know a word of English. He probably thinks we are saying how well he looks in his uniform." She smiled serenely at her husband. He put another question to Behrens, who, following Alice's remark, had glanced involuntarily at the uniform.

"What does he say?" asked Behrens miserably, knotting his forehead.

"He wants to know if you, too, are in the army."

"No, I am not," replied Behrens firmly and distinctly. "I am a stockbroker." He gazed into Rombarra's eyes, beseeching him to understand. He was trying to tell Rombarra not only that he was a stockbroker, but that he was an unwilling participant in this dreadful situation. For surely, though the count could not understand English, he must feel the impact of those appalling words beating about him. Behrens was afraid of Alice, afraid of what she would say or do next. She seemed capable of anything.

She said: "He looks clever, doesn't he? With those intense eyes and that smile. But he's only clever at lovemaking. He's jealous of me. He wouldn't let me have you here without his being present, but he's absolutely unmoral himself. Before we had been married two years I found out that he had been unfaithful to me time and again!"

She spoke composedly, her eyes, with a pleasant, friendly light in them, on Behrens' face. She had leaned back, and her

graceful arms were extended along the back of the sofa. To
Behrens their curve seemed like the outline of half-spread wings.
His forehead was flushed crimson. He stared straight at Rombarra,
striving, with that stare, to build a wall around him, to protect
him.

The little girl struggled to her feet and ran to her father,
holding up the nosegay for him to smell. Rombarra began to talk
rapidly and caressingly to her.

Behrens got out, in a muffled tone: "For the love of God,
Alice! Don't talk like that. I simply can't bear it. I'll have to get
out. Isn't it possible for me to see you alone?"

"No, no! It would be too dangerous. Besides, what would be
the good? He appears to be friendly to you, but you don't
understand him. He is sly, and he can be violent."

Behrens had an odd sensation of floating; there was a singing
sound in his ears. He wondered if he might be going to have a
stroke. He experienced, too, a feeling of deep self-pity. How
cruel of Alice to create such a ghastly situation as this! He had
suffered so much because of her in the past. He had come here
feeling that that was all over. He had been reasonably sure of
himself, prepared for a meeting that might revive a little the old
pain, but that would establish a new picture of Alice in his
memory—an Alice dignified, happy in her husband and child,
with perhaps an affectionate backward glance for the old life in
which he had had a part. His hands trembled. He tried to speak,
but even his English seemed to desert him now. He turned a
troubled gaze on her.

Her voice went out, not cool and even now, but staccato, with
little gasps, as though at any moment she might lose control of
herself:

"Of course, you were the only one I ever really loved, David.
It was just that I was carried off my feet by Gaetano. You
seemed so commonplace, so terribly uninteresting beside him. I
thought that life with you would be intolerably dull, and now—if
you only knew—how beautiful you look to me, sitting there! If
you knew how I am longing to put my arms around you, and kiss
you and kiss you!"

If Rombarra felt nothing strange in the atmosphere of the
room, the child certainly did. She got from her father's knee,
with a strange look of excitement, and began to run round and
about the three, tearing the nosegay into pieces and scattering the

violets over the marble floor. Rombarra laughed at her, clapping his hands together.

Alice bent and picked up the violets that had fallen at her feet. "I shall always keep these," she said. "The nosegay was really intended for me, wasn't it, David? Do you remember how we used to hunt for the first violets together, under last year's dead leaves? Do you remember, David?"

He nodded, gulping. "I'm not likely to forget, Alice."

At the sound of his wife's name Rombarra turned his head sharply toward them with an intense and significant gesture.

The child began to run about over the flowers, trampling them with her little feet. When she passed Behrens she threw back her head and looked up at him with a defiant and challenging gaze.

Behrens muttered: "Why do you stay with him? Why do you bear it?"

"There's the child. He would never give her up. You see what he is like with her."

"You will endure it, then? After—this meeting? All you have said today?"

"Yes—I will endure it. And I'm sorry for having made you suffer, David. But I wanted you to know. And I wanted to be unfaithful to him—he's been so unfaithful to me. And I have been unfaithful—before his very eyes. Can you understand?"

The little girl ran suddenly to her mother's knees. Alice took her up and held her close. "I must not fail Félicité," she said.

Félicité stared across at Behrens as though suddenly resentful of his presence. Rombarra regarded his wife and child with satisfaction, then turned toward Behrens with a questioning smile. Behrens rose to go.

He thought he would take advantage of the foreign custom and touch Alice's hand with his lips. It would be their last kiss. As their flesh touched he had the feeling that he was kissing the hand of a stranger. This was not the Alice he had known. He was afraid of her, and he longed to be away.

As the two men shook hands, Behrens said in his broken French: "It has been very pleasant meeting you."

This time the Italian made no attempt to respond, but he gave Behrens' hand a quick, almost sympathetic grip, and his eyes still held that look of questioning.

Behrens passed the columns and urns of the sunlit garden, and, as he reached the gate, he turned and looked back at the villa. He had felt that he was being observed. Now he saw that the three had come out on a small iron balcony. They were watching his departure, the child linking Alice and Rombarra together.

Behrens raised his hat. They waved to him. With a great sigh of relief, he strode swiftly down the street, hidden from their view now by a row of tall palms.

THE SNOB
by Morley Callaghan

It was at the book counter in the department store that John Harcourt, the student, caught a glimpse of his father. At first he could not be sure in the crowd that pushed along the aisle, but there was something about the colour of the back of the elderly man's neck, something about the faded felt hat, that he knew very well. Harcourt was standing with the girl he loved, buying a book for her. All afternoon he had been talking to her, eagerly, but with an anxious diffidence, as if there still remained in him an innocent wonder that she should be delighted to be with him. From underneath her wide-brimmed straw hat, her face, so fair and beautifully strong with its expression of cool independence, kept turning up to him and sometimes smiled at what he said. That was the way they always talked, never daring to show much full, strong feeling. Harcourt had just bought the book, and had reached into his pocket for the money with a free, ready gesture to make it appear that he was accustomed to buying books for young ladies, when the white-haired man in the faded felt hat, at the other end of the counter, turned half toward him, and Harcourt knew he was standing only a few feet away from his father.

The young man's easy words trailed away and his voice became little more than a whisper, as if he were afraid that everyone in the store might recognize it. There was rising in him a dreadful uneasiness; something very precious that he wanted to hold seemed close to destruction. His father, standing at the end of the bargain counter, was planted squarely on his two feet, turning a book over thoughtfully in his hands. Then he took out his glasses from an old, worn leather case and adjusted them on the end of his nose, looking down over them at the book. His coat was thrown open, two buttons on his vest were undone, his gray hair was too long, and in his rather shabby clothes he looked very much like a working-man, a carpenter perhaps. Such a resentment rose in young Harcourt that he wanted to cry out bitterly, "Why does he dress as if he never owned a decent suit in his life? He doesn't care what the whole world thinks of him. He never did. I've told him a hundred times he ought to wear his good clothes when he goes out. Mother's told him the same thing. He just laughs. And now Grace may see him. Grace will meet him."

So young Harcourt stood still, with his head down, feeling that something very painful was impending. Once he looked anxiously at Grace, who had turned to the bargain counter. Among those people drifting aimlessly by with hot red faces, getting in each other's way, using their elbows but keeping their faces detached and wooden, she looked tall and splendidly alone. She was so sure of herself, her relation to the people in the aisles, the clerks behind the counter, the books on the shelves, and everything around her. Still keeping his head down and moving close, he whispered uneasily, "Let's go and have tea somewhere, Grace."

"In a minute, dear," she said.

"Let's go now."

"In just a minute, dear," she repeated absently.

"There's not a breath of air in here. Let's go now."

"What makes you so impatient?"

"There's nothing but old books on that counter."

"There may be something here I've wanted all my life," she said, smiling at him brightly and not noticing the uneasiness in his face.

So Harcourt had to move slowly behind her, getting closer to his father all the time. He could feel the space that separated them narrowing. Once he looked up with a vague, sidelong glance. But his father, red-faced and happy, was still reading the book, only now there was a meditative expression on his face, as if something in the book had stirred him and he intended to stay there reading for some time.

Old Harcourt had lots of time to amuse himself, because he was on a pension after working hard all his life. He had sent John to the university and he was eager to have him distinguish himself. Every night when John came home, whether it was early or late, he used to go into his father's and mother's bedroom and turn on the light and talk to them about the interesting things that had happened to him during the day. They listened and shared this new world with him. They both sat up in their night-clothes and, while his mother asked all the questions, his father listened attentively with his head cocked on one side and a smile or a frown on his face. The memory of all this was in John now, and there was also a desperate longing and a pain within him growing harder to bear as he glanced fearfully at his father, but he thought stubbornly, "I can't introduce him. It'll be easier for everybody if he doesn't see us. I'm not ashamed. But it will be easier. It'll be more sensible. It'll only embarrass him to see Grace." By this time he knew he was ashamed, but he felt that his shame was justified, for Grace's father had the smooth, confident manner of a man who had lived all his life among people who were rich and sure of themselves. Often when he had been in Grace's home talking politely to her mother, John had kept on thinking of the plainness of his own home and of his parents' laughing, good-natured untidiness, and he resolved desperately that he must make Grace's people admire him.

He looked up cautiously, for they were about eight feet away from his father, but at that moment his father, too, looked up and John's glance shifted swiftly far over the aisle, over the counters, seeing nothing. As his father's blue, calm eyes stared steadily over the glasses, there was an instant when their glances might have met. Neither one could have been certain, yet John, as he turned away and began to talk to Grace hurriedly, knew surely that his father had seen him. He knew it by the steady calmness in his father's blue eyes. John's shame grew, and then humiliation sickened him as he waited and did nothing.

His father turned away, going down the aisle, walking erectly in his shabby clothes, his shoulders very straight, never once looking back. His father would walk slowly along the street, he knew, with that meditative expression deepening and becoming grave.

Young Harcourt stood beside Grace, brushing against her soft shoulder, and made faintly aware again of the delicate scent she used: There, so close beside him, she was holding within her everything he wanted to reach out for, only now he felt a sharp hostility that made him sullen and silent.

"You were right, John," she was drawling in her soft voice. "It does get unbearable in here on a hot day. Do let's go now. Have you ever noticed that department stores after a time can

make you really hate people?'' But she smiled when she spoke,
so he might see that she really hated no one.

"You don't like people, do you?" he said sharply.

"People? What people? What do you mean?"

"I mean," he went on irritably, "you don't like the kind of
people you bump into here, for example."

"Not especially. Who does? What are you talking about?"

"Anybody could see you don't," he said recklessly, full of a
savage eagerness to hurt her. "I say you don't like simple,
honest people, the kind of people you meet all over the city."
He blurted the words out as if he wanted to shake her, but he
was longing to say, "You wouldn't like my family. Why couldn't
I take you home to have dinner with them? You'd turn up your
nose at them, because they've no pretensions. As soon as my
father saw you, he knew you wouldn't want to meet him. I could
tell by the way he turned."

His father was on his way home now, he knew, and that
evening at dinner they would meet. His mother and sister would
talk rapidly, but his father would say nothing to him, or to
anyone. There would only be Harcourt's memory of the level
look in the blue eyes, and the knowledge of his father's pain as
he walked away.

Grace watched John's gloomy face as they walked through the
store, and she knew he was nursing some private rage, and so
her own resentment and exasperation kept growing, and she said
crisply, "You're entitled to your moods on a hot afternoon, I
suppose, but if I feel I don't like it here, then I don't like it. You
wanted to go yourself. Who likes to spend very much time in a
department store on a hot afternoon? I begin to hate every stupid
person that bangs into me, everybody near me. What does that
make me?"

"It makes you a snob."

"So I'm a snob now?" she said angrily.

"Certainly you're a snob," he said. They were at the door and
going out to the street. As they walked in the sunlight, in the
crowd moving slowly down the street, he was groping for words
to describe the secret thoughts he had always had about her.
"I've always known how you'd feel about people I like who
didn't fit into your private world," he said.

"You're a very stupid person," she said. Her face was flushed
now, and it was hard for her to express her indignation, so she
stared straight ahead as she walked along.

They had never talked in this way, and now they were both quickly eager to hurt each other. With a flow of words, she started to argue with him, then she checked herself and said calmly, "Listen, John, I imagine you're tired of my company. There's no sense in having tea together. I think I'd better leave you right here."

"That's fine," he said. "Good afternoon."

"Good-bye."

"Good-bye."

She started to go, she had gone two paces, but he reached out desperately and held her arm, and he was frightened, and pleading, "Please don't go, Grace."

All the anger and irritation had left him; there was just a desperate anxiety in his voice as he pleaded, "Please forgive me. I've no right to talk to you like that. I don't know why I'm so rude or what's the matter. I'm ridiculous. I'm very, very ridiculous. Please, you must forgive me. Don't leave me."

He had never talked to her so brokenly, and his sincerity, the depth of his feeling, began to stir her. While she listened, feeling all the yearning in him, they seemed to have been brought closer together, by opposing each other, then ever before, and she began to feel almost shy. "I don't know what's the matter. I suppose we're both irritable. It must be the weather," she said. "But I'm not angry, John."

He nodded his head miserably. He longed to tell her that he was sure she would have been charming to his father, but he had never felt so wretched in his life. He held her arm tight, as if he must hold it or what he wanted most in the world would slip away from him, yet he kept thinking, as he would ever think, of his father walking away quietly with his head never turning.

THE BEGGAR MAID
by Alice Munro

Patrick Blatchford was in love with Rose. This had become a
fixed, even furious, idea with him. He wanted to marry her. He
waited for her after classes, moved in and walked beside her, so
that anybody she was talking to would have to reckon with his
presence. He wouldn't talk when friends or classmates of hers
were around, but he would try to catch Rose's eye, so that he
could indicate by a cold, incredulous look what he thought of
their conversation. Rose was flattered but nervous. A friend of
hers once mispronounced "Metternich" in Patrick's presence,
and he said to Rose later, "How can you be friends with people
like that?"

Patrick was 24 years old, a graduate student who planned to
be a history professor. He had come to Ontario from British
Columbia, and it seemed his family was rich. He was tall, thin,
fair and almost good-looking. He had a long pale-red birthmark
dribbling like a tear down his temple and his cheek. He said it
was fading as he got older; by the time he was 40 it would have
faded away. But it was not the birthmark that cancelled out his
good looks, Rose thought. It was something else; maybe the
shrillness that kept breaking through his voice, or his startling
clumsiness, which knocked dishes off tables he did not seem
even to have touched, or his tendency to blush. There was a
sharp-edged, jumpy, disconcerting quality about him altogether.

The first time Patrick took Rose to the movies, he arrived at
Dr. Henshawe's, where she was living, half an hour early. He
wouldn't knock; he knew he was early. He sat on the step
outside the door. This was in winter; it was dark out, but there
was a little coach lamp beside the door.

"Oh, Rose! Come and look!" called Dr. Henshawe, in her
soft, amused voice, and they looked down together from the dark

window of the study. "The poor young man," said Dr. Henshawe tenderly. Dr. Henshawe was in her seventies. She was a former English professor, fastidious and lively. She had a lame leg, but a youthful and charmingly tilted head, with white braids wound around it.

She called Patrick "poor" because he was in love, and perhaps also because he was a male, doomed to push and blunder. Even from where they were standing, he looked stubborn and pitiable, determined and dependent, sitting out there in the cold. "Guarding the door," said Dr. Henshawe. "Oh, Rose!"

Rose didn't like her saying that. She didn't like her laughing at Patrick. She didn't like Patrick sitting on the steps that way, either. He was asking to be laughed at. He was the most vulnerable person she had ever known, and yet he was full of cruel judgments; he was full of conceit.

Dr. Henshawe had at one time headed the local school board, and she was a founding member of the Co-operative Commonwealth Federation. She still sat on committees, and she wrote letters to the paper, reviewed books. After she retired from the university, she began taking in scholarship students. Her house was small and perfect: polished floors; glowing rugs; Chinese vases and landscapes; black carved screens—much that Rose could not appreciate at the time.

Rose couldn't really tell how much she liked being at Dr. Henshawe's. At times she felt impatient, sitting in the dining-room with a linen napkin on her knee, eating from fine white plates on blue placemats, with the canary fluttering in its cage in the dining-room window and Dr. Henshawe directing the table conversation. (There was not a great deal to eat, however, and Rose had taken to keeping chocolate bars in her room.) "You are a scholar, Rose," Dr. Henshawe would say. "This will interest you." Then she would read aloud from the paper or, more likely, from the *Canadian Forum* or the *Atlantic Monthly*. She talked about politics, about writers. She mentioned Frank Scott and Dorothy Livesay. She said, You must read this, Rose, you must read that—which made Rose sullenly determined not to. How could she? She was reading Thomas Mann. She was reading Tolstoy.

Dr. Henshawe's house had done one thing for Rose, though. It had destroyed the naturalness, the taken-for-granted background, of home. Rose lived with her aunt and uncle in Hanratty, Ontario, a town 50 miles to the north of London, where the university was, and for her to go back there now was to go quite literally into a crude light. Her aunt and uncle had installed fluorescent tubes in the kitchen, the bathroom, the hall. In the front room they had a floor lamp whose shade was permanently wrapped in wide strips of cellophane. What Dr. Henshawe's house and her aunt and uncle's house did best, in Rose's opinion, was discredit each other. In Dr. Henshawe's charming rooms there was always for Rose the knowledge of home, a raw indigestible lump, and at home now her sense of order elsewhere exposed such embarrassing, sad poverty. Poverty was not just wretchedness, as Dr. Henshawe seemed to think; it was not just deprivation. It meant having those ugly lights and being proud of them. It meant continual talk of money and malicious talk about new things people had bought and whether they were paid for. It meant pride and jealousy flaring over something like the new pair of plastic imitation-lace curtains that Rose's aunt had bought for the front room. Of course, her aunt and uncle did not think they were poor. Poverty was what they had raised Rose up from when they had brought her to live with them at the age of ten. There was no denying that what she had known before was worse, no denying that when she came to them she was much in favour of everything their house contained—the linoleum and the wrapped lampshade and the Disney deer with a lump of artificial fern growing out of its back and the many admonitions, pious and cheerful and mildly bawdy, that hung on the walls:

Believe on the Lord Jesus Christ and thou shalt be saved.

This is my kitchen and I will do as I darned please.

More than two persons in this bed is dangerous and unlawful.

What would Patrick say to all this? Rose could not imagine. How would someone offended by a mispronunciation of "Metternich" react to her uncle's stories? Her uncle might start telling about the Displaced Person—the Belgium, he called him—who worked in the same butcher shop as he did, nervily singing French songs and cherishing notions of getting on in this new country. "Don't you get any ideas," her uncle had said to him. "Don't you think youse can come over and start workin' for us and it's goin' to end up *us* working for *youse*."

Patrick would say from time to time that since Rose's home

was only 50 miles away, he ought to go up and meet her family.

"It's only my aunt and uncle," she said once.

"But they're your guardians, aren't they?"

"I guess so."

"They took you when your father died," Patrick said.

Rose did not really know if her father was dead. She rather hoped so.

"They must be your legal guardians. Who administers what your father left? His estate?"

Estate. Rose could think of no reply.

Sometimes Dr. Henshawe would say to Rose, "Well, you are a scholar, you are not interested in that." Usually she was speaking of some activity at the college—a pep rally, a football game, a dance. And usually she was right: Rose was not interested. But Rose was not eager to admit it; she did not seek that definition of herself.

On the stairway wall hung graduation photographs of all the other girls, scholarship girls, who had lived with Dr. Henshawe. Most of them had got to be teachers, then mothers. One was a dietician, two were librarians, one was a professor of English, like Dr. Henshawe herself. Rose did not like to look at them, at their soft-focused, meekly smiling gratitude. They seemed to be urging on her some deadly secular piety. There were no actresses among them, no brassy magazine journalists; none of them had latched on to the sort of life Rose wanted for herself. Rose wanted to perform in public, though not necessarily on a stage. She wanted to be known and envied, to be slim and clever. She told Dr. Henshawe that if she had been a man she would have wanted to be a foreign correspondent.

"Then you must be one," cried Dr. Henshawe alarmingly. "The future will be wide open for women. You must concentrate on languages. You must take courses in political science. And economics. Perhaps you could get a job on the paper for the summer. I have friends there."

Rose was frightened at the idea of working on a paper, and she hated the introductory economics course; she had been looking for a way of dropping it. It was dangerous to mention things to Dr. Henshawe.

Rose had got to live with Dr. Henshawe by accident. Another girl had been picked to move in, but she came down with TB and had to go to a sanatorium. Dr. Henshawe went up to the scholarship office on the second day of registration to get the names of some other freshmen. That same day, Rose was supposed to go to a meeting of the new scholarship students. The bursar was to give a talk, telling them of ways to earn money and live cheaply, and explaining the high level of performance that would be expected of them.

As Rose was climbing the stairs to the second floor of the administration building, a girl came up beside her and said, "Are you on your way to the meeting, too?" Rose nodded, and they walked together, telling each other the details of their scholarships. Rose said she did not yet have a place to live; she was staying at the Y. She did not really have enough money to be here at all. She had a scholarship for her tuition and the county prize to buy her books and a bursary of $300 to live on. That was all.

"You'll have to get a job," the other girl said. She had a bigger bursary, because she was in science, but she was hoping to get a job in the cafeteria. She had a room in somebody's basement. She said it wasn't damp—or not very. She cooked on a hot plate. "How much does the room cost? How much does a hot plate cost?" asked Rose.

The other girl wore her hair in a roll. She wore a crêpe blouse, shiny from ironing. Her breasts were large, sagging and matronly. She probably wore a dirty pink hooked-up-the-side brassière, Rose thought.

There was a little window in the door of the meeting room. They could look through at the other scholarship winners, who were waiting. It seemed to Rose that she saw four or five girls of the same physical type as the girl who was with her, and some bright-eyed, self-satisfied, babyish-looking boys. In one glance through the little window she detected—or thought she detected— traces of eczema, stained underarms, dandruff, mouldy deposits on the teeth and crusty flakes in the corners of the eyes. There was a pall over all of them—a true, terrible pall of eagerness and docility.

"I have to go to the john," Rose said. She went back to the first floor, where the halls were crowded with ordinary students who were not on scholarships, who would not be expected to get As and be grateful and live cheaply. Enviable and innocent, they milled around the registration tables in their new university blazers, their frosh beanies, yelling reminders to each other,

confused information, nonsensical insults. Rose walked among
them feeling bitterly superior and despondent. She could see
herself working in the cafeteria—her figure, which was broad
enough already, broadened out more by the green cotton uniform, her hair stringy from the heat.

A woman stopped her. "Aren't you one of the scholarship
girls?" she said. It was the registrar's secretary, with an armload
of papers. Rose thought she was going to be reprimanded for
not being at the meeting. She was going to say she felt sick. But
the secretary said, "Come with me now; I've got somebody I
want you to meet."

Dr. Henshawe was being a charming nuisance in the office.
She was not so easily suited. She liked poor girls, bright girls,
but they had to be fairly good-looking girls. The secretary thought
Rose might just do, if she could change the sour expression on
her face. "If you put a smile on, I think this could be your lucky
day," she said, and Rose smiled obediently, though she was
quite bewildered.

So Rose was taken home and installed in the house with the
Chinese screens and vases, and told she was a scholar. She got a
job working in the library instead of in the cafeteria. Dr. Henshawe
was a friend of the head librarian. Rose worked on Saturday
afternoons, putting books away in the stacks. In the fall the
library was nearly empty on Saturdays, because of the football
games. The narrow windows were open to the leafy campus, the
football field, the dry fall country. Distant songs and shouts
came drifting in. The college buildings were not old at all, but
they were built to look old. The arts building had a tower, and
the library had casement windows which might have been designed for shooting arrows through. The buildings and the books
in the library were what pleased Rose most about the place. The
life that usually filled it, and that was now drained away, concentrated around the football field, seemed to her inappropriate
and distracting. The cheers and songs were idiotic, if you could
hear the words. What did they want to build such dignified
buildings for it they were going to sing songs like that? She
knew enough not to reveal these opinions. If anybody said to
her, "It's really awful you have to work and never get to any of
the games," she would fervently agree.

One Saturday a man grabbed her bare leg, between her sock
and her skirt. It happened in the agriculture section, down at the

bottom of the stacks. She had seen a man crouched down looking at a low shelf, farther along. As she reached up to push a book into place he passed behind her. He bent and grabbed her leg, all in one smooth, startling movement, then was gone. She could feel for quite a while where his finger had dug in. It didn't seem to her a sexual touch; it was more like a joke, though not at all a friendly one. She heard him run away, or felt him running; the metal shelves were vibrating. Then they stopped. There was no sound of him. She walked around looking between the stacks, looking in the carrels. Suppose she did see him, bumped into him around a corner, what did she intend to do? She did not know. It was simply necessary to look for him, as in one of those tense childish games like hide-and-seek. She looked down at the sturdy pinkish calf of her leg. Amazing, that somebody had wanted to blotch and punish it.

There were usually a few graduate students working in the carrels even on Saturday afternoons. More rarely, a professor. But every carrel she looked into was empty, until she came to the last one. She poked her head in freely, by this time not expecting anybody. Then she had to say she was sorry, for there was a young man with a book on his lap, books on the floor, papers all around him. She asked if he had seen anybody run past. He said no. She told him what had happened, not because she was frightened or disgusted, as he seemed afterward to think, but just because she had to tell somebody; it was so odd. She was not at all prepared for his response. His long neck and face turned red, the flush entirely absorbing a birthmark on the side of his face. He was thin and fair. He rose up without any thought for the book in his lap or the paper in front of him. The book thumped on the floor. A great sheaf of papers, pushed across the desk, upset his ink bottle.

"How vile," he said.

"Grab it," said Rose, leaning toward the ink bottle. He righted it, shoving the papers onto the floor.

"Did he hurt you?"

"No, not really."

"Come on upstairs. We'll report it."

"Oh, no."

"He can't get away with that. He shouldn't be allowed to."

"There isn't anybody to report it to," said Rose. "The librarian goes off at noon on Saturdays."

"It's disgusting," he said in a high-pitched, excitable voice and Rose, sorry now that she had told him anything, said that she had to get back to work.

"Are you really all right?" he asked.

"Oh, yes," Rose said.

"I'll be right here. Just call me if he comes back."

That was Patrick. If she had been trying to make him fall in love with her, there was no better way she could have chosen. He had many chivalric notions, she came to realize, which he pretended to mock by putting certain words and phrases in quotation marks. "The fair sex," he would say, and "damsel in distress." The pretended irony did not fool anybody.

Rose continued to see him in the library every Saturday, and often she met him walking across the campus or in the cafeteria. He made a point of greeting her with courtesy and concern, saying, "How are you?" in a way that suggested she might have suffered a further attack, or might still be recovering from the first one. He always flushed deeply when he saw her, and she thought this was because the memory of what she had told him so embarrassed him. Later, she found out it was because he was in love.

Somehow he discovered her name and where she lived. He phoned her at Dr. Henshawe's house and asked her to go to the movies with him. At first, when he said, "This is Patrick Blatchford speaking," she could not think who that was, but after a moment she recognized the high, rather aggrieved and tremulous voice. She said she would go. This was partly because Dr. Henshawe always said approvingly that Rose did not waste her time going out with boys.

Soon after they started going out, Rose said to Patrick, "Wouldn't it be funny if it was you? If it was you who grabbed my leg that day in the library?"

He did not think it would be funny. He was horrified that she could think such a thing.

"I'm only joking," said Rose wistfully. She saw it would not do. They had just been to see a Hitchcock movie, and so she said, "You know, if Hitchcock made a movie about something like that, you would be a wild insatiable leg-grabber with a split personality; the other half of you would be a timid scholar."

He didn't like that, either. "Is that how I seem to you?" he said. "A timid scholar?" It seemed to her he consciously deepened his voice, introduced a few growling notes, drew in his chin.

"I didn't say you were a timid scholar any more than a leg-grabber. It's not *you*. I was just thinking of it as an idea."

After a while he said, "I suppose I don't seem very manly."

Rose was frightened and irritated by such exposure. He took such chances; had nothing ever taught him not to take such chances? But maybe he didn't. He knew she would have to say something reassuring. In fact, she was longing not to; she wanted to say, judiciously, "Well, no. You don't." But that wouldn't actually be true. He did seem masculine to her. She believed that only a man could take those chances, could be so careless and demanding.

When Patrick asked Rose to marry him, she said, "We come from two different worlds." She felt like a character in a play, saying that. "My people are poor people. You would think the place I live in was a dump."

Now it was she who was being dishonest, pretending to throw herself on his mercy, for of course she did not expect him to say, "Oh, well, if you come from poor people and live in a dump, then I will have to revise my feelings and withdraw my offer."

"But I'm glad," said Patrick. "I'm glad you're poor. You're so lovely. You're like the Beggar Maid."

"Who?"

" 'King Cophetua and the Beggar Maid.' You know, the painting. Don't you know that painting?"

Patrick had a trick—no, it was not a trick; Patrick had no tricks. Patrick had a way of expressing surprise, fairly scornful surprise, when people did not know something he knew, and similar scorn, similar surprise, that they ever bothered to know something he did not. His arrogance and humility were both so exaggerated. The arrogance, Rose thought later, must come from being rich, though Patrick was never arrogant about that in itself. His sisters, when she met them, turned out to be the same way—disgusted with anybody who did not know about horses or sailing, and just as disgusted with anybody who knew about music, say, or politics.

Rose had no idea at the beginning how rich Patrick was. Nobody at the university believed that, though; everyone thought she had been calculating and clever. It turned out that other girls had tried for Patrick and had not struck, as she had, the necessary chord. Older girls, sorority girls who had never noticed her before began to look at her with puzzlement and respect. Even

Dr. Henshawe, when she saw that things were more serious than she had supposed, and settled Rose down for a talk about it, assumed that Rose had her eye on money. "It is no small triumph to attract the attentions of the heir to a mercantile empire," said Dr. Henshawe, being ironic and serious at the same time. "I don't despise wealth. Sometimes I wish I had some of it. I am sure you would learn to put it to good uses. But what about your ambitions, Rose? What about your degree? Can you forget all that so soon?"

"Mercantile empire" was a rather grand way of putting it. Patrick's family owned a chain of department stores in British Columbia. All Patrick had said to Rose was that his father owned some stores. When she said "two different worlds," Rose was thinking that he probably lived in some substantial house like the larger houses in Dr. Henshawe's neighbourhood. She was thinking of merchants at home. She could not realize what a coup she had made, because people at home would have considered it a coup if she had snared the butcher's son, or the jeweller's.

The first chance she had, Rose looked up the painting of the Beggar Maid in an art book in the library. She studied the maid, meek and voluptuous, with shy white feet. She showed milky surrender—helplessness and gratitude. Was that how Patrick saw her, was that how she could be? To be like that she would need the king. He looked sharp and swarthy—clever and barbaric, even in his trance of passion. He could make a puddle of her with his fierce desire. There would be no apologizing with him, none of the flinching, the lack of faith that seemed to be revealed in all her transactions with Patrick.

She could not turn Patrick down. She could not do it. It was not the amount of money she could not ignore but the amount of love he offered. She believed that she felt sorry for him. It was as if he had come up to her in a crowd carrying a large, simple, dazzling object—a huge egg, say, of solid silver, something of doubtful use and punishing weight—and was offering it to her, in fact thrusting it at her, begging her to take some of the weight off him. If she thrust it back, how could he bear it? But that explanation left out something. It left out her own greed, which was not for money, but for worship. The size, the weight, the shine of what he said was love (and she did not doubt him) had to impress her, even though she had never asked for it. It did not seem likely such an offering would come her way again.

She had always thought that this would happen, that somebody would look at her and love her, totally and helplessly. At the same time, she had thought that nobody would, nobody would ever want her at all. She would look at herself in the glass and think: wife, sweetheart. Those mild, lovely words—how could they apply to her? It was what she had dreamed of. It was not what she wanted.

She grew very tired, irritable, sleepless. She tried to think admiringly of Patrick. His lean, fair face was really very handsome, she decided. He graded papers; he presided at examinations; he was working on his thesis. There was a smell of pipe tobacco and rough wool about him, which she liked. He was 24. None of the girls she knew had a boyfriend as old as that.

Then, one day when they were walking back from a restaurant downtown, without warning she remembered him saying, "I suppose I don't seem very manly." She remembered another time, when he had said, "Do you love me? Do you really love me?" He had looked at her in a scared and threatening way. Then, when she said yes, he said how lucky he was, how lucky they were, he bet not many people loved each other as they did. Now she shivered with irritation and misery. She was sick of herself as much as of him; she was sick of the picture they made at this moment, walking across a snowy downtown park, her bare hand snuggled in his, in his pocket. Some outrageous and cruel things were shouted inside her. But she could not take her hand out and speak the truth. Instead, she started tickling and teasing him.

Outside Dr. Henshawe's back door, in the snow, she kissed him, tried to make him open his mouth. She did scandalous things to him. When he kissed her, his lips were so soft, his tongue was shy; instead of holding her, he seemed to collapse over her. She could not find the force in him.

"You're lovely," he said. "You have lovely skin. Such fair eyebrows. You're so delicate."

She was pleased to hear that; anybody would be. But she said warningly, "I'm not so delicate. I'm really quite large."

"You don't know how I love you. There's a book I have called *The White Goddess*. Every time I see the title I think of you, because your skin is so white."

Rose wriggled away from him. She bent down and got a handful of snow from a drift by the steps and clapped it on his head.

"My white god," she said.

He shook the snow out. She scooped some more and threw it at him. He didn't laugh; he was surprised and alarmed. She brushed the snow from his eyebrows and licked it off his ears. She was laughing, though she felt desperate rather than merry.

"Dr. *Hen*shawe," Patrick hissed at her. The tender poetic voice, which he used for rhapsodizing about her, could break into remonstrance, exasperation, with no steps at all between. "Dr. Henshawe will hear you!"

"Dr. Henshawe says you are an honourable young man," said Rose dreamily. "I think she's in love with you." She blew at the snow in his hair. "Why don't you go in and deflower her? I bet she's a virgin. That's her window. Why don't you?" She rubbed his hair, then slipped her hand inside his overcoat and rubbed the front of his pants. "You're excited," she said triumphantly. She had never done or said such a thing to a boy, or a man, before.

"Shut up," said Patrick. Rose raised her head and in a loud whisper pretended to call toward an upstairs window, "Dr. Henshawe! Come and see what Patrick's got for you!"

To stop her, to keep her quiet, Patrick had to struggle with her. He got a hand over her mouth and with the other hand beat her away from his zipper. As soon as he began to fight her she was relieved, but she could not stop yet; she had to resist. She was still afraid she might really be able to get the better of him. She was quite strong.

But he was stronger. He forced her to her knees, and then pushed her face down in a snowdrift. He pulled her arms back and rubbed her face in the snow. Then he let her go and almost spoiled it. "Are you all right?" he said. "Are you? I'm sorry. Rose?"

She staggered up and shoved her snowy face into his. "Kiss me! I love you!"

"Do you. *Do* you?"

Then the light came on, flooding them and the trampled snow, and Dr. Henshawe was calling over their heads.

"Rose! Rose!" She called in a patient, encouraging voice, as if Rose were lost in a fog somewhere and needed directing home.

"Do you love him, Rose?" said Dr. Henshawe when she came in. "Now, do you?" Her voice was full of doubt and seriousness. Rose took a deep breath and answered as if filled with calm emotion, "Yes, I do."

"Well, then," said Dr. Henshawe.

Patrick shared an apartment with two other graduate students. He lived plainly, did not own a car or belong to a fraternity. Ordinarily, his clothes were shabby. His friends were the sons of teachers and ministers. He said that his father had all but disowned him for becoming an intellectual. He said he would never go back to business.

Rose and Patrick began to go to his apartment in the early afternoons, when both the other students were out. The apartment was cold. They undressed quickly and got into Patrick's bed. They clung together, shivering. Rose giggled. She was continually playful. When they began to make love in earnest, she switched at once to being loving, eager, passionate. The first few times, she was so busy that she hardly noticed that she didn't feel anything. It was enough for her that they were doing this. They were doing what other lovers did. The fear she had felt that they would not manage it, that there was a great humiliation in store, made her triumphant; she never thought to ask for pleasure as well. So when pleasure presented itself, their fifth or sixth time together, she was thrown out of gear, her counterfeit passion silenced.

Patrick said, "What's the matter?"

"Nothing!" she said, making herself radiant and attentive once more. But the new developments interfered, and she had finally to give into them, more or less disregarding Patrick. When she could take note of him again, she overwhelmed him with gratitude; she was really grateful now, and she wanted to be forgiven—though she could not say so—for all her pretending and her doubts.

Why should she doubt so much, she thought, lying pleasurably in bed while Patrick went to make some instant coffee. It was partly Patrick's doing; his chivalry and self-abasement, along with his scolding, did discourage her. But it was partly her own conviction that anyone who would fall in love with her must be hopelessly lacking, must be finally revealed as a fool. So she took note of whatever was foolish about Patrick, even though she consciously looked for things that were masterful, admirable. That much she could see; perhaps she could change it. At this moment, in his bed, in his room—surrounded by his books and clothes, his shoe-brushes, his typewriter, some tacked-up cartoons torn out of magazines—she could see him as a moderate, likeable, independent, even humorous person. If only we could be ordinary, she was thinking. If only, when he came back in, he would not start thanking her and fondling and worshipping her, making her nervous. She didn't like worship, really; she only liked the idea of it. On the other hand, she didn't like it when he started to correct and criticize her. Patrick loved her, but what did he love? Not her Huron County accent, which he was trying hard to change (though she was sometimes mutinous and unreasonable, declaring in the face of all evidence that she did not have an accent, and that everybody talked the way she did). Not her jittery sexual boldness. His relief at her virginity matched hers at his competence. She could make him flinch at her vulgarity. All the time, moving or speaking, she was damaging herself in his eyes; yet he loved her. He looked right through her, through all the distractions she was creating, and loved some obedient image that Rose herself could not see. And he had hopes. Her accent could be eliminated, her friends could be discredited and removed, her vulgarity could be discouraged.

What about all the rest of her? Her energy, her laziness, her vanity, her discontent, her ambitions. She concealed all that; he had no idea. For all her doubts, she did not want him to fall out of love with her.

They made two trips. First they went to British Columbia, on the train, during the Easter holidays. His parents sent Patrick his ticket. He paid for Rose's, though it took almost all the money he had in the bank. He told his parents she had bought it herself. He did not want them to know she could not afford it.

Patrick's parents lived on Vancouver Island, near Sidney. In front of the house, about half an acre of clipped green lawn— green so early in the year; Rose had never imagined such a thing—sloped down to a stone wall and a narrow pebbly beach. The house was half stone, half stucco-and-timber. The windows of the living-room, the dining-room, the den all faced the sea, and because of the strong winds that sometimes blew onshore they were made of thick glass—plate glass, Rose supposed, like the windows of the automobile showroom at home. The seaward wall of the dining-room was all windows, curving out in a gentle bay, and you looked through the thick curved glass as through the bottom of a bottle. The sideboard, too, had a smooth curving belly, and seemed as big as a boat. Thickness was noticeable everywhere—in towels and rugs and cutlery, and in silences. There was a terrifying amount of luxury and unease. After a day or so Rose became so discouraged that her wrists and ankles felt weak. Picking up her knife and fork was a chore; cutting and chewing the roast beef was almost beyond her; she got short of breath climbing the stairs.

The first morning, Patrick's mother had taken her for a walk in the grounds, pointing out the greenhouse, the cottage where "the couple" lived (a charming, ivied, shuttered cottage, bigger than Dr. Henshawe's house). His mother showed Rose the rose garden, the kitchen garden. There were many low stone walls. "Patrick built them," said his mother. She explained things with an indifference that bordered on distaste. "He built all these walls."

Rose's own voice came out full of false assurance, eager and inappropriately enthusiastic. "He must be a true Scot," she said. The Blatchfords had come from Glasgow. "Weren't the best stonemasons from Scotland? Maybe he had stonemason ancestors!" She cringed later at the thought of these efforts, the pretense of ease and gaiety, as cheap and imitative as her clothes.

"No," said Patrick's mother. "No, I don't think they were stonemasons." Something like fog went out from her: affront, disapproval, dismay. Rose thought that perhaps she had been offended by the suggestion that her husband's family might have worked with their hands. When she got to know her better—or had observed her longer; it was impossible to get to know her—Rose understood that in conversation Patrick's mother disliked anything fanciful, speculative, abstract. (She also, of course, disliked Rose's chatty tone.) Any interest beyond a factual consideration of the matter at hand—food, weather, invitations, furniture, servants—apparently struck her as sloppy, ill-bred, dangerous. It was all right to say "This is a warm day" but not "This day reminds me of when we used to . . ."

She was the only child of one of the early lumber barons of Vancouver Island. She had been born in a now-vanished northern settlement. But whenever Patrick tried to get her to talk about the past, whenever he asked, whenever he asked her for the simplest information—what steamers went up the coast, when the settlement was abandoned, what was the route of the first railway—she would say irritably, "I don't know. How should I know about that?" This irritation was the strongest note that ever got into her voice.

Neither did Patrick's father care for this concern about the past. Many things—most things—about Patrick seemed to strike him as bad signs.

"What do you want to know all that for?" he shouted down the table one evening when Patrick asked about the beginnings of the store. He was a short, square-shouldered man, red-faced, astonishingly belligerent. Patrick looked like his mother, who was tall, pale, elegant in the most muted way possible—as if her clothes, her makeup, her style were all chosen with an ideal neutrality in mind.

"Because I am interested in history," said Patrick pompously, with a giveaway break in his voice.

"Because . . . I . . . am . . . interested . . . in . . . history," said his sister Marion, in immediate parody, break and all. "History."

The sisters, Joan and Marion, were younger than Patrick but older than Rose. At an earlier meal they had questioned her.

"Do you ride?" they asked.

"No."

"Do you sail?"

"No."

Play tennis? Play golf? Play badminton?

No. No. No.

"She is probably an intellectual genius, like Patrick," the father said. And Patrick, to Rose's horror and embarrassment, began to shout at the table in general an account of Rose's scholarships, her prizes, her superiority. What did he hope for? Did he really think this bragging would convince them? Against Patrick, against his bragging, his so-called intellectual interests, his scorn for sports and television, the family seemed united. But this alliance was only temporary. The father's dislike of his daughters seemed minor only in comparison with his dislike of Patrick. He railed at them too—about the time they wasted on sports, the cost of their horses and boats and equipment. They wrangled with each other on obscure questions of scores and damages. All complained to the mother about the food, which was plentiful and delicious. She seldom spoke at all. Rose had never imagined so much true malevolence concentrated in one place. Her uncle was a bigot and a grumbler and a household tyrant, her aunt was a whiner; but compared to Patrick's family they were jovial and content.

"Are they always like this?" she said to Patrick. "Is it me? They don't like me."

"They don't like you because I chose you," said Patrick with some satisfaction. "That's the way they are."

They lay on the stony beach after dark, in their raincoats, and hugged and kissed uncomfortably. Patrick said, "You see why I need you? I need you so much!"

Then Rose took Patrick home. It was just as bad as she had thought it would be. Her aunt had gone to great trouble, cooking scalloped potatoes, turnips, big pork-and-beef sausages. Patrick hated coarse-textured food, and made no pretense of eating it. The table was spread with a plastic cloth; they ate under the fluorescent light. The centrepiece was new and special for the occasion—a plastic swan with slits in the wings, in which were stuck fancily folded paper napkins. When he was reminded to take one, Rose's uncle grunted and refused. Otherwise he was on dismally good behaviour. Word had reached this house of Rose's triumph. It came through people they had to respect, there in town; if it had come just from outside, they would not have believed it. Rose's uncle's boss, the butcher, had heard it from his wife, whose sister was married to a dentist who had a son at the university.

Rose tried to start some conversation. She talked brightly, unnaturally, rather as if she were an interviewer trying to draw out an amusing local couple. She was ashamed on more levels than she could count. Ashamed for the food and the plastic table-cloth and her aunt and uncle; ashamed for Patrick, the gloomy snob, who frowned so unkindly when her aunt passed the toothpick holder; ashamed for herself and the way she sounded. With Patrick there, she didn't dare slip back into an accent closer to theirs. That accent jarred on her now, anyway. It seemed not just a different way of pronouncing some vowels but a different approach to talking. Talking was shouting, the words separate and emphasized so people could bombard each other with them. And the things people said were like lines from some hackneyed rural comedy. "Wal, if a feller took a notion to," they said. They said that. Seeing them through Patrick's eyes, hearing them through his ears, she had to be disbelieving.

Rose tried to get them to talk about local history—some things she thought Patrick might be interested in. Presently her aunt did begin to talk, though the conversation took another direction from anything Rose had intended.

"The line we lived on," her aunt said to Patrick, "the twelfth line, it was the worst in creation for suicides."

"A line is a township road," Rose explained. She had misgivings, and rightly, for then Patrick got to hear about a man who had cut his own throat from ear to ear; a man who had shot himself once and not done enough damage, so he loaded up and fired again and did it right; a man who had hanged himself using the kind of chain you hitch a tractor with, so it was a wonder his head was not torn off. Rose's aunt presented all this to Patrick with a garrulous, shy politeness. These were her credentials. Having had these things happen nearby, having known some of the people they happened to, made her feel worthy of attention. But she was not self-important; she wanted to share, she hoped to please.

"You were right," said Patrick afterward. "It is a dump. You must be glad to escape. Of course, they're not your real parents."

Rose thought of her real parents and her real home—the torn dark window blinds, the poor farm, the bad luck, the dishpan with the rag plug in it. Her father had walked to town one day and then walked on, or got on a freight—they never knew. Her mother had ulcerated sores on her legs, and went to hospital, where she died. Patrick must be imagining for her something more genteel than her aunt and uncle could provide, something like the homes of his poor friends: a few books about, a tea tray, mended linen, worn good taste; proud, tired, educated people. What a coward he was, thought Rose angrily, but she knew that she herself was the coward. She was unable to think of her early childhood, that dark time, without such shame—hating it, hating herself for carrying it with her. When her aunt and uncle took her, she had been lousy. Her aunt had soaked her head in kerosene. Nevertheless, now that Rose was sure of getting away, a layer of loyalty and protectiveness was hardening around every memory she had of home—even around the worst, the inadmissible memories.

Not long after they got back, Patrick gave Rose a diamond ring and announced that he was giving up the academic life for her sake. He would start learning about his father's business.

"But you hate that," Rose said.

"I can't afford to take that attitude when I have a wife to support."

It seemed that Patrick's desire to marry, even to marry Rose, had been taken by his father as a sign of sanity. Great streaks of generosity were mixed in with all the ill-will in that family. His father offered a job in one of the stores, offered to buy them a house. Patrick was as incapable of turning down this offer as Rose was of turning down his. He did not know yet that he would make a far cleverer businessman than scholar. He liked the idea of sacrificing, "going into harness," for Rose.

"Will we have a house like your parents'?" she asked.

"Well, maybe not at first, not quite so—" Patrick said.

"I don't want a house like that!"

"We'll have whatever you like."

Provided it's not a *dump*, thought Rose.

Girls she hardly knew stopped her and asked to see her ring, admired it and wished her happiness. She went home for a weekend, and met the dentist's wife on the main street. "Oh, Rose, isn't it wonderful," she said. "When are you coming back here again? The ladies of the town want to give a tea for you!" The dentist's wife was a powerful woman who had never spoken to Rose in her life before. Paths were opening now, barriers were softening. And Rose—oh, this was the worst of it—instead of cutting the dentist's wife, Rose was blushing and skittishly flashing her diamond and saying yes, what a lovely idea. When people said how happy she must be, she did think herself happy. It was as simple as that; she dimpled and sparkled. "Where will you live?" they said, and Rose said, "Oh, in British Columbia." That added more magic to the tale. "Is it really beautiful there?" they said. "Is it never winter?"

"Oh, yes!" cried Rose. "Oh, no!"

One morning, Rose woke early, got up and dressed, and let herself out the side door. It was too early for the buses to be running. She walked through the city to Patrick's apartment. She walked across the park. Around the South African War Memorial a pair of greyhounds were leaping and playing while an old woman stood by, holding their leashes. The sun was just up, shining on their silver hides. The grass was wet. Daffodils and narcissus grew in the park like wild flowers.

Patrick came to the door in his grey-and-maroon-striped pyjamas, tousled, frowning sleepily. "What's the matter?" he asked.

She couldn't say it. He pulled her into the apartment. She put her arms around him and hid her face against his chest and in a stagey way said, "Please. Please let me not marry you."

"Are you sick?" Patrick said. "What's the matter?"

"Please let me not marry you," repeated Rose with even less conviction.

"You're crazy."

She didn't blame him for thinking so. Her voice sounded unnatural, wheedling and silly. As soon as he opened the door, as soon as she faced the fact of him, his sleepy eyes, his pyjamas, she saw that what she had come to do was enormous, impossible.

"Are you upset?" said Patrick. "What's happened?"

"Nothing."

"How did you get here?"

"Walked."

She had been fighting back a need to go to the bathroom. It seemed that if she went to the bathroom she would destroy some of the strength of her case. But she freed herself; she said, "Wait a minute."

When she came out he had the electric kettle going and was measuring out instant coffee. He looked decent and bewildered.

"I'm not really awake," he said. "Now, sit down. First of all, are you premenstrual?"

"No," she said. But she realized with dismay that she was, and that he might be able to figure it out, because a month ago they had been worried she might be pregnant.

"Well, if you're not premenstrual and nothing's happened to upset you, then what is all this about?"

"I don't want to get married," said Rose, backing away from the cruelty of "I don't want to marry you."

"When did you come to this decision?" he asked.

"Long ago," she said. "I don't know. . . . This morning."

They were talking in whispers. Rose looked at the clock. It was a little after seven. "When do they get up?" she said, meaning the other graduate students.

"About eight o'clock."

"Is there milk?" Rose went to the refrigerator.

"Quiet with the door," Patrick said, too late.

"I'm sorry," said Rose in a strange, silly voice.

"We went for a walk last night," Patrick said. "Everything was fine. You come this morning and tell me you don't want to get married. *Why* don't you want to get married?"

"I just don't. I don't want to be married."

"What *do* you want to do?"

"I don't know."

Patrick kept staring at her sternly, drinking his coffee. "Well, I know," he said at last.

"What?"

"I know who's been talking to you."

"Nobody has been talking to me."

"Oh, no? Well, I bet Dr. Henshawe has."

"No," Rose said.

"Some people don't have a very high opinion of her," Patrick said. "They think she has an influence on girls. She doesn't like the girls who live there to have boyfriends. You told me."

"That's not it."

"What did she say to you, Rose?"

"She didn't say anything." Rose began to cry.

"Are you sure?"

"Oh, Patrick, listen, please. I can't marry you. Please, I don't know why. I can't. Please believe me, I can't," babbled Rose, weeping.

Patrick said, "Sh-h-h, you'll wake them up," and he lifted her out of her chair and took her to his room, where she sat on the bed. He shut the door. She held herself, and rocked back and forth.

"What is it, Rose?" he said. "What's the matter? Are you sick?"

"It's just so hard to tell you."

"Tell me what?"

"What I just did tell you."

"I mean, have you found out you have TB or something?"

"No."

"Is there something in your family you haven't told me?" said Patrick encouragingly. "Insanity?"

"No." Rose rocked and wept.

"So what is it?"

"I don't love you," said Rose. "I don't love you. I don't love you." She fell on the bed and put her head in the pillow. "I'm so sorry. I'm so sorry. I can't help it."

After a few moments Patrick said, "Well, if you don't love me you don't love me. I can't force you to." His voice sounded high and spiteful, though the words were reasonable. "I just wonder if you know what you *do* want," he continued. "I don't think you do. I don't think you have any idea what you want. You're just in a state."

"I don't have to know what I want to know what I don't want!" said Rose angrily, turning over.

"Sh-h-h. We have to stop. They'll be waking up soon."

"I never loved you. I never wanted to. It was a mistake."

"All right. All right. You made your point." Patrick's face was so white the birthmark stood out like a cut.

"Why am I supposed to love you? Why do you act as if there was something wrong with me if I didn't? You despise me. You despise my background and think you're doing me such a great favour—"

"I fell in love with you," said Patrick. "I don't despise you. Oh, Rose. I worship you."

"You're a sissy," said Rose. "You're a prude." She jumped up with great pleasure as she said this. She felt full of energy. "You don't even know how to make love right," she went on. "I always wanted to get out of this from the very first. I felt sorry for you. You won't look where you're going; you're always knocking things over, just because you can't be bothered. You can't be bothered noticing anything, you're so wrapped up in yourself. And you're always bragging. You don't even know how to brag right, if you want to impress people; you do it in such a stupid way, all they do is laugh at you."

Patrick sat on the bed and looked up at her, his face open to whatever she would say. She wanted to beat and beat him, to say worse and worse, uglier and crueller things. She took a breath, drew in air, to stop the things she felt rising.

"I don't want to see you ever," she said viciously. But at the door she turned and said in a normal and regretful voice, "Goodbye."

Patrick wrote her a note: "I don't understand what happened the other day and I want to talk to you about it. But I think we should wait for two weeks and not see or talk to each other, and find out how we feel at the end of that time."

Rose had forgotten all about her ring. When she came out of Patrick's apartment building that morning she was still wearing it. She couldn't go back, and she didn't want to send it to him through the mail; it was too valuable. She continued to wear it, because she did not want to have to tell Dr. Henshawe what had happened. She was relieved to get Patrick's note. She thought that she could give him the ring when they met.

She thought about what Patrick had said about Dr. Henshawe. No doubt there was some truth in it, or else why would she be so reluctant to let Dr. Henshawe know she had broken her engagement? She told her that she was not seeing Patrick while she studied for her exams. She told no one that her situation had changed. She did not like to give up being envied.

She tried to think what to do next. She could not stay on at Dr. Henshawe's. She had to escape from Patrick; she had to escape from Dr. Henshawe, too. She did not want to stay on at the university, surrounded by girls who had always said to each other what a fluke it was, her getting Patrick. She would have to get a job.

The head librarian had offered her a job for the summer, but that was perhaps at Dr. Henshawe's suggestion. Once Rose moved out, the offer might not hold. Instead of studying for her exams, Rose knew, she ought to be downtown, applying for work as a filing clerk at the insurance offices, applying at Bell Telephone, at the department stores. The idea terrified her. She kept on studying. That was the one thing she really knew how to do. She was a scholarship student, after all.

The next Saturday afternoon, when she was working in the library, she saw Patrick. She did not see him by accident. She went down to the bottom floor, trying not to make any noise on the spiralling metal staircase. There was a place in the stacks where she could stand, almost in darkness, and see into his carrel. She did that. She couldn't see his face, but she saw his long pink neck and the old plaid shirt he wore on Saturdays. She was no longer irritated by him, no longer frightened by him; she was free. She could look at him as she would look at anybody; she could appreciate him. He had behaved well. He had not tried to rouse her pity, he had not bullied her, he had not molested her with pitiful phone calls and letters. He had not come and sat on Dr. Henshawe's doorstep. He was an honourable person, and he would never know how she acknowledged that, how much she liked him for it. The things she had said to him filled her with shame. And they were not even true. He did know how to make love. She was so moved, so gentled, by the sight of him that she wanted to give him something, some surprising bounty; she wished to undo all his unhappiness.

Then she had a compelling picture of herself. She was running softly into his carrel, she was throwing her arms around him from behind, she was giving everything back to him. Would he take it, would he still want it? She saw them laughing and crying, explaining, forgiving. This was a violent temptation for her; it was barely resistible. She had an impulse to hurl herself, whether it was off a cliff or into a warm bed of welcoming grass and flowers she really could not tell.

The temptation was not resistible after all. She gave in to it.

When Rose afterward reviewed and talked about this moment in her life (for, like most people nowadays, she talked freely about her private decisions—about her life—to friends and lovers and party acquaintances whom she might never see again, and they did the same), she said comradely compassion had overcome her; she was never proof against a bare, bent neck. Then she went further into it and said greed, greed. She had run to him and clung to him and overcome his suspicions and kissed and cried and reinstated herself with him simply because she did not know how to do without his love and his looking after her: she was frightened of the world; she had not been able to think out any other plan for herself. When she was seeing life in economic terms, or was talking with people who did, she said that only middle-class people had choices; only people with good shoes and the price of a train ticket to Toronto could afford to run away. At least if you were a girl, she said, and in my day.

At other times she said it was really vanity. It was vanity pure and simple—to resurrect him, to bring him back his happiness. To see if she had the power to do that. She could not resist the test of power. She explained that she had paid for it. They were married eleven years, they had two daughters; and during those years the scenes of the first breakup and reconciliation were periodically repeated. She said over again all the things she had said the first time, and the things she had held back, and many other things that occurred to her. She beat her head against the bedpost, she smashed a gravy-boat through the dining-room window. Then she was so weakened, so sickened by what she had done, that she lay in bed, shivering; she begged and begged for his forgiveness. Sometimes she would attack him, and he would beat her. The next morning they would get up early and make a special breakfast; they would sit eating bacon and eggs and drinking filtered coffee, worn out, bewildered, treating each other with shamefaced kindness. What do you think triggers the reaction, they would say. Do you think we ought to take a holiday? A waste, a sham, those efforts, as it turned out, but they worked for the moment. Rose and Patrick ended up saying that they supposed most married people went through this; indeed, they seemed to know mostly people who did. They could not separate until enough damage had been done—until nearly mortal damage had been done—to keep them apart. And until Rose had a job and was making her own money; so perhaps there was a very simple reason after all.

What Rose never said to anybody was that she sometimes thought it had not been pity or greed or cowardice or vanity but something quite different, like a vision of happiness. In view of everything else she had told, she could not tell that. She didn't mean just that they had bearable, ordinary times between eruptions, long busy times of wallpapering and vacationing and children's illnesses and meals and shopping, but that sometimes, without reason or warning, happiness—the possibility of happiness—would surprise them. It was as if they were in different though identical-seeming skins, as if there existed a perfectly kind and innocent Rose and Patrick, so rarely visible, in the shadow of their usual selves. Perhaps it was this Patrick she had seen when she was free of him, invisible to him, looking into his carrel. She should have left him there.

She knew that was how she had seen him, because it happened again. She was in the Toronto airport, in the middle of the night. This was about nine years after she and Patrick were divorced. Rose had become well known by this time; her face was familiar all over the country. She had a television program on which she interviewed politicians, actors, writers and many ordinary people, who were angry about something the government or the police or a company or a union had done to them. Sometimes she talked to people who had seen strange sights—UFOs or sea monsters—or who had unusual accomplishments or collections, or kept up obsolete customs.

She was travelling alone. No one was meeting her. She had just flown in from Yellowknife. She was tired and bedraggled. She saw Patrick standing at a coffee bar, with his back to her. He wore a raincoat. He was heavier than he had been, but she knew him at once. And she had the same feeling that this was the person she was bound to—that by a certain magical yet possible trick they could find and trust each other, and that to begin again all she had to do was go up and touch him on the shoulder, surprise him with his happiness.

She did not, of course, but she did stop. She was standing still when he turned around, heading for one of the little plastic tables and curved seats grouped in front of the coffee bar. All his skinniness and shabbiness, his prim authoritarianism were gone;

he had smoothed out, filled out into such a modish, agreeable, responsible, slightly complacent-looking man. His birthmark had faded. Rose thought how haggard and strange she must look, in her rumpled trenchcoat, her long, greying hair fallen forward around her face, old mascara smudged under her eyes.

He made a face at her. It was a truly hateful, savagely warning face—infantile, self-indulgent, yet calculated; it was like an explosion of disgust and loathing. It was hard to believe. But she had seen it.

Sometimes when Rose was talking to someone in front of the television cameras she would sense the desire in them to make a face. She could sense it in all sorts of people—in skilful politicians and witty liberal bishops and honoured humanitarians, in housewives who had witnessed natural disasters and in workmen who had performed rescues or been cheated out of disability pensions. They were longing to sabotage themselves, to make a face or say a dirty word. Was this the face they all wanted to make—to show somebody, to show everybody? They wouldn't do it, though; they wouldn't get the chance. Special circumstances were required: a lurid, unreal place, the middle of the night; a staggering, unhinging weariness; the sudden, hallucinatory appearance of your true enemy.

Violent Encounters

THE MOOSE AND THE SPARROW
by Hugh Garner

From the very beginning Moose Maddon picked on him. The kid was bait for all of Maddon's cruel practical jokes around the camp. He was sent back to the toolhouse for left-handed saws, and down to the office to ask the pay cheater if the day's mail was in, though the rest of us knew it was only flown out every week.

The kid's name was Cecil, and Maddon used to mouth it with a simpering mockery, as if it pointed to the kid being something less than a man. I must admit though that the name fitted him, for Cecil was the least likely lumberjack I've seen in over twenty-five years in lumber camps. Though we knew he was intelligent enough, and a man too, if smaller than most of us, we all kidded him, in the good-natured way a bunkhouse gang will. Maddon however always lisped the kid's name as if it belonged to a woman.

Moose Maddon was as different from Cecil as it is possible for two human beings to be and still stay within the species. He was a big moose of a man, even for a lumber stiff, with a round flat unshaven face that looked down angrily and dourly at the world. Cecil on the other hand was hardly taller than an axe-handle, and almost as thin. He was about nineteen years old, with the looks of an inquisitive sparrow behind his thick horn-rimmed glasses. He had been sent out to the camp for the summer months by a distant relative who had a connection with the head office down in Vancouver.

That summer we were cutting big stuff in an almost inaccessible stand of Douglas fir about fifty miles out of Nanaimo. The logs were catted five miles down to the river where they were bunked waiting for the drive. Cecil had signed on as a whistle punk, but after a few days of snarling the operation with wrong

125

signals at the wrong time and threatening to hang the rigging-slingers in their own chokers, he was transferred to Maddon's gang as a general handyman. Besides going on all the ridiculous and fruitless errands for Moose, he carried the noon grub to the gangs from the panel truck that brought it out from camp, made the tea and took the saws and axes in to old Bobbins, the squint eye, to be sharpened.

For the first two weeks after he arrived, the jokes were the usual ones practised on a greenhorn, but when they seemed to be having little or no effect on his bumbling habits and even temper Moose devised more cruel and intricate ones. One night Moose and a cohort of his called Lefevre carried the sleeping Cecil, mattress and all, down to the river and threw him in. The kid almost drowned, but when he had crawled up on shore and regained his breath he merely smiled at his tormentors and ran back to the bunkhouse, where he sat shivering in a blanket on the springs of his bunk till the sun came up.

Another time Moose painted a wide mustache with tar on Cecil's face while he slept. It took him nearly a week to get it all off, and his upper lip was red and sore-looking for longer than that.

Nearly all of us joined in the jokes on Cecil at first, putting a young raccoon in his bunk, kicking over his tea water, hiding his clothes or tying them in knots, all the usual things. It wasn't long though until the other men noticed that Moose Maddon's jokes seemed to have a grim purpose. You could almost say he was carrying out a personal vendetta against the kid for refusing to knuckle under or cry "Uncle." From then on everybody but Moose let the kid alone.

One evening as a few of us sat outside the bunkhouse shooting the guff, Moose said, "Hey, Cecil dear, what do you do over on the mainland?"

"Go to school," Cecil answered.

Moose guffawed. "Go to school? At your age!"

Cecil just grinned.

"What school d'ya go to, Cecil? Kindergarten?" Moose asked him, guffawing some more.

"No."

"You afraid to tell us?"

"No."

"Well, what school d'ya go to?"

"U.B.C."

"What's that, a hairdressin' school?"

"No, the university."

"University! You!"

Moose, who was probably a Grade Four dropout himself, was flabbergasted. I'm sure that up until that minute he'd been living in awe of anybody with a college education.

"What you takin' up?" he asked, his face angry and serious now.

"Just an arts course," Cecil said.

"You mean paintin' pictures an' things?"

"No, not quite," the kid answered.

For once Moose had nothing further to say.

From then on things became pretty serious as far as Moose and Cecil were concerned. On at least two occasions the other men on the gang had to prevent Moose from beating the boy up, and old Bobbins even went so far as to ask Mr. Semple, the walking boss, to transfer the youngster to another gang. Since learning that Cecil was a college boy, Moose gave him no peace at all, making him do jobs that would have taxed the strength of any man in the camp, and cursing him out when he was unable to do them, or do them fast enough.

The kid may not have been an artist, as Moose had thought, but he could make beautiful things out of wire. Late in the evenings he would sit on his bunk and fashion belt-buckles, rings and tie-clips from a spool of fine copper wire he'd found in the tool shed. He made things for several of the men, always refusing payment for them. He used to say it gave him something to do, since he couldn't afford to join in the poker games.

One evening late in the summer as I was walking along the river having an after-supper pipe, I stumbled upon Cecil curled up on a narrow sandy beach. His head was buried in his arms and his shoulders were heaving with sobs. I wanted to turn around without letting him know he'd been seen, but he looked so lonely crying there by himself that I walked over and tapped him on the shoulder.

He jumped as if I'd prodded him with a peavey, and swung around, his eyes nearly popping from his head with fright. The six weeks he'd spent working under Moose Maddon hadn't done his nerves any good.

"It's all right, kid," I said.

"Oh! Oh, it's you, Mr. Anderson!"

He was the only person in camp who ever called me anything but "Pop."

"I don't mean to butt in," I said. "I was just walking along here, and couldn't help seeing you. Are you in trouble?"

He wiped his eyes on his sleeve before answering me. Then he turned and stared out across the river.

"This is the first time I broke down," he said, wiping his glasses.

"Is it Moose?"

"Yes."

"What's he done to you now?"

"Nothing more than he's been doing to me all along. At first I took it—you know that, Mr. Anderson, don't you?"

I nodded.

"I thought that after I was out here a couple of weeks it would stop," he said. "I expected the jokes that were played on me at first. After all I was pretty green when I arrived here. When they got to know me the other men stopped, but not that—that Moose."

He seemed to have a hard time mouthing the other's name.

"When are you going back to school?" I asked him.

"In another couple of weeks."

"Do you think you can stand it until then?"

"I need all the money I can make, but it's going to be tough."

I sat down on the sand beside him and asked him to tell me about himself. For the next ten or fifteen minutes he poured out the story of his life; he was one of those kids who are kicked around from birth. His mother and father had split up while he was still a baby, and he'd been brought up in a series of foster homes. He'd been smart enough, though, to graduate from high school at seventeen. By a miracle of hard work and self-denial he'd managed to put himself through the first year of university, and his ambition was to continue on to law school. The money he earned from his summer work here at the camp was to go towards his next year's tuition.

When he finished we sat in silence for a while. Then he asked me, "Tell me, Mr. Anderson, why does Maddon pick on me like he does?"

I thought about his question for a long time before answering it. Finally I said, "I guess that deep down Moose knows you are smarter than he is in a lot of ways. I guess he's—well, I guess you might say he's jealous of you."

"No matter what I do, or how hard I try to please him, it's no good."

"It never is," I said.

"How do you mean?"

I had to think even longer this time. "There are some men, like Moose Maddon, who are so twisted inside that they want to take it out on the world. They feel that most other men have had better breaks than they've had, and it rankles inside them. They try to get rid of this feeling by working it out on somebody who's even weaker than they are. Once they pick on you there's no way of stopping them short of getting out of their way or beating it out of their hide."

Cecil gave me a wry grin. "I'd never be able to beat it out of the—the Moose's hide."

"Then try to keep out of his way."

"I can't for another two weeks," he said. "I'm afraid that before then he'll have really hurt me."

I laughed to reassure him, but I was afraid of the same thing myself. I knew that Moose was capable of going to almost any lengths to prevent Cecil leaving the camp without knuckling under at least once; his urge seemed to me to be almost insane. I decided to talk to George Semple myself in the morning, and have the boy flown out on the next plane.

"I don't think Moose would go as far as to really hurt you," I told him.

"Yes he would! He would, Mr. Anderson. I know it! I've seen the way he's changed. All he thinks about any more are ways to make me crawl. It's no longer a case of practical jokes; he wants to kill me!"

My reassuring laugh stuck in my throat this time. "In another two weeks, son, you'll be back in Vancouver, and all this will seem like a bad dream."

"He'll make sure I leave here crippled," Cecil said.

We walked back to the camp together, and I managed to calm him down some.

The next day I spoke to Semple, the walking boss, and convinced him we should get the boy out of there. There was never any thought of getting rid of Moose, of course. Saw bosses were worth their weight in gold, and the top brass were calling for more and more production all the time. Whatever else Moose was, he was the best production foreman in the camp. When Semple spoke to Cecil, however, the kid refused to leave. He said he'd made up his mind to stick it out until his time was up.

Though my gang was working on a different side than Maddon's, I tried to keep my eye on the boy from then on. For a week things went on pretty much as usual, then one suppertime Cecil came into the dining hall without his glasses. Somebody asked him what had happened, and he said there'd been an accident, and that Moose had stepped on them. We all knew how much of an accident it had been; luckily the kid had an old spare pair in his kit. Few of his gang had a good word for Moose any more, which only seemed to make him more determined to take his spite out on the kid.

That evening I watched Cecil fashioning a signet ring for one of the men out of wire and a piece of quartz the man had found. The way he braided the thin wire and shaped it around a length of thin sapling was an interesting thing to see. Moose was watching him too, but pretending not to. You could see he hated the idea of Cecil getting along so well with the other men.

"I was going to ask you to make me a new watch strap before you left," I said to Cecil. "But it looks like you're running out of wire."

The kid looked up. "I still have about twenty-five feet of it left," he said. "That'll be enough for what I have in mind. Don't worry, Mr. Anderson, I'll make you the watch strap before I leave."

The next afternoon there was quite a commotion over where Maddon's gang were cutting, but I had to wait until the whistle blew to find out what had happened. Cecil sat down to supper with his right hand heavily bandaged.

"What happened?" I asked one of Maddon's men.

"Moose burned the kid's hand," he told me. "He heated the end of a saw blade in the tea fire, and then called the kid to take it to the squint eye to be sharpened. He handed the hot end to Cecil, and it burned his hand pretty bad."

"But—didn't any of you?"

"None of us was around at the time. When we found out, big Chief went after Moose with a cant hook, but the rest of us held him back. He would have killed Moose. If Maddon doesn't leave the kid alone, one of us is going to have to cripple him for sure."

Moose had been lucky that The Chief, a giant Indian called Danny Corbett, hadn't caught him. I made up my mind to have

Cecil flown out in the morning without fail, no matter how much he protested.

That evening the kid turned in early, and we made sure there was always one of us in the bunkhouse to keep him from being bothered by anybody. He refused to talk about the hand-burning incident at all, but turned his head to the wall when anybody tried to question him about it. Moose left shortly after supper to drink and play poker in Camp Three, about a mile away through the woods.

I woke up during the night to hear a man laughing near the edge of the camp, and Maddon's name being called. I figured it was Moose and Lefevre coming home drunk from Camp Three, where the bull cook bootlegged homebrew.

When I got up in the morning, Cecil was already awake and dressed, sitting on the edge of his bunk plaiting a long length of his copper wire, using his good hand and the ends of the fingers of the one that was burned.

"What are you doing up so early?" I asked him.

"I went to bed right after chow last night, so I couldn't sleep once it got light." He pointed to the plaited wire. "This is going to be your watch strap."

"But you didn't need to make it now, Cecil," I said. "Not with your hand bandaged and everything."

"It's all right, Mr. Anderson," he assured me. "I can manage it okay, and I want to get it done as soon as I can."

Just as the whistle blew after breakfast one of the jacks from Camp Three came running into the clearing shouting that Moose Maddon's body was lying at the bottom of a deep, narrow ravine outside the camp. This ravine was crossed by means of a fallen log, and Moose must have lost his footing on it coming home drunk during the night. There was a free fall of more than forty feet down to a rocky stream bed.

None of us were exactly broken-hearted about Moose kicking off that way, but the unexpectedness of it shocked us. We all ran out to the spot, and the boys rigged a sling from draglines and hauled the body to the top of the ravine. I asked Lefevre if he'd been with Moose the night before, but he told me he hadn't gone over to Camp Three. Later in the day the district coroner flew out from Campbell River or somewhere, and after inspecting the log bridge made us rig a hand-line along it. He made out a certificate of accidental death.

When they flew the body out, Cecil stood with the rest of us on the river bank, watching the plane take off. If I'd been in his place I'd probably have been cheering, but he showed no emotion at all, not relief, happiness, or anything else.

He worked on my watch strap that evening, and finished it the next day, fastening it to my watch and attaching my old buckle to it. It looked like a real professional job, but when I tried to pay him for it he waved the money aside.

It was another week before Cecil packed his things to leave. His hand had begun to heal up nicely, and he was already beginning to lose the nervous twitches he'd had while Moose was living. When he was rowed out to the company plane, all the boys from his bunkhouse were on the river bank to see him go. The last we saw of Cecil was his little sparrow smile, and his hand waving to us from the window.

One day in the fall I went out to the ravine to see how the handline was making it. It still shocked me to think that Maddon, who had been as sure-footed as a chipmunk, and our best man in a log-rolling contest, had fallen to his death the way he had. Only then did I notice something nobody had looked for before. In the bark of the trunks of two small trees that faced each other diagonally across the fallen log were burn marks that could have been made by wire loops. A length of thin wire rigged from one to the other would have crossed the makeshift footbridge just high enough to catch a running man on the shin, and throw him into the ravine. Maddon could have been running across the log that night, if he'd been goaded by the laughter and taunts of somebody waiting at the other end. I remembered the sound of laughter and the shouting of Maddon's name.

I'm not saying that's what happened, you understand, and for all I know nobody was wandering around outside the bunkhouses on the night of Maddon's death, not Cecil or anybody else. Still, it gives me a queer feeling sometimes, even yet, to look down at my wrist. For all I know I may be the only man in the world wearing the evidence of a murder as a wristwatch strap.

THE MURDERER
by Yvette Naubert

Although he was known as one of the best shots on the police force, Lieutenant Gilbert Leroy was not an aggressive man. Indeed he had been a rather timid child of a conciliatory nature, not at all rowdy, but shrewd. He knew how to keep cool under any circumstances. Like all boys, he had had an arsenal of toy weapons, was very good at "killing" the enemy, quick to yell, "You're dead. I killed you," but always in play, without the slightest animosity toward anyone. When he started with the police force, he enjoyed target practice and quickly became a sharpshooter, always hitting the target whether he was running, lying down, or even in more dangerous positions. Soon he was admirably sure of himself. He was certain that when he had to draw his revolver out of its holster some day to shoot a fleeing bandit in the leg, he wouldn't miss.

At the wheel of the police car he patrolled the streets of a district inhabited mostly by immigrants who, in general, were citizens with respect for the law since they were never sure how it was administered. Hardly anything ever happened. Sometimes a new father would spread the word of his son's birth by turning his stereo up full blast in the middle of the night, a quarrel, usually in a foreign language, might break out between neighbours, or there might be a burglary in an apartment. Gilbert would arrive on the scene, calm everybody down in his reassuring way, restore things to normal, then return to the station. He would stretch out like a big cat, yawn, and joke with his fellow officers while he drank a Coca-Cola and filled out his report. Society can't do without conscientious, loyal policemen. Gilbert Leroy was as self-assured as the Rock of Gibraltar.

Like all policemen for whom black is black and white is white, Gilbert seldom questioned himself or the other officers.

Since he became a policeman, he had lost a certain naiveté; he knew that the words honesty and dishonesty were only a matter of degree, but thieves were thieves, that is to say, people who had to be caught in the act, manacled, and thrown in prison. Motives were for the judges, lawyers and psychiatrists to figure out. Gilbert Leroy didn't have much faith in psychiatrists who often complicated simple cases with their involved and obscure diagnoses.

He had been fortunate to find a rare pearl, a young lady who was still a virgin at the age of twenty-three. He loved and respected his fiancée and intended to do so until they were married. He was very discreet about this. None of his colleagues knew he wasn't sleeping with his fiancée. It was true that he often had her in his dreams but it was always a corpse he held in his arms. This bothered and worried him. He didn't think he had a tendency to necrophilia. Surely these detestable dreams would be over when he married in a few months' time.

One day his office received a call. Four armed men were in the process of robbing a bank and were holding the staff and customers hostage. The policemen jumped into their cars and took off at full speed, sirens wailing. Gilbert, his hands gripping the steering wheel, managed the speeding car with confidence and impeccable self-control. As if endowed with a second sight, he perceived obstacles before they came into his path.

In front of the bank, the police drew their revolvers as they got out of their vehicles. Shooting started immediately. Gilbert took a step forward, revolver in hand, but after a bullet whizzed close by him, he ran for cover behind his car, taking time to examine the situation. He could see that the action on the part of the police was dangerous and didn't make much sense. They were shooting wild, endangering the lives of the innocent people who were being held prisoner in the bank.

Gilbert soon singled out the one who seemed to be the leader of the masked bandits; he was giving orders and firing more calmly than the others. The policeman carefully took aim and fired. The bandit ducked, but behind him another man collapsed, clutching his throat.

The fusillade lasted about ten minutes. Two bandits were seriously wounded and two others surrendered. Only one policeman was injured, his cheek grazed by a bullet. Gilbert entered the bank and went to the spot where he had seen the man fall. He was lying curled up on his side, eyes wide open, a gaping hole in his throat. Even before he looked, Gilbert knew the man was dead and he knew that he had killed him.

"It's Mr. Tremblay, our accountant," said a voice. "How awful!"

Gilbert looked up at the two bandits being led away in handcuffs. Without his mask, the one Gilbert had aimed at looked young, even innocent. Before going out, he turned and smiled at the policeman.

Later, after the wounded had been taken to the hospital, the dead man to the morgue, and the others, suffering from shock, treated on the spot, Gilbert Leroy drove back to the police station at a normal speed. He stopped at red lights and waited for pedestrians before turning at intersections. His hands trembled lightly on the steering wheel.

"I wonder who killed the accountant," said his colleague who was sitting beside him.

"I did."

The other man turned his head so quickly Gilbert thought he could hear the bones cracking.

"That's not true, Lieutenant. Not you."

At the station, there was the same outburst of astonishment, disbelief. Lieutenant Gilbert Leroy couldn't have killed a man by mistake. He must be intimating his own guilt to protect someone else who fired at the same time and missed. The chief called him into his office and closed the door.

"Lieutenant, is it true what they tell me?"

"Yes, it's true."

"What happened, then?"

"I don't know. I don't know."

All he could do was repeat the words: he didn't know, he didn't understand. He had aimed at the bandit but an innocent man was dead, that was all.

"I'll resign."

"Out of the question. It's an accident. It's not your fault."

"But if one of the bandits had killed Tremblay, the accountant, what would happen to him?"

"He would certainly be tried and convicted. Why do you think those guys were armed?"

"And what about us, Captain?"

The chief of police looked his lieutenant right in the eye.

Slowly, his face assumed an unaccustomed expression. Deep down, very deep down, there was a flicker of indecision. Gilbert had the feeling that his chief was rapidly withdrawing from him even though he was still sitting there in the chair before him.

"Do you put yourself on the same level as those bandits, Lieutenant?"

"We carry revolvers on our person and we shoot on occasion. We kill, too."

"Take a few days rest, Lieutenant. It's Wednesday today. Don't come back to work until next Monday."

Gilbert sent flowers and visited the funeral home where a crowd of the curious, attracted by the drama, had assembled. Before the casket he asked the widow and her four children for forgiveness.

"It wasn't your fault," replied the woman, who was in tears. "You were doing your duty."

He attended the funeral, even accompanied the remains to the cemetery. Gilbert didn't take part in the ceremonies. He wasn't concerned with that. He went out of a sense of duty, to prove his good will and especially his innocence. Of the event he remembered only one thing: the bandit's smile. That smile was with him constantly and sometimes he would turn around quickly, certain he would see the bandit behind him even though he knew he was in prison. He was dreading the day he would be called as a witness and find himself once again in the presence of the thief. On that day he was sure he would find out what the future held for him. Gilbert Leroy was afraid for the first time in his life.

He went around in a daze, went to work every day but his heart wasn't in it. He spent every evening in his room, stretched out on the bed, gazing at the ceiling. He refused to answer the phone, even when his fiancée called. She came to the house several times and had long talks with Gilbert's mother but he refused to let her into his room and said he would see her later. At night he stayed in darkness, eyes wide open until sleep overcame him. Even during his sleep, the mocking smile haunted him.

On the day of the trial, as soon as he walked into the Court House, his colleagues came and shook his hand.

"How's it going, Lieutenant?"

"Fine."

The judge, the lawyers, witnesses, journalists, and the curious already filled the public gallery. Gilbert sat down apart from the others and waited. When the bandit came in flanked by two policemen, Gilbert's hands started to tremble and he had a knot in his throat. The boy held his head high, his lip curled back like a dog ready to bite. He looked insolently around the room, his gaze stopping at Gilbert. Once again the bandit smiled.

On the witness stand, the policeman swore the usual oath on the Bible and answered the lawyer's questions. He coldly related the events in every detail, omitting nothing, when suddenly he stopped answering. Rather, he answered questions he alone could hear. He was no longer answering; someone else had taken over his body, was telling him what to say; the young bandit was looking at a living being, not something mechanical like a robot. Yes, he had always had the desire to kill. As a little boy, he had liked killing and shooting games. The training he had received and the target practice he had had to do accentuated these tendencies, had made him one of the most dangerous men in society, a murderer protected by the law. He had killed a man; now he wanted to be tried as the criminal he was.

There was a general uproar. The robed lawyers fidgeted, the policemen got edgy, journalists ran to the telephones, the judge rapped on his desk. The young bandit, eyes wide open, was no longer smiling.

Some policemen came up to Gilbert, silently surrounding him, forming a barricade as if to protect him from society, from justice, and from himself. Gilbert thrust them aside, left the room and the Court House.

He went and stood in front of the building where his fiancée was working as a shorthand typist. He had been directing traffic on work days at that corner for the last three years. How many times had he nearly been knocked down by some angry maniac's car? Now he understood that many potential killers don't dare fulfill their desire.

At five o'clock the building disgorged its human cargo. The doors were hardly big enough to let the flood of people out. Most of them ran off like fugitives from justice. Gilbert thought, "How many of them are just like me, only waiting for the chance?" But, to tell the truth, that thought didn't bother him very much.

"Gilbert! What a nice surprise!"

She was already there, very close to him, happy, her face held up for his kiss, but he didn't feel he had the right to embrace this young woman or any other. He took her arm and led her off to his car which he had parked in a nearby street.

"What's the matter, Gilbert?"

Before deciding to speak, he took the time to put her into the car and get in himself.

"Jeanine, I killed a man."

"I know, Gilbert, but it was an accident. You were a police-man on duty. It's not your fault."

"Yes, it is my fault. No, it wasn't an accident. You forget, you all forget that I am a sharpshooter and I never miss. There-fore, I killed because I wanted to. I am a dangerous man. And that's why I don't want to marry you, Jeanine. You are a fine young woman and you should not marry a murderer. You would never be safe with me. Who knows? Perhaps I will kill again, especially since I know I'm so well protected by the law."

"I think you are humiliated, especially because you, a sharp-shooter, as you say, missed the mark the first time you shot at someone."

"I aimed before I fired. I took good aim before pressing the trigger."

She moved closer to him, put her hand on his thigh and her head on his shoulder.

"Let's go to my place. We can talk more comfortably there."

"I've told you everything, Jeanine."

"But I haven't told you everything, Gilbert."

Since his confession at the Court House he had nothing more to say. He had never been a very talkative man and now he wanted to keep quiet and have silence around him. His fiancée's attitude was disconcerting. Instead of accepting what he had to say immediately, as he had expected, she seemed to be drawing even closer to him.

"Help yourself while I take off my coat. I'll be right back."

He wasn't thirsty. He felt very calm and clear-headed, with no needs or desires. He sat down in a chair and looked around as if for the first time at this living-room where two girls lived. There was nothing out of the ordinary, nothing particular which might attract your attention. He heard the water running in the bath-room and a little later, Jeanine's voice calling him from the bedroom. She had pulled back the bedclothes and was standing there in the nude waiting for him.

"Why, Jeanine?"

"Hush, Gilbert. Come here."

Later, he came to understand that she had desired the murderer. She even admitted it indirectly.

"I didn't want to leave you tonight without being in your arms."

She was even more beautiful than he had imagined. She had soft dark skin and on her right thigh was a beauty mark in the shape of a black circle about the same size as a bullet from a revolver. This birthmark fascinated Gilbert, deeply troubled him. In it he saw some sort of foreboding or warning. He realized that, in these few minutes, his love had come to an end.

A lump was hardening in his throat and as he drove along in his car, he had an odd feeling of emptiness as if he were waking up after a long sleep in a dead city populated by visible ghosts. All of a sudden he found himself opposite the bank where the holdup had taken place. Through the window he could see the exact spot where the bandit was standing when he fired. He hadn't made a mistake; he had aimed and pressed the trigger at the very moment the accountant stood up. He had never wanted to kill the bandit, just at most to wound him, but not to kill him. Willingly and knowingly he had killed the innocent man who stood up at that fatal, precise moment.

Now Gilbert had to choose a lawyer. He knew several and experience had taught him that he shouldn't go to the most honest but to the cleverest.

"I'll get out of it," he said to himself, "like any other criminal who knows how to circumvent justice."

After his confession in court, he thought he would soon be arrested but no one came to apprehend him. He seemed to have been forgotten. At the station, his fellow officers nodded to him from a distance, then immediately returned to whatever they had been doing. Not at all good naturedly the captain received him.

"What's this you said at the trial yesterday, Lieutenant? A cock-and-bull story. If people listened to you, we'd have to resign en masse. To hear you talk, we're all murderers."

"But, Captain, I didn't accuse you or any other officers. I told the truth as it concerns me and I demand to be tried accordingly."

"Tried? But who's talking about committing you to trial?"

The police chief was turning a ballpoint pen round and round in his hands, a worried look and an angry scowl on his face. Gilbert understood his distress and wanted to exonerate him from

any blame. He even pitied him as if he were discovering that this
man he had admired was weak and impotent.

"You have always been an excellent policeman, Lieutenant. I
must confess I don't understand your public confession at all.
When you joined the force you knew you were taking certain
risks: among others, the risk of killing and being killed."

"I was trained to kill and I liked it. Even to the most coward-
ly, a revolver gives the feeling of great power because he knows
he's holding the lives of other people in his hands. I have been
trained to kill and have carried a revolver on my person for
years. If it wasn't to be used, then what was it for?"

On the whole, he knew of very few who sincerely wanted to
serve society. Most of them were really only interested in their
pay and their benefits. Several were even in collusion with
thieves whom they would be ready to shoot at the first opportunity. But that was their concern. It was he alone, Gilbert Leroy,
criminal, killer, murderer, who should be tried. He had killed an
unarmed, innocent man. He had aimed at that man, not at the
bandit. The bandit was his equal, his brother; he had never
wanted to kill him. They were both of the same race; they
belonged to the same clan. The young bandit had smiled at him,
had even guessed the truth before he did.

"Can't you simply let it pass as wounded pride? Could it not
be that the humiliation of having missed your aim, you, a
sharpshooter, is driving you to blame yourself, Lieutenant?"

"Captain, that's exactly why I didn't miss, because I am a
sharpshooter. If I killed the accountant, it's because I aimed at
him. I don't know why but I aimed at his throat and didn't
miss."

The police chief listened to him as he turned the ballpoint pen
in his hands. A frown was gathering between his thick eyebrows.
Gilbert had the feeling that every word he uttered was like
digging another shovel of earth to deepen the trench. When he
left, he put his letter of resignation, his badge and his revolver
on the chief's desk. The captain kept turning the ballpoint pen in
his hands, and long after Gilbert had left, he continued to do so,
his eyes riveted on the badge and the revolver.

The Leroy home became a target for photographers, newspaper,
television, and movie reporters. The phone never stopped ringing
even after the number was changed. Gilbert's brothers and sisters
were harassed constantly, his nieces and nephews were snubbed
and insulted at school. Students demonstrated in support of the

policeman, waving placards and shouting slogans such as: "Christ or Barabbas—The police . . . as they really are—A policeman tells the truth, the whole truth and nothing but the truth." They organised a sit-in in front of the Court House but were quickly dispersed by the police. There were other groups who, on the contrary, defended the police force in general, and condemned Lieutenant Gilbert Leroy. Gilbert's parents, unable to put up with this oppression, went to stay in the country.

Gilbert took no part whatsoever in these events. He waited with a deep inner peace. He ate well, slept well, and since the authorities refused to incarcerate him, he was absolutely free to come and go as he pleased. Children would run after him, trying to get his autograph, and more than one young girl openly made advances to him.

Jeanine was no longer his fiancée. She was a murderer's mistress. Also, she had discovered his real personality and the less he loved her, the more she desired him. She would often take his right hand in hers, hold it against her cheek, her breasts, her stomach, would kiss the five fingers which held the revolver and linger over the index finger. She too had become a different person to Gilbert. Her soft skin took on a greenish hue, like decomposing flesh. Sometimes he imagined he was a hundred yards away, taking aim at the beauty spot on her thigh, sinking a bullet into it. Then he remembered the dreams he used to have when Jeanine was only his fiancée. The memory of those dreams troubled him more than the dreams themselves.

There wasn't a lawyer who would take his case, knowing he would have the whole police force on his back. Besides, why did he need a lawyer when he wasn't accused of a crime?

The trial of the two bandits (the other two had died as a result of their injuries) took place without Gilbert being called a second time as a witness. He was present at each session, listened to his former colleagues take the oath and calmly relate the facts, certain they would not be accused of having killed two men. One of them, with a flash of wit, even made the audience laugh.

The young bandit remained completely indifferent throughout the whole trial. He didn't even hear what was said. Now he entered the room, his expression devoid of any sarcasm, would find Gilbert, then look at him with hatred. The ex-policeman would have liked to make him understand that he didn't hate anyone, that he loved him like a brother.

The bandit was sentenced to twenty-five years in prison; his partner who was older and had a longer record, to a few years more. After he was sentenced, before he disappeared forever, the young man looked at Gilbert one last time, and once again, Gilbert understood the meaning of that look.

He went back home, ate some bread, some ham and cheese, drank two cups of tea. Then he turned on the hanging lamp in the windowless dining room. He arranged the table and chairs so as to imitate as much as possible a courtroom at the Court House. He stood behind one of the chairs as if he were in the prisoner's box. Mentally he repeated the words of the trial and uttered aloud the fateful word:

"Guilty."

He was alone, incredibly alone. No one was near him, no policeman to lead him to the place of execution, no padre to prepare him, no hangman to put him to death. He had to do it all by himself. He looked in an old Roman prayer book for the appropriate prayers and stumbled onto the words of absolution he had heard sung so often in Latin when Latin was still the language of the church. He read them aloud in French so he could really understand and absorb the meaning of the words:

> Deliver me, O Lord, from everlasting death
> on this day of terror:
> When the heavens and the earth will be shaken.
> As you come to judge the world by fire.
> I am in fear and trembling
> at the judgment and wrath that is to come.
> That day will be a day of wrath, of misery,
> and of ruin:
> A day of grandeur and great horror:
> Eternal rest grant unto them, O Lord,
> and let perpetual light shine upon them.
> Deliver me, O Lord, from everlasting
> death on that day of terror.
> Lord have mercy.
> Christ have mercy.
> Lord have mercy.

He went toward the extreme penalty with profound peace of mind. He had never felt so at peace. For the first time in his life, he was in perfect harmony with himself.

He fastened the rope around one of the beams; since it was a rather low ceiling, only a short piece of rope was left hanging. Gilbert had only to raise himself on tip toe to put the noose around his neck. Then he quickly flexed his knees and tugged violently.

For a minute or two, his body turned round and round on the tips of his toes. His knees were nearly touching the floor.

SOME OF HIS BEST FRIENDS
by Harold Horwood

*Odd, he thought, this circle of black faces flecked with white,
like foam on an angry sea. Was it just contrast that made teeth
stand out like that, or were they really whiter than other people's?
That young one there, now . . . so like Jimmie in a way. . . .*

*Could he talk his way out of this jam, he wondered? Could
he? Or was he in for real trouble? He was used to trouble—it
was almost his business. But this young negro really disturbed
him—a face that should have been gentle, but wasn't. . . .*

The boy at first had been just one of the crowd—a smooth,
oval face, not light or dark, somewhere in the middle range
of the swirling mob of color that seemed to collect around
tourists like ants at a picnic. They were a nuisance, but pleas-
ing, too, in a flattering sort of way, always smiling, always
willing to do any odd job for a handful of coppers or a
piece of silver. The local people said the tourists spoiled them
by overpaying.

At home they kept mostly to one side of the street, though
he'd often mixed with large crowds of all sorts. Here they
flowed around you, jostled, rubbed shoulders, and their carefree
spirit was infectious, or perhaps it was the atmosphere of the
islands that was infectious—blessed by sun, cooled by trade
winds, shaded by palms.

The little town came down by steps to the blue circle of the
harbor, spreading itself across the lower slopes of the dead
volcanoes that rose behind it, and, except on banana-boat days,
seemed always to be half asleep. The slopes had spice planta-
tions rooted in their black and crumbling soil, and workers under
nutmeg boughs looked down on schooners and ketches moored at
the shopside quay, or out to the toy fortress at the harbor mouth.

He drove a small rented car of ancient British make, always expecting it to give its last hiccup, but it continued, surprisingly, to respond to his touch. It was the car, above all, that attracted the following of young natives, all of them insisting that there was no way he could manage without a chauffeur, guide, car-polisher and messenger-boy. He tried at first to farm out these jobs piecemeal, but the boy Jimmie seemed forever at the fore-front of the applicants. Fifteen or sixteen, bright, neat, freshly scrubbed, always wearing a broad-brimmed hat, clean blue shirt and immaculate white shorts, it was he who usually got the nod and the shilling piece for his services. Gradually, the boy be-came a fixture.

He was staying at the time in a comfortable little tourist home on a terrace overlooking the town. Two ladies of middle years, who hoped the climate might do something for their asthma and bursitis, were also guests there. But since he was the only one with a car, he usually parked it between the poin-settias near the front door. A vacationing journalist, he felt justifiably lazy, so he spent hours just sitting or lying around, listening to the tree toads, absorbing the sensuous beauty of his surroundings, and letting his mind ramble. He was so engaged, with the pleasant splash of water from the garden path weaving itself into his reverie, when his meditation was interrupted by the hostess—an Englishwoman of reduced circumstances but good family, as he had been assured by the other guests.

"Pardon me, sir," she said. "Would you ask your manservant to do that job around at the back?"

"Manservant?" he said, jumping up. "I haven't . . ." Then he really heard the splashing of the hose for the first time, and rushed out front to find Jimmie, shirt and shorts folded and laid on the steps, engaged in an orgy of car-washing.

"My god, Jim, what are you doing?"

"Needs a wash, Boss," the boy said, flashing a captivating grin. At that moment one of the lady guests appeared at the gate.

"But for Christ's sake, you can't run around like that in public!"

"Why not, Boss?" The grin grew broader. "Don't expect me to get my clothes all wet, do you?"

This logic, he realized, might be sound enough in the Carib-bean, where nobody seemed to notice whether colored boys wore any clothes or not. The lady guest, he was relieved to see, walked quietly past without turning a hair. She'd been nursing her ailments on this island for a long time.

"Put on your shorts," he said quietly. "You can have an extra dollar for a spare pair if you need it. And I'll move the car around to the back. You can look after it there any way you want."

The boy became his shadow, following him everywhere on silent bare feet. Intelligent, unobtrusive, but with a flash of humor in his wide-set eyes, he earned every cent of his modest wage merely by steering his employer away from the common tourist pitfalls and keeping the indigents at bay. Uninvited, he penetrated the shell of cynicism, and lodged himself in the man's heart.

Why should he remind me of Jimmie, he thought? That sneer . . . that almost ape-like look, not really a bit like the boy at all . . . those ugly lines of hatred on his face. What the hell have we done to them, anyway? They didn't get like that just for fun. And is there any way we can change it? Is it too late to do anything about it now? Would they let us, if we tried?

"Why'd ja come here, Whitey? You one o' them cats from the *Chronicle, lookin' for a story? Why'd ja come here, man?*"

"Yes, I'm from the *Chronicle." Fighting to keep the voice level. "I'm not looking for a story, though. I'm here to help. I'm with you. I'm on your side in this thing." They didn't believe him, he could see. "I'm . . . I'm your friend." He tried to smile, but could feel how false it must look, could hear the false ring of his own voice.*

"Don't need no friends like you, man."

The soft accents, the boy's voice, singing, to the splash of the hose, as he gave the car its morning bath on the wide, flat stones of the terrace; trips into the hills and down to the beaches; wading in the shallows collecting coral, the boy amazed at his delight in such trivial things; talking with a native potter high in the hills, where Jimmie had brought him; talking with plantation workers while the boy squatted in the shade nibbling a piece of cane; sampling potent native liquor on a back-country farm where no tourist was supposed to go.

He'd hinted, once or twice, that he'd like to meet the boy's family, and finally, on a hot afternoon when the trade wind moved sluggishly through the palm heads, Jimmie took him to a small side street in the lower part of town where the little houses crowded one another like the steps of a stair, their splayed roofs making a gay and exotic pattern like a picture out of Asia or from some remote corner of the Balkans.

The narrow road was noisy with the joy of living. Bright-plumed chickens, skinny dogs and dusky children all squabbled and played together on the pavement. A slim girl with a shy smile and an erotic walk picked her way through the litter of life underfoot, her tight cotton dress of scarlet and saffron showing every curve and movement of a body just arriving at its brief moment of perfection. Out of the windowless and sometimes doorless houses poured a tide of Latin music from radios that seemed to be playing endlessly, adding their joyous babble to the general chorus.

It might have been called a slum—but what a great slum to live in! The people were poor, certainly, but how they enjoyed themselves! Loudly demonstrative and emotional, but relaxed as well, they seemed to savor the bittersweet taste of life with a gusto never known to the dreary and respectable subdivisions of his native city.

They turned in at a house much like dozens of others. The boy's father was there—a loafer and drinker, probably, and maybe a bully, too, judging by the bottles in the garbage bucket and the strap on the wall. To the white man he was overrespectful, obsequious, quite unlike Jimmie, who performed his services with cheerful dignity, as though doing a favor.

"My poor wife she die, three, four year ago," he explained in a plaintive voice. "My girl now, she manage. . . ."

The voice droned on, self-pitying, but the visitor wasn't listening at all. The room was more crowded than any he could remember—a huge cook stove, a treadle sewing machine, a wind-up gramophone, not to mention six children younger than Jimmie, a cat, a parrot, and a fighting cock in a crate, the whole menagerie apparently managed by his older sister, a girl of about seventeen. She seemed cheerful and competent—far more grown-up than her father—but despite eyes that were soft and lovely, her beauty was already marred by overwork—tough and stringy where she should have been soft and full, her face, under its coat of dark bronze, already showing lines of strain. Before she was twenty-five, he thought sadly, the marks of age would be etched around her eyes.

The children at first were as shy as young goats—which he thought strange, for if he'd met them on a beach they would have come crowding around offering to stage fights for his

camera and hoping for a coin or two. However, they plunged
into his bag of goodies with devastating gusto, and before the
evening was over the younger ones were climbing into his arms.
Everything about the children delighted him.

There had to be a party for "Jimmie's Boss" the girl decided,
so he stayed through the evening and ate a strange dish of rice
and fish with flavorings that he'd never tasted before, and drank
something called orange wine that he'd never even heard of. As
the night covered the narrow street, neighbors came drifting in,
and there were lights and laughter, and they sat on the steps,
listening to a youngster from next door pluck the strings of a
guitar and sing a ballad learned from a calypso troupe. A woman
walking through the dusk with a huge basket on her head took up
the song and sang it alternately with the boy on the steps,
grinning as she finished each verse. Another woman, certainly
old enough to be a grandmother, came peddling along on a
bicycle, her flowered yellow dress glowing like neon in the
shafts of light from the houses. . . .

*The young one might not really be dangerous, he decided. If it
weren't for the others . . . But some of the older ones sure
looked like thugs—a broken nose, scarred faces, a mark that
might have been made by half a bottle. Toughs, he thought. Real
nigger toughs. Once held in check by fear, now turned loose, not
knowing what to do with their freedom. What have we done to
them, and is there any way to help them remake themselves? Or
would they even want to? Can they ever do it alone? He wasn't
really afraid of them, he decided. He'd been in tight spots
before. Main thing was to keep your cool, no matter what. . . .*

*Then he saw, with a cold chill, the piece of chain hanging out
of the pocket. The circle getting tighter. Like wild animals, he
thought, running in a pack. Alone, they'd be scared as rabbits.*

*"Look, you guys, I've been working on your side for years—
schools, housing, job opportunities—the whole bit. I'm a columnist, see? I'm doing everything I can to help."*

No answer. No response. Just the tightening circle.

*Why can't I talk to them? Why can't I explain? Why won't they
listen? Just drawing nearer, tighter, slowly, remorselessly. For
the first time, he began to feel real fear crawling around down
in his belly.*

In the glowing night the children came clustering around him
to say goodbye, shy no longer, open, responsive, eager to share

his love (yes, he decided reflectively, love). And impulsively he invited them all on a picnic that weekend, a motor trip to Grenville Bay on the other side of the island. The prospect seemed almost too much for the young ones to imagine. Some of them had never been outside the town, scarcely away from its crowded waterfront. The promise of this prodigious journey of twenty-odd miles seemed to them like an invitation to the far side of the moon.

The weather, as always, was perfect, and the trip through the green and spice-scented mountains was lovely and memorable, though he could never remember how they managed to crowd nine people into the little car, or how they negotiated the twisting road without one of the shouting youngsters falling through a window into a ravine.

They saw the great, plunging, east-coast surf, which some of them had never heard of, and they looked down on green-and-brown villages from the god-like height of extinct volcanoes. They drank fresh lime juice that was cheap, plentiful and delicious, and soda pop that was expensive, scarce and vile-tasting. There was an ice-cream machine run by a gasoline engine, and there was a dingy little pavilion where he and Jimmie and the girl had a drink with a stiff shot of rum in it, and ice that cost more than the rum. And the children ran and shouted on the sand, as though it were the first morning of creation, instead of a tired old afternoon of the earth's eventide, in what he suspected might be the shadow of man's last reckoning.

The lightning of the first blow caught him unawares, rocked his whole body in an apocalypse of shock and pain. He hadn't expected it to start so suddenly. . . . I did nothing to provoke them . . . nothing. They can't really be doing this . . . it's some kind of mistake . . . Christ, how I've always hated blood, emergency wards, casualties, the obscene sight of battered bodies on the ugly fringes of the police beat . . . how I hated it when I had to cover that beat years ago!

"Please . . ." he sputtered, "please . . ."

"That blood in yer mouth, Whitey? How's it taste, man? You used to drinkin' blood, ain't ja, white boy?"

Then the second blow . . . lights dancing in his head, swimming . . .

The stars were coming out like lamps as they returned that evening, the excitement running low at last. They stopped by the little house in the narrow street. And then the children came to him one by one and kissed him. He touched their faces with his fingertips, feeling infinite tenderness, and a deep conviction that the human race really was one family, that these children, with their beautiful, satin-dark skins, tight curls and sombre eyes, were really and in truth *his* children. He was sure they felt the same family tie with him, even with a light-skinned stranger from a world so alien they could barely begin to imagine its outlines.

After that he saw them often, and the parting, when it came, was painful. They watched him go, certain that he would return, for he lacked the courage to tell them of the thousands of miles of ocean that separated his bleak northern city from their bright little island, or that his chances of seeing them for at least two or three years were small indeed.

Some months later, back in the smog, sitting over his typewriter, wrapped in the smell of ink and newsprint, he picked a letter with a gaudy foreign stamp from a pile of mail placed on his desk by a copy boy. It was addressed in a childish hand, written in the uncertain English of a young West Indian negro with scanty book learning. It said the things that people say in letters—the stilted, toneless things that you learn to say in school. But just at the end, instead of the formal greeting that he expected, there was simplicity and truth.

"Come again soon. We all love you. Your friend Jimmie."

And there were the stars coming out overhead, like ruddy lamps in the sky of a burning ghetto. The edges of tall buildings reached for them like dragons' teeth.

The line of duty, he thought . . . hazards of the job . . . a three-column head on page one:

NEWSPAPER VETERAN
VICTIM OF RACE RIOT

Pity he couldn't write the story . . . pity . . . what did we know of pity? And what else did they do, he wondered, before they killed you? What else did they do?

THE IRON MEN
by Farley Mowat

As I sat in the doorway of my tent watching Hekwaw at work, my glance travelled from the quick motions of his lean hands, sending a knife blade gleaming over white wood, to his rapt face. Black hair hung long and lank over his brow, shadowing his eyes.

Dreaming over his task, he seemed neither to see nor hear the world around him—a world of rolling tundra, of looming hills, of rushing rivers and still lakes; a world of caribou, white wolves, black ravens and a myriad birds. The world that we, in our ignorance, chose to call the Barrenlands. It was Hekwaw's world but for the moment he was unaware of it, intent on giving new life to a memory out of another age.

The long arctic sun was lying on the rim of the horizon before he rose and came toward me carrying the product of memory. It was a thing made of antler bone, black spruce and caribou sinew . . . and it had no place upon those northern plains. It was a crossbow, a weapon used by the Scythians in Asia Minor three thousand years ago and one that dominated the medieval battle-fields of Europe until the age of gunpowder.

Some days earlier Hekwaw had been recalling stories from the ancient times of his people and he had spoken of a weapon I did not recognize. I questioned him until he drew a picture of it in the sand. I could not believe what he showed me, for it seemed impossible that his ancestors, isolated in the central arctic, could have discovered a weapon known to no other native American people. I asked him if he could make one of the weapons and he nodded. Now the crossbow was a reality.

Laying an unfeathered wooden bolt in the groove, he drew back the sinew string with both hands and lodged it in a cross-ways slit. On the shadowed river a red-throated loon dipped and swam. There was a sudden, resonant vibration on the still air. The bolt whirred savagely over the river and the loon flashed its wings in a dying flurry.

Hekwaw lowered the bow, placed it carefully beside him and squatted on his heels to light his stained old soapstone pipe. He did not wait for my questions but began a tale which had been called back to life across many centuries by the vibrant song of the crossbow.

Ai-ya! But this is a weapon! It came to us in distant times but I keep the memory of it because my fathers' fathers were men to whom it was given to remember. So it is that I can speak of the Innuhowik.

They were beings who seemed more than human, yet death could fell them. They were bearded, but their beards were not black like those of the Godbringers—they were yellow and sometimes brown and looked as bright as copper. The eyes of some were brown also, but most were of the colour of the eastern sky just before sunrise, or the deep ice of the winter lakes. Their voices boomed and rumbled, and they spoke no words my people understood.

We never knew what land they came from, only that it lay eastward beyond salt waters which they travelled over in boats many times the length of a kayak.

In those days my people lived, as they had always lived, far inland and so they did not witness the arrival of the Innuhowik. The tents of my forbears stood along the shores of *Innuit Ku,* River of Men, which flows north out of the forests. My people avoided the forests for these belonged to the *Itkilit,* the Indians as you call them. In spring when the caribou migrated north out of their lands, the Itkilit sometimes followed, and when they came upon one of our camps there would be fighting. Afterwards they would withdraw into the shelter of the trees. We feared them, but the tundra plains were ours by right, as the forests were theirs by right, and so our southernmost camps stood only a few days' journey from the place where Innuit Ku emerges from the shadows of the trees.

One late-summer day when the leaves of the dwarf willows were already darkening, a young boy lay on the crest of a hill close to the most southerly Innuit camp. It was his task to give warning if the canoes of the Itkilit should appear. When he saw something moving far to the south he did not wait to be sure what it was. He came running like a hare over the rocky plain and his cry pierced into the skin tents of the families who lived at that place.

It was past noon and the men were mostly resting in the cool tents, but at the sound of the boy's cry they ran out into the blazing light. Women clutched their babies and quickly led the older children into the broken hills beyond the River.

The people had chosen the site of that camp with care. A little distance to the south of it the River roared through a narrow gorge, tossing great plumes of spray high into the air. Neither canoe nor kayak could pass through unless it stayed close to the cliffs on the western side. And men lying on top of these western cliffs could look directly down upon the only safe channel. It was to this gorge that the Innuit men hurried when the boy gave the alarm. Beside each man was a pile of frost-shattered rocks, jagged edged and as heavy as one man could lift. These were the best weapons we could muster against the Itkilit, for in those times my people had not good bows because the only wood available to us was of a kind too weak and too soft.

The men atop the cliff had not long to wait before something came into sight far up the River. As it plunged toward them they stared fearfully, but they were perplexed too. It was a boat they saw—not a canoe—and one such as no Innuit had ever imagined. It was as long as three kayaks, as broad as the length of a man, and built of thick wooden planks. The beings it carried were stranger still. All save one sat with their backs to the front of the boat and pulled at long paddles set between wooden pins. There were eight of them, sitting in pairs. The ninth stood in the back facing the rest and holding another long paddle thrust out behind. He held the gaze of my people for he wore a shining metal cap on his head and under it his face was almost hidden by a long yellow beard. Polished iron sheets on his breast caught reflections from the swift waters and sent lights into the eyes of the men on the cliffs.

These strange ones were almost upon the Innuit, but my people were so bewildered they did not know how to act. Were these *men* below them? Or spirits? If they were spirits they could not be killed. They *could*, however, be angered, then there would be no way of knowing what they might do.

The big wooden boat swept into the gorge and was steered into the western channel by the tall man at the stern whose bellowing voice could be heard even above the roar of the

waters. From the cliffs high above, my people watched . . . and
did nothing, and the strangers passed on down the River.

As the Innuit began to rise to their feet, one of them yelled,
and they all looked where he pointed. Three long, bark canoes
had appeared upriver, and this time there was no doubt who
came into our lands. They were Itkilit, dressed in scraped hides
and wearing the faces of death, and driving their canoes as
swiftly as wolves racing after a deer.

There was barely time for my people to snatch up the sharp
rocks lying beside them. As the canoes flew past below, they
came under a hail of boulders that smashed bark boats and men's
bones. Two of the canoes broke apart like the skulls of rabbits
under the blows of an axe.

The River was red that day; but from out of the spray of the
gorge, one canoe emerged. The Innuit men ran to the shore,
tossed their swift kayaks into the stream and gave chase.

Great falls block the River only a few miles downstream from
the gorge, and it was toward the falls that the last canoe, holed
by stones and with some of its men wounded, was being driven.
When the funnelling current above the falls was reached, the
Itkilit saw death ahead and knew death was behind them. At the
last moment they turned out of the current and drove their
sinking canoe ashore. They leapt up the bank toward a ridge of
rocks from whose shelter they hoped to defend themselves from
the Innuit.

They did not reach that ridge. It was already held by the
iron-clad strangers who had also been warned by the current and
by the roar of falling water and had gone to the shore. These
strange ones rose up from behind the rocks of the ridge and
charged down upon the Itkilit roaring like bears, thrusting with
great long knives, and slashing with iron axes. Only a few Itkilit
got back to the River. They flung themselves into it and were
swept over the falls.

The strangers—they whom we later called Innuhowik, Iron
Men—stood watching the kayaks where they hovered in the
current. Perhaps my people seemed as terrifying to their eyes as
they had seemed to ours, but they were brave. One of them came
slowly to the shore carrying no weapon in his hands. At his
approach the kayaks nervously moved out of the backwater and
away from the land. The yellow-bearded leader of the Innuhowik
came to the water's edge, and my people wondered at his size
for he stood a head taller than any of them. They watched as he

drew a short knife from his belt and held it out, handle first, toward the kayakers.

It was a man named Kiliktuk who paddled cautiously toward the spot and, reaching out his long, double-bladed paddle, touched the handle of the knife. The stranger smiled and laid the knife on the paddle blade so Kiliktuk could draw it to him without touching shore.

Soon all the kayaks were beached and the men who were my forefathers were crowded around the Innuhowik fingering their tools and weapons. It was clear the strangers were not ill-disposed to the Innuit, so they were brought back to the camp. Far into that night the song-drums sounded while Innuit and Innuhowik sat together by the fires and feasted on caribou meat and fish. It is remembered that the strangers ate like men—like hungry men—and that they looked at our women with the eyes of men.

As to what happened after, the stories speak of many things. They tell especially of the strength of the Innuhowik, and of the wonderful tools and weapons they possessed. These were mostly of iron, which was unknown to the Innuit except as hard, heavy stones which sometimes fell from the skies.

After they had been in the camp for a few days, the Innuhowik began asking questions by means of drawings in the sand, and by signs, and the people understood that they wished to know if Innuit Ku led to the sea in the east. When they had been made to know that it did not, but led instead to the northern seas from which the ice seldom passes, they became unhappy. They talked with one another in loud voices, but at last they came to an agreement and let us understand they wished to remain with us for a time.

We were glad to have them stay. They soon gave up wearing their own clothing of thick cloth and metal plates and put on the soft caribou-skin garments our women made for them. When the cold weather began they even put aside their horned iron caps which made them look like muskox bulls.

The Innuhowik knew many secret things. They could make fire by striking iron on rock and they had small blue stones that could tell them where the sun was even though the sky was black with clouds. But although they had much wisdom, there were many things in our land which were strange to them. We taught each other, and perhaps it was they who had the most to learn.

Their leader's name was Koonar. He could carry whole carcasses of caribou for many miles. He could split the skull of even the great brown bear when he wielded his long iron blade. His mind was just as strong, and in only a little time he could understand and speak our tongue. From Koonar's lips my people heard the story of how the Innuhowik came to our River. It was told that they sailed out of the northeast in their long wooden ships until they reached the coast of the sea which lies far to the east of us. Some of them stayed there guarding their ships while others took smaller boats and went inland up the rivers, though what it was they sought we never learned.

Koonar's boat went far south into unknown lands and travelled upon lakes and rivers running through the forests. But one night there was trouble with the Itkilit, and they fought, and some of the Innuhowik perished, as did many of the Itkilit. Koonar turned back but found his old way now barred by the Itkilit and so the Innuhowik followed new rivers north, hoping to be able to turn east to the shores where the long ships waited. When they were five days' travel to the south of the first Innuit camps, they came upon two tents of Itkilit and surprised the people in them, killing all except a young boy who escaped and carried word to other Itkilit camps. Then Koonar and his men were pursued into our land as I have already told.

Koonar lived in Kiliktuk's tent, where also lived Airut who was Kiliktuk's daughter. She was a fine young woman with full, round cheeks and a laughing voice. She had been married once but her man had been killed when his kayak was holed on a rapid in the River. Kiliktuk hoped Airut would seem good in Koonar's sight so that Koonar might become a son in that tent. Yet Koonar, alone of his men, seemed not to desire a woman, and so he did not take Airut though she was willing.

One day in the month when the snows come, Koonar went to a cache near the deer crossing place to bring back some meat stored there. He was returning with two whole gutted carcasses on his shoulders when he slipped and fell among the rocks with such force that one of his thigh bones was shattered. He was carried into Kiliktuk's tent with pieces of bone sticking out of the flesh, and even his own men believed he would die. He was sick for a long time; and it may be that he lived only because Airut refused to let death take him away, and because Kiliktuk who was a great shaman could command the help of the spirits.

Koonar recovered but he never walked freely again nor did he regain his great strength, for it seemed the injury he had suffered had eaten into his heart. Truly he was changed, for now it came about that the hopes of Kiliktuk were realized. Koonar took Airut as his wife, even as his men had all taken wives, and after that my people believed the Innuhowik would stay forever in the camps of the Innuit.

The people were wrong. When the snows were thick on the land and the rivers were solidly frozen, the Innuhowik gathered in a big snowhouse the people had built for them and spent many days talking together. What all that talk came to in the end was that the Innuhowik decided to forsake their women and go away from the land of my people. They had made up their minds to travel eastward over the tundra plains, using some of our dogs and sleds.

My people were not willing that the Innuhowik should do this, for they needed their dogs and they were also angry on behalf of the women. It seemed it would come to a fight, until Koonar stepped in. He said if my people would assist the Innuhowik to go, he himself would remain and all the gifts he could make would be ours.

Do you wonder why he agreed to stay? My people wondered too. Perhaps he believed his injuries would make him a burden to his fellows; or perhaps it was because the woman, Airut, was with child.

In the worst time of winter, when the blizzards rule the land, the eight Innuhowik left our camps, driving dog sleds eastward in search of the salt sea and their own big ships. No word was ever heard of them again, not even by our cousins, the sea people, who live along the coasts. I think that in the dark depths of the winter nights their magic failed them and they perished.

So now the tale of the Innuhowik becomes the tale of Koonar, of Airut, and of the children she bore. First was the boy Hekwaw, whose name I bear, born in the spring. A year later Airut had a girl child who was called Oniktok, but afterwards she had no more children. Koonar seemed content with his life, even though he was so crippled he could hardly leave his tent or his snowhouse. The other men of the camp hunted the meat that fed Koonar and his family, but they were glad to do this because Koonar was well liked. He did not laugh as much as he had done when his own men were still with us, and he spent many hours playing

Innuhowik games. He taught these to his son, and one of them
was still played in my own grandfather's time. Many small
squares were marked out on the snow or on a piece of deer hide,
and each man had a number of stones . . . but now that game is
forgotten.

Kiliktuk was the man closest to Koonar, since both were
shamans who knew many magical things and understood each
other's minds. Koonar would often talk of things he had
seen in distant places. Sometimes he told of great battles
on land and sea fought with such weapons that men's blood
flowed like spring freshets. It was remembered that, when
he spoke of such things, his face would become terrible
and most people were afraid to remain in his presence even
though such talk of great killings of men could not easily
be believed.

Things went well in the many camps along the River until the
child, Hekwaw, was in his eighth year and had become a very
promising boy and a source of much pride to his father. After
the snows began that autumn, Kiliktuk decided that a journey
must be made south to cut trees for new sleds, kayak frames,
tent poles and other wooden things that were needed. In earlier
times this had been considered a dangerous venture, one to be
made only when a large number of Innuit from many camps
could band together for protection in case the Itkilit attacked the
wood gatherers. But since the Itkilit had suffered so heavily at
the gorge and the Killing Falls, it was thought they would not
now be anxious to fight.

Because of his crippled leg, Koonar could not leave the camps
in order to teach Hekwaw, his son, the ways of men on the land,
so Kiliktuk had become the boy's teacher. Now he asked that
Hekwaw accompany the wood-gathering party in order that he
might learn the nature of the southern country. Koonar loved his
son and wished him to become a foremost man, so he did not
oppose this. The boy took his place on Kiliktuk's long sled, and
a big party of men, some women and other boys set off to the
south. They passed through the country of little sticks to the end
of a big lake stretching far into the forests. Here they made
camp.

Each morning thereafter the men drove south on the ice of the
lake to where good timber grew on its shores. Before dark they
would return to the travel camp where the women would greet

them with trays of hot soup and boiled meat. At first some men stayed at the camp during the day to guard it, but when no signs of Itkilit were seen these men went also to help with the cutting.

On the sixth day, while the Innuit men were far down the lake, a band of Itkilit came running on snowshoes out of the small woods near the camp. When the Innuit men returned again in the evening, they found three women and three boys, Hekwaw among them, dead in the snow.

Kiliktuk and his companions did not pursue the Itkilit into the thick cover of the forests, knowing they would be helpless against the long bows, spitting their arrows from hiding. They were afraid that the slaughter of their women and children was planned to draw them into an ambush. So they wrapped the remains of the dead ones in caribou skins, loaded the sleds, and started north.

The sounds of their lamentings were heard in the river camps even before the dog teams were seen. It is remembered that when Kiliktuk entered Koonar's igloo he took an iron knife Koonar had given him and thrust it partway into his own chest, inviting Koonar to drive it home into his heart.

The fury of Koonar at the loss of his son was of a kind unknown to my people. It was of a kind unknown in our land. Koonar did not lament his dead, as my people did; he burned and roared in the grip of madness, and so terrifying was he that none dared come near him for the space of many days and nights. Then he grew silent . . . silent and cold, with a chill more dreadful than his fury. At last he ordered the people to bring him muskox horns, the best and hardest dry wood, plaited caribou sinews, and some other things.

He worked in his snowhouse for three days and when he was done he held in his hand the father of this bow which I have made—although what I have done is but the crude work of a child compared to what Koonar wrought.

For a long time after that he ordered the lives of the people in the camp as if they were no more than dogs. He drove each hunter to make a crossbow. If a man did not make it well enough, Koonar struck him and forced him to do it again. It is unthinkable for one of us to strike another, for to do so is to show that you are truly a madman; yet the people endured Koonar's madness, for their awe of him was the awe one has of a devil.

When each man had a crossbow and a supply of bolts, Koonar dragged himself out of the snowhouse and made them set up 'targets and practise shooting, day after day. Although it is not in my people's nature to give themselves in this way to such a task, they were afraid to resist.

With the coming of the long night which is the heart of winter, Kiliktuk, obeying Koonar's will, chose the ten best marksmen and ordered them to prepare dogs and gear for a long journey. Six teams were hitched to six sleds and the chosen men left the camps, heading south along the frozen river. Kiliktuk was in the lead, and on his sled lay Koonar, well wrapped in muskox robes against the brittle cold.

It is told how these men boldly drove into the forests, Koonar having banished both fear and caution from their hearts. For seven days they drove southward among the trees, and in the evening of the seventh day they came in sight of the smoking tents of a big band of Itkilit upon a lake shore.

The Innuit would have preferred to draw back and wait for dawn before attacking, but Koonar would allow no delay. The sleds spread out and were driven at full speed across the intervening ice straight into the heart of the Itkilit camp. They came so swiftly, the Itkilit dogs hardly had time to howl an alarm before the sleds halted in a line and the Innuit men jumped off, bows in hand.

Many of the Itkilit came spilling out of their tents without even stopping to seize their own weapons, for they could not believe they would be attacked so boldly. They were met by the whine and whirr and thud of the bolts.

Many Itkilit died that night. The Innuit would not have harmed the women and children but Koonar demanded that everyone who could be caught be killed. When the slaughter was over, Koonar ordered the tents of the Itkilit burned down so that those who had escaped into the forests would die of starvation and frost.

While the flames were still leaping, the Innuit turned their teams northward. They drove with hardly a pause until the trees began to thin and the plains stretched ahead.

Only then did they make camp. Koonar was so exhausted that he could not move from his sled where he lay with eyes closed, singing strange songs in a voice that had lost most of its strength. When Kiliktuk tried to give him a drink of meat soup he thrust it aside, spilling it on the snow. It is remembered that there was no joy in that camp. Too much blood had been shed and there was darkness in the hearts of the men of my people.

At dawn the sleds drove north again, but when they were almost in sight of the home camps Kiliktuk's sled turned aside from the trail. He motioned the others forward, bidding them carry the news of the battle.

Late that night a man stepped out of his snowhouse at the home camp to relieve himself and saw something that made him shout until everyone in the camp came outside. To the north a tongue of fire thrust upward as if to join the flickering green flames of the spirit lights. The long roll of snow-covered hills by the Killing Falls emerged briefly from the darkness. The people were still watching in astonishment when a sled came swiftly into camp from northward. On it rode Kiliktuk . . . and he was alone.

He was asked many questions, but neither then nor later did he tell the people how the last of the Innuhowik departed. Only to his grandson, the son of Koonar's daughter, did he tell that tale. That child also was called Hekwaw and he was the father of my father's fathers, and it was through them that I heard how Kiliktuk drove Koonar down the River to the place where the Innuhowik's old boat was still cached among the rocks. It was from them I heard how Kiliktuk tenderly placed Koonar in that boat and piled bundles of dry willow scrub around him. Then Kiliktuk put the flint and steel in Koonar's hands and parted from the stranger who had become his son.

Kiliktuk drove away as he had been ordered to do, and when he looked back, flames were already lifting above the boat. So the last of the Innuhowik went from our lands to that place of warriors where, he had told us, his people go at the end of their time.

There followed many years and many generations during which my people prospered because of the gift of this bow. We no longer feared the Itkilit and in our pride and strength went against them. We drove them south into the forests for such a distance that, after a time, they were hardly even remembered. Our camps spread over the whole width and breadth of the plains.

But in the time of my grandfather's grandfather, the strangers returned.

This time they came not to our country but to the forested lands in the south, and there they made friends with the Itkilit. They did not wear iron on their breasts or on their heads, and they were not called Innuhowik. They were *your* people, who are called *Kablunait*. The Kablunait brought gifts to the Itkilit, and foremost of these was the gun.

Then the Itkilit considered what we had done to them in times they had never forgotten.

They came north out of the forests again, first in small bands and then in hundreds, and Koonar's gift failed us. They killed us from great distances with their guns and they roamed so widely over our lands that my people had to flee north almost to the coasts of the frozen seas.

It seemed as if the guns brought by the Kablunait would mean an end to my people, and so it might have happened. But one summer the Itkilit failed to appear on the plains; and as summer followed summer and they still failed to return, my people began to move slowly south and recover their land.

The Itkilit stopped coming against us because they were dead in their thousands; dead from a fire that burned in their bodies, rotting the flesh so they stank like old corpses while life still lingered within them. This we know, for that fire, which was another gift from the Kablunait, afterwards swept out over the plains and my people also died in their thousands.

Now the Itkilit are no more than a handful scattered through the dark shadows of the forests; and the wide country where my people once dwelt is nearly empty of men.

So it ends. . . . But this bow I hold in my hand is where it began.

Darkness had fallen and the fire was nearly out. Hekwaw stirred the coals until the fire was reborn under the touch of the night wind. His face was turned from me as he dropped the crossbow onto the flames, and I could barely hear his words:

"Take back your gift, Koonar. Take it back to the lands of the Innuhowik and the Kablunait . . . its work here is done."

A FIELD
OF WHEAT
by Sinclair Ross

It was the best crop of wheat that John had ever grown; sturdy, higher than the knee, the heads long and filling well; a still, heat-hushed mile of it, undulating into a shimmer of summer-colts and crushed horizon blue. Martha finished pulling the little patch of mustard that John had told her about at noon, stood a minute with her shoulders strained back to ease the muscles that were sore from bending, then bunched up her apron filled with the yellow-blossomed weeds and started towards the road. She walked carefully, placing her feet edgeways between the rows of wheat to avoid trampling and crushing the stalks. The road was only a few rods distant, but several times she stopped before reaching it, holding her apron with one hand close against her skirts, luxuriant and tall. Once she looked back, her eyes shaded, across the wheat to the dark fallow land beside it. John was there; she could see the long, slow-settling plume of dust thrown up by the horses and the harrow-cart. He was a fool for work, John. This year he was farming the whole section of land without help, managing with two outfits of horses, one for the morning and one for the afternoon; six, and sometimes even seven hours a shift.

It was John who gave such allure to the wheat. She thought of him hunched black and sweaty on the harrow-cart, twelve hours a day, smothering in dust, shoulders sagged wearily beneath the glare of sun. Her fingers touched the stalks of grain again and tightened on a supple blade until they made it squeak like a mouse. A crop like this was coming to him. He had had his share of failures and setbacks, if ever a man had, twenty times over.

Martha was thirty-seven. She had clinched with the body and

substance of life; had loved, borne children—a boy had died—
and yet the quickest aches of life, travail, heartbrokenness, they
had never wrung as the wheat wrung. For the wheat allowed no
respite. Wasting and unending it was struggle, struggle against
wind and insects, drought and weeds. Not an heroic struggle to
give a man courage and resolve, but a frantic, unavailing one.
They were only poor, taunted, driven things; it was the wheat
that was invincible. They only dreaded, built bright futures;
waited for the first glint of green, watched timorous and eager
while it thickened, merged, and at last leaned bravely to a ripple
in the wind; then followed every slip of cloud into the horizon,
turned to the wheat and away again. And it died tantalizingly
sometimes, slowly: there would be a cool day, a pittance of rain.

Or perhaps it lived, perhaps the rain came, June, July, even
into August, hope climbing, wish-patterns painted on the future.
And then one day a clench and tremble to John's hand; his voice
faltering, dull. Grasshoppers perhaps, sawflies or rust; no matter,
they would grovel for a while, stand back helpless, then go on
again. Go on in bitterness and cowardice, because there was
nothing else but going-on.

She had loved John, for these sixteen years had stood close
watching while he died—slowly, tantalizingly, as the parched
wheat died. He had grown unkempt, ugly, morose. His voice
was gruff, contentious, never broke into the deep, strong laughter that used to make her feel she was living at the heart of
things. John was gone, love was gone; there was only wheat.

She plucked a blade; her eyes travelled hungrily up and down
the field. Serene now, all its sting and torment sheathed. Beautiful, more beautiful than Annabelle's poppies, then her sunsets.
Theirs—all of it. Three hundred acres ready to give perhaps a
little of what it had taken from her—John, his love, his lips
unclenched.

Three hundred acres. Bushels, thousands of bushels, she
wouldn't even try to think how many. And prices up this year. It
would make him young again, lift his head, give him spirit.
Maybe he would shave twice a week as he used to when they
were first married, buy new clothes, believe in himself again.

She walked down the road towards the house, her steps quick-
ening to the pace of her thoughts until the sweat clung to her face
like little beads of oil. It was the children now, Joe and Annabelle: this winter perhaps they could send them to school in town
and let them take music lessons. Annabelle, anyway. At a pinch

Joe could wait a while; he was only eight. It wouldn't take
Annabelle long to pick up her notes; already she played hymn
tunes by ear on the organ. She was bright, a real little lady for
manners; among town people she would learn a lot. The farm
was no place to bring her up. Running wild and barefoot, what
would she be like in a few years? Who would ever want to marry
her but some stupid country lout?

John had never been to school himself; he knew what it meant
to go through life with nothing but his muscles to depend upon;
and that was it, dread that Annabelle and Joe would be handi-
capped as he was, that was what had darkened him, made him
harsh and dour. That was why he breasted the sun and dust a
frantic, dogged fool, to spare them, to help them to a life that
offered more than sweat and debts. Martha knew. He was a
slow, inarticulate man, but she knew. Sometimes it even vexed
her, brought a wrinkle of jealousy, his anxiety about the children, his sense of responsibility where they were concerned. He
never seemed to feel that he owed her anything, never worried
about her future. She could sweat, grow flat-footed and shapeless, but that never bothered him.

Her thoughts were on their old, trudging way, the way they
always went; but then she halted suddenly, and with her eyes
across the wheat again found freshening promise in its quiet
expanse. The children must come first, but she and John—mightn't
there be a little of life left for them too? A man was young at
thirty-nine. And if she didn't have to work so hard, if she could
get some new clothes, maybe some of the creams and things that
other women had . . .

As she passed through the gate, Annabelle raced across the
yard to meet her. "Do you know what Joe's done? He's taken
off all his clothes and he's in the trough with Nipper!" She was
a lanky girl, sunburned, barefoot, her face oval and regular, but
spoiled by an expression that strained her mouth and brows into
a reproachful primness. It was Martha who had taught her the
expression, dinning manners and politeness into her, trying to
make her better than the other little girls who went to the country
school. She went on, her eyes wide and aghast, "And when I
told him to come out he stood right up, all bare, and I had to
come away."

"Well, you tell him he'd better be out before I get there."

"But how can I tell him? He's all bare."

Then Joe ran up, nothing on but little cotton knee-pants,

strings of green scum from the water-trough still sticking to his face and arms. "She's been peekin'." He pointed at Annabelle. "Nipper and me just got into the trough to get cooled off, and she wouldn't mind her own business."

"Don't you tell lies about me." Annabelle pounced on him and slapped his bare back. "You're just a dirty little pig anyway, and the horses don't want to drink after you've been in the trough."

Joe squealed, and excited by the scuffle Nipper yelped and spattered Martha with a spray of water from his coat and tail. She reached out to cuff him, missed, and then to satisfy the itch in her fingers seized Joe and boxed his ears. "You put your shirt on and then go and pick peas for supper. Hurry now, both of you, and only the fat ones, mind. No, not you, Annabelle." There was something about Annabelle's face, burned and countrified, that changed Martha's mind. "You shell the peas when he gets them. You're in the sun too much as it is."

"But I've got a poppy out and if he goes to the garden by himself he'll pick it—just for spite." Annabelle spun round, and leaving the perplexity in her voice behind her, bolted for the garden. The next minute, before Martha had even reached the house, she was back again triumphant, a big fringed pink and purple poppy in her hand. Sitting down on the doorstep to admire the gaudy petals, she complained to herself, "They go so fast—the first little winds blows them all away." On her face, lengthening it, was bitten deeply the enigma of the flowers and the naked seed-pods. Why did the beauty flash and the bony stalks remain?

Martha had clothes to iron, and biscuits to bake for supper; Annabelle and Joe quarrelled about the peas until she shelled them herself. It was hot—heat so intense and breathless that it weighed like a solid. An ominous darkness came with it, gradual and unnoticed. All at once she turned away from the stove and stood strained, inert. The silence seemed to gather itself, hold its breath. She tried to speak to Nipper and the children, all three sprawled in a heap alongside the house, but the hush over everything was like a raised finger, forbidding her.

A long immobile minute; suddenly a bewildering awareness that the light was choked; and then, muffled, still distant, but charged with resolution, climaxing the stillness, a slow, long brooding heave of thunder.

Martha darted to the door, stumbled down the step and around

the corner of the house. To the west there was no sky, only a
gulf of blackness, so black that the landscape seemed slipping
down the neck of a funnel. Above, almost overhead, a heavy,
hard-lined bank of cloud swept its way across the sun-white blue
in august, impassive fury.

"Annabelle!" She wanted to scream a warning, but it was a
bare whisper. In front of her the blackness split—an abrupt,
unforked gash of light as if angry hands had snatched to seal the
rent.

"Annabelle! Quick—inside—!" Deep in the funnel shaggy
thunder rolled, emerged and shook itself, then with hurtling
strides leaped up to drum and burst itself on the advancing peak
of cloud.

"Joe, come back here!" He was off in pursuit of Nipper, who
had broken away from Annabelle when she tried to pull him into
the house. "Before I warm you!"

Her voice broke. She stared into the blackness. There it
was—the hail again—the same white twisting little cloud against
the black one—just as she had seen it four years ago.

She craned her neck, looking to see whether John was coming. The wheat, the acres and acres of it, green and tall, if only
he had put some insurance on it. Damned mule—just work and
work. No head himself and too stubborn to listen to anyone else.

There was a swift gust of wind, thunder in a splintering
avalanche, the ragged hail-cloud low and close. She wheeled,
with a push sent Annabelle toppling into the house, and then ran
to the stable to throw open the big doors. John would turn the
horses loose—surely he would. She put a brace against one of
the doors, and bashed the end into the ground with her foot.
Surely—but he was a fool—such a fool at times. It would be just
like him to risk a runaway for the sake of getting to the end of
the field.

The first big drops of rain were spitting at her before she
reached the house. Quietly, breathing hard, she closed the door,
numb for a minute, afraid to think or move. At the other side of
the kitchen Annabelle was tussling with Joe, trying to make him
go down cellar with her. Frightened a little by her mother's
excitement, but not really able to grasp the imminence of danger,
she was set on exploiting the event; and to be compelled to seize
her little brother and carry him down cellar struck her imagination as a superb way of crystallizing for all time the dread-
fulness of the storm and her own dramatic part in it. But

Martha shouted at her hoarsely, "Go and get pillows. Here, Joe, quick, up on the table." She snatched him off his feet and set him on the table beside the window. "Be ready now when the hail starts, to hold the pillow tight against the glass. You, Annabelle, stay upstairs at the west window in my room."

The horses were coming, all six at a break-neck gallop, terrified by the thunder and the whip stripes John had given them when he turned them loose. They swept past the house, shaking the earth, their harness jangling tinny against the brattle of thunder, and collided headlong at the stable door.

John, too; through Joe's legs Martha caught sight of his long, scarecrow shape stooped low before the rain. Distractedly, without purpose, she ran upstairs two steps at a time to Annabelle. "Don't be scared, here comes your father!" Her own voice shook, craven. "Why don't you rest your arms? It hasn't started yet."

As she spoke there was a sharp, crunching blow on the roof, its sound abruptly dead, sickening, like a weapon that has sunk deep into flesh. Wildly she shook her hands, motioning Annabelle back to the window, and started for the stairs. Again the blow came; then swiftly a stuttered dozen of them.

She reached the kitchen just as John burst in. With their eyes screwed up against the pommelling roar of the hail they stared at each other. They were deafened, pinioned, crushed. His face was a livid blank, one cheek smeared with blood where a jagged stone had struck him. Taut with fear, her throat aching, she turned away and looked through Joe's legs again. It was like a furious fountain, the stones bouncing high and clashing with those behind them. They had buried the earth, blotted out the horizon; there was nothing but their crazy spew of whiteness. She cowered away, put her hands to her ears.

Then the window broke, and Joe and the pillow tumbled off the table before the howling inrush of the storm. The stones clattered on the floor and bounded up to the ceiling, lit on the stove and threw out sizzling steam. The wind whisked pots and kettles off their hooks, tugged at and whirled the sodden curtains, crashed down a shelf of lamps and crockery. John pushed Martha and Joe into the next room and shut the door. There they found Annabelle huddled at the foot of the stairs, round-eyed, biting her nails in terror. The window she had been holding was broken too; and she had run away without closing the bedroom door, leaving a wild tide of wind upstairs to rage unchecked. It was rocking the whole house, straining at the walls. Martha ran up to close the door, and came down whimpering.

There was hail heaped on the bed, the pictures were blown off the walls and broken, the floor was swimming; the water would soak through and spoil all the ceilings.

John's face quietened her. They all crowded together, silent, averting their eyes from one another. Martha wanted to cry again, but dared not. Joe, awed to calmness, kept looking furtively at the trickle of blood on his father's face. Annabelle's eyes went wide and glassy as suddenly she began to wonder about Nipper. In the excitement and terror of the storm they had all forgotten him.

When at last they could go outside they stumbled over his body on the step. He had run away from Joe before the storm started, crawled back to the house when he saw John go in, and crouching down against the door had been beaten lifeless. Martha held back the children, while John picked up the mangled heap and hurried away with it to the stable.

Neither Joe nor Annabelle cried. It was too annihilating, too much like a blow. They clung tightly to Martha's skirts, staring across the flayed yard and garden. The sun came out, sharp and brilliant on the drifts of hail. There was an icy wind that made them shiver in their thin cotton clothes. "No, it's too cold on your feet." Martha motioned them back to the step as she started towards the gate to join John. "I want to go with your father to look at the wheat. There's nothing anyway to see."

Nothing but the glitter of sun on hailstones. Nothing but their wheat crushed into little rags of muddy slime. Here and there an isolated straw standing bolt upright in headless defiance. Martha and John walked to the far end of the field. There was no sound but their shoes slipping and rattling on the pebbles of ice. Both of them wanted to speak, to break the atmosphere of calamity that hung over them, but the words they could find were too small for the sparkling serenity of wasted field. Even as waste it was indomitable. It tethered them to itself, so that they could not feel or comprehend. It had come and gone, that was all; before its tremendousness and havoc they were prostrate. They had not yet risen to cry out or protest.

It was when they were nearly back to the house that Martha started to whimper. "I can't go on any longer; I can't, John. There's no use, we've tried." With one hand she clutched him and with the other held her apron to her mouth. "It's driving me out of my mind. I'm so tired—heart-sick of it all. Can't you see?''

He laid his big hands on her shoulders. They looked at each other for a few seconds, then she dropped her head weakly against his greasy smock. Presently he roused her. ''Here come Joe and Annabelle!'' The pressure of his hands tightened. His bristly cheek touched her hair and forehead. ''Straighten up, quick, before they see you!''

It was more of him than she had had for years. ''Yes, John, I know—I'm all right now.'' There was a wistful little pull in her voice as if she would have had him hold her there, but hurriedly instead she began to dry her eyes with her apron. ''And tell Joe you'll get him another dog.''

Then he left her and she went back to the house. Mounting within her was a resolve, a bravery. It was the warming sunlight, the strength and nearness of John, a feeling of mattering, belonging. Swung far upwards by the rush and swell of recaptured life, she was suddenly as far above the desolation of the storm as a little while ago she had been abject before it. But in the house she was alone; there was no sunlight, only a cold wind through the broken window; and she crumpled again.

She tried to face the kitchen, to get the floor dried and the broken lamps swept up. But it was not the kitchen; it was tomorrow, next week, next year. The going on, the waste of life, the hopelessness.

Her hands fought the broom a moment, twisting the handle as if trying to unscrew the rusted cap of a jar; then abruptly she let it fall and strode outside. All very fine for John: he'd talk about education for Joe and Annabelle, and she could worry where the clothes were to come from so that they could go clean and decent even to the country school. It made no difference that she had wanted to take out hail insurance. He was the one that looked after things. She was just his wife; it wasn't for her to open her mouth. He'd pat her shoulder and let her come back to this. They'd be brave, go on again, forget about the crop. Go on, go on—next year and the next—go on till they were both ready for the scrap-heap. But she'd had enough. This time he'd go on alone.

Not that she meant it. Not that she failed to understand what John was going through. It was just rebellion. Rebellion because their wheat was beaten to the ground, because there was this brutal, callous finish to everything she had planned, because she had will and needs and flesh, because she was alive. Rebellion, not John at all—but how rebel against a summer storm, how find the throat of a cloud?

So at a jerky little run she set off for the stable, for John. Just that she might release and spend herself, no matter against whom or what, unloose the fury that clawed within her, strike back a blow for the one that had flattened her.

The stable was quiet, only the push of hay as the horses nosed through the mangers, the lazy rub of their flanks and hips against the stall partitions; and before its quietness her anger subsided, took time for breath. She advanced slowly, almost on tiptoe, peering past the horses' rumps for a glimpse of John. To the last stall, back again. And then there was a sound different from the stable sounds. She paused.

She had not seen him the first time she passed because he was pressed against one of the horses, his head pushed into the big deep hollow of its neck and shoulder, one hand hooked by the fingers in the mane, his own shoulders drawn up and shaking. She stared, thrust out her head incredulously, moved her lips, but stood silent. John sobbing there, against the horse. It was the strangest, most frightening moment of her life. He had always been so strong and grim; had just kept on as if he couldn't feel, as if there were a bull's hide over him, and now he was beaten.

She crept away. It would be unbearable to watch his humiliation if he looked up and saw her. Joe was wandering about the yard, thinking about Nipper and disconsolately sucking hailstones, but she fled past him, head down, stricken with guilty shame as if it were she who had been caught broken and afraid. He had always been so strong, a brute at times in his strength, and now—

Now—why now that it had come to this, he might never be able to get a grip on himself again. He might not want to keep on working, not if he were really beaten. If he lost heart, if he didn't care about Joe and Annabelle any more. Weeds and pests, drought and hail—it took so much fight for a man to hold his own against them all, just to hold his own, let alone make headway.

"Look at the sky!" It was Annabelle again, breathless and ecstatic. "The far one—look how it's opened like a fan!"

Withdrawn now in the eastern sky the storm clouds towered, gold-capped and flushed in the late sunlight, high, still pyramids of snowiness and shadow. And one that Annabelle pointed to,

apart, the farthest away of them all, this one in bronzed slow
splendour spread up mountains high to a vast, plateau-like summit.

Martha hurried inside. She started the fire again, then nailed a
blanket over the broken window and lit the big brass parlour
lamp—the only one the storm had spared. Her hands were quick
and tense. John would need a good supper tonight. The biscuits
were water-soaked, but she still had the peas. He liked peas.
Lucky that they had picked them when they did. This winter they
wouldn't have so much as an onion or potato.

The Trouble with Families . . .

PENNY IN THE DUST
by Ernest Buckler

My sister and I were walking through the old sun-still fields the
evening before my father's funeral, recalling this memory or
that—trying, after the fashion of families who gather again in the
place where they were born, to identify ourselves with the
strange children we must have been.

"Do you remember the afternoon we thought you were lost?"
my sister said. I did. That was as long ago as the day I was
seven, but I'd had occasion to remember it only yesterday.

"We searched everywhere," she said. "Up in the meeting-
house, back in the blueberry barrens—we even looked in the
well. I think it's the only time I ever saw Father really upset. He
didn't even stop to take the oxen off the wagon tongue when
they told him. He raced right through the chopping where Tom
Reeve was burning brush, looking for you—right through the
flames almost; they couldn't do a thing with him. And you up in
your bed, sound asleep!

"It was all over losing a penny or something, wasn't it?" she
went on, when I didn't answer. It was. She laughed indulgently.
"You were a crazy kid, weren't you."

I was. But there was more to it than that. I had never seen a
shining new penny before that day. I'd thought they were all
black. This one was bright as gold. And my father had given it
to me.

You would have to understand about my father, and that is the
hard thing to tell. If I say that he worked all day long but never
once had I seen him hurry, that would make him sound like a
stupid man. If I say that he never held me on his knee when I
was a child and that I never heard him laugh out loud in his life,
it would make him sound humourless and severe. If I said that
whenever I'd be reeling off some of my fanciful plans and he'd

177

come into the kitchen and I'd stop short, you'd think that he was distant and that in some kind of way I was afraid of him. None of that would be true.

There's no way you can tell it to make it sound like anything more than an inarticulate man a little at sea with an imaginative child. You'll have to take my word for it that there was more to it than that. It was as if his sure-footed way in the fields forsook him the moment he came near the door of my child's world and that he could never intrude on it without feeling awkward and conscious of trespass; and that I, sensing that but not understanding it, felt at the sound of his solid step outside, the child-world's foolish fragility. He would fix the small spot where I planted beans and other quick-sprouting seeds before he prepared the big garden, even if the spring was late; but he wouldn't ask me how many rows I wanted and if he made three rows and I wanted four, I couldn't ask him to change them. If I walked behind the load of hay, longing to ride, and he walked ahead of the oxen, I couldn't ask him to put me up and he wouldn't make any move to do so until he saw me trying to grasp the binder.

He, my father, had just given me a new penny, bright as gold.

He'd taken it from his pocket several times, pretending to examine the date on it, waiting for me to notice it. He couldn't offer me *anything* until I had shown some sign that the gift would be welcome.

"You can have it if you want it, Pete," he said at last.

"Oh, thanks," I said. Nothing more. I couldn't expose any of my eagerness either.

I started with it, to the store. For a penny you could buy the magic cylinder of "Long Tom" popcorn with Heaven knows what glittering bauble inside. But the more I thought of my bright penny disappearing forever into the black drawstring pouch the storekeeper kept his money in, the slower my steps lagged as the store came nearer and nearer. I sat down in the road.

It was that time of magic suspension in an August afternoon. The lifting smells of leaves and cut clover hung still in the sun. The sun drowsed, like a kitten curled up on my shoulder. The deep flour-fine dust in the road puffed about my bare ankles, warm and soft as sleep. The sound of the cowbells came sharp and hollow from the cool swamp.

I began to play with the penny, putting off the decision. I would close my eyes and bury it deep in the sand; and then, with my eyes still closed, get up and walk around, and then come back to search for it. Tantalizing myself, each time, with the excitement of discovering afresh its bright shining edge. I did that again and again. Alas, once too often.

It was almost dark when their excited talking in the room awakened me. It was Mother who had found me. I suppose when it came dusk she thought of me in my bed other nights, and I suppose she looked there without any reasonable hope but only as you look in every place where the thing that is lost has ever lain before. And now suddenly she was crying because when she opened the door there, miraculously, I was.

"Peter!" she cried, ignoring the obvious in her sudden relief, "*where* have you been?"

"I lost my penny," I said.

"You lost your penny . . . ? But what made you come up here and hide?"

If Father hadn't been there, I might have told her the whole story. But when I looked up at Father, standing there like the shape of everything sound and straight, it was like daylight shredding the memory of a silly dream. How could I bear the shame of repeating before him the childish visions I had built in my head in the magic August afternoon when almost anything could be made to seem real, as I buried the penny and dug it up again? How could I explain that pit-of-the-stomach sickness which struck through the whole day when I had to believe, at last, that it was really gone? How could I explain that I wasn't really hiding from *them*? How, with the words and the understanding I had then, that this was the only possible place to run from that awful feeling of loss?

"I lost my penny," I said again. I looked at Father and turned my face into the pillow. "I want to go to sleep."

"Peter," Mother said. "It's almost nine o'clock. You haven't had a bite of supper. Do you know you almost scared the *life* out of us?"

"You better get some supper," Father said. It was the only time he had spoken.

I never dreamed that he would mention the thing again. But the next morning when we had the hay forks in our hands, ready to toss out the clover, he seemed to postpone the moment of actually leaving for the field. He stuck his fork in the ground and brought in another pail of water, though the kettle was chock full. He took out the shingle nail that held a broken yoke strap together and put it back in exactly the same hole. He went into the shed to see if the pigs had cleaned up all their breakfast.

And then he said abruptly: "Ain't you got no idea where you lost your penny?"

"Yes," I said, "I know just about."

"Let's see if we can't find it," he said.

We walked down the road together, stiff with awareness. He didn't hold my hand.

"It's right here somewhere," I said. "I was playin' with it, in the dust."

He looked at me, but he didn't ask me what game anyone could possibly play with a penny in the dust.

I might have known he would find it. He could tap the alder bark with his jackknife just exactly hard enough so it wouldn't split but so it would twist free from the notched wood, to make a whistle. His great fingers could trace loose the hopeless snarl of a fishing line that I could only succeed in tangling tighter and tighter. If I broke the handle of my wheelbarrow ragged beyond sight of any possible repair, he could take it and bring it back to me so you could hardly see the splice if you weren't looking for it.

He got down on his knees and drew his fingers carefully through the dust, like a harrow; not clawing it frantically into heaps as I had done, covering even as I uncovered. He found the penny almost at once.

He held it in his hand, as if the moment of passing it to me were a deadline for something he dreaded to say, but must. Something that could not be put off any longer, if it were to be spoken at all.

"Pete," he said, "you needn'ta hid. I wouldn'ta beat you."

Beat me? Oh, Father! You didn't think that was the reason . . . ? I felt almost sick. I felt as if I had struck *him*.

I had to tell him the truth then. Because only the truth, no matter how ridiculous it was, would have the unmistakable sound truth has, to scatter that awful idea out of his head.

"I wasn't hidin', Father," I said, "honest. I was . . . I was buryin' my penny and makin' out I was diggin' up treasure. I was makin' out I was findin' gold. I didn't know what to *do* when I lost it, I just didn't know where to *go*. . . ." His head was bent forward, like mere listening. I had to make it truer still.

"I made out it was gold," I said desperately, "and I—I was

makin' out I bought you a mowin' machine so's you could get your work done early every day so's you and I could go in to town in the big automobile I made out I bought you—and everyone'd turn around and look at us drivin' down the streets. . . ." His head was perfectly still, as if he·were only waiting with patience for me to finish. "*Laugh*in' and *talk*in'," I said. Louder, smiling intensely, com*pell*ing him, by the absolute conviction of some true particular, to believe me.

He looked up then. It was the only time I had ever seen tears in his eyes. It was the only time in my seven years that he had ever put his arm around me.

I wondered, though, why he hesitated, and then put the penny back in his own pocket.

Yesterday I knew. I never found any fortune and we never had a car to ride in together. But I think he knew what that would be like, just the same. I found the penny again yesterday, when we were getting out his good suit—in an upper vest pocket where no one ever carries change. It was still shining. He must have kept it polished.

I left it there.

BENNY
by Mordecai Richler

When Benny was sent overseas in the autumn of 1941 his father, Garber, decided that if he had to yield one son to the army it might just as well be Benny, who was a dumbie and wouldn't push where he shouldn't; Mrs. Garber thought, he'll take care, my Benny will watch out; and Benny's brother Abe proclaimed, "When he comes back, I'll have a garage of my own, you bet, and I'll be able to give him a job." Benny wrote every week, and every week the Garbers sent him parcels full of good things a St. Urbain Street boy should always have, like salami and pickled herring and *shtrudel*. The food parcels never varied and the letters—coming from Camp Borden and Aldershot and Normandy and Holland—were always the same too. They began— "I hope you are all well and good"—and ended—"don't worry, all the best to everybody, thank you for the parcel."

When Benny came home from the war in Europe, the Garbers didn't make an inordinate fuss, like the Shapiros did when their first-born son returned. They met him at the station, of course, and they had a small dinner for him.

Abe was overjoyed to see Benny again. "Atta boy," was what he kept saying all evening, "Atta boy, Benny."

"You shouldn't go back to the factory," Mr. Garber said. "You don't need the old job. You can be a help to your brother Abe in his garage."

"Yes," Benny said.

"Let him be, let him rest," Mrs. Garber said. "What'll happen if he doesn't work for two weeks?"

"Hey, when Artie Segal came back," Abe said, "he told me that in Italy there was nothing that a guy couldn't get for a couple of Sweet Caps. Was he shooting me the bull or what?"

Benny had been discharged and sent home not because the war

was over, but because of the shrapnel in his leg. He didn't limp too badly and he wouldn't talk about his wound or the war, so at first nobody noticed that he had changed. Nobody, that is, except Myerson's daughter, Bella.

Myerson was the proprietor of Pop's Cigar & Soda, on St. Urbain, and any day of the week you could find him there seated on a worn, peeling kitchen chair playing poker with the men of the neighbourhood. He had a glass eye and when a player hesitated on a bet, he would take it out and polish it, a gesture that never failed to intimidate. His daughter, Bella, worked behind the counter. She had a clubfoot and mousey brown hair and some more hair on her face, and although she was only twenty-six, it was generally agreed that she would end up an old maid. Anyway she was the one—the first one—to notice that Benny had changed. The very first time he appeared in Pop's Cigar & Soda after his homecoming, she said to him, "What's wrong, Benny?"

"I'm all right," he said.

Benny was short and skinny with a long narrow face, a pulpy mouth that was somewhat crooked, and soft black eyes. He had big, conspicuous hands which he preferred to keep out of sight in his pockets. In fact he seemed to want to keep out of sight altogether and whenever possible, he stood behind a chair or in a dim light so that the others wouldn't notice him. When he had failed the ninth grade at F.F.H.S. Benny's class master, a Mr. Perkins, had sent him home with a note saying: "Benjamin is not a student, but he has all the makings of a good citizen. He is honest and attentive in class and a hard worker. I recommend that he learn a trade."

When Mr. Garber had read what his son's teacher had written, he had shaken his head and crumpled up the bit of paper and said—"A trade?"—he had looked at his boy and shaken his head and said—"A trade?"

Mrs. Garber had said stoutly, "Haven't you got a trade?"

"Shapiro's boy will be a doctor," Mr. Garber had said.

"Shapiro's boy," Mrs. Garber had said.

Afterwards, Benny had retrieved the note and smoothed out the creases and put it in his pocket, where it had remained.

The day after his return to Montreal, Benny showed up at Abe's garage having decided that he didn't want two weeks off. That pleased Abe a lot. "I can see that you've matured since

you've been away," Abe said. "That's good. That counts for
you in this world."

Abe worked extremely hard, he worked night and day, and he
believed that having Benny with him would give his business an
added kick. "That's my kid brother Benny," Abe used to tell
the taxi drivers. "Four years in the infantry, two of them up
front. A tough *hombre*, let me tell you."

For the first few weeks Abe was pleased with Benny. "He's
slow," he reported to their father, "no genius of a mechanic, but
the customers like him and he'll learn." Then Abe began to
notice things. When business was slow, Benny, instead of taking
advantage of the lull to clean up the shop, used to sit shivering in
a dim corner, with his hands folded tight on his lap. The first
time Abe noticed his brother behaving like that, he said, "What's
wrong? You got a chill?"

"No. I'm all right."

"You want to go home or something?"

"No."

Whenever it rained, and it rained often that spring, Benny was
not to be found around the garage, and that put Abe in a foul
temper. Until one day during a thunder shower, Abe tried the
toilet door and discovered that it was locked. "Benny," he
yelled, "you come out, I know you're in there."

Benny didn't answer, so Abe fetched the key. He found
Benny huddled in a corner with his head buried in his knees,
trembling, with sweat running down his face in spite of the cold.

"It's raining," Benny said.

"Benny, get up. What's wrong?"

"Go away. It's raining."

"I'll get a doctor, Benny."

"No. Go away. Please, Abe."

"But Benny . . ."

Benny began to shake violently, just as if an inner whip had
been cracked. Then, after it had passed, he looked up at Abe
dumbly, his mouth hanging open. "It's raining," he said.

The next morning Abe went to see Mr. Garber. "I don't know
what to do with him," he said.

"The war left him with a bad taste," Mrs. Garber said.

"Other boys went to the war," Abe said.

"Shapiro's boy," Mr. Garber said, "was an officer."

"Shapiro's boy," Mrs. Garber said. "You give him a vacation, Abe. You insist. He's a good boy. From the best."

Benny didn't know what to do with his vacation, so he slept in late, and began to hang around Pop's Cigar & Soda.

"I don't like it, Bella," Myerson said, "I need him here like I need a cancer."

"Something's wrong with him psychologically," one of the card players ventured.

But obviously Bella enjoyed having Benny around and after a while Myerson stopped complaining. "Maybe the boy is serious," he confessed, "and with her club foot and all that stuff on her face, I can't start picking and choosing. Besides, it's not as if he was a crook. Like Huberman's boy."

"You take that back. Huberman's boy was a victim of circumstances. He was taking care of the suitcase for a stranger, a complete stranger, when the cops had to mix in."

Bella and Benny did not talk much when they were together. She used to knit, he used to smoke. He would watch silently as she limped about the store, silently, with longing, and consternation. The letter from Mr. Perkins was in his pocket. Occasionally, Bella would look up from her knitting. "You feel like a cup coffee?"

"I wouldn't say no."

Around five in the afternoon he would get up, Bella would come round the counter to give him a stack of magazines to take home, and at night he would read them all from cover to cover and the next morning bring them back as clean as new. Then he would sit with her in the store again, looking down at the floor or at his hands.

One day instead of going home around five in the afternoon, Benny went upstairs with Bella. Myerson, who was watching, smiled. He turned to Shub and said: "If I had a boy of my own, I couldn't wish for a better one than Benny."

"Look who's counting chickens," Shub replied.

Benny's vacation dragged on for several weeks and every morning he sat down at the counter in Pop's Cigar & Soda and every evening he went upstairs with Bella, pretending not to hear the wise-cracks made by the card players as they passed. Until one afternoon Bella summoned Myerson upstairs in the middle of a deal. "We have decided to get married," she said.

"In that case," Myerson said, "you have my permission."

"Aren't you even going to say luck or something?" Bella asked.

"It's your life," Myerson said.

They had a very simple wedding without speeches in a small synagogue and after the ceremony was over Abe whacked his younger brother on the back and said, "Atta boy, Benny. Atta boy."

"Can I come back to work?"

"Sure you can. You're the old Benny again. I can see that."

But his father, Benny noticed, was not too pleased with the match. Each time one of Garber's cronies congratulated him, he shrugged his shoulders and said, "Shapiro's boy married into the Segals."

"Shapiro's boy," Mrs. Garber said.

Benny went back to the garage, but this time he settled down to work hard and that pleased Abe enormously. "That's my kid brother Benny," Abe took to telling the taxi drivers, "married six weeks and he's already got one in the oven. A quick worker, I'll tell you."

Benny not only settled down to work hard, but he even laughed a little, and, with Bella's help, began to plan for the future. But every now and then, usually when there was a slack period at the garage, Benny would shut up tight and sit in a chair in a dark corner. He had only been back at work for three, maybe four, months when Bella went to speak to Abe. She returned to their flat on St. Urbain, her face flushed and triumphant. "I've got news for you," she said to Benny. "Abe is going to open another garage on Mount Royal and you're going to manage it."

"But I don't want to, I wouldn't know how."

"We're going to be partners in the new garage."

"I'd rather stay with Abe."

Bella explained that they had to plan for their child's future. Their son, she swore, would not be brought up over a cigar & soda, without so much as a shower in the flat. She wanted a fridge. If they saved, they could afford a car. Next year, she said, after the baby was born, she hoped there would be sufficient money saved so that she could go to a clinic in the United States to have an operation on her foot. "I was to Dr. Shapiro yesterday and he assured me there is a clinic in Boston where they perform miracles daily."

"He examined you?" Benny asked.

"He was very, very nice. Not a snob, if you know what I mean."

"Did he remember that he was at school with me?"

"No," Bella said.

Bella woke at three in the morning to find Benny huddled on the floor in a dark corner with his head buried in his knees, trembling. "It's raining," he said. "There's thunder."

"A man who fought in the war can't be scared of a little rain."

"Oh, Bella, Bella, Bella."

She attempted to stroke his head but he drew sharply away from her.

"Should I send for a doctor?"

"Shapiro's boy maybe?" he asked, giggling.

"Why not?"

"Bella," he said. "Bella, Bella."

"I'm going next door to the Idelsohns to phone for the doctor. Don't move. Relax."

But when she returned to the bedroom he had gone.

Myerson came round at eight in the morning. Mr. and Mrs. Garber were with him.

"Is he dead?" Bella asked.

"Shapiro's boy, the doctor, said it was quick."

"Shapiro's boy," Mrs. Garber said.

"It wasn't the driver's fault," Myerson said.

"I know," Bella said.

GINGERBREAD BOY
by Phyllis Gotlieb

Benno was sitting in the closet with the door closed. It was dark and stuffy, and the toe of a shoe was digging into the base of his spine, but he liked the closeness. He had been grown in a tank as narrow as this closet, in dark warm liquids. He had no true memory of that time, but he closed his eyes and imagined that he could remember the warmth, and the love and kindness that seemed to be around him then. . . .

There was a thump and a yell of laughter, and he blinked. Poppy and her ball. She had nothing to worry about. He had been playing with her a few minutes ago. He would throw the ball, and she would miss it and run after it, shrieking.

"Come on, Benno, throw it, Benno!" And Benno threw it, mouth drawn in the thin ironical line that served him for a smile.

Finally, running to catch it, she overreached herself and fell. She sat there a minute, lower lip shoved out and mouth drawn down at the corners into a deep inverted U before it opened into a howl.

"No, no, Poppy. Don't cry, lovey." Benno pulled her up as Mrs. Peretto came running into the room.

"Benno, what did you . . ." She bit off the words and grabbed the child. "What happened, sweetie?"

Benno said quietly, "Mrs. Peretto, why don't you ask Poppy *what I did to her*?"

The woman twisted to face him and he saw that she was trembling. She loosened her hold on the little girl and stood up.

"*Mrs. Peretto*, Benno? Not 'Mom,' Benno?" Her eyes filled. "I . . . I don't know what's got into you. . . ." She hurried out of the room.

But she had left the child behind—*afraid to let me know she doesn't trust me*—and Poppy, sorrow forgotten, trotted over to

188

Benno and yanked at his trouser-leg. "C'mon, c'mon, Benno, let's play some more."

"No more for now, Poppy," Benno gently detached the sticky fingers, "go find your mummy."

So he went and sat down in the closet with the door shut and brooded. He would have enjoyed one of Wenslow's cigars right now, but the closet was no place to smoke it. Anyway, the whole business was no good. But as he was about to get up he heard another sound: Mrs. Peretto dialing the intercom. He stayed still.

"Helen? Oh . . . fine, I guess . . . nothing really new, but I've been having a little bit of trouble too . . . the thing is, I can't even say it's anything I haven't made up in my own mind. I'm just . . . just getting to be a little scared. . . ."

Benno waited till he was sure she had gone. If she knew he skulked in closets and listened to private conversations it wouldn't have helped at all. He always went into closets when he felt moody, but he didn't care to advertise it.

As he opened the door, he saw himself in the full-length glass, the image of a broad, stocky twelve-year-old boy.

But he was five years old, not twelve. He had been made in this shape and he would die in it: pseudo-male and sterile, hairless except for the strong dark line of brow and the close-cropped head of hair so dark and wiry it looked artificial. Even the temper of his skin was dark and sullen.

He ran a hand over his face. He had been grown from a piece of Peretto's flesh, so the features were Peretto's; but Peretto was a man, and Benno a second-hand copy pretending to be his child.

He sneered at the image and slipped out of the house.

Peretto and Wenslow shared one of the shabby portables in Administration; it contained the lab where Benno had been born, and a small private office. When Benno reached it he was glad to find Peretto in and Wenslow out.

As he closed the door behind him, Peretto looked up. "What's eating you, Benno?"

"Not me," said Benno. "You."

"I don't think I'm giving you any trouble. What is it?"

"Mrs. Peretto thinks I've got it in for Poppy, or something. She thought I hurt her when she fell today."

Peretto shrugged. "Parents always worry about jealousy problems between older and younger children."

Benno helped himself in Wenslow's humidor and lit up.

"She's not worried. She's frightened. I heard her saying so to Mrs. Metzner on the phone. She's scared of me."

Peretto said hesitantly, "That's not so, Benno. . . . I think she's feeling a little guilty . . . like a lot of the rest of us."

"Because it's hard to keep loving made-up things like us when you've got real kids of your own."

"We put a lot of love into you—"

"But that was different. That was when you thought you couldn't have any kids."

"Earth was pretty hot when we left. We couldn't be sure we wouldn't be sterile forever. We had to have something, Benno."

"So now you've got something and you're stuck with it." Benno looked out of the window where the yellow sun of Skander V was shining on experimental plots and groves of trees, on Residential, on the dunes and the salt lake and the rest of the Colony beyond. "And it makes you sick to look at us and think you wanted and loved us."

"Benno!"

"But it's true. Dickon told me Wenslow said that to him."

"Oh, Wenslow!"

"Well, maybe you don't like him so much either. But you and he are on the same side."

"Do we have to pick sides?"

"We can't help it. A lot of the guys are talking funny, too."

Peretto waited. The androids were unable to lie and he did not want to make Benno compromise himself.

Benno said uncomfortably, "About Bimbo Harrington."

"But you know he drowned. We couldn't do anything for him."

"Nobody ever saw his body."

"It wasn't a thing to see. He—the android body decomposes so—we can't do anything about . . ."

"Well, they think—" Benno began, but the door opened. Wenslow came in.

His pale eyes flashed and his thin nostrils twitched at the smoke in the air. "At the cigars again, I see, Benno," he said pleasantly.

Benno blew a mouthful of smoke into his face and walked out. He heard the voices through the closed door:

"I swear to God if that thing belonged to me—"

Peretto interrupted wearily: "You leave cigars around because you get a good snide laugh out of seeing him smoke them. If he manages to do it without amusing you, too bad for you. Now let's quit niggling and get to work."

"And then she said, 'I don't know what's got into you, you always called me Mom until—' "

"And if you tried it, she'd twist your ears off for you, the bitch!"

Benno watched the bitter face across the campfire and realized that Dickon had probably paid very heavily for his own enjoyment in blowing smoke at Wenslow. He would have to be more careful of his pleasures in the future.

He said, trying to keep peace, "The Perettos aren't bad, Dickon. You have to be fair to them."

The shadows in Dickon's eyes were as deep as the humps of the dunes against the night sky. "You can say that, smoking cigars and turning yourself into a clown to suck up to them."

"If I did that, I'd be selling my soul," said Benno. "But if I left off smoking when I like it just for fear of anything they might do, I'd be selling it twice over."

"Soul! I'd like to see you show me where you've got a soul!"

"Nothing *you* could see! Oh hell, I guess if I had to live with the Wenslows I'd be as big a bastard as you are." Dickon answered him in kind, and he waited for a slackening. "But don't you see? They loved us and made us love them, so they think we've got immortal souls. That's the only thing that's keeping them from wiping us out."

"What makes you think they haven't started wiping us out already?" Rudi Metzner asked. "What about Bimbo?"

"I asked Peretto about that today," Benno said slowly. "He said he'd drowned."

"And you believed him? Sure he drowned. But it was in one of those tanks, you can bet. Did you know they'd started up the tanks again? What's your guess about what they're doing?"

"I don't get you."

"Take a look in one of those tanks," said Dickon. "Try it in the middle of the night, sneak around the back where the guard won't see you. You'll see they've got a thing in there, something new they're making, and I'll bet they started it with Bimbo. Maybe Peretto and Wenslow wouldn't bloody their hands on us, but that don't stop them from making a new kind of android to do their work, a killer that's not so scared of souls! Take a look and see."

"I'll promise this," said Benno. "You try messing around with the Perettos and I'll kill you dead, Dickon, because *you* haven't got the soul of a flea!"

The stars were dim beyond the two moons that made the shadows shift and fall; rustling trees covered his footsteps in the grass.

He cursed them, he didn't believe them, he had sworn he wouldn't go. But here he was. He had wakened in the night as if he had planned it, and dressed and crept out. He paused: if his world broke now he would never be able to love the Perettos again, and there was nothing else. He went on.

At the back of the fence he had the whole building between himself and the guard. He climbed the chicken-wire and dropped down silently. He knew that the lock of the tank-room window was broken. No one was worried about theft; the guard was there only to prevent the disturbance of delicate adjustments in the equipment.

He pushed at the window; it creaked but the wind covered the noise.

Inside it was very dark, but he knew the room well. Two steps and he found the bank of switches on the first tank. One dim light was all he dared. The glimmer inside, faint as it was, showed that one was empty. He pressed back the toggle and moved on to the peephole of the next. That one was empty too, and he began to hope. The third—

He was afraid to turn on more than one light, and the liquid was cloudy, but there was definitely a creature there.

In a second it became sensitive to the light and began turning and threshing. The cloudiness enveloped it again but he had seen it. Sickened, he turned the light out and groped for the window.

He dropped down and climbed the wire without caring where he went or whether he was caught.

A few steps away from the fence a group of figures emerged from the bushes and surrounded him.

"Couldn't resist, eh, Benno?"

"What do you want?" he whispered.

"We had a bet on you," said Dickon, grinning. "Go ahead, tell us what you saw there."

After a moment, he said, "All right. I saw something there— but not clearly enough to tell what it was."

"But we told you what it was and you know. Go on, don't you?"

"Yes," said Benno.

"Not feelin' so snotty now, are you, Benno?"

Hurrah for our side. He would have hit out at them, but there were too many. He turned to find the weak point in the circle, but they were his equals.

"Let me go," he said.

"Okay, for now. But remember, we'll be calling on you one day. You'll come."

He ran, and their laughter followed him.

It was afternoon; with Poppy swinging on his hand Benno tramped along the stretch of sand that threaded through the tufted dunes and separated the back gardens of Residential from the lake. The sun was shining, but not for Benno.

He tried to tell himself that he had no proof of anything, but he felt weak inside in the face of Dickon's hatred of the humans.

"Let's dig here," said Poppy, "and we'll find the treasure." Benno sat down while she went to work. Her presence was Mrs. Peretto's way of saying: I was a fool yesterday and didn't mean what I said. If that was the case, he had nothing to fear there. He looked around. The beach was quiet, the waters rippled sluggishly.

A few houses down, a woman came through the back gate and out onto the sand, a naked baby tucked under one arm and a flannel blanket under the other. Mrs. Harrington. She was wearing brief red shorts and a fluffy blouse; a black ponytail bobbed on her tanned neck.

She trotted down to one of the usndecks near the water and sat there, sloshing her feet while the baby kicked on the blanket beside her, gurgling.

Then Harrington, out from work, swung down the garden, leaped over the gate, and ran across the sands. He grabbed the ponytail, pulled his wife's head back, and kissed her upside-down face. He whispered in her ear, gesturing back toward the house. She shushed him, glancing at Benno and Poppy. He cajoled; she resisted. Finally she shrugged, tucked up the baby, and followed him back to the house. Benno could hear them giggling as they went.

"When I get big I'm going to be a mummy," said Poppy. "And you can be the daddy, Benno."

"Yeh," said Benno.

He crouched, trapped in the amber of twelve-year-old boy-hood on Skander V. Peretto had said, "We would have made you—complete, if we could. We just don't know enough. . . ."

Benno, watching the Harringtons, knew well enough what he would never be.

Poppy put aside her pail and shovel and came over to him, bracing herself between his knees and resting her forehead against his. Her breath was like apples; she scratched his face gently and he kissed her, rich with the pleasure of feeling a living being against him. *This is all I'm good for.* He hugged her as she giggled, and ruffled his hair in her neck, grunting like the wild pigs the colonists hunted for sport.

Someone shrieked behind him: "You filthy beast! Let go of that child at once, do you hear?"

He was so taken by surprise that he fell back in the sand, pulling Poppy on top of him. Mrs. Wenslow was standing over him, fists tight, face contorted.

"Dirty, dirty thing! Wait till they hear about this! Peretto's darling! I'll tell them different, you filthy—"

Benno righted himself and ran, leaving Poppy howling behind him. The woman knew he wasn't, he couldn't—! But there was no arguing with that— He ran.

In the hills there were caves hidden behind thickets of low gnarled trees. . . .

He squatted, nursing his hurt as the sun sank and the moons swung by. He thought and thought till his mind turned sickly and his head ached. Was he as innocent as he had always believed? He was afraid to search the unexplored reaches of his mind, but he knew for sure that his loins were empty and he cursed himself and his makers.

Exhausted at last, he groped in his pocket for one of the cigars he had filched the day before. He stared at it, shrugged and lit it.

He sat smoking and watching the stars as they filtered in and out of the leaves. He didn't know what he was waiting for.

"Put that out, you nut! You want to get caught?"

Benno peered out; he saw nothing but stars and branches. "Dickon?" he called tentatively.

Pushing aside the boughs, Dickon slipped in and sat beside him. "Go on, put it out. They'll see us a mile off."

"I don't care."

"I do, God damn it, the thing's suffocating me."

Benno mashed it out. "You wouldn't have found me without it."

"Now they're not going to find *us*," said Dickon. "What happened? I was out hunting and they rounded us up and sent us to bring you in. Huh!"

"I was playing with Poppy, horsing around. Somebody thought it was something dirty."

"Boy, I love you for that!" Dickon thumped him on the back. "It's what I've been waiting for—but I never thought you'd be the one. Who was it? Not Peretto?"

"No. It was Mrs. Wenslow."

Benno was shocked by the silence. No sneers, no laughter. He turned to look for Dickon's face in the dark, and thought suddenly: *he loves them.*

Dickon said in a low voice, "Nobody'd play with that scrawny kid of theirs. They got him so he's scared to let out a peep."

"I'm sorry, Dickon."

"What for, you bloody fool? What do you mean?"

"Nothing," said Benno.

Dickon raised his head. "Listen, there they are! Halloo! Halloo!" he called softly down the hill.

"Who?"

"The rest of us! I've got two dozen down there, only ten missing." He divided the branches and called, "Come on up, you guys, I found him!"

"But what—" Benno began, but Dickon was waving the others in.

"Hi!" they cried. "What was all the business about?"

Dickon guffawed. "He was horsing with the Peretto brat and they thought—" He elaborated to an extent that made Benno glad the darkness hid his flushed face. Their eyes glittered in the dimness: they were staring at him with respect.

"Gee, lemme touch you! You been holding out on us, Benno? Maybe you got—"

"Shut up, shut up for God's sake!" Benno snarled. "He's feeding you a line. I'm just the same as you are, dammit!" His people!

Dickon laughed again, nastily. "All right, forget it for now.

We've got to get the others together and we can start out."

"Start out for what?" Benno felt the incredulous stares around him.

"You all there? What d'you think we got these guns for? We're all set to knock the lot of them off the planet!"

Benno caught his breath. "Just on account of this thing with me?"

"Who else? Think we're gonna let 'em get away with it?"

Benno gaped at their set faces in the dusk. "But they're not mad at you, you damn fools!"

"What do you mean? Think you're going to back out after getting us all up here?"

"I didn't. You came after me." He tried to keep his voice level. "They got nothing against you. I just came up here to think for a while. Let me go back and take my lumps and we'll forget the whole business."

"Forget it!" Dickon swung up the rifle. "You're coming down with us right now! I'm giving the orders and you're gonna do it!"

"Yeah? You want to fight, okay. But you don't pin it on me." Benno grasped the rifle barrel and pulled it to his chest. "Go on. Kill me."

Dickon stood indecisive. Everyone knew that if Benno were dead the whole affair would collapse. Then he pulled the rifle out of Benno's hands and set it aside. "The kid wants to take his lumps," he sneered. "Okay . . . put the guns away and give him what he wants!"

Words rattled at him: ". . . betbetbetterterter i-i-idededea . . ." He shook his head and the words rolled around inside it as he pulled himself out of his sleep or coma, he never knew which.

Mist was pushing into the cave. The trees outside seemed clotted with cobwebs. His lids were heavy and crusted, his body felt flayed to the bone, sore in every joint, muscle, nerve. His tongue pulled away from his palate with a wrench and his arms flopped like dying fishes. He looked at them and saw that the wrists were bound.

". . . don't know why I never thought of it before . . ." Benno moved his head again and nearly groaned. There was no comfort in the sickly early dawn rolling by in wet drifts of fog.

"Much better idea," Dickson was saying. "We can't just run

down there waving guns. They'd knock us off in an hour. But if we pick up one of their brats they'll come after us. They'll never know where to find us in all these holes and we can do what we like with them.''

Benno pulled himself up till he sat hunched over his knees. He didn't dare touch his face, even to rub his eyes.

"All we have to decide is whose kid," said one of the others.

"The creep's up," said Dickon. "Knock him on the head, somebody."

"Leave him alone, Dickon, he never hurt you." Dickon cocked an eyebrow at the speaker and went back to his plan.

"Whose! Think anybody'd miss Wenslow's brat? We want Peretto's. They'll put it on Benno, and if he gets killed, nobody'll worry."

Benno stared at Dickon with horror and pity. His personality had degenerated like a child's in a tantrum, leaving only an idiot rage. The other androids were shifting about, looking at each other.

Finally, Rudi said, "We didn't figure on anybody getting killed in this, Dickon."

Dickon turned on him: "What did you think, you were playing tiddleywinks?"

"We wanted to get even a bit, get them under our thumb and give them a scare—"

"Yeah, and end up with love and kisses and an all-day sucker!"

Benno said, "Isn't that what *you* want, Dickon?"

"You shut up! Keep your mouth out of this!" He was almost sobbing. "I could kill you. I could kill you now so—damn—easy—"

"No you couldn't, Dickon," Rudi said quietly.

"Jesus, a bunch of cupcakes! I used to think you wanted to be men! I'll do it, I'll do it myself, damn you, and I'll pull you in with me! Watch, you'll see I'll split the whole damn planet in two!"

He leaped out and flung himself down the slope with a crash of branches and was lost in the mist.

"Oh, God," Rudi said. He was about to follow, but Benno cried out, "Don't do it! It's too thick to find him in that."

"But if he hurts the kid they'll wipe us all out!"

"Undo my hands." They freed him.

"What do you think you can do?"

"I shouldn't have run off in the first place." Benno peered into the mist: it was settling slowly like water down a clogged drain. "He won't get much of a head start in that. If I can reach Peretto he'll listen to me."

"But you're a mess."

Benno rubbed his wrists. "We'll all be pretty messy if I don't go."

Rudi said, "We've got the guns—"

"We'd end up killing somebody. Besides . . . this is between the Wenslows and me, and that's how it'll have to be settled."

"What do you want us to do?"

"Oh, wait around here half an hour, and when you get back tell them I got away. That way your tongue won't tie up on you. It's true as far as it goes."

"But hell, they'll know there's something fishy there!"

"Sure, but they won't do anything about it." Benno rubbed his sore head. "They might even respect you for sticking up for me."

Rudi said awkwardly, "Don't rub it in, Benno. Here, take a gun anyway."

"Nuts. I don't want to shoot anybody. Or give them an excuse to shoot me."

He scrambled down, aching at every move, catching drunkenly at the dripping branches. At the bottom he stopped to get his breath and pull his ripped clothes together.

How would Dickon go about stealing a child from the midst of Residential?

The children usually played outside after breakfast when the mist had cleared and the grass dried off a little. Sometimes the androids took care of them after their work in the fields and vegetable gardens. Today there would be no androids, and perhaps the children would not be trusted outdoors. Would the humans be expecting an attack? Dickon wouldn't care; he was set for any risk.

Benno cut over toward the lakeshore and the dunes, in spite of the possibility of ambush. There weren't enough men to hide behind every dune. As the sun came out he climbed a rise and checked his direction. The quarry might have changed plans a hundred times already, but with Dickon's anger, and the rifle under his arm, Benno thought the chance was small.

He dipped in and out among the dunes. He couldn't see

anyone else on the sands, but he knew his dark moving figure would be eminently noticeable. Scrambling along, he glanced uneasily at the buildings as he passed them. If Dickon had headed for Administration in an attempt to attack Wenslow there would have been some noise and running about. There was only a waiting quiet. He had to assume that Dickon, like himself, was still skulking. But there was very little time.

Here, now, was the place where he and Poppy had been— yesterday? And where Mrs. Wenslow—he closed his mind . . . but where, also, he had watched the Harringtons with lewd eyes as they whispered. . . .

—don't start on me here, Bob, for God's sake. There's Benno and Poppy over there watching us.

A kid and an android? What's it got to do with them?

I don't know . . . some of those androids . . .

Some of those androids lie awake at night, listening for sounds of love.

Benno lay on the grass-tufted dune, the sun had risen. The throbbing aches in his body washed away, he was comfortable. The warmth of the sun told him this was all he could ever want. Men were hateful, he did not need them, but the warmth and the sun . . .

Dickon! Where was Dickon? He leaped up, afraid that he had slept an hour, and what Dickon could have done in that time— but the sun hadn't moved; his drowsiness had only stretched the moment. But the danger of sleep was real. He shook his head and rubbed his eyes.

Then he saw his first man, back down where the sundecks began. It was too far to tell whether he was armed, but he was moving east and heading for Benno. Benno scrambled for the next hillock. The man speeded up. *That's done it.* He'd never make the last quarter-mile at this rate. He gave up and began to run.

". . . or I'll shoot!" came the end of a yell. Benno thought he was a liar. The noise of the shot knocked him off his feet with fright. He scurried on, glancing back once to see the pursuer running, not stopping to aim. *Because I'm not armed.* He had no idea how to stop Dickon without a gun, but if he had brought one he would have been dead by now. He looked back again. Now there were two of them. Good, let's have a race!

He cut north, straight through the trees, and made a beeline across the central green, gathering pursuers and frightening children with his torn clothes and beaten face.

Then he heard a shriek from back of the Perettos'.

In the yard he found Dickon. Poppy screaming under one arm, rifle in the other hand, Mrs. Peretto at bay. Benno pulled up, stopped by the look on Dickon's face. As if he had evolved from some other feral animal, and were now reverting to it.

Benno screamed, "Dickon! Dickon!" and without thinking tore up a lump of sod from the border edge and threw it. It struck Dickon in the face, but almost before it struck Benno heard the sound of a rifle, and Dickon fell, shot through the heart.

Behind them Wenslow lowered the rifle.

Dickon sprawled grotesquely, his face tamed at last and his mouth full of dirt.

I didn't have to do that to him. . . . He looked up at Wenslow's savage face, Dickon's counterpart. *I'm the only one who's sorry.* . . . He was cold and sick.

Poppy flung herself against him; she had wet her pants in fright and her hands grabbed his hair like balls of sticky resin, but his arms went tightly around her. Peretto's hand was on his shoulder, Mrs. Peretto crowding at his side. . . .

Peretto said, half-teasing, half-rueful, "You love him more than us, hey, Poppy?"

Wenslow snarled, "He has perverted her!"

Benno was packing. Since nearly all he owned had been given him by humans, he was too proud to take everything he wanted. But he had a knife, the clothes he wore, a few things he had made himself. . . . He left off a moment, went over to the window and looked out.

Below, the children were playing, and he watched their wheeling patterns on the grass; their cries were like birdcalls in the misty verge of evening. . . .

When I grow up I'm going to be a mummy. And—

The door opened. Peretto came in and closed it behind him. His eyes took in the colored handkerchief in the best tradition spread out with Benno's possessions.

"You need an icebag for that face," he said. "I brought it."

"I don't want it." But he took it and held it to his swollen jaw.

Peretto drew in on his cigarette and let the coil of smoke drift away on his words. "Why are you running away?"

"You saw what he did. You heard what he said."

"Do you know anyone who agrees with him?"

Benno looked away. "They're all afraid of us."

"You've shown them not to be. The rest are back and there won't be any more trouble . . . you know, you didn't have to go running off yesterday, nobody believed that woman."

"I—I'm not going because of her."

"You're running away so you can be by yourself and pretend to be a man."

"That's a lousy thing to say!"

"You're an android, Benno," Peretto said gently. "You can only be a man between the ears."

"I'm nothing." They stared at each other, two cloudy images beyond the looking-glass.

"The men and women who have androids love them—"

"They ruin them and kill them!"

Peretto sighed. "There were some wild stories flying around about what was in the tank, weren't there? Dickon started most of them."

"What of it?"

"Only that the Harringtons wanted another android. Another Bimbo."

"Oh . . ." said Benno. Then he sneered. "So he can mind the baby while they—" He clapped his hands over his mouth and sat down on the bed, trembling.

Peretto's voice was almost a whisper. "You sounded exactly like Wenslow when you said that. You even looked like him."

Benno saw a black gulf falling away before him, the goal he had been running for, a cave in the hills where he would eat hate till his soul was consumed, his humanity gone, and he had become the animal looking out of Dickon's eyes when he died.

"What am I to do?" He clasped his aching head in his hands.

"Dammit, Benno, what can I tell you? You have to do the best you can to live without envy or hate. . . ."

When he looked up Peretto was gone. The dark was rising to blend him with the room, the house, the Colony. There was nothing else. All he could ever have was here.

He sat there while the moons rose and swung in their eccentric orbits. When he stood up he did not unpack his bundle. Not yet. But he left it behind him on the table and went down to the Perettos.

THE DEAD CHILD
by Gabrielle Roy

Why then did the memory of that dead child seek me out in the very midst of the summer that sang?

When till then no intimation of sorrow had come to me through the dazzling revelations of that season.

I had just arrived in a very small village in Manitoba to finish the school year as replacement for a teacher who had fallen ill or simply, for all I know, become discouraged.

The principal of the Normal School had called me to his office towards the end of my year's study. "Well," he said, "there's a school available for the month of June. It's not much but it's an opportunity. When the time comes for you to apply for a permanent position, you'll be able to say you've had experience. Believe me, it's a help."

And so I found myself at the beginning of June in that very poor village—just a few shacks built on sand, with nothing around it but spindly spruce trees. "A month," I asked myself, "will that be long enough for me to become attached to the children or for the children to become attached to me? Will a month be worth the effort?"

Perhaps the same calculation was in the minds of the children who presented themselves at school that first day of June—"Is this teacher going to stay long enough to be worth the effort?" —for I had never seen children's faces so dejected, so apathetic, or perhaps sorrowful. I had had so little experience. I myself was hardly more than a child.

Nine o'clock came. The room was hot as an oven. Sometimes in Manitoba, especially in the sandy areas, an incredible heat settles in during the first days of June.

Scarcely knowing where or how to begin, I opened the attendance book and called the roll. The names were for the most part

202

very French and today they still return to my memory, like this, for no reason: Madeleine Bérubé, Josephat Brisset, Emilien Dumont, Cécile Lépine. . . .

But most of the children who rose and answered "Present, mamzelle," when their names were called had the slightly narrowed eyes, warm colouring and jet black hair that told of métis blood.

They were beautiful and exquisitely polite; there was really nothing to reproach them for except the inconceivable distance they maintained between themselves and me. It crushed me. "Is this what children are like then," I asked myself with anguish, "untouchable, barricaded in some region where you can't reach them?"

I came to the name Yolande Chartrand.

No one answered. It was becoming hotter by the minute. I wiped a bit of perspiration from my forehead. I repeated the name and, when there was still no answer, I looked up at faces that seemed to me completely indifferent.

Then from the back of the classroom, above the buzzing of flies, there arose a voice I at first couldn't place. "She's dead, mamzelle. She died last night."

Perhaps even more distressing than the news was the calm level tone of the child's voice. As I must have seemed unconvinced, all the children nodded gravely as if to say, "It's true."

Suddenly a sense of impotence greater than any I can remember weighed upon me.

"Ah," I said, lost for words.

"She's already laid out," said a boy with eyes like coals. "They're going to bury her for good tomorrow."

"Ah," I repeated.

The children seemed a little more relaxed now and willing to talk, in snatches and at long intervals.

A boy in the middle of the room offered, "She got worse the last two months."

We looked at one another in silence for a long time, the children and I. I now understood that the expression in their eyes that I had taken for indifference was a heavy sadness. Much like this stupefying heat. And we were only at the beginning of the day.

"Since Yolande . . . has been laid out," I suggested, "and she was your schoolmate . . . and would have been my pupil

. . . would you like . . . after school at four o'clock . . . for us to go and visit her?''

On the small, much too serious faces there appeared the trace of a smile, wary, still very sad but a sort of smile just the same.

"It's agreed then, we'll go to visit her, her whole class."

From that moment, despite the enervating heat and the sense that haunted us all, I feel sure, that human efforts are all ulti-mately destined to a sort of failure, the children fixed their attention as much as possible on what I was teaching and I did my best to rouse their interest.

At five past four I found most of them waiting for me at the door, a good twenty children but making no more noise than if they were being kept in after school. Several of them went ahead to show me the way. Others pressed around me so closely I could scarcely move. Five or six of the smaller ones took me by the hand or the shoulder and pulled me forward gently as if they were leading a blind person. They did not talk, merely held me enclosed in their circle.

Together, in this way, we followed a track through the sand. Here and there thin spruce trees formed little clumps. The air was now barely moving. In no time the village was behind us—forgotten, as it were.

We came to a wooden cabin standing in isolation among the little trees. Its door was wide open, so we were able to see the dead child from quite far off. She had been laid out on rough boards suspended between two straight chairs set back to back. There was nothing else in the room. Its usual contents must have been crowded into the only other room of the house for, besides a stove and table and a few pots on the floor, I could see a bed and a mattress piled with clothes. But no chairs. Clearly the two used as supports for the boards on which the dead child lay were the only ones in the house.

The parents had undoubtedly done all they could for their child. They had covered her with a clean sheet. They had given her a room to herself. Her mother, probably, had arranged her hair in the two very tight braids that framed the thin face. But some pressing need had sent them away: perhaps the purchase of a coffin in town or a few more boards to make her one them-selves. At any rate, the dead child was alone in the room that had been emptied for her—alone, that is to say, with the flies. A faint odour of death must have attracted them. I saw one with a blue body walk over her forehead. I immediately placed myself

near her head and began to move my hand back and forth to
drive the flies away.

The child had a delicate little face, very wasted, with the
serious expression I had seen on the faces of most of the children
here, as if the cares of the adults had crushed them all too early.
She might have been ten or eleven years old. If she had lived a
little longer, I reminded myself, she would have been one of my
pupils. She would have learned something from me. I would
have given her something to keep. A bond would have been
formed between me and this little stranger—who knows, perhaps
even for life.

As I contemplated the dead child, those words "for life"—as
if they implied a long existence—seemed to me the most rash
and foolish of all the expressions we use so lightly.

In death the child looked as if she were regretting some poor
little joy she had never known. I continued at least to prevent the
flies from settling upon her. The children were watching me. I
realized that they now expected everything from me, though I
didn't know much more than they and was just as confused. Still
I had a sort of inspiration.

"Don't you think Yolande would like to have someone with
her always till the time comes to commit her to the ground?"

The faces of the children told me I had struck the right note.

"We'll take turns then, four or five around her every two
hours, until the funeral."

They agreed with a glow in their dark eyes.

"We must be careful not to let the flies touch Yolande's
face."

They nodded to show they were in agreement. Standing around
me, they now felt a trust in me so complete it terrified me.

In a clearing among the spruce trees a short distance away, I
noticed a bright pink stain on the ground whose source I didn't
yet know. The sun slanted upon it, making it flame, the one
moment in this day that had been touched by a certain grace.

"What sort of girl was she?" I asked.

At first the children didn't understand. Then a boy of about
the same age said with tender seriousness, "She was smart,
Yolande."

The other children looked as if they agreed.

"And did she do well in school?"

"She didn't come very often this year. She was always being
absent."

"Our teacher before last this year said Yolande could have done well."

"How many teachers have you had this year?"

"You're the third, mamzelle. I guess the teachers find it too lonesome here."

"What did Yolande die of?"

"T.B., mamzelle," they replied with a single voice, as if this was the customary way for children to die around here.

They were eager to talk about her now. I had succeeded in opening the poor little doors deep within them that no one perhaps had ever much wanted to see opened. They told me moving facts about her brief life. One day on her way home from school—it was in February; no, said another, in March— she had lost her reader and wept inconsolably for weeks. To study her lesson after that, she had to borrow a book from one of the others—and I saw on the faces of some of them that they'd grudged lending their readers and would always regret this. Not having a dress for her first communion, she entreated till her mother finally made her one from the only curtain in the house: "the one from this room . . . a beautiful lace curtain, mamzelle."

"And did Yolande look pretty in her lace curtain dress?" I asked.

They all nodded deeply, in their eyes the memory of a pleasant image.

I studied the silent little face. A child who had loved books, solemnity and decorous attire. Then I glanced again at the astonishing splash of pink in the melancholy landscape. I realized suddenly that it was a mass of wild roses. In June they open in great sheets all over Manitoba, growing from the poorest soil. I felt some alleviation.

"Let's go and pick some roses for Yolande."

On the children's faces there appeared the same slow smile of gentle sadness I had seen when I suggested visiting the body.

In no time we were gathering roses. The children were not yet cheerful, far from that, but I could hear them at least talking to one another. A sort of rivalry had gripped them. Each vied to see who could pick the most roses or the brightest, those of a deep shade that was almost red.

From time to time one tugged at my sleeve, "Mamzelle, see the lovely one I've found!"

On our return we pulled them gently apart and scattered petals over the dead child. Soon only her face emerged from the pink drift. Then—how could this be?—it looked a little less forlorn.

The children formed a ring around their schoolmate and said of her without the bitter sadness of the morning, "She must have got to heaven by this time."

Or, "She must be happy now."

I listened to them, already consoling themselves as best they could for being alive.

But why, oh why, did the memory of that dead child seek me out today in the very midst of the summer that sang?

Was it brought to me just now by the wind with the scent of roses?

A scent I have not much liked since the long ago June when I went to that poorest of villages—to acquire, as they say, experience.

THE LOST SALT GIFT
OF BLOOD
by Alistair McLeod

Now in the early evening the sun is flashing everything in gold. It bathes the blunt grey rocks that loom yearningly out toward Europe and it touches upon the stunted spruce and the low-lying lichens and the delicate hardy ferns and the ganglia-rooted moss and the tiny tough rock cranberries. The grey and slanting rain squalls have swept in from the sea and then departed with all the suddenness of surprise marauders. Everything before them and beneath them has been rapidly, briefly, and thoroughly drenched and now the clear droplets catch and hold the sun's infusion in a myriad of rainbow colours. Far beyond the harbour's mouth more tiny squalls seem to be forming, moving rapidly across the surface of the sea out there beyond land's end where the blue ocean turns to grey in rain and distance and the strain of eyes. Even farther out, somewhere beyond Cape Spear, lies Dublin and the Irish coast; far away but still the nearest land and closer now than is Toronto or Detroit to say nothing of North America's more western cities; seeming almost hazily visible now in imagination's mist.

Overhead the ivory white gulls wheel and cry, flashing also in the purity of the sun and the clean, freshly washed air. Sometimes they glide to the blue-green surface of the harbour, squawking and garbling; at times almost standing on their pink webbed feet as if they would walk on water, flapping their wings pompously against their breasts like over-conditioned he-men who have successfully passed their body-building courses. At other times they gather in lazy groups on the rocks above the harbour's entrance murmuring softly to themselves or looking also quietly out toward what must be Ireland and the vastness of the sea.

The harbour itself is very small and softly curving, seeming like a tiny, peaceful womb nurturing the life that now lies within it but which originated from without; came from without and through the narrow, rock-tight channel that admits the entering and withdrawing sea. That sea is entering again now, forcing itself gently but inevitably through the tightness of the opening and laving the rocky walls and rising and rolling into the harbour's inner cove. The dories rise at their moorings and the tide laps higher on the piles and advances upward toward the high-water marks upon the land; the running moon-drawn tides of spring.

Around the edges of the harbour brightly coloured houses dot the wet and glistening rocks. In some ways they seem almost like defiantly optimistic horseshoe nails: yellow and scarlet and green and pink; buoyantly yet firmly permanent in the grey unsundered rock.

At the harbour's entrance the small boys are jigging for the beautifully speckled salmon-pink sea trout. Barefootedly they stand on the tide-wet rocks flicking their wrists and sending their glistening lines in shimmering golden arcs out into the rising tide. Their voices mount excitedly as they shout to one another encouragement, advice, consolation. The trout fleck dazzlingly on their sides as they are drawn toward the rocks, turning to seeming silver as they flash within the sea.

It is all of this that I see now, standing at the final road's end of my twenty-five-hundred-mile journey. The road ends here— quite literally ends at the door of a now abandoned fishing shanty some six brief yards in front of where I stand. The shanty is grey and weatherbeaten with two boarded-up windows, vanishing wind-whipped shingles and a heavy rusted padlock chained fast to a twisted door. Piled before the twisted door and its equally twisted frame are some marker buoys, a small pile of rotted rope, a broken oar and an old and rust-flaked anchor.

The option of driving my small rented Volkswagen the remaining six yards and then negotiating a tight many-twists-of-the-steering-wheel turn still exists. I would be then facing toward the west and could simply retrace the manner of my coming. I could easily drive away before anything might begin.

Instead I walk beyond the road's end and the fishing shanty and begin to descend the rocky path that winds tortuously and narrowly along and down the cliff's edge to the sea. The small stones roll and turn and scrape beside and beneath my shoes and after only a few steps the leather is nicked and scratched. My toes press hard against its straining surface.

As I approach the actual water's edge four small boys are jumping excitedly upon the glistening rocks. One of them has made a strike and is attempting to reel in his silver-turning prize. The other three have laid down their rods in their enthusiasm and are shouting encouragement and giving almost physical moral support: "Don't let him get away, John," they say. "Keep the line steady." "Hold the end of the rod up." "Reel in the slack." "Good." "What a dandy!"

Across the harbour's clear water another six or seven shout the same delirious messages. The silver-turning fish is drawn toward the rock. In the shallows he flips and arcs, his flashing body breaking the water's surface as he walks upon his tail. The small fisherman has now his rod almost completely vertical. Its tip sings and vibrates high above his head while at his feet the trout spins and curves. Both of his hands are clenched around the rod and his knuckles strain white through the water-roughened redness of small-boy hands. He does not know whether he should relinquish the rod and grasp at the lurching trout or merely heave the rod backward and flip the fish behind him. Suddenly he decides upon the latter but even as he heaves his bare feet slide out from beneath him on the smooth wetness of the rock and he slips down into the water. With a pirouetting leap the trout turns glisteningly and tears itself free. In a darting flash of darkened greenness it rights itself within the regained water and is gone. "Oh damn!" says the small fisherman, struggling upright onto his rock. He bites his lower lip to hold back the tears welling within his eyes. There is a small trickle of blood coursing down from a tiny scratch on the inside of his wrist and he is wet up to his knees. I reach down to retrieve the rod and return it to him.

Suddenly a shout rises from the opposite shore. Another line zings tautly through the water throwing off fine showers of iridescent droplets. The shouts and contagious excitement spread anew. "Don't let him get away!" "Good for you." "Hang on!" "Hang on!"

I am caught up in it myself and wish also to shout some enthusiastic advice but I do not know what to say. The trout curves up from the water in a wriggling arch and lands behind the boys in the moss and lichen that grow down to the sea-washed rocks. They race to free it from the line and proclaim about its size.

On our side of the harbour the boys begin to talk. "Where do you live?" they ask and is it far away and is it bigger than St. John's? Awkwardly I try to tell them the nature of the North American midwest. In turn I ask them if they go to school. "Yes," they say. Some of them go to St. Bonaventure's which is the Catholic school and others go to Twilling Memorial. They are all in either grade four or grade five. All of them say that they like school and that they like their teachers.

The fishing is good they say and they come here almost every evening. "Yesterday I caught me a nine-pounder," says John. Eagerly they show me all of their simple equipment. The rods are of all varieties as are the lines. At the lines' ends the leaders are thin transparencies terminating in grotesque three-clustered hooks. A foot or so from each hook there is a silver spike knotted into the leader. Some of the boys say the trout are attracted by the flashing of the spike; others say that it acts only as a weight or sinker. No line is without one.

"Here, sir," says John, "have a go. Don't get your shoes wet." Standing on the slippery rocks in my smooth-soled shoes I twice attempt awkward casts. Both times the line loops up too high and the spike splashes down far short of the running, rising life of the channel.

"Just a flick of the wrist, sir," he says, "just a flick of the wrist. You'll soon get the hang of it." His hair is red and curly and his face is splashed with freckles and his eyes are clear and blue. I attempt three or four more casts and then pass the rod back to the hands where it belongs.

And now it is time for supper. The calls float down from the women standing in the doorways of the multicoloured houses and obediently the small fishermen gather up their equipment and their catches and prepare to ascend the narrow upward-winding paths. The sun has descended deeper into the sea and the evening has become quite cool. I recognize this with surprise and a slight shiver. In spite of the advice given to me and my own precautions my feet are wet and chilled within my shoes. No place to be unless barefooted or in rubber boots. Perhaps for me no place at all.

As we lean into the steepness of the path my young companions continue to talk, their accents broad and Irish. One of them used to have a tame sea gull at his house, had it for seven years. His older brother found it on the rocks and brought it home. His grandfather called it Joey. "Because it talked so much," explains John. It died last week and they held a funeral about a mile away from the shore where there was enough soil to dig a grave. Along the shore itself it is almost solid rock and there is no ground for a grave. It's the same with people they say. All week they have been hopefully looking along the base of the cliffs for another sea gull but have not found one. You cannot kill a sea gull they say, the government protects them because they are scavengers and keep the harbours clean.

The path is narrow and we walk in single file. By the time we reach the shanty and my rented car I am wheezing and badly out of breath. So badly out of shape for a man of thirty-three; sauna baths do nothing for your wind. The boys walk easily, laughing and talking beside me. With polite enthusiasm they comment upon my car. Again there exists the possibility of restarting the car's engine and driving back the road that I have come. After all, I have not seen a single adult except for the women calling down the news of supper. I stand and fiddle with my keys.

The appearance of the man and the dog is sudden and unexpected. We have been so casual and unaware in front of the small automobile that we have neither seen nor heard their approach along the rock-worn road. The dog is short, stocky and black and white. White hair floats and feathers freely from his sturdy legs and paws as he trots along the rock looking expectantly out into the harbour. He takes no notice of me. The man is short and stocky as well and he also appears as black and white. His rubber boots are black and his dark heavy worsted trousers are supported by a broadly scarred and blackened belt. The buckle is shaped like a dory with a fisherman standing in the bow. Above the belt there is a dark navy woollen jersey and upon his head a toque of the same material. His hair beneath the toque is white as is the three-or-four-day stubble on his face. His eyes are blue and his hands heavy, gnarled, and misshapen. It is hard to tell from looking at him whether he is in his sixties, seventies, or eighties.

"Well, it is a nice evening tonight," he says, looking first at John and then to me. "The barometer has not dropped so perhaps fair weather will continue for a day or two. It will be good for the fishing."

He picks a piece of gnarled grey driftwood from the roadside and swings it slowly back and forth in his right hand. With desperate anticipation the dog dances back and forth before him, his intense eyes glittering at the stick. When it is thrown into the harbour he barks joyously and disappears, hurling himself down the bank in a scrambling avalanche of small stones. In seconds he reappears with only his head visible, cutting a silent but rapidly advancing *V* through the quiet serenity of the harbour. The boys run to the bank's edge and shout encouragement to him—much as they had been doing earlier for one another. "It's farther out," they cry, "to the right, to the right." Almost totally submerged, he cannot see the stick he swims to find. The boys toss stones in its general direction and he raises himself out of the water to see their landing splashdowns and to change his wide-waked course.

"How have you been?" asks the old man, reaching for a pipe and a pouch of tobacco and then without waiting for an answer, "perhaps you'll stay for supper. There are just the three of us now."

We begin to walk along the road in the direction that he has come. Before long the boys rejoin us accompanied by the dripping dog with the recovered stick. He waits for the old man to take it from him and then showers us all with a spray of water from his shaggy coat. The man pats and scratches the damp head and the dripping ears. He keeps the returned stick and thwacks it against his rubber boots as we continue to walk along the rocky road I have so recently travelled in my Volkswagen.

Within a few yards the houses begin to appear upon our left. Frame and flat-roofed, they cling to the rocks looking down into the harbour. In storms their windows are splashed by the sea but now their bright colours are buoyantly brave in the shadows of the descending dusk. At the third gate, John, the man, and the dog turn in. I follow them. The remaining boys continue on; they wave and say, "So long."

The path that leads through the narrow whitewashed gate has had its stone worn smooth by the passing of countless feet. On either side there is a row of small, smooth stones, also neatly whitewashed, and seeming like a procession of large white eggs or tiny unbaked loaves of bread. Beyond these stones and also on either side, ther are some cast-off tires also whitewashed and serving as flower beds. Within each whitened circumference the colourful low-lying flowers nod; some hardy strain of pansies or perhaps marigolds.T he path leads on to the square green house, with its white borders and shutters. On one side of the wooden doorstep a skate blade has been nailed, for the wiping off of feet, and beyond the swinging screen door there is a porch which

smells saltily of the sea. A variety of sou'westers and rubber
boots and mitts and caps hang from the driven nails or lie at the
base of the wooden walls.

Beyond the porch there is the kitchen where the woman is at
work. All of us enter. The dog walks across the linoleum-covered
floor, his nails clacking, and flings himself with a contented sigh
beneath the wooden table. Almost instantly he is asleep, his coat
still wet from his swim within the sea.

The kitchen is small. It has an iron cookstove, a table against
one wall and three or four handmade chairs of wood. There is
also a wooden rocking-chair covered by a cushion. The rockers
are so thin from years of use that it is hard to believe they still
function. Close by the table there is a wash-stand with two pails
of water upon it. A wash-basin hangs from a driven nail in its
side and above it is an old-fashioned mirrored medicine cabinet.
There is also a large cupboard, a low-lying couch, and a window
facing upon the sea. On the walls a barometer hangs as well as
two pictures, one of a rather jaunty young couple taken many
years ago. It is yellowed and rather indistinct; the woman in a
long dress with her hair done up in ringlets, the man in a serge
suit that is slightly too large for him and with a tweed cap pulled
rakishly over his right eye. He has an accordion strapped over
his shoulders and his hands are fanned out on the buttons and
keys. The other picture is of the Christ-child. Beneath it is
written, "Sweet Heart of Jesus Pray for Us."

The woman at the stove is tall and fine featured. Her grey hair
is combed briskly back from her forehead and neatly coiled with
a large pin at the base of her neck. Her eyes are as grey as the
storm scud of the sea. Her age, like her husband's, is difficult to
guess. She wears a blue print dress, a plain blue apron and
low-heeled brown shoes. She is turning fish within a frying pan
when we enter.

Her eyes contain only mild surprise as she first regards me.
Then with recognition they glow in open hostility which in turn
subsides and yields to self-control. She continues at the stove
while the rest of us sit upon the chairs.

During the meal that follows we are reserved and shy in our
lonely adult ways; groping for and protecting what perhaps may
be the only awful dignity we possess. John, unheedingly, talks
on and on. He is in the fifth grade and is doing well. They are
learning percentages and the mysteries of decimals; to change a
percent to a decimal fraction you move the decimal point two

places to the left and drop the percent sign. You always, always do so. They are learning the different breeds of domestic animals: the four main breeds of dairy cattle are Holstein, Ayrshire, Guernsey, and Jersey. He can play the mouth organ and will demonstrate after supper. He has twelve lobster traps of his own. They were originally broken ones thrown up on the rocky shore by storms. Ira, he says nodding toward the old man, helped him fix them, nailing on new lathes and knitting new headings. Now they are set along the rocks near the harbour's entrance. He is averaging a pound a trap and the "big" fishermen say that that is better than some of them are doing. He is saving his money in a little imitation keg that was also washed up on the shore. He would like to buy an outboard motor for the small reconditioned skiff he now uses to visit his traps. At present he has only oars.

"John here has the makings of a good fisherman," says the old man. "He's up at five most every morning when I am putting on the fire. He and the dog are already out along the shore and back before I've made tea."

"When I was in Toronto," says John, "no one was ever up before seven. I would make my own tea and wait. It was wonderful sad. There were gulls there though, flying over Toronto harbour. We went to see them on two Sundays."

After the supper we move the chairs back from the table. The woman clears away the dishes and the old man turns on the radio. First he listens to the weather forecast and then turns to short wave where he picks up the conversations from the offshore fishing boats. They are conversations of catches and winds and tides and of the women left behind on the rocky shores. John appears with his mouth organ, standing at a respectful distance. The old man notices him, nods, and shuts off the radio. Rising, he goes upstairs, the sound of his feet echoing down to us. Returning he carries an old and battered accordion. "My fingers have so much rheumatism," he says, "that I find it hard to play anymore."

Seated, he slips his arms through the straps and begins the squeezing accordion motions. His wife takes off her apron and stands behind him with one hand upon his shoulder. For a moment they take on the essence of the once young people in the photograph. They begin to sing:

> Come all ye fair and tender ladies
> Take warning how you court your men

They're like the stars on a summer's morning
First they'll appear and then they're gone.

I wish I were a tiny sparrow
And I had wings and I could fly
I'd fly away to my own true lover
And all he'd ask I would deny.

Alas I'm not a tiny sparrow
I have not wings nor can I fly
And on this earth in grief and sorrow
I am bound until I die.

John sits on one of the home-made chairs playing his mouth
organ. He seems as all mouth-organ players the world over: his
right foot tapping out the measures and his small shoulders now
round and hunched above the cupped hand instrument.

"Come now and sing with us, John," says the old man.

Obediently he takes the mouth organ from his mouth and
shakes the moisture drops upon his sleeve. All three of them
begin to sing, spanning easily the half century of time that
touches their extremes. The old and the young singing now their
songs of loss in different comprehensions. Stranded here, alien
of my middle generation, I tap my leather foot self-consciously
upon the linoleum. The words sweep up and swirl about my
head. Fog does not touch like snow yet it is more heavy and
more dense. Oh moisture comes in many forms!

All alone as I strayed by the banks of the river
Watching the moonbeams at evening of day
All alone as I wandered I spied a young stranger
Weeping and wailing with many a sigh.

Weeping for one who is now lying lonely
Weeping for one who no mortal can save
As the foaming dark waters flow silently past him
Onward they flow over young Jenny's grave.

Oh Jenny my darling come tarry here with me
Don't leave me alone, love, distracted in pain
For as death is the dagger that plied us usunder
Wide is the gulf, love, between you and I.

* * *

After the singing stops we all sit rather uncomfortably for a moment. The mood seeming to hang heavily upon our shoulders. Then with my single exception all come suddenly to action. John gets up and takes his battered school books to the kitchen table. The dog jumps up on a chair beside him and watches solemnly in a supervisory manner. The woman takes some navy yarn the colour of her husband's jersey and begins to knit. She is making another jersey and is working on the sleeve. The old man rises and beckons me to follow him into the tiny parlour. The stuffed furniture is old and worn. There is a tiny wood-burning heater in the centre of the room. It stands on a square of galvanized metal which protects the floor from falling, burning coals. The stovepipe rises and vanishes into the wall on its way to the upstairs. There is an old-fashioned mantelpiece on the wall behind the stove. It is covered with odd shapes of driftwood from the shore and a variety of exotically shaped bottles, blue and green and red, which are from the shore as well. There are pictures here too: of the couple in the other picture; and one of them with their five daughters; and one of the five daughters by themselves. In that far-off picture time all of the daughters seem roughly between the ages of ten and eighteen. The youngest has the reddest hair of all. So red that it seems to triumph over the non-photographic colours of lonely black and white. The pictures are in standard wooden frames.

From behind the ancient chesterfield the old man pulls a collapsible card table and pulls down its warped and shaky legs. Also from behind the chesterfield he takes a faded checkerboard and a large old-fashioned matchbox of rattling wooden checkers. The spine of the board is almost cracked through and is strengthened by layers of adhesive tape. The checkers are circumferences of wood sawed from a length of broom handle. They are about three quarters of an inch thick. Half of them are painted a very bright blue and the other half an equally eye-catching red. "John made these," says the old man, "all of them are not really the same thickness but they are good enough. He gave it a good try."

We begin to play checkers. He takes the blue and I the red. The house is silent with only the click-clack of the knitting needles sounding through the quiet rooms. From time to time the old man lights his pipe, digging out the old ashes with a flattened nail and tamping in the fresh tobacco with the same nail's head.

The blue smoke winds lazily and haphazardly toward the low-beamed ceiling. The game is solemn as is the next and then the next. Neither of us loses all of the time.

"It is time for some of us to be in bed," says the old woman after a while. She gathers up her knitting and rises from her chair. In the kitchen John neatly stacks his school books on one corner of the table in anticipation of the morning. He goes outside for a moment and then returns. Saying good-night very formally he goes up the stairs to bed. In a short while the old woman follows, her footsteps travelling the same route.

We continue to play our checkers, wreathed in smoke and only partially aware of the muffled footfalls sounding softly above our heads.

When the old man gets up to go outside I am not really surprised, any more than I am when he returns with the brown, ostensible vinegar jug. Poking at the declining kitchen fire, he moves the kettle about seeking the warmest spot on the cooling stove. He takes two glasses from the cupboard, a sugar bowl and two spoons. The kettle begins to boil.

Even before tasting it, I know the rum to be strong and overproof. It comes at night and in fog from the French islands of St. Pierre and Miquelon. Coming over in the low-throttled fishing boats, riding in imitation gas cans. He mixes the rum and the sugar first, watching them marry and dissolve. Then to prevent the breakage of the glasses he places a teaspoon in each and adds the boiling water. The odour rises richly, its sweetness hung in steam. He brings the glasses to the table, holding them by their tops so that his fingers will not burn.

We do not say anything for some time, sitting upon the chairs, while the sweetened, heated richness moves warmly through and from our stomachs and spreads upward to our brains. Outside the wind begins to blow, moaning and faintly rattling the window's whitened shutters. He rises and brings refills. We are warm within the dark and still within the wind. A clock strikes regularly the strokes of ten.

It is difficult to talk at times with or without liquor; difficult to achieve the actual act of saying. Sitting still we listen further to the rattle of the wind; not knowing where nor how we should begin. Again the glasses are refilled.

"When she married in Toronto," he says at last, "we figured that maybe John should be with her and with her husband. That maybe he would be having more of a chance there in the city.

But we would be putting it off and it weren't until nigh on two years ago that he went. Went with a woman from down the cove going to visit her daughter. Well, what was wrong was that we missed him wonderful awful. More fearful than we ever thought. Even the dog. Just pacing the floor and looking out the window and walking along the rocks of the shore. Like us had no moorings, lost in the fog or on the ice-floes in a snow squall. Nigh sick unto our hearts we was. Even the grandmother who before that was maybe thinking small to herself that he was trouble in her old age. Ourselves having never had no sons only daughters."

He pauses, then rising goes upstairs and returns with an envelope. From it he takes a picture which shows two young people standing self-consciously before a half-ton pickup with a wooden extension ladder fastened to its side. They appear to be in their middle twenties. The door of the truck has the information: "Jim Farrell, Toronto: Housepainting, Eavestroughing, Aluminum Siding, Phone 535-3484," lettered on its surface.

"This was in the last letter," he says. "That Farrell I guess was a nice enough fellow, from Heartsick Bay he was.

"Anyway they could have no more peace with John than we could without him. Like I says he was here too long before his going and it all took ahold of us the way it will. They sent word that he was coming on the plane to St. John's with a woman they'd met through a Newfoundland club. I was to go to St. John's to meet him. Well, it was all wrong the night before the going. The signs all bad; the grandmother knocked off the lampshade and it broke in a hunnerd pieces—the sign of death; and the window blind fell and clattered there on the floor and then lied still. And the dog runned around like he was crazy, moanen and cryen worse than the swiles does out on the ice, and throwen hisself against the walls and jumpen on the table and at the window where the blind fell until we would have to be letten him out. But it be no better for he runned and throwed hisself in the sea and then come back and howled outside the same window and jumped against the wall, splashen the water from his coat all over it. Then he be runnen back to the sea again. All the neighbours heard him and said I should bide at home and not go to St. John's at all. We be all wonderful scared and not know what to do and the next mornen, first thing I drops me knife.

"But still I feels I has to go. It be foggy all the day and everyone be thinken the plane won't come or be able to land.

And I says, small to myself, now here in the fog be the bad luck and the death but then there the plane be, almost like a ghost ship comen out the fog with all its lights shinen. I think maybe he won't be on it but soon he comen through the fog, first with the woman and then see'n me and starten to run, closer and closer till I can feel him in me arms and the tears on both our cheeks. Powerful strange how things will take one. That night they be killed."

From the envelope that contained the picture he draws forth a tattered clipping:

Jennifer Farrell of Roncesvalles Avenue was instantly killed early this morning and her husband James died later in emergency at St. Joseph's Hospital. The accident occurred about 2 A.M. when the pickup truck in which they were travelling went out of control on Queen St. W. and struck a utility pole. It is thought that bad visibility caused by a heavy fog may have contributed to the accident. The Farrells were originally from Newfoundland.

Again he moves to refill the glasses. "We be all alone," he says. "All our other daughters married and far away in Montreal, Toronto, or the States. Hard for them to come back here, even to visit; they comes only every three years or so for perhaps a week. So we be hav'n only him."

And now my head begins to reel even as I move to the filling of my own glass. Not waiting this time for the courtesy of his offer. Making myself perhaps too much at home with this man's glass and this man's rum and this man's house and all the feelings of his love. Even as I did before. Still locked again for words.

Outside we stand and urinate, turning our backs to the seeming gale so as not to splash our wind-snapped trousers. We are almost driven forward to rock upon our toes and settle on our heels, so blow the gusts. Yet in spite of all, the stars shine clearly down. It will indeed be a good day for the fishing and this wind eventually will calm. The salt hangs heavy in the air and the water booms against the rugged rocks. I take a stone and throw it against the wind into the sea.

Going up the stairs we clutch the wooden bannister unsteadily and say good-night.

The room has changed very little. The window rattles in the

wind and the unfinished beams sway and creak. The room is full of sound. Like a foolish Lockwood I approach the window although I hear no voice. There is no Catherine who cries to be let in. Standing unsteadily on one foot when required I manage to undress, draping my trousers across the wooden chair. The bed is clean. It makes no sound. It is plain and wooden, its mattress stuffed with hay or kelp. I feel it with my hand and pull back the heavy patchwork quilts. Still I do not go into it. Instead I go back to the door which has no knob but only an ingenious latch formed from a twisted nail. Turning it, I go out into the hallway. All is dark and the house seems even more inclined to creak where there is no window. Feeling along the wall with my outstretched hand I find the door quite easily. It is closed with the same kind of latch and not difficult to open. But no one waits on the other side. I stand and bend my ear to hear the even sound of my one son's sleeping. He does not beckon any more than the nonexistent voice in the outside wind. I hesitate to touch the latch for fear that I may waken him and disturb his dreams. And if I did what would I say? Yet I would like to see him in his sleep this once and see the room with the quiet bed once more and the wooden chair beside it from off an old wrecked trawler. There is no boiled egg or shaker of salt or glass of water waiting on the chair within this closed room's darkness.

Once though there was a belief held in the outports, that if a girl would see her own true lover she should boil an egg and scoop out half the shell and fill it with salt. Then she should take it to bed with her and eat it, leaving a glass of water by her bedside. In the night her future husband or a vision of him would appear and offer her the glass. But she must only do it once.

It is the type of belief that bright young graduate students were collecting eleven years ago for the theses and archives of North America and also, they hoped, for their own fame. Even as they sought the near-Elizabethan songs and ballads that had sailed from County Kerry and from Devon and Cornwall. All about the wild, wide sea and the flashing silver dagger and the lost and faithless lover. Echoes to and from the lovely, lonely hills and glens of West Virginia and the standing stones of Tennessee.

Across the hall the old people are asleep. The old man's snoring rattles as do the windows; except that now and then there are catching gasps within his breath. In three or four short hours he will be awake and will go down to light his fire. I turn and walk back softly to my room.

Within hre bed the warm sweetness of the rum is heavy and intense. The darkness presses down upon me but still it brings no sleep. There are no voices and no shadows that are real. There are only walls of memory touched restlessly by flickers of imagination.

Oh I would like to see my way more clearly. I, who have never understood the mystery of fog. I would perhaps like to capture it in a jar like the beautiful childhood butterflies that always die in spite of the airholes punched with nails in the covers of their captivity—leaving behind the vapours of their lives and deaths; or perhaps as the unknowing child who collects the grey moist condoms from the lovers' lanes only to have them taken from him and to be told to wash his hands. Oh I have collected many things I did not understand.

And perhaps now I should go and say, oh son of my *summa cum laude* loins, come away from the lonely gulls and the silver trout and I will take you to the land of the Tastee Freeze where you may sleep till ten of nine. And I will show you the elevator to the apartment on the sixteenth floor and introduce you to the buzzer system and the yards of the wrought-iron fences where the Doberman pinscher runs silently at night. Or may I offer you the money that is the fruit of my collecting and my most success-ful life? Or shall I wait to meet you in some known or unknown bitterness like Yeats's Cuchulain by the wind-whipped sea or as Sohrab and Rustum by the future flowing river?

Again I collect dreams. For I do not know enough of the fog on Toronto's Queen St. West and the grinding crash of the pickup and of lost and misplaced love.

I am up early in the morning as the man kindles the fire from the driftwood splinters. The outside light is breaking and the wind is calm. John tumbles down the stairs. Scarcely stopping to splash his face and pull on his jacket, he is gone, accompanied by the dog. The old man smokes his pipe and waits for the water to boil. When it does he pours some into the teapot then passes the kettle to me. I take it to the wash-stand and fill the small tin basin in readiness for my shaving. My face looks back from the mirrored cabinet. The woman softly descends the stairs.

"I think I will go back today," I say while looking into the mirror at my face and at those in the room behind me. I try to emphasize the "I." "I just thought I would like to make this trip—again. I think I can leave the car in St. John's and fly back directly." The woman begins to move about the table, setting out the round white plates. The man quietly tamps his pipe.

The door opens and John and the dog return. They have been down along the shore to see what has happened throughout the night. "Well, John," says the old man, "what did you find?"

He opens his hand to reveal a smooth round stone. It is of the deepest green inlaid with veins of darkest ebony. It has been worn and polished by the unrelenting restlessness of the sea and buffed and burnished by the gravelled sand. All of its inadequacies have been removed and it glows with the lustre of near perfection.

"It is very beautiful," I say.

"Yes," he says, "I like to collect them." Suddenly he looks up into my eyes and thrusts the stone toward me. "Here," he says, "would you like to have it?"

Even as I reach out my hand I turn my head to the others in the room. They are both looking out through the window to the sea.

"Why, thank you," I say. "Thank you very much. Yes, I would. Thank you. Thanks." I take it from his outstretched hand and place it in my pocket.

We eat our breakfast in near silence. After it is finished the boy and dog go out once more. I prepare to leave.

"Well, I must go," I say, hesitating at the door. "It will take me a while to get to St. John's." I offer my hand to the man. He takes it in his strong fingers and shakes it firmly.

"Thank you," says the woman. "I don't know if you know what I mean but thank you."

"I think I do," I say. I stand and fiddle with the keys. "I would somehow like to help or keep in touch but . . ."

"But there is no phone," he says, "and both of us can hardly write. Perhaps that's why we never told you. John is getting to be a pretty good hand at it though."

"Good-bye," we say again, "good-bye, good-bye."

The sun is shining clearly now and the small boats are putt-putting about the harbour. I enter my unlocked car and start its engine. The gravel turns beneath the wheels. I pass the house and wave to the man and woman standing in the yard.

On a distant cliff the children are shouting. Their voices carol down through the sun-washed air and the dogs are curving and dancing about them in excited circles. They are carrying something that looks like a crippled gull. Perhaps they will make it well. I toot the horn. "Good-bye," they shout and wave, "good-bye, good-bye."

The airport terminal is strangely familiar. A symbol of impermanence, it is itself glisteningly permanent. Its formica surfaces have been designed to stay. At the counter a middle-aged man in mock exasperation is explaining to the girl that it is Newark he wishes to go to, *not* New York.

There are not many of us and soon we are ticketed and lifting through and above the sun-shot fog. The meals are served in tinfoil and in plastic. We eat above the clouds looking at the tips of wings.

The man beside me is a heavy-equipment salesman who has been trying to make a sale to the developers of Labrador's resources. He has been away a week and is returning to his wife and children.

Later in the day we land in the middle of the continent. Because of the changing time zones the distance we have come seems eerily unreal. The heat shimmers in little waves upon the runway. This is the equipment salesman's final destination while for me it is but the place where I must change flights to continue even farther into the heartland. Still we go down the wheeled-up stairs together, donning our sunglasses, and stepping across the heated concrete and through the terminal's electronic doors. The salesman's wife stands waiting along with two small children who are the first to see him. They race toward him with their arms outstretched. "Daddy, Daddy," they cry, "what did you bring me? What did you bring me?"

THE END OF THE WORLD
by Mavis Gallant

I never like to leave Canada, because I'm disappointed every time. I've felt disappointed about places I haven't even seen. My wife went to Florida with her mother once. When they arrived there, they met some neighbors from home who told them about a sign saying "No Canadians." They never saw this sign anywhere, but they kept hearing about others who did, or whose friends had seen it, always in different places, and it spoiled their trip for them. Many people, like them, have never come across it but have heard about it, so it must be there somewhere. Another time I had to go and look after my brother Kenny in Buffalo. He had stolen a credit card and was being deported on that account. I went down to vouch for him and pay up for him and bring him home. Neither of us cared for Buffalo.

"What have they got here that's so marvellous?" I said.

"Proust," said Kenny.

"What?"

"Memorabilia," he said. He was reading it off a piece of paper.

"Why does a guy with your education do a dumb thing like swiping a credit card?" I said.

"Does Mother know?" said Kenny.

"Mum knows, and Lou knows, and I know, and Beryl knows. It was in the papers, 'Kenneth Apostolesco, of this city . . .' "

"I'd better stay away," my brother said.

"No, you'd better not, for Mum's sake. We've only got one mother."

"Thank God," he said. "Only one of each. One mother and one father. If I had more than one of each, I think I'd still be running."

It was our father who ran, actually. He deserted us during the

225

last war. He joined the Queen's Own Rifles, which wasn't a Montreal regiment—he couldn't do anything like other people, couldn't even join up like anyone else—and after the war he just chose to go his own way. I saw him downtown in Montreal one time after the war. I was around twelve, delivering prescriptions for a drugstore. I knew him before he knew me. He looked the way he had always managed to look, as if he had all the time in the world. His mouth was drawn in, like an old woman's, but he still had his coal black hair. I wish we had his looks. I leaned my bike with one foot on the curb and he came down and stood by me, rocking on his feet, like a dancer, and looking off over my head. He said he was night watchman at a bank and that he was waiting for the Army to fix him up with some teeth. He'd had all his teeth out, though there wasn't anything wrong with them. He was eligible for new ones provided he put in a claim that year, so he though he might as well. He was a bartender by profession, but he wasn't applying for anything till he'd got his new teeth. "I've told them to hurry it up," he said. "I can't go round to good places all gummy." He didn't ask how anyone was at home.

I had to leave Canada to be with my father when he died. I was the person they sent for, though I was the youngest. My name was on the back page of his passport: "In case of accident or death notify WILLIAM APOSTOLESCO. Relationship: Son." I was the one he picked. He'd been barman on a ship for years by then, earning good money, but he had nothing put by. I guess he never expected his life would be finished. He collapsed with a lung hemorrhage, as far as I could make out, and they put him off at a port in France. I went there. That was where I saw him. This town had been shelled twenty years ago and a lot of it looked bare and new. I wouldn't say I hated it exactly, but I would never have come here of my own accord. It was worse than Buffalo in some ways. I didn't like the food or the coffee, and they never gave you anything you needed in the hotels—I had to go out and buy some decent towels. It didn't matter, because I had to buy everything for my father anyway—soap and towels and Kleenex. The hospital didn't provide a thing except the bedsheets, and when a pair of those was put on the bed it seemed to be put there once and for all. I was there twenty-three days and I think I saw the sheets changed once. Our grandfathers had been glad to get out of Europe. It took my father to go back. The hospital he was in was an old convent or monastery. The beds were so close together you could hardly get a chair between them. Women patients were always wandering around the men's wards, and although I wouldn't swear to it, I think some of them had their beds there, at the far end. The patients were given crocks of tepid water to wash in, not by their beds but on a long table in the middle of the ward. Anyone too sick to get up was just out of luck unless, like my father, he had someone to look after him. I saw beetles and cockroaches, and I said to myself, This is what a person gets for leaving home.

My father accepted my presence as if it were his right—as if he hadn't lost his claim to any consideration years ago. So as not to scare him, I pretended my wife's father had sent me here on business, but he hardly listened, so I didn't insist.

"Didn't you drive a cab one time or other?" he said. "What else have you done?"

I wanted to answer, "You know what I've been doing? I've been supporting your wife and educating your other children, practically singlehanded, since I was twelve."

I had expected to get here in time for his last words, which ought to have been "I'm sorry." I thought he would tell me where he wanted to be buried, how much money he owed, how many bastards he was leaving behind, and who was looking out for them. I imagined them in ports like this, with no-good mothers. *Somebody* should have been told—telling me didn't mean telling the whole world. One of the advantages of having an Old Country in the family is you can always say the relations that give you trouble have gone there. You just say, "He went back to the Old Country," and nobody asks any questions. So he could have told me the truth, and I'd have known and still not let the family down. But my father never confided anything. The trouble was he didn't know he was dying—he'd been told, in fact, he was getting better—so he didn't act like a dying man. He used what breath he had to say things like "I always liked old Lou," and you would have thought she was someone else's daughter, a girl he had hardly known. Another time he said, "Did Kenny do well for himself? I heard he went to college."

"Don't talk," I said.

"No, I mean it. I'd like to know how Kenny made out."

He couldn't speak above a whisper some days, and he was careful how he pronounced words. It wasn't a snobbish or an English accent—nothing that would make you grit your teeth. He just sounded like a stranger. When I was sent for, my mother said, "He's dying a pauper, after all his ideas. I hope he's satisfied." I didn't answer, but I said to myself, This isn't a question of satisfaction. I wanted to ask her, "Since you didn't get along with him and he didn't get along with you, what did you go and have three children for?" But those are the questions you keep to yourself.

"What's your wife like?" my father croaked. His eyes were interested. I hadn't been prepared for this, for how long the mind stayed alive and how frivolous it went on being. I thought he should be more serious. "*Wife*," my father insisted. "What about her?"

"Obedient" came into my head, I don't know why; it isn't important. "Older than me," I said, quite easily, at last. "Better educated. She was a kindergarten teacher. She knows a lot about art." Now, why that, of all the side issues? She doesn't like a bare wall, that's all. "She prefers the Old Masters," I said. I was thinking about the Scotch landscape we've got over the mantelpiece.

"Good, good. Name?"

"You know—*Beryl*. We sent you an announcement, to that place in Mexico where you were then."

"That's right. Beryl." "Burrull" was what he actually said.

I felt reassured, because my father until now had sounded like a strange person. To have "Beryl" pronounced as I was used to hearing it made up for being alone here and the smell of the ward and the coffee made of iodine. I remembered what the Old Master had cost—one hundred and eighty dollars in 1962. It must be worth more now. Beryl said it would be an investment. Her family paid for half. She said once, about my father, "One day he'll be sick; we'll have to look after him." "We can sell the painting," I said. "I guess I can take care of my own father."

It happened—I was here, taking care of him; but he spoiled it now by saying, "You look like you'd done pretty well. That's not a bad suit you've got on."

"Actually," I said, "I had to borrow from Beryl's father so as to get here."

I thought he would say, "Oh, I'm sorry," and I had my next answer ready about not begrudging a cent of it. But my father closed his eyes, smiling, saving up more breath to talk about nothing.

"I liked old Lou," he said distinctly. I was afraid he would ask, "Why doesn't she write to me?" and I would have to say, "Because she never forgave you," and he was perfectly capable of saying then, "Never forgave me for what?" But instead of that he laughed, which was the worst of the choking and wheezing noises he made now, and when he had recovered he said, "Took her to Eaton's to choose a toy village. Had this shipment in, last one in before the war. Summer '39. The old man saw the ad, wanted to get one for the kid. Old man came—each of us had her by the hand. Lou looked round, but every village had something the matter, as far as Her Royal Highness was concerned. The old man said, 'Come on, Princess, hurry it up,' but no, she'd of seen a scratch, or a bad paint job, or a chimney too big for a cottage. The old man said, 'Can't this kid make up her mind about anything? She's going to do a lot more crying than laughing,' he said, 'and that goes for you, too.' He was wrong about me. Don't know about Lou. But she was smart that time—not to want something that wasn't perfect."

He shut his eyes again and breathed desperately through his mouth. The old man in the story was his father, my grandfather.

"Nothing is perfect," I said. I felt like standing up so everyone could hear. It wasn't sourness but just the way I felt like reacting to my father's optimism.

Some days he seemed to be getting better. After two weeks I was starting to wonder if they hadn't brought me all this way for nothing. I couldn't go home and come back later, it had to be now; but I couldn't stay on and on. I had already moved to a cheaper hotel room. I dreamed I asked him, "How much longer?" but luckily the dream was in a foreign language—so foreign I don't think it was French, even. It was a language no one on earth had ever heard of. I wouldn't have wanted him to understand it, even in a dream. The nurses couldn't say anything. Sometimes I wondered if they knew who he was—if they could tell one patient from another. It was a big place, and poor. These nurses didn't seem to have much equipment. When they needed sterile water for anything, they had to boil it in an old saucepan. I got to the doctor one day, but he didn't like it. He had told my father he was fine, and that I could go back to Canada any time—the old boy must have been starting to wonder why I was staying so long. The doctor just said to me, "Family business is of no interest to me. You look after your duty and I'll look after mine." I was afraid that my dream showed on my face and that was what made them all so indifferent. I didn't know how much time there was. I wanted to ask my father why he thought everything had to be perfect, and if he still stood by it as a way of living. Whenever he was reproached about something—by my mother, for instance—he just said, "Don't make my life dark for me." What could you do? He certainly made her life dark for her. One year when we had a summer cottage, he took a girl from the village, the village tramp, out to an island in the middle of the lake. They got caught in a storm coming back, and around fifty people stood on shore waiting to see the canoe capsize and the sinners drown. My mother had told us to stay in the house, but when Kenny said, to scare me, "I guess the way things are, Mum's gone down there to drown herself," I ran after her. She didn't say anything to me, but took her raincoat off and draped it over my head. It would have been fine if my father had died then—if lightning had struck him, or the canoe gone down like a stone. But no, he waded ashore—the slut, too—and someone even gave her a blanket. It was my mother that was blamed, in a funny way. "Can't you keep your husband home?" this girl's father said. I remember that same summer some other woman saying to her, "You'd better keep your husband away from my daughter. I'm telling you for your own good, because my husband's got a gun in the house." Someone did say, "Oh, poor Mrs. Apostolesco!" but my mother only answered, "If you think that, then I'm poor for life." That was only one of the things he did to her. I'm not sure if it was even the worst.

It was hard to say how long he had been looking at me. His lips were trying to form a word. I bent close and heard, "Sponge."

"Did you say 'sponge'? Is 'sponge' what you said?"

"Sponge," he agreed. He made an effort: "Bad night last night. Awful. Wiped everything with my sponge—blood, spit. Need new sponge."

There wasn't a bed table, just a plastic bag that hung on the bedrail with his personal things in it. I got out the sponge. It needed to be thrown away, all right. I said, "What color?"

"Eh?"

"This," I said, and held it up in front of him. "The new one. Any special color?"

"Blue." His voice broke out of a whisper all at once. His eyes were mocking me, like a kid seeing how far he can go. I thought he would thank me now, but then I said to myself, You can't expect anything; he's a sick man, and he was always like this.

"Most people think it was pretty good of me to have come here," I wanted to explain—not to boast or anything, but just for the sake of conversation. I was lonely there, and I had so much trouble understanding what anybody was saying.

"Bad night," my father whispered. "Need sedation."

"I know. I tried to tell the doctor. I guess he doesn't understand my French."

He moved his head. "Tip the nurses."

"You don't mean it!"

"Don't make me talk." He seemed to be using a reserve of breath. "At least twenty dollars. The ward girls less."

I said, "Jesus God!" because this was new to me and I felt out of my depth. "They don't bother much with you," I said, talking myself into doing it. "Maybe you're right. If I gave them a present, they'd look after you more. Wash you. Maybe they'd put a screen around you—you'd be more private then."

"No, thanks," my father said. "No screen. Thanks all the same."

We had one more conversation after that. I've already said there were always women slopping around in the ward, in felt slippers, and bathrobes stained with medicine and tea. I came in and found one—quite young, this one was—combing my father's hair. He could hardly lift his head from the pillow, and still she thought he was interesting. I thought, Kenny should see this.

"She's been telling me," my father gasped when the woman had left. "About herself. Three children by different men. Met a North African. He adopts the children, all three. Gives them his name. She has two more by him, boys. But he won't put up with a sick woman. One day he just doesn't come. She's been a month in another place; now they've brought her here. Man's gone. Left the children. They've been put in all different homes, she doesn't know where. Five kids. Imagine."

I thought, You left us. He had forgotten; he had just simply forgotten that he'd left his own.

"Well, we can't do anything about her, can we?" I said. "She'll collect them when she gets out of here."

"If she gets out."

"That's no way to talk," I said. "Look at the way she was

talking and walking around . . ." I could not bring myself to
say, "and combing your hair." "Look at how *you* are," I said.
"You've just told me this long story."

"She'll seem better, but she'll get worse," my father said.
"She's like me, getting worse. Do you think I don't know what
kind of ward I'm in? Every time they put the screen around a
patient, it's because he's dying. If I had t.b., like they tried to
make me believe, I'd be in a t.b. hospital."

"That just isn't true," I said.

"Can you swear I've got t.b.? You can't."

I said without hesitating, "You've got a violent kind of t.b.
They had no place else to put you except here. The ward might
be crummy, but the medicine . . . the e dical care . . ." He
closed his eyes. "I'm looking you straight in the face," I said,
"and I swear you have this unusual kind of t.b., and you're
almost cured." I watched, without minding it now, a new kind
of bug crawling along the base of the wall.

"Thanks, Billy," said my father.

I really was scared. I had been waiting for something without
knowing what it would mean. I can tell you how it was: it was
like the end of the world. "I didn't realize you were worried," I
said. "You should of asked me right away."

"I knew you wouldn't lie to me," my father said. "That's
why I wanted you, not the others."

That was all. Not long after that he couldn't talk. He had
deserted the whole family once, but I was the one he abandoned
twice. When he died, a nurse said to me, "I am sorry." It had
no meaning, from her, yet only a few days before it was all I
thought I wanted to hear.

Magic, Symbols and Fantasies

THE SORCERER
by Roch Carrier
(translated by Sheila Fischman)

In the evening the bus came back from town. Sometimes it would stop and we'd watch a child from the village, as they used to say, who'd been away for a long time, get off with his suitcases and look around as though he had arrived in a foreign place.

The village was built on the side of a hill. Because of the difference in levels, we could lie in the grass on the slope and have our eyes at street level. Discreetly spreading the blades of grass, we could see without being seen. We could spy on life.

One evening the bus stopped in front of us. The powerful brakes gripped the steel of the wheels and made them shriek. The door opened and we saw shoes covered with grey spats on which broad striped trousers fell; the man placed his foot, in its spat, on the pavement and emerged from the shadows inside the bus. He was wearing a top hat like the magicians who came to put on shows. His coat with tails, as we called his jacket, came down to his calves. There was a white bow-tie around his neck and he carried a leather case like old Doctor Robitaille. The bus set off again. Only then did we notice that the man's face was black.

Was he some practical joker who'd covered his face with black as we did the day before Lent to fool the grownups? We knew that Africa was full of Black people, we knew they had them in the United States and on the trains, but it wasn't possible that a Black man had got on the bus and come to our village.

"Either he isn't a real nigger or he's got the wrong village," I said to my friend Lapin, who was lying flat in the grass like a hunter watching his prey.

"Look how white his teeth are; that's proof he's a real nigger."

Without moving his feet, his feet in their grey spats, the Black man looked up towards the top of the mountain, then down towards the bottom, contemplating for a moment. With his leather case, his jacket open to the wind, his black fingers pinching the brim of his top hat, he began to walk towards the top of the mountain. Lapin and I waited a bit before coming out of our hiding-place so we wouldn't be seen. Then, from a distance, we followed the Black man. Other people were following him too, but they hid in their houses, behind curtains that closed after he'd gone by. A short distance from the place where he'd got off the bus was La Sandwich Royale, one of our two restaurants. The Black man stopped, looked up towards the top of the mountain, then down towards the bottom and, dragging his feet in their spats he went into La Sandwich Royale. A terrible cry rang out and already the wife of the owner of La Sandwich Royale was hopping onto the street, arms raised, in tears and squealing as loud as the butcher's pigs.

"She's a woman," Lapin explained, "it's normal for her to be scared like that."

"A nigger in the missionaries' magazine and a nigger you see right across from you isn't the same thing."

The frightened woman didn't want to go back by herself where the Black man was. Lapin and I had approached the window and our noses were pressed to the glass. The Black man was sitting at a table.

"The nigger's waiting," Lapin noted.

Several people had come running at the sound of the panic-stricken woman's cries. Pouce Pardu, who'd been in the war, in the Chaudière Regiment, had done everything a man can do in a lifetime. He said:

"Me, I'm not afraid of Black men."

He went inside. The grownups approached the window and, like Lapin and me, they saw Pouce Pardu come up to the Black man, talk to him, laugh, make the Black man smile, sit down with him, give him his hand. We saw the Black man hold the brave man's hand for a long time, hold it open, bring it close to his eyes. The wife of the owner of La Sandwich Royale had stopped screaming but she was still trembling.

Through the window we'd seen Pouce Pardu take back his open hand and offer a banknote to the Black man. The owner's wife was somewhat reassured, because she said:

"I'll go back inside if you'll come with me."

We went in, Lapin and I and the other little boys and the grownups who were looking in the window; Pouce Pardu announced:

"That nigger can just look at your hand and tell your future and your past."

"Ask him what he wants to eat," said the wife of the owner of La Sandwich Royale.

Another former soldier, who'd fought the war in Newfoundland and who feared nothing either, said:

"The future, I know: I ain't got one. I'm going to ask the nigger to tell me my past."

We'd seen the Black man bend over the soldier's open palm and whisper. After him, other people ventured to approach the Black man and later that evening cars came from the neighbouring villages, filled with people who'd come to see the Black man and who wanted to learn what lay in the future. Lapin and I no longer called him the Black man, but the Sorcerer. For only a sorcerer can know the future: a sorcerer or God. God, of course, wouldn't be black. . . .

The next day Lapin and I, crouching in the grass, saw the Black man reappear; we saw him come down from the mountain with his top hat, his spats and his jacket open to the wind. Lapin and I, flat against the ground, held our breath and watched the sorcerer pass: with his white teeth he was smiling like a true devil. So then Lapin and I had no need to talk to each other in order to understand. We took pebbles from our pockets and threw them at him with all the strength of our small white arms.

Several years later I was in Montreal where I was wearing myself out trying to sell my first pieces of writing. One afternoon I was going to a newspaper to try to sell a story entitled "The Princess and the Fireman," when I noticed, on the other side of the street, a Black man wearing a top hat and grey spats, striped trousers and a tailcoat. I hadn't forgotten the Black man of my childhood. Running through the traffic, I crossed rue Sainte-Catherine. It was the Black man of my childhood, the one we'd thrown stones at because of his black skin, his unusual hat, his ridiculous spats, his strange knowledge; it was the same man, old now, bent over, his hat battered, his hair white, his spats soiled and his leather case worn thin. It was the same man! The white bow-tie was greyish now.

"Monsieur! Monsieur!" I called out. "Will you read my hand?" I asked as I caught up with him.

He put his case on the sidewalk, rested his back against the building. I held out my open hand. He didn't look at me, but bent over to see the lines of my palm. After a minute of absorbed silence he said:

"I can read that there's something you're sorry about."

THE GRECIAN URN
by W. P. Kinsella

CHAPTER ONE
A Japanese red herring

The mail slot in the door to my house is taped open. It measures
9½" × 1¼" and is 11" above the step. There is an empty Japanese
orange box on the front step, and a three-inch-thick foam pillow
on the floor just inside the door. I have placed food and water on
the floor at strategic locations throughout the house, in red
plastic dishes that once belonged to our cat.

My son argues that with winter fast approaching it is uneco-
nomical to have the mail slot taped open. He is nineteen, in
second year university, majoring in civil engineering and doing
very well. He has a very attractive girlfriend named Tanya, with
a dark red, pouty mouth and exceedingly large breasts. My son
often asks just exactly what it is that I expect to come through
the slot. I tell him to trust his father.

Recently, and inexplicably to everyone but myself, I have
committed some rather bizarre little crimes. To explain to the
authorities the perfectly logical reasons for my criminal activity
would, as I see it, be far worse than simply accepting the
consequences. Explanation would cause me to reveal a story far
too ludicrous to be believed. It is, I contend, far better to let
everyone concerned assume that for reasons unknown, I Charles
Bristow, age 49, have gone a little, no, more than a little,
strange. I am, I must admit, a particularly inept criminal. It is, I
suppose, because I have had no practice. Until very recently I
was a most average member of the community.

Suddenly becoming a criminal, and an inept one at that, is to
say the least a traumatic experience. As a sort of last resort,
perhaps in the way of therapy, although I am not at all sure about

that, I am doing my best to convince everyone except my son that I am mentally deranged. I think I am going to try to blame my misfortune on the male menopause, about which I read a very interesting article in a back issue of the Reader's Digest.

A few weeks ago, if anyone had told me that I would be attempting to convince people that I am insane, I would have laughed at them. Widowed for some two years, I lived quietly in my own home, mortgage-free, with my son. I was employed as a minor bureaucrat in the city civil service, and had held my position for some 30 years. I am currently under suspension without pay, pending disposition of the criminal charges against me. I gardened, bowled Tuesday nights, attended a church-sponsored friendship gathering on Saturday evenings, and subscribed to a book of the month club.

As yet I have refused to discuss Allan or the urn while I am being held for psychiatric evaluation here at the J. Walter Ives Institute for the Emotionally Disturbed. Everyone knows about the urn. No one knows about Allan. The first time I was arrested, the night I broke the Grecian Urn, I was let out on bail, charged with wilful damage and possession of burglar tools, to wit: a hammer and chisel. The next time the charge was trespassing by night, followed by loitering, followed by a second trespassing by night charge, at which time my bail was rescinded and I was remanded in custody for fourteen days for psychiatric evaluation. Seven of those days have passed.

I have submitted to a battery of tests: described my feelings toward my parents, tried to remember if I was bottle- or breast-fed, played with blocks and looked at ink blots.

Unthinkingly, I chose to use the hospital phone to call my son and plead with him to leave the mail slot open. When all rational arguments failed I ordered him to leave it open, reminding him that I paid his tuition to university as well as the utility bills.

My son complains that Tanya won't come to the house since she learned of my strange behaviour. I sympathize with him. She used to come over Tuesdays and Saturdays, my nights out. It was seldom mentioned between us, but I could always tell because the air would be heavy with her perfume when I arrived home. Soon after Tanya began visiting our home regularly, my son took to washing his own sheets. I am quite proud of him.

The phone was apparently tapped. The doctors were smiling like slit throats the next day. They must also have talked to my son, for they were inordinately interested in the Japanese orange box on the front step. I denied everything, even phoning my son. However, during the interview I doodled a number of Japanese flags on the paper in front of me and also wrote, *Remember Pearl Harbor*, in a tiny, cramped hand, quite unlike my own. As I left the room, nonchalantly whistling "Over There," they converged on the paper like baying hounds.

At supper that evening, when a Toyota commercial came on the television, I began flipping carrots at the TV.

CHAPTER TWO
The All-Blue streetcar

I suppose it was logical that Allan should have come to me for help. Outside of Viveca I was probably the only living person who knew. Beatrice may have suspected but we never discussed the matter.

Allan's secret. What exactly is it that I know? That seems to be a real point of contention. I really only know what Allan has told me and what I think I have seen.

I never liked Allan. I didn't like him in 1943 and I don't like him today. I do like Viveca. I would do anything for Viveca. She was the only reason I tried to help Allan.

I have lived in this city all my life. I joined the Army on my sixteenth birthday, 3 October, 1942. Two months later I met Allan, or rather Allan sought me out as a friend. He was lonely. I have never liked to be unkind to anyone. I tolerated him. He had the look of an English schoolboy, cheeks like two apples floating in a pail of white paint, very blond hair, pale blue eyes, a mouth that looked like he was wearing lipstick.

"My parents came over when the war started. Money, you know. Horrified that I joined up."

I was noncommittal.

"I can do some rather unusual things," he said.

I started to tell him I was not interested but instead remained silent.

"My family is unique," he persisted. "We all have powers. They begin at puberty, reach full potential by about 30, then decline to nothing by 50."

"So what?" I said. My father fought with the IRA, claimed to have killed seven Black and Tans. "There'll Always Be an England," was not my favourite song. Allan was somehow insulted that he could not rouse my curiosity, but it didn't keep him at bay for long. He offered no demonstration of his uniqueness. I continued to reluctantly accept him as my friend. It was a few weeks later, on top of a railway trestle, in a streetcar that had jumped the tracks, that I got to observe Allan in action.

The All-Blue streetcar was not, as the name may suggest, painted blue. Instead of having names and destinations the streetcars bore a small metal plate about a foot square on the front and rear. If one wished to get around the city, one learned quickly that the All-Blue streetcar travelled west to south, the Red-and-White streetcar went east to south, while the Green-and-Red went east to west.

On a dismal March night in 1943 we were travelling to a movie on the south side of the city. The All-Blue streetcar had to cross the river valley on top of a railway bridge. Halfway across the car bucked and pitched sideways. We were seated, Allan and I, at about the middle of the car, the only other passengers two girls about our age who were sitting at the very back. I thought we were certainly going to die. I could already feel the streetcar hurtling the 400 feet toward the ice of the river below. The lights went out as the car swung sideways, the rear of the car hanging out over the water. At the last instant the front wheels caught on the outside track and the car hung, balancing like a poorly constructed teeter-totter. The conductor scrambled to safety. Allan and I edged toward the front. I looked back. The two girls were huddled together in the back corner. An instant later they were beside us and the four of us climbed from the front of the car, the white-faced motorman helping us down on to the deck of the bridge.

There is documentation of the incident, if not of Allan's act of moving the girls to safety. On the front page of the 15 March, 1943 issue of a long-extinct daily newspaper is a photograph of two servicemen and two girls. My copy, yellow with age, is framed and hangs on the wall of my bedroom. The photograph was captioned The Survivors. The short blond youth with the chipmunk cheeks is Allan, the taller, raw-boned young man is me. The girls! If I could produce even one of them to document the events of that night. One person in the world who could testify that my recent actions are not those of a madman. The girl beside me in the photo, the pale, blondish girl about whose waist I have my arm, protecting her as best I could from the bitter wind, is Beatrice. We were married in 1946. She died in 1974.

The girl beside Allan, the one with green eyes and wine-coloured hair spreading over her shoulders, is Viveca.

CHAPTER THREE
J. Walter Ives is a tranvestite.

Day nine. I have taken to writing short notes and dropping them around the hospital. The attendants are all spies as are most of the inmates.

Last night, they brought into my room a whimpering drunk who smelled like wet newspaper.

"Why are you here?" he asked me. He had little red eyes like a rat. A spy's question if I ever heard one.

"I go around killing drunks," I said, which ended the conversation.

My first note read: I am capable of great destruction. It was signed with a triangular Japanese flag. Triangles have great significance to the doctors here. At every opportunity I work the conversation around to the male menopause. A black doctor with an Afro moustache and a red-and-yellow caftan listened for some time before saying, "I'm a rat man myself, and rats don't have no male menopause. I don't believe in none of that jive."

Beware the Ides of March: I left taped to my pillow. That afternoon one of the doctors carried a copy of *Julius Caesar* with many little bookmarks in it.

Isn't everybody a chipmunk? I wrote that on a piece of cardboard and slipped it into a deck of playing cards in the recreation room, in place of the jack of diamonds which I cleverly concealed in the toe of my slipper.

A large, jolly looking man with bushy eyebrows and eyes as blue as bachelor buttons, sits beside me in the recreation room. "I am a latent homosexual," he says, placing his hand on my knee.

CHAPTER FOUR
Cosmo perfume

Neither Allan nor I ever saw any action during the war. We spent our entire time stationed in our own city, although those who joined up both before and after us were shipped off to

Europe, many never to return. Perhaps Allan had something to do with it. I never asked him. I am not a very curious person.

After the adventure on the All-Blue streetcar, the four of us became friends. I must reluctantly admit that of the two girls I preferred Viveca. That, of course, was all it was, a preference. Allan and Viveca became inseparable. Like Allan, Viveca was an outgoing person. Besides being beautiful she had enormous vitality. Beatrice was the quiet one. On the assumption that likes attract we were paired together.

A significant, I believe that is the word Allan used to describe Viveca, no powers of her own, but extremely susceptible to his. Once or twice, when we were alone in barracks, Allan gave small demonstrations of his abilities. He made objects fall from shelves, stopped and started my pocket watch several times while seated in a chair across the room. Once he shattered the glass in my shaving mirror simply by staring at it. I was not particularly impressed. I asked if he could make money. He said he couldn't. He said he could, if he wished, dematerialize and inhabit inanimate objects. He said he could live inside a silver dollar, or a tree, or the fender of a bus. He said that because of Viveca's susceptibility to his powers, he could allow her to experience the same phenomena. It seemed to me to be an extremely silly thing to do and I told him so.

Allan tried his best to convert me to his point of view. He said that he and Viveca would travel the world, being able to inhabit great works of art. He had, he said, the command of a dimension of which ordinary mortals were unaware. He could step, not only into paintings or sculpture, but could come alive in the time and place that the work represented. It seemed like a lot of trouble to me. I envied Allan only Viveca. Once, at a dance hall, I took Viveca's hand to lead her to the dance floor. I could feel her pulse throbbing like something alive. She placed herself extraordinarily close to me as we danced. I could feel her breasts against the front of my uniform. Her perfume had the odour of cosmos, those tall pale pink and mauve flowers that sway beautifully in gardens like delicate children. I thought of kissing her. I'm certain she wouldn't have minded. But Allan would have, and Beatrice. I don't mean to belittle Beatrice. She was a good and faithful wife to me and as loving as her fragile health would permit. She gave me a fine son and many years of devotion.

"I wish things were different," I said to Viveca as we danced. "I wish that you and I might . . "

She moved back slightly to look into my face. Her laugh was joyful, like wind chimes, and I remember her words, but I remember more the liquid green of her eyes and the pink tip of her tongue peeking between her lips.

"Dear Charles," she said. "You are of another world."

After the war ended we saw less and less of Allan and Viveca. Sometime late in 1945 they left and we never heard from them again. That is until the night before I was first arrested.

CHAPTER FIVE
Only you Dick daring . . .

It was Viveca who came to the door. She was eighteen when I had last seen her, she looked no more than 25 now; 26, she told me later. It was, she had decided, the ideal age. She held her hand out to me. The pulse was there, throbbing like a bird between us.

It embarrassed me to see her looking so young. I have not aged particularly gracefully. It would be a kindness to say that I have the average appearance of a man dramatically close to 50.

Viveca spent little time on amenities. Allan was in trouble, she told me, and because Allan was in trouble so was she. They needed the help of a third party. Would I be it?

I am sure that Allan, with his inordinate perceptions, knew how I felt about Viveca. That was why he sent her ahead. He knew I could refuse her nothing. It was quite extraordinary, her reappearance after some 30 years. In recent times, and especially since my wife passed away, I have been fantasizing more and more about Viveca. I remember Allan once describing to me certain, to say the least, avant-garde, sexual practices, and intimating rather strongly that he and Viveca . . .

"Allan must talk with you," Viveca said.

I agreed. Allan was like Dorian Grey; he looked scarcely older than when I last saw him. Side by side we could be mistaken for father and son. There was a desperate tone in his voice as he talked to me, a sense of urgency with just a hint of panic. I found great pleasure in Allan's distress. I tried to remain very calm and feign disinterest, but secretly I was greatly stimulated. I recalled Viveca in my arms, Allan talking of his uniqueness disappearing at age 50. Perhaps, just perhaps, there was a chance.

I would pretend to help but then at the last moment . . . I would have followed Viveca over Niagara Falls in a teacup.

His powers were virtually gone, Allan explained. He and Viveca had spent the last 30 years doing exactly as they said they would. They had passed like needles through the history of the world. They had visited nearly every time and civilization by means of inhabiting paintings and other original works of art. With Allan's time running out they had decided on a final resting place: a Grecian Urn that was the feature exhibit of a travelling display currently showing at our museum. It was, Allan stated, the urn to which John Keats had written his immortal ode "On a Grecian Urn." I had no reason to doubt him as I had seen it advertised as such in our newspaper.

"Why me?" I asked. "Surely you've made this transfer of dimension thousands of times before?"

It seemed that they had attempted the transfer a few weeks before, in another city, and failed. Allan had been able to send Viveca on her journey but had no energy left to transport himself, and had barely been able to return Viveca to her natural form. They wanted me along as a safeguard in case something went wrong again. A mere precaution, they assured me. Allan had been conserving his energy for several weeks and everything would go well. Both went into ecstasies about the life ahead of them on the urn. The tranquillity, beauty, peace, they sounded to me like acquaintances of mine who had recently taken up organic gardening. They quoted lavishly from Keats' poem, assured me that they both realized that they would be totally unable to cope with the everyday world without Allan's powers, and that the ultimate in nth dimensional living was waiting for them on the urn.

I was not about to argue with them although my mind was in turmoil. I tried to think of ways that I could trick Allan into leaving Viveca behind. However, I am hardly a devious person, and as I watched Viveca's face as she described the joys that lay ahead of her, her eyes flashed, and she laughed often, the magic bell-like laughter of long ago. Her perfume was the same and my thoughts moved to the rows and rows of gentle cosmos that had graced my garden the last few summers. I would help them both. It would be the last act of love I could ever perform for Viveca.

CHAPTER SIX
The importance of triangles

Day twelve. Had a long session with one of the doctors today. He reviewed the results of my tests.

"You are as sane as I am," he told me.

He is the one with the copy of *Julius Caesar*, who puts great stock in the importance of triangles.

CHAPTER SEVEN
Blue gnats

The three of us visited the museum that same evening. The Grecian Urn was the central exhibit. They pointed out to me the spot they intended to occupy on the urn. They were as happy as if they were merely going on a holiday. I have a scant knowledge of art, but even to my untrained eye the urn was impressive. It stood some four feet high and there were three bands on it, each displaying a number of raised figures in Greek dress, in various postures, among pastoral scenery.

I arranged to accompany them to the museum the following night. It was difficult to get close to the urn. It was behind crimson ropes and there was a constant line of people filing past. We waited until closing time. The circular hall was empty. Allan shook hands with me and gave me a few last moment instructions. Viveca kissed me, her mouth a swarming thing. Was I wrong to interpret the kiss as much more than one old friend saying goodbye to another?

"Would you check the exit-way, Charles," Allan said to me.

I walked the length of the red carpet to the doorway, looked outside to be certain that we were alone. When I turned Allan and Viveca were gone: all that was left for me to see was a small swarm of bluish stars no larger than gnats disappearing into the side of the urn in a tornado shape. The urn was several feet distant from the restraining ropes. I looked carefully around, crawled under the ropes and approached the urn. In the area that Allan and Viveca had pointed out to me were two new figures, a boy and a girl, looking as though they had been part of the urn since it was created. The operation appeared to have been a success. I was just bending to inspect them closely when a startled security guard entered the display hall.

"What are you doing?" he demanded.

I stuttered an illogical reply.

"The museum is closed for the night, sir," he said with an air of authority. He looked carefully at me, then all around the exhibit hall. "I thought I heard voices," he said. "Are you sure you're alone?"

"I was checking for gnats," I said, and laughing hysterically, fled from the building.

CHAPTER EIGHT
The limits of psychiatry

Day thirteen. Another session with the doctors. Three listened; one spoke. The spokesman's eyes were small hazel triangles. Their consensus of opinion was that I am trying to con them.

After a long discussion about doctor-patient relationships, I admitted that I was trying to con them, and told them the complete story from start to finish. Then I asked their advice. They suggested that when I go to court I plead temporary insanity and not try to tell the judge my story.

"He might think you're crazy," the spokesman said.

They intend to certify me sane. Something is wrong.

CHAPTER NINE
Meanwhile, back at the museum

Twice the following evening I went through the line-up to view the urn. It was impossible for me to get beyond the restraining ropes. I merely stood and stared at the figures on the third band of the urn until the people behind pushed me on. Allan had given me certain instructions to follow and in order to do my job I had to get very close to Allan and Viveca. I had no choice but to wait until the museum closed. I hid in an alcove, then at the first opportunity rushed to the urn. I looked closely at the new figures. They seemed to fit in well. I traced the outline of Viveca's body with my index finger. As instructed I put my ear close to the figures.

"Help!" hissed Allan in the voice of a movie cartoon mouse.

"What's wrong?"

"Everything. This urn is not genuine. Seventeenth century at the latest. No character. No dimension . . ."

"There's no one around. Come on out."

"I can't."

"Why not?"

"My powers are weak. It may be weeks, even months. . . ."

"You'll just have to rest up."

"The urn is being moved to another city day after tomorrow . . . and by the way keep your hands off Viveca, I saw what you did."

"Viveca's being awfully quiet."

As I spoke I touched Viveca again. I could feel her warmth and smell the faint odour of cosmos.

"Remember it is I who maintain her in this dimension," he said in an agitated voice, like a tape being played at the wrong speed. Then he told me what I must do. Detailed instructions on how to rescue him and Viveca. He had barely finished when the security guard appeared.

"You again," he said.

"It is such a treasure," I said. "I only wanted to get a close look at it."

"If I catch you around here again I'm going to have to take you in."

I apologized for inconveniencing him and slunk away.

The following evening I hid in the washroom of the museum. Feeling like a fool, I stood on a toilet seat when the security guard checked the washroom at closing time. After waiting a suitable length of time I took the hammer and chisel that Allan had instructed me to bring and made my way to the urn.

Ever so carefully I worked at chipping the two small figurines from the face of the urn. I deliberately released Viveca first, placed her gently in the side pocket of my suit, then went to work to free Allan. As I had his figure nearly liberated, my chisel slipped ever so slightly and the urn cracked and split into a number of pieces. I managed to catch Allan as the urn disintegrated. Remarkably, his only injury was a very small piece broken from his right foot.

Regardless of what the security guard told the police, it was not me who was screaming and cursing incoherently. At the sound of the urn breaking and Allan screaming in his tiny voice, the security guard ran into the exhibit area. He said something original like, "What's going on here?" Then he drew his pistol and pointed it very unsteadily at me. I bent over and placed Allan among the ruins of the urn. "You had better put up your hands," said the guard as he advanced on me. I complied.

"Come over here with me so I can watch you while I call the police," he said, pointing to a desk and chairs a few yards distant. He looked at me closely. "You're the man who was talking to the urn." He was about 60, pink-cheeked, with a military haircut and a small white moustache like a skiff of snow below his nose. On his dark blue uniform he wore a name tag: Charles Stoddard—Security.

"Dear Charles," I said. "You are of another world."

CHAPTER TEN
After the fall

The day after I was first arrested I stayed home from work. It was the first day I had missed in eight years. I told my son I had gotten drunk and fallen against the urn and that I had no idea why I was in the museum. He looked at me skeptically for he knows that I virtually never drink. My lawyer, the one who I called to post bail for me the previous night, insisted at the time I submit to a breath analysis. My blood-alcohol reading was 0.00%.

CHAPTER ELEVEN
Putting a cloud in a suitcase

They are holding Viveca as evidence. I was searched at the police station after my arrest. I'm afraid I made rather a fool of myself.

"It's a religious object," I wailed. "You can't deny me my religion."

"Looks like a piece of the vase he busted," said a young cop. He was built like a middle guard and looked like a teenager. The whole police force was very young.

"Be brave, Viveca," I said to her as I passed her to the police officer. I could feel her pulse beating very rapidly. The middle guard slipped her into an envelope and licked the flap with a beefy tongue.

I demanded that he leave air holes in the envelope. I'm afraid I may have become a little hysterical about it. Reluctantly he took a pen and poked a few holes in the envelope.

"You're not going to put her in a safe! You mustn't put her in an airtight place of any kind." I tried to remain composed, but my voice was quite out of control.

"Trust me, Mr. Bristow," the officer said.

"You can call a lawyer now," the man on the desk informed me. Then turning to one of the officers, said, "It must be a full moon. They come out from under their rocks whenever there's a full moon."

The moment I got home I taped open the mail slot and made the other preparations I have described. While the security guard was phoning the police, Allan limped from the display area to the far wall, and while the deceased urn was being examined and I was being handcuffed and led out of the museum he slipped along the baseboard and out the front doors. I can only assume that he will try to make his way back to my home. It doesn't seem reasonable that he will go anywhere else, for it will be very difficult for a four-inch tall plaster figure about ⅜ of an inch thick to get much attention from anyone who does not believe in him. Allan gave me so many instructions that after my arrest they all seemed to have blurred and merged with the actual conversations I had with Allan and Viveca. I do seem to recall him saying that after his removal from the urn he would require nourishment, but I can't be certain. I put out food and water just in case.

Now that I'm willing to tell the truth I find it would be easier to stuff a cloud into a suitcase than to get anyone to take me seriously. I pleaded with my lawyer to have Viveca returned to me. I told him to have the museum people check and they would find that she was not a part of the broken urn. He promised he would look into it but from the tone of his voice I could tell he was humouring me. From the hospital I phoned the museum director and pleaded with him to view the piece of evidence the police were holding. I insisted that he compare it with photographs of the urn. I'm afraid I may have become a little hysterical again. He took no action, I suppose considering the source of the call. Over the telephone I have become quite friendly with the middle guard at the police station, his name is Rourke and our families come from a similar part of Ireland. He assures me that Viveca is being kept in an airy bottom drawer.

CHAPTER TWELVE
Meanwhile, back at J.W.I.

I keep having a dream. Sometimes I have it in the daytime,
therefore I suppose I would have to say it is a fantasy as
well as a dream. The water dishes that I left in my house
for Allan's use are large red plastic ones. They are some
four inches off the ground. Since Allan is only about four
inches tall, my calculations indicate that he would have great
difficulty getting a drink without falling in. I should phone
my son and have him change the dishes for saucers. Yet I
do not. My dream is that my son phones me to say that he
has found (a) a four-inch plaster figure in Greek dress submerged in the water dish, or (b) a full-grown man of about
50, who must have had an extremely difficult time drowning
himself in less than three inches of water.

Assuming that doctors like to hear about dreams, I discussed
this one with them. They are not concerned because they don't
believe my original story. Their professional advice is to try not
to think about it.

The night following my first arrest I went back to the museum
grounds to look for Allan. My concern was not really for Allan
but that he is the only one who can release Viveca. I spent a
good deal of time searching the foliage around the building
and skulking about the grounds, until a greasy-looking kid
with a widow's peak, driving a Toyota with a frothing Doberman in the back seat, shone a spotlight on me. Trespassing
by night. The following afternoon I was arrested for loitering about the grounds. I tried to be more careful that night
but the kid with the Doberman got me again, hence my banish-
ment to J. Walter Ives.

CHAPTER THIRTEEN
Sayanora

My fourteen days are up. The doctors come to say goodbye.
They explain that according to their analysis of my handwriting I
am perfectly sane.

"There are other dimensions," I assure them, "of which you are incapable of understanding. In fact . . ."

I am interrupted by the head nurse who advises me that there is a phone call from my son. The head nurse says that he sounds very agitated.

BLOODFLOWERS
by W. D. Valgardson

Danny Thorson saw Mrs. Poorwilly before he stepped off the
freight boat onto Black Island. He couldn't have missed her. She
was fat and had thick, heavy arms and legs. She stood at the
front of the crowd with her hands on her hips.

"You the new teacher?" Mrs. Poorwilly said.

"Yes, I'm—"

Mrs. Poorwilly cut him off by waving her arm at him and
saying, "Put your things on the wheelbarrow. Mr. Poorwilly
will take them up to the house. Board and room is $50 a month.
We're the only ones that give it. That's Mr. Poorwilly."

Mrs. Poorwilly waved her hand again, indicating a small man
who was standing behind an orange wheelbarrow. He had a
round, red face, and his hair was so thin and blond that from ten
feet away he looked bald.

Danny piled his suitcases and boxes onto the wheelbarrow. He
was tired and sore from the trip to the island. The bunk had been
too short. The weather had been bad. For the first three days of
the trip, he hadn't been able to hold anything down except
coffee.

When the wheelbarrow was full, Mr. Poorwilly took his hands
out of his pockets. They were twisted into two rigid pink hooks.
He slipped them through two metal loops that had been nailed to
the handles of the wheelbarrow, then lifted the barrow on his
wrists.

At the top of the first rise, Mr. Poorwilly stopped. As if to
reassure Danny, he said, "Mrs. Poorwilly's a good cook. We've
got fresh eggs all winter, too."

Danny glanced back. Mrs. Poorwilly was swinging cases of

tinned goods onto the dock. Her grey hair blew wildly about her face.

They started off again. As there were no paths on the bare granite, Danny followed Mr. Poorwilly. They walked along a ridge, dropped into a hollow. The slope they had to climb was steep, so Danny bent down, caught the front of the wheelbarrow and pulled as Mr. Poorwilly pushed. They had just reached the top when they met an elderly, wasted man who was leaning heavily on the shoulder of a young girl as he shuffled along.

Danny was so surprised by the incongruity of the pair that he stared. The girl's black hair fell to her shoulders, making a frame for her face. She looked tired, but her face was tanned and her mouth was a warm red. Her cheeks were pink from the wind. She stopped when she saw Danny.

The man with her made no attempt to greet them. His breath came in ragged gasps. His dark yellow skin was pulled so tightly over his face that the bone seemed to be pushing through. His eyes protruded and the whites had turned yellow. He gave the girl's shoulder a tug. They started up again.

When they had passed, Danny said, "Who was that? The girl is beautiful."

"Sick Jack and his daughter. It's his liver. Mrs. Poorwilly helps Adel look after him. She says he won't see the spring. He'll be the second. How are you feeling after the trip? You look green."

"I feel green. It was nine days in hell. The boat never quit rolling."

"Good thing you're not going back with them, then." Mr. Poorwilly twisted his head toward the dock to indicate who he meant. "Sunrise was red this morning. There'll be a storm before dawn tomorrow."

Mr. Poorwilly slipped his hands back into the metal loops. "Sorry to be so slow, but the arthritis causes me trouble. Used to be able to use my hands but not anymore. It's a good thing I've got a pension from the war. Getting shot was the best thing has ever happened to me."

Danny noticed a small, red flower growing from a crack in the rock. When he bent down to get a better look, he saw that the crack was filled with brown stems. He picked the flower and held it up. "What is it?"

"Bloodflower," Mr. Poorwilly replied. "Only thing that grows on the island except lichen. Shouldn't pick it. They say it brings bad luck. If you cut your finger or make your nose bleed, it'll be OK."

Danny laughed. "You don't believe that, do you?"

"Mrs. Poorwilly says it. She knows quite a bit about these things."

When they reached the house, Danny unloaded his belongings and put them into his bedroom. Mr. Poorwilly left him and went back to the dock for the supplies Mrs. Poorwilly had been unloading.

While the Poorwillys spent the day sorting and putting away their winter's supplies, Danny walked around the island. What Mr. Poorwilly said was true. Nothing grew on the island except lichen and bloodflowers. Despite the cold, patches of red filled the cracks that were sheltered from the wind.

The granite of the island had been weathered smooth, but there was nowhere it was truly flat. Three-quarters of the island's shoreline fell steeply into the sea. Only in scattered places did the shoreline slope gently enough to let Danny walk down to the water. To the west the thin blue line of the coast of Labrador was just barely visible. Two fishing boats were bobbing on the ocean. There were no birds except for some large grey gulls that rose as he approached and hovered in the air until he was well past them. He would have liked to have them come down beside him so he could have touched them, but they rose on the updrafts. He reached toward them and shouted for them to come down, then laughed at himself and continued his exploring.

Except for the houses and the fish sheds, the only other buildings were the school and the chicken roost behind the Poorwillys. All the buildings were made from wood siding. Because of the rock, there were no basements. Rock foundations had been put down so the floors would be level.

Most of the houses showed little more than traces of paint. The Poorwillys' and Mary Johnson's were the only ones that had been painted recently. Danny knew the other house belonged to Mary Johnson because it had a sign with her name on it. Below her name it said, "General store. Post office. Two-way radio."

Danny explored until it started to get dark, then went back to the Poorwillys.

"Heard you've been looking around," Mrs. Poorwilly said. "If you hadn't come back in another five minutes, I would have sent Mr. Poorwilly to bring you back."

"There's no danger of getting lost." Danny was amused at her concern.

"No," Mrs. Poorwilly agreed, "but you wouldn't want to slip and fall in the dark. You're not in a city now with a doctor down the street. You break a leg or crack your skull and you might have to wait two, three weeks for the weather to clear enough for a plane to come. You don't want to be one of the three."

Danny felt chastised, but Mrs. Poorwilly dropped the subject. She and Mr. Poorwilly spent all during supper asking him about the mainland. As they talked, Mrs. Poorwilly fed her husband from her plate. He sat with his hands in his lap. There were no directions given or taken about the feeding. Both Mr. and Mrs. Poorwilly were anxious to hear everything he had to tell them about the mainland.

When he got a chance, Danny said, "What'd you mean 'one of the three'?"

"Trouble always comes in threes. Maybe you didn't notice it on the mainland because things are so complicated. On the island you can see it because it's small and you know everybody. There's just 35 houses. Somebody gets hurt, everybody knows about it. They can keep track. Three, six, nine, but it never ends unless it's on something made up of threes."

"You'll see before the winter is out. Last month the radio said Emily died in the sanatorium. TB. Now Sick Jack's been failing badly. He's got to be a hard yellow and he's lost all his flesh. He dies, then there'll be one more thing to end it. After that, everything will be OK."

Mrs. Poorwilly made her pronouncement with all the assuredness of an oracle. Danny started on his dessert.

"Mr. Poorwilly says you think Adel's a nice bit of fluff."

Danny had started thinking about the book on mythology he'd been reading at summer school. The statement caught him off guard. He had to collect his thoughts, then he said, "The girl with the long dark hair? I only caught a glimpse of her, but she seemed to be very pretty."

"When her father goes, she'll be on her own," Mr. Poorwilly said. "She's a good girl. She works hard."

"Does she have any education?"

"Wives with too much education can cause a lot of trouble," Mrs. Poorwilly said. "They're never satisfied. The young fellows around here and on the coast have enough trouble without that."

Danny tried not to show his embarrassment. "I was thinking in terms of her getting a job on the mainland. If her spelling is good and she learned to type, she could get a government job."

"Might be that she'll go right after her father. No use making plans until we see what the winter brings." Mr. Poorwilly turned to his wife for confirmation. "It's happened before."

Mrs. Poorwilly nodded as she scraped the last of the pudding from the dish and fed it to her husband.

"What you want is what those people had that I was reading about. They used to ward off evil by choosing a villager to be king for a year. Then so the bad luck of the old year would be done with, they killed him in the spring."

"They weren't Christians," Mr. Poorwilly said.

"No," Danny replied. "They gave their king anything he wanted. A woman, food, gifts, everything, since it was only for a year. Then when the first flowers bloomed, they killed him."

"Must have been them Chinese," Mr. Poorwilly said.

"No. Europeans. But it was a long time ago."

"Have you ever ridden on a train?" Mrs. Poorwilly asked. "Mr. Poorwilly and I rode on a train for our honeymoon. I remember it just like yesterday."

Mr. and Mrs. Poorwilly told him about their train ride until it was time to go to bed. After Danny was in bed, Mr. Poorwilly stuck his head through the curtain that covered the doorway. In a low voice, he said, "Don't go shouting at the sea gulls when you're out walking. Most of the people here haven't been anywhere and they'll think you're sort of funny."

"OK," Danny said. Mr. Poorwilly's head disappeared.

The next day Mrs. Poorwilly had everyone in the village over to meet Danny. As fast as Danny met the women and children, he forgot their names. The men were still away fishing or working on the mainland. Mr. Poorwilly and Danny were the only men until Adel brought Sick Jack.

Sick Jack looked even thinner than he had the day before. The yellow of his skin seemed to have deepened. As soon as he had shaken Danny's hand, he sat down. After a few minutes, he fell into a doze and his daughter covered him with a blanket she had brought.

Mrs. Poorwilly waited until Sick Jack was covered, then brought Adel over to see Danny.

"This is Adel. She'll come for coffee soon, and you can tell her about the trains and the cities. She's never been off the island."

Adel blushed and looked at the floor. "Certainly," Danny said. "I've a whole set of slides I'm going to show Mr. and Mrs. Poorwilly. If you wanted, you could come and see them."

Adel mumbled her thanks and went to the side of the room. She stayed beside her father the rest of the evening, but Danny glanced at her whenever he felt no one was looking at him.

She was wearing blue jeans and a heavy blue sweater that had been mended at the elbows and cuffs with green wool. It was too large for her so Danny assumed that it had belonged to her father or one of the other men. From what Mrs. Poorwilly had said, Danny had learned that Adel and her father were given gifts of fish and second-hand clothing. When the men went fishing, they always ran an extra line for Sick Jack.

In spite of her clothing, Adel was attractive. Her hair was as black as he had remembered it and it hung in loose, natural waves. Her eyes were a dark blue. Underneath the too-large sweater, her breasts made soft, noticeable mounds.

She left before Danny had a chance to speak to her again, but he didn't mind as he knew he'd see her during the winter.

For the next two weeks, busy as he was, Danny couldn't help but notice the change in the village. The men returned at all hours, in all kinds of weather. Mostly they came two and three at a time, but now and again a man would come by himself, his open boat a lonely black dot on the horizon.

Most of the men brought little news that was cheerful. The fishing had been bad. Many of them were coming home with the absolute minimum of money that would carry them until spring. No one said much, but they all knew that winter fishing would be necessary to keep some of the families from going hungry. In a good year, the winter fishing provided a change in diet for people sick of canned food. This year the fishing wouldn't be so casual.

By the end of September the weather had turned bitterly cold.

The wind blew for days at a time. The houses rocked in the wind. Danny walked the smallest children to their homes. The few days the fishermen were able to leave the island, there were no fish. Some of the men tried to fish in spite of the weather, but most of the time they were able to do little more than clear the harbour before having to turn around.

The evening Sick Jack died, Danny had gone to bed early. The banging on the door woke him. Mr. Poorwilly got up and answered the door. Danny heard the muttered talk, then Mr. Poorwilly yelled the news to Mrs. Poorwilly. They both dressed and left right away. Danny would have offered to go with them, but he knew that he would just be in the way so he said nothing.

Mrs. Poorwilly was back for breakfast. As she stirred the porridge, she said, "She's alone now. We washed him and dressed him and laid him out on his bed. She's a good girl. She got all his clothes out and would have helped us dress him, but I wouldn't let her. Mr. Poorwilly is staying with her until some of the women come to sit by the body. If the weather holds, we'll have the funeral tomorrow."

"Why not have the funeral while the weather stays good? It could change tomorrow."

"Respect," Mrs. Poorwilly said. "But it's more than that, too. I wouldn't say it to her, but it helps make sure he's dead. Once just around when I married, Mrs. Milligan died. She was 70. Maybe older. They rushed because the weather was turning. They were just pushing her over the side when she groaned. The cold did it. She died for good the next week, but since then we like to make sure."

Danny went to the funeral. The body was laid out on the bed with a shroud pulled to its shoulders. Mary Johnson sang "The Old Rugged Cross." Mrs. Poorwilly held the Bible so Mr. Poorwilly could read from it. Adèl sat on a kitchen chair at the foot of the bed. She was pale and her eyes were red, but she didn't cry.

When the service was over, one of the fishermen pulled the shroud over Sick Jack's head and tied it with a string. They lifted the body onto a stretcher they had made from a tarpaulin and a pair of oars. The villagers followed them to the harbour.

They laid the body on the bottom of the boat. Three men got in. As the boat swung through the spray at the harbour's mouth, Danny saw one of the men bend and tie an anchor to the shrouded figure.

Mrs. Poorwilly had coffee ready for everyone after the service. Adel sat in the middle of the kitchen. She still had a frozen look about her face, but she was willing to talk.

Sick Jack's death brought added tension to the village. One day in class while they were reading a story about a robin that had died, Mary Johnson's littlest boy said, "My mother says somebody else is going to die. Maybe Miss Adel now that her father's gone."

Danny had been sharp with him. "Be quiet. This is a Grade Three lesson. You're not even supposed to be listening. Have you done your alphabet yet?"

His older sister burst out, "That's what my mother said. She said—"

Danny cut her off. "That's enough. We're studying literature, not mythology. Things like that are nothing but superstition."

That night Danny asked about Adel. Mrs. Poorwilly said, "She's got a settlement coming from the mine where he used to work. It's not much. Maybe $500 or $600. Everybody'll help all they can, but she's going to have to get a man to look after her."

During November, Danny managed to see Adel twice. The first time, she came for coffee. The second time, she came to see Danny's slides of the mainland. Danny walked her home the first time. The second time, Mrs. Poorwilly said, "That's all right, Mr. Thorson. I'll walk with her. There's something I want to get from Mary Johnson's."

Danny was annoyed. Mrs. Poorwilly had been pushing him in Adel's direction from the first day he had come. Then, when he made an effort to be alone with her, she had stepped between them.

Mrs. Poorwilly was back in half an hour with a package of powdered milk.

Danny said, "I would have got that for you, Mrs. Poorwilly."

"A man shouldn't squeeze fruit unless he's planning on buying," she replied.

Adel walked by the school a number of times when he was there. He got to talk to her, but she was skittish. He wished that she was with him in the city. There, at least, there were dark corners, alley-ways, parks, even doorsteps. On the island, you couldn't do anything without being seen.

At Christmas the villagers held a party at the school. Danny showed his slides. Afterwards they all danced while Wee Jimmy played his fiddle. Danny got to dance with Adel a good part of the night.

He knew that Mrs. Poorwilly was displeased and that everyone in the village would talk about his dancing for the rest of the year, but he didn't care. Adel had her hair tied back with a red ribbon. The curve of her neck was white and smooth. Her blouse clung to her breasts and was cut low enough for him to see where the soft curves began. Each time he danced with one of the other women, Danny found himself turning to see what Adel was doing. When the party was over, he walked Adel home and kissed her goodnight. He wanted her to stay with him in the doorway, but she pulled away and went inside.

Two days before New Year's, Mrs. Poorwilly's prediction came true. The fishing had remained poor, but Michael Fairweather had gone fishing in a heavy sea because he was one of those who had come back with little money. Two hundred yards from the island his boat capsized.

Danny had gone to school on the pretext of doing some work, but what he wanted was some privacy. He had been sitting at the window staring out to sea when the accident happened. He had seen the squall coming up. A violent wind whipped across the waves and behind it a white, ragged line on the water raced toward the island. Michael Fairweather was only able to turn his boat halfway round before the wind and sleet struck.

Danny saw the boat rise to the crest of a wave, then disappear, and Michael was hanging on to the keel. Danny bolted from the room, but by the time he reached the dock, Michael had disappeared.

The squall had disappeared as quickly as it had come. Within half an hour the sea was back to its normal rolling. The fishermen rowed out of the harbour and dropped metal bars lined with hooks. While one man rowed, another held the line at the back of the boat. As Danny watched, the boats crossed back and forth until it was nearly dark.

They came in without the body. Danny couldn't sleep that night. In the morning, when a group of men came to the Poorwillys, Danny answered the door before Mr. Poorwilly had time to get out of his bedroom. The men had come for the loan of the Poorwillys' rooster.

Mrs. Poorwilly nestled the rooster in her jacket on the way to the dock, then tied it to Mr. Poorwilly's wrist with a leather thong. Mr. Poorwilly stepped into the front of the skiff. The rooster hopped onto the bow. With that the other men climbed into their boats and followed Mr. Poorwilly and the rooster out of the harbour.

"What are they doing?" Danny asked.

Mrs. Poorwilly kept her eyes on the lead boat, but she said, "When they cross the body, the rooster will crow."

Danny turned and stared at the line of boats. In spite of the wind, the sun was warm. The rooster's feathers gleamed in the sun. Mr. Poorwilly stood as still as a wooden figurehead. The dark green and grey boats rose and fell on the waves. Except for the hissing of the foam, there was no sound.

Danny looked away and searched the crowd for Adel. He had looked for a third time, when Mrs. Poorwilly, without turning, said, "She won't come for fear the current will have brought her father close to shore. They might bring him up."

All morning and into the afternoon the boats crossed and recrossed the area in front of the harbour in a ragged line. No one left the dock. The women with small babies didn't come down from their houses, but Danny could see them in their doorways.

As the day wore on, Danny became caught up in the crossing and recrossing of the boats. None of the men dragged their hooks. The only time the men in the rear of the boats moved was to change positions with the men at the oars.

When the cock crew, the sound caught Danny by surprise. The constant, unchanging motion and the hissing of the spray had drawn him into a quiet trance. It had been as if the boats and he had been there forever.

The sound was so sharp that some of the women cried out. The men with the iron bars covered with hooks threw them into the sea, and shoved the coils of rope after them. They didn't want to pass the spot where the cock crew until the hooks were on the bottom. The bars disappeared with little spurts of white foam. Danny could hear the rope rubbing against the side of the boat as it was pulled hand over hand.

"It's him," Mrs. Poorwilly said. "God have mercy, they've got him."

Danny turned back. It was true. Instead of a white shroud, the men were pulling a black bundle into the boat.

The funeral was bad. Marj Fairweather cried constantly and tried to keep the men from taking the body. As they started to leave, she ran to the dresser for a heavy sweater, then sat in the middle of the floor, crying and saying, "He'll be so cold. He'll be so cold."

In spite of Marj, the tension in the community eased after the funeral was over. People began to visit more often, and when they came they talked more and stayed longer.

Adel came frequently to the Poorwillys. When she came, she talked to the Poorwillys, but she watched Danny. She wasn't open about it, but when Danny looked at her, she let her eyes linger on him for a second before turning away. She had her colour back and looked even better than before. Most of the time, Danny managed to walk her home. Kissing her was not satisfactory because of the cold and the bulky clothes between them, but she would not invite him in and there was no privacy at the Poorwillys. In spite of the walks and goodnight kisses, she remained shy when anyone else was around.

The villagers had expected the weather and the fishing to improve. If anything, the weather became worse. Ice coated the boats. The wind blew night and day. Often, it only stopped in the hour before dawn.

Then, without warning, Marj Fairweather sent her children to the Poorwillys, emptied a gas lamp on herself and the kitchen floor, and lit a match.

This time there was no funeral. The entire village moved in a state of shock. While one of the sheds was fixed up for the children, Marj's remains were hurried to sea and dumped in the same area as her husband's.

The village drew into itself. The villagers stayed in their own houses. When they came to the door, they only stayed long enough to finish their business. The men quit going to the dock. Most of them pulled their boats onto the island and turned them over.

A week after the fire, Danny arrived to find his room stripped of his belongings. Mrs. Poorwilly waited until he had come into the kitchen. "Mr. Poorwilly and I decided to take two of the Fairweather children. We'll take the two youngest. A fourteen-year-old can't take care of six kids."

Danny was too stunned to say anything. Mrs. Poorwilly continued. "Some of us talked about it. We hope you don't mind, but there's nothing else to do. Besides, there's going to be no money from the mine. Adel needs your board and room worse than we do. We'll keep the Fairweather children for nothing."

When Danny didn't reply, Mrs. Poorwilly added, "We got

help moving your things. We gave Adel the rest of this month's
money.''

Danny hesitated for a moment, but there was nothing to say.
He went outside.

He knocked at Adel's door. She let him in. "Mrs. Poorwilly
says you're to stay with me now.''

"Yes, she told me," Danny said.

Adel showed him to his bedroom. All his clothes had been
hung up and his books had been neatly piled in one corner. He
sat on the edge of the bed and tried to decide what to do. He
finally decided he couldn't sit in the bedroom for the next five
months and went back into the kitchen.

The supper was good, but Danny was too interested in Adel to
pay much attention. In the light from the oil lamp, her eyes
looked darker than ever. She was wearing a sweater with a
V-neck. He could see the soft hollow of her throat and the
smooth skin below her breastbone. Throughout supper he told
her about the mainland and tried to keep his eyes above her
neck.

The next morning when he went to school, he expected to see
a difference in the children's attitudes. Twice he turned around
quickly. Each time the children had all been busy writing in their
notebooks. There was no smirking or winking behind their hands.
At noon, he said, "In case any of you need to ask me something, there's no use your going to the Poorwillys. I'm staying at
Miss Adel's now.''

The children solemnly nodded their heads. He dismissed them
and went home for lunch.

Adel was at home. She blushed and said, "The women at the
sheds said I should come home early now that I've got you to
look after. Since the men aren't fishing there isn't much to do.''

"That's very good of them," Danny replied.

Danny and Adel were left completely alone. He had expected
that some of the villagers would drop by, but no one came to
visit. Danny and Adel settled into a routine that was disturbed
only by Danny's irritation at being close to Adel. Adel shied
away from him when he brushed against her. At the end of the
second week, she accepted his offer to help with the dishes.
They stood side by side as they worked. Danny was so distracted
by Adel's warmth and the constant movement of her body that
the dishes were only half dried.

Danny put his hand on Adel's shoulder and turned her toward

him. She let him pull her close. There was no place to sit or lie
in the kitchen so he picked her up and carried her to the
bedroom. She didn't resist when he undressed her. After he
made love to her, he fell asleep. When he woke up, Adel had
gone to her own bed.

Danny took Adel to bed with him every evening after that, but
during the night she always slipped away to her own bedroom.
At the beginning of the next week, they had their first visitor.
Mrs. Poorwilly stopped by to see how they were doing. They
had been eating supper when she arrived. Normally, they would
have been finished eating, but Adel had been late in coming
from the fish sheds. The weather had improved enough for the
men to go fishing. Mrs. Poorwilly accepted a cup of coffee and
sat and talked to them for an hour.

It was as if her coming had been a signal. After that, villagers
dropped by in the evenings to talk for a little while. They nearly
always brought something with them and left it on the table.
Danny had wanted to protest, but he didn't know what to say
that wouldn't embarrass their visitors so he said nothing.

Adel stopped going back to her own bed. Danny thought about
getting married but dismissed the idea. He was comfortable with
things the way they were.

The day Danny started to get sick he should have known
something was wrong. He had yelled at the children for no
particular reason. When Adel had come home, he had been
grouchy with her. The next day his throat had been sore, but he
had ignored it. By the end of the day, he was running a temperature and his knees felt like water.

Adel had been worried, but he told her not to call Mrs.
Poorwilly. Their things had become so mixed together that it was
obvious they were using the same bedroom.

For the next few days he was too sick to protest about anything. Mrs. Poorwilly came frequently to take his temperature
and to see that Adel kept forcing whisky and warm broth into
him. All during his sickness Danny was convinced that he was
going to die. During one afternoon he was sure that he was dead
and that the sheets were a shroud.

The crisis passed and he started to cough up phlegm, but he
was so weak that it was an effort for him to lift his head. The
day he was strong enough to sit up and eat in the kitchen, Mrs.
Poorwilly brought him a package of hand-rolled cigarettes.

"Nearly everyone is coming to see you tomorrow. They'll all bring something in the way of a present. It's a custom. Don't say they shouldn't or they'll think you feel their presents aren't good enough."

Danny said that he understood.

The school children came first with hand-carved pieces of driftwood. He admired the generally shapeless carvings, and after the first abortive attempt carefully avoided guessing at what they were supposed to be.

After the children left, the McFarlans came. Mr. McFarlan had made a shadow box from shingle. He had scraped the shingle with broken glass until the grain stood out. Inside the box he had made a floor of lichen and pebbles. Seagulls made from clam shells sat on the lichen.

His wife stretched a piece of black cloth over the end of a fish box. On it she had glued boiled fish bones to form a picture of a boat and man.

Someone brought a tin of pears, another brought a chocolate bar. One of the men brought half a bottle of whisky.

Each visitor stayed just long enough to inquire how Danny felt, wish him well and leave a present on the table. When the last visitor had gone, Danny was exhausted. Adel helped him to bed.

He felt much better by the end of the week, but when he tried to return to work, Mrs. Poorwilly said, "Mary Johnson's doing a fine job. Not as good as you, of course, but the kids aren't suffering. If you rush back before you're ready, everybody will take it that you think she's doing a poor job. If you get sick again, she won't take over."

Adel returned to work at the sheds, but the women sent her home. The weather had held and there was lots of fish, but they said she should be at home looking after Danny.

At first it was ideal. They had little to do except sit and talk or make love. Danny caught up on his reading. They both were happy, but by the end of March their confinement had made them both restless.

To get out of the house, Danny walked to Mrs. Poorwilly's. While they were having coffee, Danny said, "I guess everyone must have got the flu."

"No," Mrs. Poorwilly replied, "just some colds among the children. Adel and you making out all right?"

"Yes," Danny said.

"Her mother was a beauty, you know. I hope you didn't mind moving, but these things happen."

"No, I didn't mind moving."

They sat for five minutes before Danny said, "Could I ask you something? I wouldn't want anyone else to know."

Mrs. Poorwilly nodded her assent.

"Mary Johnson is doing such a good job that I thought I might ask her to radio for a plane. Maybe it would be a good idea for me to take Adel to the mainland for a week."

"Any particular reason?"

"Yes. If she wants, I'll marry her."

"Haven't you asked her?"

Danny shook his head. It had never occurred to him that she might say no.

"Wait until you ask her. The superintendent will want a reason. You'll have to tell him over the radio and everyone will know. You wouldn't want to tell him and then have her turn you down."

Adel was standing at the window when he returned. He put his arms around her. "You know, I think we should get married."

Adel didn't answer.

"Don't you want to marry me?" he asked.

"Yes. I do. But I've never been off the island. You won't want to stay here always."

"We can stay for a couple of years. We'll go a little at a time. We can start with a week on the mainland for a honeymoon. We'll go somewhere on a train."

That evening he went to Mary Johnson's. Mary tried to raise the mainland operator, but the static was so bad that no contact could be made. Danny kept Mary at the radio for half an hour. He left when she promised to send one of the children with a message if the radio cleared.

Danny returned the next night, but the static was just as bad. Mary promised to send for him as soon as the call went through.

A week went by. The weather continued to improve. Danny checked the thermometer. The temperature was going up a degree every two days.

At the end of the week he returned to Mary's. The radio wasn't working at all. One of the tubes needed to be replaced. He left. Halfway home he decided to go back and leave a message for the plane. The radio might work just long enough for a message, but not long enough for him to be called to the set. When he came up to the house, he was sure that he heard the radio. He banged on the front door. Mary took her time coming. When she opened the door, he said, "I heard the radio. Can you send a message right away?"

Mary replied that he must have just heard the children talking.

Danny insisted on her trying to make the call. She was annoyed, but she tried to get through. When she had tried for five minutes, Danny excused himself and left.

He walked part-way home, then turned and crept back over the rock.

The windows were dark. He lay in the o llow of rock behind the house until the cold forced him to leave.

In the morning, he went to the dock to talk to the fishermen. He offered to pay any one of them triple the normal fare to take him down to the coast. They laughed and said they would bring him some fresh fish for supper.

When he had continued insisting that he wanted to leave, they said that a trip at this time of year was impossible. Even planes found it difficult to land along the coast. A boat could be crushed in the pack ice that was shifting up and down the shore.

Danny told Adel about the radio and the boats. She sympathized with him, but agreed with the men that it was hopeless to try and make the trip in an open boat.

"Besides," she said, "the freight boats will be coming in a month or so."

True to their word, the fishermen sent a fresh fish. Danny tried to pay the boy who brought it, but he said that he had been told not to accept anything. Danny had put the money into the boy's hand. The boy had gone, but a few minutes later he returned and put the money in front of the door.

Late that afternoon, Danny walked to the dock. After looking around to see that no one was watching, he bent down and looked at the rope that held one of the boats. He untied it, then tied it again.

He returned to the house and started gathering his heavy clothing. When Adel came into the room, she said, "What are you going to do?"

"I'm leaving."

"Is the plane coming?"

"I'm taking myself. I've had enough. I'm not allowed to work. You're not allowed to work. Everyone showers us with things they won't let us pay for. I try to use the radio, but it never works." He turned to face her. "It always worked before."

"Sometimes it hasn't worked for weeks," Adel replied. "Once it was six weeks. It's the change in temperature."

"But it works. The other night I heard it working. Then when I asked Mary Johnson to call, she said it was just the children talking."

"Mary told me," Adel said. "You made her very upset. She thinks you're still not feeling well."

"I'm feeling fine. Just fine. And I'm leaving. I don't know what's going on here, but I'm getting out. I'm going to get a plane and then I'm coming back for you."

"You said we could leave a little at a time."

"That was before this happened. What if something goes wrong? Three people have died. One of them died right before my eyes and I couldn't do anything about it. What if we needed a doctor? Or a policeman? What if someone took some crazy notion into his head?"

Danny took Sick Jack's nor'westers off a peg. He laid out the clothes he wanted and packed two boxes with food. He lay awake until three o'clock, then slipped outside and down to the boats.

The boats were in their usual places. He reached for the rope of the first boat. His hand closed on a heavy chain. Danny couldn't believe it. He jumped onto the boat and ran his hand around the chain. He climbed out and ran from boat to boat. Every boat was the same. He tried to break the chains loose. When they wouldn't break, he sat on the dock and beat his hands on the chains. When he had exhausted himself, he sat with his face pressed into his hands.

In the morning, Mary sent one of the boys to tell Danny that the radio had worked long enough for her to send a message. It hadn't been confirmed, but she thought it might have been heard. For the rest of the day, Danny was elated, but as the days passed and the plane did not appear, he became more and more depressed. Adel kept saying that the plane would come, but Danny doubted if it would ever come.

The weather became quite mild. Danny walked to the dock every day. The chains were still on the boats. He had spent an hour on the dock staring at the thin blue line that was the mainland and was walking back to Adel's when he noticed that the snow had melted away from some of the cracks in the granite. The cracks were crammed with closely packed leaves.

He paused to pick a leaf. *April the first,* he thought, *April the first will come and we'll be able to go.* Then, as he stared at the small green leaf in his hand, he realized that he was wrong. It was weeks later that the first freight boat came.

The rest of the day he tried to make plans for Adel and himself, but he could not concentrate. The image of thousands and thousands of bloodflowers kept spilling into his mind.

THE LOONS
by Margaret Laurence

Just below Manawaka, where the Wachakwa River ran brown and noisy over the pebbles, the scrub oak and grey-green willow and chokecherry bushes grew in a dense thicket. In a clearing at the centre of the thicket stood the Tonnerre family's shack. The basis of this dwelling was a small square cabin made of poplar poles and chinked with mud, which had been built by Jules Tonnerre some fifty years before, when he came back from Batoche with a bullet in his thigh, the year that Riel was hung and the voices of the Metis entered their long silence. Jules had only intended to stay the winter in the Wachakwa Valley, but the family was still there in the thirties, when I was a child. As the Tonnerres had increased, their settlement had been added to, until the clearing at the foot of the town hill was a chaos of lean-tos, wooden packing cases, warped lumber, discarded car tires, ramshackle chicken coops, tangled strands of barbed wire and rusty tin cans.

The Tonnerres were French halfbreeds, and among themselves they spoke a *patois* that was neither Cree nor French. Their English was broken and full of obscenities. They did not belong among the Cree of the Galloping Mountain reservation, further north, and they did not belong among the Scots-Irish and Ukrainians of Manawaka, either. They were, as my Grandmother MacLeod would have put it, neither flesh, fowl, nor good salt herring. When their men were not working at odd jobs or as section hands on the C.P.R., they lived on relief. In the summers, one of the Tonnerre youngsters, with a face that seemed totally unfamiliar with laughter, would knock at the doors of the town's brick houses and offer for sale a lard-pail full of bruised wild strawberries, and if he got as much as a quarter he would grab the coin and run before the customer had time to change her mind. Sometimes old Jules, or his son Lazarus, would get mixed up in a Saturday-night brawl, and would hit out at whoever was nearest, or howl drunkenly among the offended shoppers on Main Street, and then the Mountie would put them for the night in the barred cell underneath the Court House, and the next morning they would be quiet again.

Piquette Tonnerre, the daughter of Lazarus, was in my class at school. She was older than I, but she had failed several grades, perhaps because her attendance had always been sporadic and her interest in school-work negligible. Part of the reason she had missed a lot of school was that she had had tuberculosis of the bone, and had once spent many months in hospital. I knew this because my father was the doctor who had looked after her. Her sickness was almost the only thing I knew about her, however. Otherwise, she existed for me only as a vaguely embarrassing presence, with her hoarse voice and her clumsy limping walk and her grimy cotton dresses that were always miles too long. I was neither friendly nor unfriendly towards her. She dwelt and moved somewhere within my scope of vision, but I did not actually notice her very much until that peculiar summer when I was eleven.

"I don't know what to do about that kid," my father said at dinner one evening. "Piquette Tonnerre, I mean. The damn bone's flared up again. I've had her in hospital for quite a while now, and it's under control all right, but I hate the dickens to send her home again."

"Couldn't you explain to her mother that she had to rest a lot?" my mother said.

"The mother's not there," my father replied. "She took off a few years back. Can't say I blame her. Piquette cooks for them, and she says Lazarus would never do anything for himself as long as she's there. Anyway, I don't think she'd take much care of herself, once she got back. She's only thirteen, after all. Beth, I was thinking—what about taking her up to Diamond Lake with us this summer? A couple of months rest would give that bone a much better chance."

My mother looked stunned.

"But Ewen—what about Roddie and Vanessa?"

"She's not contagious," my father said. "And it would be company for Vanessa."

"Oh dear," my mother said in distress, "I'll bet anything she has nits in her hair."

"For Pete's sake," my father said crossly, "do you think Matron would let her stay in the hospital for all this time like that? Don't be silly, Beth."

Grandmother MacLeod, her delicately featured face as rigid as a cameo, now brought her mauve-veined hands together as though she were about to begin a prayer.

"Ewen, if that half-breed youngster comes along to Diamond Lake, I'm not going," she announced. "I'll go to Morag's for the summer."

I had trouble in stifling my urge to laugh, for my mother brightened visibly and quickly tried to hide it. If it came to a choice between Grandmother MacLeod and Piquette, Piquette would win hands down, nits or not.

"It might be quite nice for you, at that," she mused. "You haven't seen Morag for over a year, and you might enjoy being in the city for a while. Well, Ewen dear, you do what you think best. If you think it would do Piquette some good, then we'll be glad to have her, as long as she behaves herself."

So it happened that several weeks later, when we all piled into my father's old Nash, surrounded by suitcases and boxes of provisions and toys for my ten-month-old brother, Piquette was with us and Grandmother MacLeod, miraculously, was not. My father would only be staying at the cottage for a couple of weeks, for he had to get back to his practice, but the rest of us would stay at Diamond Lake until the end of August.

Our cottage was not named, as many were, "Dew Drop Inn" or "Bide-a-Wee," or "Bonnie Doon." The sign on the roadway bore in austere letters only our name, MacLeod. It was not a large cottage, but it was on the lakefront. You could look out the windows and see, through the filigree of the spruce trees, the water glistening greenly as the sun caught it. All around the cottage were ferns, and sharp-branched raspberry bushes, and moss that had grown over fallen tree trunks. If you looked carefully among the weeds and grass, you could find wild strawberry plants which were in white flower now and in another month would bear fruit, the fragrant globes hanging like miniature scarlet lanterns on the thin hairy stems. The two grey squirrels were still there, gossiping at us from the tall spruce beside the cottage, and by the end of the summer they would again be tame enough to take pieces of crust from my hands. The broad moose antlers that hung above the back door were a little more bleached and fissured after the winter, but otherwise everything was the same. I raced joyfully around my kingdom, greeting all the places I had not seen for a year. My brother, Roderick, who had not been born when we were here last summer, sat on the car rug in the sunshine and examined a brown spruce cone, meticulously turning it round and round in his small and curious hands. My mother and father toted the luggage from car to cottage, exclaiming over how well the place had wintered, no broken windows, thank goodness, no apparent damage from storm-felled branches or snow.

Only after I had finished looking around did I notice Piquette. She was sitting on the swing, her lame leg held stiffly out, and her other foot scuffing the ground as she swung slowly back and forth. Her long hair hung black and straight around her shoulders, and her broad coarse-featured face bore no expression—it was blank, as though she no longer dwelt within her own skull, as though she had gone elsewhere. I approached her very hesitantly.

"Want to come and play?"

Piquette looked at me with a sudden flash of scorn.

"I ain't a kid," she said.

Wounded, I stamped angrily away, swearing I would not speak to her for the rest of the summer. In the days that followed, however, Piquette began to interest me, and I began to want to interest her. My reasons did not appear bizarre to me. Unlikely as it may seem, I had only just realised that the Tonnerre family, whom I had always heard called half-breeds, were actually Indians, or as near as made no difference. My acquaintance with Indians was not extensive. I did not remember ever having seen a real Indian, and my new awareness that Piquette sprang from the people of Big Bear and Poundmaker, of Tecumseh, of the Iroquois who had eaten Father Brebeuf's heart— all this gave her an instant attraction in my eyes. I was a devoted reader of Pauline Johnson at this age, and sometimes would orate aloud and in an exalted voice, *West Wind, blow from your prairie nest; Blow from the mountains, blow from the west*—and so on. It seemed to me that Piquette must be in some way a daughter of the forest, a kind of junior prophetess of the wilds, who might impart to me, if I took the right approach, some of the secrets which she undoubtedly knew—where the whippoorwill made her nest, how the coyote reared her young, or whatever it was that it said in Hiawatha.

I set about gaining Piquette's trust. She was not allowed to go swimming, with her bad leg, but I managed to lure her down to the beach—or rather, she came because there was nothing else to do. The water was always icy, for the lake was fed by springs, but I swam like a dog, thrashing my arms and legs around at such speed and with such an output of energy that I never grew cold. Finally, when I had had enough, I came out and sat beside Piquette on the sand. When she saw me approaching, her hand squashed flat the sand castle she had been building, and she looked at me sullenly, without speaking.

"Do you like this place?" I asked, after a while, intending to lead on from there into the question of forest lore.

Piquette shrugged. "It's okay. Good as anywhere."

"I love it," I said. "We come here every summer."

"So what?" Her voice was distant, and I glanced at her uncertainly, wondering what I could have said wrong.

"Do you want to come for a walk?" I asked her. "We wouldn't need to go far. If you walk just around the point there, you come to a bay where great big reeds grow in the water, and all kinds of fish hang around there. Want to? Come on."

She shook her head.

"You dad said I ain't supposed to do no more walking than I got to."

I tried another line.

"I bet you know a lot about the woods and all that, eh?" I began respectfully.

Piquette looked at me from her large dark unsmiling eyes.

"I don't know what in hell you're talkin' about," she replied. "You nuts or somethin'? If you mean where my old man, and me, and all them live, you better shut up, by Jesus, you hear?"

I was startled and my feelings were hurt, but I had a kind of dogged perseverance. I ignored her rebuff.

"You know something, Piquette? There's loons here, on this lake. You can see their nests just up the shore there, behind those logs. At night, you can hear them even from the cottage, but it's better to listen from the beach. My dad says we should listen and try to remember how they sound, because in a few years when more cottages are built at Diamond Lake and more people come in, the loons will go away."

Piquette was picking up stones and snail shells and then dropping them again.

"Who gives a good goddamn?" she said.

It became increasingly obvious that, as an Indian, Piquette

was a dead loss. That evening I went out by myself, scrambling through the bushes that overhung the steep path, my feet slipping on the fallen spruce needles that covered the ground. When I reached the shore, I walked along the firm damp sand to the small pier that my father had built, and sat down there. I heard someone else crashing through the undergrowth and the bracken, and for a moment I thought Piquette had changed her mind, but it turned out to be my father. He sat beside me on the pier and we waited, without speaking.

At night the lake was like black glass with a streak of amber which was the path of the moon. All around, the spruce trees grew tall and close-set, branches blackly sharp against the sky, which was lightened by a cold flickering of stars. Then the loons began their calling. They rose like phantom birds from the nests on the shore, and flew out onto the dark still surface of the water.

No one can ever describe that ululating sound, the crying of the loons, and no one who has heard it can ever forget it. Plaintive, and yet with a quality of chilling mockery, those voices belonged to a world separated by aeons from our neat world of summer cottages and the lighted lamps of home.

"They must have sounded just like that," my father remarked, "before any person ever set foot here."

Then he laughed. "You could say the same, of course, about sparrows, or chipmunks, but somehow it only strikes you that way with the loons."

"I know," I said.

Neither of us suspected that this would be the last we would ever sit here together on the shore, listening. We stayed for perhaps half an hour, and then we went back to the cottage. My mother was reading beside the fireplace. Piquette was looking at the burning birch log, and not doing anything.

"You should have come along," I said, although in fact I was glad she had not.

"Not me," Piquette said. "You wouldn't catch me walkin' way down there jus' for a bunch of squawkin' birds."

Piquette and I remained ill at ease with one another. I felt I had somehow failed my father, but I did not know what was the matter, nor why she would not or could not respond when I suggested exploring the woods or playing house. I thought it was probably her slow and difficult walking that held her back. She

stayed most of the time in the cottage with my mother, helping
her with the dishes or with Roddie, but hardly ever talking. Then
the Duncans arrived at their cottage, and I spent my days with
Mavis, who was my best friend. I could not reach Piquette at
all, and I soon lost interest in trying. But all that summer she
remained as both a reproach and a mystery to me.

That winter my father died of pneumonia, after less than a
week's illness. For some time I saw nothing around me, being
completely immersed in my own pain and my mother's. When I
looked outward once more, I scarcely noticed that Piquette
Tonnerre was no longer at school. I do not remember seeing her
at all until four years later, one Saturday night when Mavis and I
were having Cokes in the Regal Café. The jukebox was booming
like tuneful thunder, and beside it, leaning lightly on its chrome
and its rainbow glass, was a girl.

Piquette must have been seventeen then, although she looked
about twenty. I stared at her, astounded that anyone could have
changed so much. Her face, so stolid and expressionless before,
was animated now with a gaiety that was almost violent. She
laughed and talked very loudly with the boys around her. Her
lipstick was bright carmine, and her hair was cut short and
frizzily permed. She had not been pretty as a child, and she was
not pretty now, for her features were still heavy and blunt. But
her dark and slightly slanted eyes were beautiful, and her skin-
tight skirt and orange sweater displayed to enviable advantage a
soft and slender body.

She saw me, and walked over. She teetered a little, but it was
not due to her once-tubercular leg, for her limp was almost gone.

"Hi, Vanessa." Her voice still had the same hoarseness.
"Long time no see, eh?"

"Hi," I said. "Where've you been keeping yourself, Piquette?"

"Oh, I been around," she said. "I been away almost two
years now. Been all over the place—Winnipeg, Regina, Saska-
toon. Jesus, what I could tell you! I come back this summer, but
I ain't stayin'. You kids goin' to the dance?"

"No," I said abruptly, for this was a sore point with me. I
was fifteen, and thought I was old enough to go to the Saturday-
night dances at the Flamingo. My mother, however, thought
otherwise.

"Y'oughta come," Piquette said. "I never miss one. It's just
about the on'y thing in this jerkwater town that's any fun. Boy,

you couldn' catch me stayin' here. I don' give a shit about this place. It stinks."

She sat down beside me, and I caught the harsh over-sweetness of her perfume.

"Listen, you wanna know something, Vanessa?" she confided, her voice only slightly blurred. "Your dad was the only person in Manawaka that ever done anything good to me."

I nodded speechlessly. I was certain she was speaking the truth. I knew a little more than I had that summer at Diamond Lake, but I could not reach her now any more than I had then. I was ashamed, ashamed of my own timidity, the frightened tendency to look the other way. Yet I felt no real warmth towards her—I only felt that I ought to, because of that distant summer and because my father had hoped she would be company for me, or perhaps that I would be for her, but it had not happened that way. At this moment, meeting her again, I had to admit that she repelled and embarrassed me, and I could not help despising the self-pity in her voice. I wished she would go away. I did not want to see her. I did not know what to say to her. It seemed that we had nothing to say to one another.

"I'll tell you something else," Piquette went on. "All the old bitches an' biddies in this town will sure be surprised. I'm gettin' married this fall—my boyfriend, he's an English fella, works in the stockyards in the city there, a very tall guy, got blond wavy hair. Gee, is he ever handsome. Got this real classy name. Alvin Gerald Cummings—some handle, eh? They call him Al."

For the merest instant, then, I saw her. I really did see her, for the first and only time in all the years we had both lived in the same town. Her defiant face, momentarily, became unguarded and unmasked, and in her eyes there was a terrifying hope.

"Gee, Piquette—" I burst out awkwardly, "that's swell. That's really wonderful. Congratulations—good luck—I hope you'll be happy—"

As I mouthed the conventional phrases, I could only guess how great her need must have been, that she had been forced to seek the very things she so bitterly rejected.

When I was eighteen, I left Manawaka and went away to college. At the end of my first year, I came back home for the summer. I spent the first few days talking non-stop with my mother, as we exchanged all the news that somehow had not found its way into letters—what had happened in my life and what had happened here in Manawaka while I was away. My mother searched her memory for events that concerned people I knew.

"Did I ever write you about Piquette Tonnerre, Vanessa?" she asked one morning.

"No, I don't think so," I replied. "Last I heard of her, she was going to marry some guy in the city. Is she still there?"

My mother looked perturbed, and it was a moment before she spoke, as though she did not know how to express what she had to tell and wished she did not need to try.

"She's dead," she said at last. Then, as I stared at her, "Oh, Vanessa, when it happened, I couldn't help thinking of her as she was that summer—so sullen and gauche and badly dressed. I couldn't help wondering if we could have done something more at that time—but what could we do? She used to be around in the cottage there with me all day, and honestly, it was all I could do to get a word out of her. She didn't even talk to your father very much, although I think she liked him in her way."

"What happened?" I asked.

"Either her husband left her, or she left him," my mother said. "I don't know which. Anyway, she came back here with two youngsters, both only babies—they must have been born very close together. She kept house, I guess, for Lazarus and her brothers, down in the valley there, in the old Tonnerre place. I used to see her on the street sometimes, but she never spoke to me. She'd put on an awful lot of weight, and she looked a mess, to tell you the truth, a real slattern, dressed any old how. She was up in court a couple of times—drunk and disorderly, of course. One Saturday night last winter, during the coldest weather, Piquette was alone in the shack with the children. The Tonnerres made home brew all the time, so I've heard, and Lazarus said later she'd been drinking most of the day when he and the boys went out that evening. They had an old woodstove there—you know the kind, with exposed pipes. The shack caught fire, Piquette didn't get out, and neither did the children."

I did not say anything. As so often with Piquette, there did not seem to be anything to say. There was a kind of silence around the image in my mind of the fire and the snow, and I wished I could put from my memory the look that I had seen once in Piquette's eyes.

I went up to Diamond Lake for a few days that summer, with Mavis and her family. The MacLeod cottage had been sold after my father's death, and I did not even go to look at it, not wanting to witness my long-ago kingdom possessed now by strangers. But one evening I went down to the shore by myself.

The small pier which my father had built was gone, and in its place there was a large and solid pier built by the government, for Galloping Mountain was now a national park, and Diamond Lake had been re-named Lake Wapakata, for it was felt that an Indian name would have a greater appeal to tourists. The one store had become several dozen, and the settlement had all the attributes of a flourishing resort—hotels, a dance-hall, cafés with neon signs, the penetrating odours of potato chips and hot dogs.

I sat on the government pier and looked out across the water. At night the lake at least was the same as it had always been, darkly shining and bearing within its black glass the streak of amber that was the path of the moon. There was no wind that evening, and everything was quiet all around me. It seemed too quiet, and then I realized that the loons were no longer here. I listened for some time, to make sure, but never once did I hear that long-drawn call, half mocking and half plaintive, spearing through the stillness across the lake.

I did not know what had happened to the birds. Perhaps they had gone away to some far place of belonging. Perhaps they had been unable to find such a place, and had simply died out, having ceased to care any longer whether they lived or not.

I remembered how Piquette had scorned to come along, when my father and I sat there and listened to the lake birds. It seemed to me now that in some unconscious and totally unrecognised way, Piquette might have been the only one, after all, who had heard the crying of the loons.

A TRAVEL PIECE
by Margaret Atwood

Annette is wiped right out. She never used to be this wiped out after a job; she supposes it's the medication. Any kind of a pill is a drain on the system, she doesn't like taking them but there you are.

She chews on one of the vacu-packed peanuts, thumbing through the travel brochure from the seat pocket, letting her mind drift among the coloured pictures. Thirty-six vacations in the sun, described in glowing terms, with the prices, all-inclusive it says but of course there are extras. *A gem of an island almost undiscovered by tourists, with brilliant white sand beaches and bluegreen lagoons complemented by the friendliness of the people.* Annette is returning from just such an island and she too writes pieces like this, but hers are not advertisements, they're for the newspaper and, when she gets lucky, for the glossy magazines as well, so the things she writes have to be less bland: little anecdotes, the personal touch, details on where to eat and how good the service is, jokes told by the barman if any, where to go shopping for bargains, all those straw hats and curios, out-of-the-way things you might do, such as climbing an extinct volcano or cooking a parrot-fish on a coral reef, if you had the energy and the desire. Increasingly she doesn't, but she puts herself through the paces anyway, she would consider it cheating to recommend these things without having done them. This is what makes her a good travel writer, among other things; and she has a knack for discovering local oddities, she knows what to look for, she has an eye for detail.

She's learned though that she has to strike the right balance between what she manages to notice, spontaneously and candidly— and she always takes a camera with her, just in case, though for

the glossies they usually send down their own photographer—
and what she chooses to leave out. For instance, by lifting her
head slightly she can read: LIFE JEST INDER FRONT OF YOUR SEAT. It
says LIFE JEST because the lettering, which is embroidered right
into the cloth of the pocket, has been worn away by the
outgoing and incoming thighs of countless passengers. It would
strike a humorous note but she can't use it; the airline company
would resent the implication that its planes were falling to pieces
and that would be it for the complimentary tickets.

People, she found, did not want any hint of danger in the kind
of articles it was her business to write. Even the ones who would
never go to the places she described, who could not afford it, did
not want to hear about danger or even unpleasantness; it was as
if they wanted to believe that there was somewhere left in the
world where all was well, where unpleasant things did not
happen. An unspoiled Eden; that had been a useful phrase.
Once, it seemed a long time ago, staying home meant safety,
though tedium as well, and going to the places that were her
specialty—the Caribbean, the northern half of South America,
Mexico—meant adventure, threat, pirates, brigands, lawlessness.
Now it was the reverse, home was the dangerous place and
people went on vacation to snatch a few weeks of uneventfulness.
If small black beads of oil were appearing on the white sand
beaches, if the barman's niece had stabbed her husband, if things
were stolen or it rained, they did not want to know about it; if
they felt like disasters or crimes they could read about them in
the other pages of the newspaper. So she did not report such
things and she tried her best not to notice them. There was that
pig on the beach in Mexico, being killed by a man who didn't
know how to do it properly, because some tourist had wanted a
Polynesian feast. That was the sort of thing you had to filter out.
Her job was to be pleased, and she did this well, she was evenly
tanned and in trim physical shape, she had direct blue eyes and a
white smile and was good at asking interested, polite questions
and coping with minor emergencies, such as lost suitcases,
cheerfully and without becoming irritated. She seldom had
trouble; there was something about her, an air of profession-
alism, she was too thorough to be an ordinary tourist; those in
the industry sensed it would be bad for business to upset
her.

So she went her way undisturbed among the green trees, along the white beaches, between the blue sky and the indecently blue ocean, which more and more lately had come to seem like a giant screen, flat and with pictures painted on it to create the illusion of solidity. If you walked up to it and kicked it, it would tear and your foot would go right through, into another space which Annette could only visualize as darkness, a night in which something she did not want to look at was hiding. Things were being kept from her, she had begun to feel, especially in lobbies and in cars taking her to and from airports; people were watching her, as if they were aware of this. It was the constant surveillance that was exhausting her, and the effort she had been making not to find out.

She attempted once to describe these feelings to her husband, but the attempt was not a success. Her capacity for being easily pleased, delighted even, had pervaded their marriage as well as her job, and he reacted at first with a kind of restrained, offended outrage, as if she had complained to the maître d' about a wine. Very well, madam, it shall be replaced, and a look that says: Stupid bitch. Jeff seemed hurt that she was not totally and altogether happy, that she had been coming home from her trips too tired to go out for special little dinners with him, that she crawled into bed and remained there between her mock vacations, emerging only long enough to plod through the required exercises at the typewriter. When she said, "Sometimes I feel I'm not alive," he took it as a comment on his love-making, and she had to spend half an hour reassuring him, telling him that wasn't what she meant; she'd been talking about her job. But his view of her job was that it was a lucky accident, she was a very fortunate girl to have a job like that. He himself was interning at a hospital—she'd put him through medical school on her own salary—and he felt abused and overworked. He could not understand why she wanted to stay home more; finally he swiped the pills for her, telling her they would steady her nerves. Which they have, she supposes, but then her nerves have not been unsteady, quite the contrary. It's the unbroken calm, both within and without, that is getting to her. Real events happen to other people, she thinks, why not me? And then there's her conviction that they are happening, all around her, but that they're being kept from her.

Once she took Jeff along with her, to Bermuda, though they couldn't really afford it as his way had to be paid, of course. She thought it would be good for them, he would see what she really did and stop idealizing her; she felt that perhaps he had married her because of her tan, he found her glamorous. And it would be fun to get away together. But it hadn't been. All he'd wanted to do was lie in the sun and he'd refused to eat the pumpkin soup, he was a meat and potatoes man. "Relax," he kept telling her, "why don't you just lie down beside me and relax?" He hadn't understood why she needed to go shopping, to explore the markets, to visit all the possible beaches and restaurants. "It's my job," she told him, to which he replied, "Some job, I should have a job like that." "You're not suited for it," she said, thinking of the fuss he had made over the fried plantain. He could not understand that being pleased was hard work, and he thought she was being too friendly with the taxi drivers.

The plane starts to tilt down as Annette is finishing her martini. Jeff told her she should go easy on mixing the pills and liquor, but one wouldn't hurt, so dutifully she ordered only one. For a minute or two no one notices; then the stewardesses are at their posts and a blurred, alarmed voice is coming through the intercom, but as usual it's inaudible, and half of it is in French anyway. Hardly anyone is screaming. Annette takes off her high-heeled shoes, Cuban actually, they're better for walking, slips them under the seat, and rests her forehead on her knees, protecting it with her arms. She's following the instructions on the card tucked into the seat pocket; there's a diagram on it too, about how to blow up the life vest by pulling the knobs. When the girls went through their routine at the beginning of the flight she didn't watch; she hasn't watched for a long time.

By twisting her head to the right she can see the card sticking out of the pocket of the seat next to her, and the edge of the vomit bag as well; they don't say *vomit* but *discomfort*, which fits. Next to the vomit bag is a man's knee. Nothing seems to be happening so Annette looks up to see what's going on. A lot of the people don't have their heads down on their knees the way they've been told, they're sitting bolt upright, just staring, as if they're watching a movie. The man next to Annette is white as a sheet. She asks him if he wants a Rolaid, but he doesn't, so she eats one herself. She carries a small arsenal of patent medicines with her on these trips, laxatives, cold remedies, vitamin C, aspirins; everything you can get she's had a dose of at one time or another.

The plane is going down in a long glide, it's a lot easier than she would have expected. There's a faint smell of burning rubber, that's all, no explosions; she feels hardly any discomfort, though her ears are popping. The descent is silent too because the engines aren't working, and except for one woman who is still screaming half-heartedly and another who is crying, none of the passengers is making much noise.

"Where you from?" the man beside her says, abruptly, perhaps it's the only thing he can think of to say to a woman on an airplane, no matter what the circumstances; but before Annette can answer there's a jolt that knocks her teeth together, it isn't at all like hitting water. More like a slightly bumpy runway, as if the sea is hard, like cement.

It must have damaged the loudspeakers though, because the blurred voices have stopped. The passengers crowd into the aisles, released, their mingled voices rising excitedly, like children let out of school. Annette thinks they are being remarkably calm, though real panic, with stampeding feet and people being trampled on, is difficult when the aisle is so narrow. She always notes the locations of the emergency exits and tries to sit near one but she has not managed it this time, so she decided to wait in her seat until the jam is over. The back door appears to be stuck so everyone is shoving to the front. The man sitting beside her is trying to elbow his way into the lineup, which is like a supermarket queue, they even have bundles. Annette folds her hands and looks out through the oval porthole window but all she can see is the surface of the ocean, flat as a parking lot; there isn't even any smoke or flames.

When the aisle is clearer she stands up, lifts the seat as the instruction card has told her and takes out the life vest. She has noticed that many people, in their rush to get out, have been forgetting to do this. She collects her coat from the overhead rack, which is still crammed with other coats, abandoned by their owners. The sun is shining as brightly as ever, but it may cool off at night. She has the coat with her because when she steps off the plane at the other end it will still be winter. She picks up her camera bag and her large purse, which doubles as a flight bag; she's familiar with the advantages of travelling light, she once did a fashion piece on crushable dresses.

Between the First Class cabin at the front and the Tourist Class is the tiny kitchen. As she goes through it, at the tail end of the line, Annette sees a rack of lunch trays, with plastic-wrapped sandwiches and desserts with snap-on lids. The drink trolley is there too, parked out of the way. She takes several of the sandwiches, three bottles of ginger ale and a handful of vacu-packed peanuts and stuffs them into her purse. She does this as much because she is hungry as for any other reason, but she is thinking, too, that they may need provisions. Though they will certainly be picked up soon, the plane must have sent out a distress signal. They will be rescued by helicopters. Still, it will be nice to have some lunch. She considers momentarily taking a bottle of liquor too, from the drink trolley, but rejects this as a bad idea. She remembers having read magazine articles about delirious sailors.

When she gets to the chute leading down from the open doorway she hesitates. The blue watery surface below her is dotted with round orange discs. Some of them have already made considerable headway, or have they been blown? From a distance the scene lookes delightful, with the orange circles twirling on the sea like wading pools filled with happy children. Though she's a little disappointed; she knows this is an emergency but so far everything has been so uneventful, so orderly. Surely an emergency ought to feel like one.

She would like to take a picture of the scene, with the orange against the blue, two of her favourite colours. But someone at the bottom is calling to her to hurry up, so she sits on the chute, placing her knees together so her skirt won't blow up, holds her purse, her camera and her folded coat firmly on her lap, and pushes off. It's like going down a slide, the kind they used to have in parks.

Annette finds it odd that she should be the last one off the plane. Surely the captain and the stewardesses ought to have remained on board until all the passengers were safely off, but there is no sign of them. She doesn't have much time to think about this, however, because the round boat is in a state of confusion, there seem to be a lot of people on it and someone is shouting orders. "Row," the voice says, "we've got to get away from here . . . the suction!"

Annette wonders what he is talking about. There are only two paddles in any case so she settles herself out of the way and watches while a couple of men, the owner of the voice and a younger man, paddle at either side of the boat as if their lives

depended on it. The boat moves up and down with the waves,
which are not large, it rotates—one of the men must be stronger
than the other, Annette thinks—and it moves gradually away
from the plane, in the direction of the afternoon sun. Annette
feels as though she's being taken for a boat-ride; she leans back
against the swelling rubber side of the boat and enjoys it. Behind
them, the plane settles imperceptibly lower. Annette thinks it
would be a good idea to get a picture of it, for use when they are
rescued and she can write up the story, and she opens her camera
bag, takes out her camera and adjusts the lens; but when she
squirms around so she can get a better view, the plane is gone.
She thinks it ought to have made a noise of some kind, but they
are quite a distance from where it was.

"No sense in getting too far away from the crash site," says
the man who has been giving the orders. There's something
military about him, Annette decides; maybe it's the trimmed
moustache or the fact that he's older. He and the other man ship
their paddles and he begins to roll a cigarette, taking the papers
and tobacco from his breast pocket. "I suggest we introduce
ourselves," he says; he's used to directing.

There are not as many people in the boat as Annette at first
supposed. There's the two men, the one who says he's in
insurance (though Annette doubts this), and the younger one,
who has a beard and claims to teach at a free school; the older
man's wife, who is plump and kind-looking and keeps saying
"I'm all right," although she isn't, she's been crying quietly to
herself ever since they've been in the boat; an overly tanned
woman of forty-five or so who gives no clue as to her occupation, and a boy who says he's a university student. When it
comes to Annette's turn she says, "I write a food column for one
of the newspapers." In fact she did this for a couple of months,
before she got onto the travel page, so she knows enough about
it to be able to back it up. Still, she is surprised at herself for
lying and can't imagine why she did. The only reason she can
think of is that she hasn't believed the stories of any of the
others, except the plump, crying woman, who could not possibly
be anything other than what she so obviously is.

"We've been damn lucky," says the older man, and they all
agree.

"What are we supposed to do now?" says the tanned woman.

"Just sit around and wait to be rescued, I guess," the bearded schoolteacher says, with a nervous laugh. "It's an enforced vacation."

"It'll just be a matter of hours," says the older man. "They're more efficient about these things than they used to be."

Annette volunteers the information that she has some food and they all congratulate her for being so resourceful and foresighted. She provides the wrapped sandwiches and they divide them up equally; they pass around one of the bottles of ginger ale to wash them down. Annette doesn't say anything about the peanuts or the other two bottles of ginger ale. She does say, however, that she has some seasick pills if anyone needs one.

She's about to toss the plastic sandwich trays overboard, but the older man stops her. "No, no," he says, "can't throw those away. They might come in handy." She can't imagine what for, but she does as he says.

The plump woman has stopped crying and has become quite talkative; she wants to know all about the food column. In fact they are now a festive bunch, chattering away as if they are on a huge sofa in a recreation room, or in the waiting room of an airport where the flights have been temporarily held up. There's the same atmosphere of time being passed, from necessity but with superficial cheer. Annette is bored. For a moment she thought something real had happened to her but there is no danger here, it is as safe in this lifeboat as everywhere else, and the piece she would write about it would come out sounding the same as her other pieces. *For exploring the Caribbean, a round orange lifeboat strikes an unusual note. The vistas are charming, and you have a body-to-body contact with the sea which is simply not possible in any other kind of boat. Take some sandwiches and plan to stay out for lunch!*

The sun sets in its usual abrupt, spectacular fashion, and it's not until then that they begin to get worried. No helicopters have appeared, and none of the other lifeboats is in sight. Perhaps they paddled away too quickly. They haven't even heard any sounds of distant rescue operations. But "They'll be along, all right," the older man says, and his wife suggests they have a singsong. She begins with "You Are My Sunshine," warbling in a church soprano, and continues through a repertoire of once-popular favourites: "On Top of Old Smokey," "Good Night Irene." The others join in, and Annette is momentarily amazed by the numbers of words to these songs that she herself can remember. She goes to sleep during one of the choruses, her winter coat pulled over her; she's glad she brought it.

She awakens feeling groggy and clogged. She can't believe they're all still on the boat, it's beginning to get annoying, and she is boiling hot under her coat. The rubber of the lifeboat is hot too and there's no wind, the sea is as flat as the palm of your hand with only a sickening groundswell. The others are sprawled listlessly around the boat's circumference, their legs in awkward tangles here and there. Annette thinks to herself they'd be better off with fewer people in the boat, but immediately censors this. The two women are still asleep; the plump one, the singer, lies with her mouth open, snoring slightly. Annette rubs her eyes; the lids feel dry and gritty. She seems to remember getting up in the night and squatting perilously over the edge of the boat; someone else must have made this effort and failed, or not made it at all, for there is a faint smell of urine. She is very thirsty.

The older man is awake, smoking in silence; so is the one with the beard. The student is drowsing still, curled in a heap, like a puppy.

"What should we do?" Annette asks.

"Stick it out till they come for us," says the older man. He doesn't look so military any more with his day's growth of stubble.

"Maybe they won't come," says the bearded man. "Maybe we're in the Bermuda whatchamacallit. You know, where those ships and planes vanish without a trace. What made the plane go down, anyway?"

Annette looks at the sky, which is more like a flat screen than ever. Maybe this is what has happened, she thinks, they've gone through the screen to the other side; that's why the rescuers can't see them. On this side of the screen, where she thought there would be darkness, there is merely a sea like the other one, with thousands of castaways floating around in orange lifeboats, lost and waiting to be rescued.

"The main thing," says the older man, "is to keep your mind occupied." He flicks his cigarette butt into the water. Annette expects to see a shark emerge and snap it up, but none does. "First off, we'll all get sunstroke if we aren't careful." He's right, they are all quite red.

He wakes the others and puts them to work constructing a shade, which they make from Annette's winter coat and the men's suit jackets, the buttons of one inserted into the button-holes of the next. They prop it up with the paddles, lashing it on with neckties and stockings, and sit under it, with a fleeting sense of accomplishment. It's hot and stuffy, but it is out of the sun. Again at his suggestion the men turn out their pockets and the women empty their purses, "to see what we've got to work with," the older man says. Annette has forgotten everyone's name and suggests they introduce themselves again, which they do. Bill and Verna, Julia, Mike and Greg. Julia has a pounding headache and takes several of Annette's aspirins-with-codeine. Bill is going through the assortment of handkerchiefs, keys, compacts, lipsticks, travel-sized bottles of hand lotion, pills and chewing gum. He had appropriated the two remaining bottles of ginger ale and the peanuts, which he says will have to be rationed. For breakfast he lets them each have a Chiclet and a cough drop, to suck on. After that they take turns brushing their teeth, with Annette's toothbrush. She's the only one who has travelled light and thus has all her toiletries with her. The others used suitcases, which of course went down in the hold of the plane.

"If it rains," Bill says, "this boat is perfect for catching water," but it does not look like rain.

Bill has a lot of good ideas. In the afternoon he spends some time fishing, with a hook made from a safety-pin and a line of dental floss. He catches nothing. He says they could attract seagulls by flashing Annette's camera lens at them, if there were any seagulls. Annette is lethargic, although she keeps prodding herself, reminding herself that this is important, this may be the real thing, now that they have not been rescued.

"Were you in the war?" she asks Bill, who looks smug that she has noticed.

"You learn to be resourceful," he says. Towards evening they share out one of the bottles of ginger ale, and Bill allows them three peanuts each, telling them to scrape the salt off before eating them.

Annette goes to sleep thinking of a different story; it will have to be different now. She won't even have to write it, it will be her story As Told To, with a picture of herself, emaciated and sunburned but smiling bravely. Tomorrow she should take some pictures of the others.

During the night, which they spend under the sunshade, now a communal blanket, there is a scuffle. It's Greg the student and Bill, who has hit him and now claims he was making a try for the last bottle of ginger ale. They shout angrily at each other until Verna says it must have been a mistake, the boy was having a bad dream. All is quiet again but Annette is awake, she gazes up at the stars, you can't see stars like that in the city.

After a while there is heavy breathing, surely she's imagining it, but there's a distinct sound of furtive copulation. Who can it be? Julia and Mike, Julia and Greg? Not Verna, surely, in her corset which Annette is positive she has not taken off. Annette is a little disappointed that no one has made a pass at her, if that sort of thing is going around. But it was probably initiated by Julia, that suntanned solitary voyager, this must be what she goes on vacations for. Annette thinks of Jeff, wonders how he reacted to the fact that she is missing. She wishes he was here, he would be able to do something, though she doesn't know what. They could make love, anyway.

In the morning she scans their faces for signs, revealing clues as to who did what, but finds nothing. They brush their teeth once more, then rub hand lotion onto their faces, which is refreshing. Bill passes round a package of Tums and more cough drops; he's saving the peanuts and the ginger ale for the evening meal. He devises a strainer out of his shirt and trails it over the side of the boat, to catch plankton, he says. He brings in some messy green stuff, squeezes out the salt water, and chews a handful thoughtfully. The others each take a mouthful, except Julia who says she can't swallow it. Verna tries, but spits hers out. Annette gets it down; it's salty and tastes of fish. Later, Bill does manage to catch a small fish and they eat chunks of that also; the hot fish smell mingles with the other smells, unwashed bodies and slept-in clothes, which are rubbing against Annette's nerves. She's irritable, she's stopped taking the pills, maybe that's why.

Bill has a knife, and with it he slices the plastic sandwich trays in two, then cuts slits in them to make sun goggles, "like the Eskimos," he says. He has definite leadership ability. He unravels part of Verna's sweater, then twists the pink wool to make the strings to tie them with. They have abandoned the coat sunshade, it was too hot and the paddles had to be held upright all the time, so they fasten the plastic trays over their faces. They smear their noses and lips and the exposed parts of their fore-heads with lipstick from the purse collection; Bill says it will be protection against sunburn. Annette is disturbed by the effect, these masks and bloody markings. What bothers her is that she can't tell any more who these people are, it could be anyone behind the white plastic faces with slit eyes. But she must look like that too. It is exotic though, and she is still functioning well enough to think of taking a picture, though she doesn't take it. She ought to, for the same reason she's kept her watch conscien-tiously wound up, it would help morale by implying there is a future. But suddenly there's no point.

About two o'clock Greg, the student, starts thrashing around. He lunges for the side of the boat and tries to get his head into the sea. Bill throws himself on top of him and after a minute Mike joins him. They hold Greg down on the bottom of the boat. "He was drinking sea water," Mike says, "I saw him, early this morning." The boy is gasping like a fish, and he looks like a fish too in his impersonal plastic face. Bill removes the mask, and the human features glare up into his. "He's delirious," Bill says. "If we let him up, he'll jump overboard." Bill's plastic mask turns, pointing itself toward the other members of the group. No one says anything, but they are thinking, Annette knows what they are thinking because she is thinking the same thing. They can't hold him down forever. If they let him up, he will die, and not only that, he will be lost to them, wasted. They themselves are dying slowly of thirst. Surely it would be better to . . . Verna is rummaging, slowly and painfully, like a crip-pled bumblebee, in the heap of clothing and debris; what is she looking for? Annette feels she is about to witness something mundane and horrible, doubly so because it will be bathed not in sinister blood-red lightning but in the ordinary sunlight she has walked in all her life; some tacky ritual put on for the tourists, tacky because it is put on for tourists, for those who are not responsible, for those who make the lives of others their transient spectacle and pleasure. She is a professional tourist, she works at being pleased and at not participating; at sitting still and watch-ing. But they are going to slit his throat, like that pig on the beach in Mexico, and for once she does not find it quaint and unusual. "Stay out of it," the man in the light-green suit had said to his wife, who was sentimental about animals. Could you stay out by wishing to?

I can always say it wasn't me, I couldn't help it, she thinks, visualizing the newspaper interview. But there may not be one, and she is therefore stuck in the present, with four Martians and one madman waiting for her to say something. So this is what goes on behind her back, so this is what it means to be alive, she's sorry she wondered. But the sky is not flat any more, it's bluer than ever and recedes away from her, clear but unfocused. You are my sunshine, Annette thinks; when skies are grey. The quality of the light has not changed. Am I one of them or not?

CONTRIBUTORS

Margaret Atwood (1939–)

In Margaret Atwood's second novel, *Surfacing* (1972), two inept moviemakers shoot nonsense sequences, mistakenly believing that, as "new Renaissance men," they can undertake any technical challenge and carry it off. The novel reveals them both to be doltish failures, but their dreamed-of Renaissance versatility is actually realized in their creator.

Margaret Atwood was born and grew up in Ottawa. She took a B.A. degree from the University of Toronto, an A.M. from Radcliffe College, and did further graduate studies in English literature at Harvard. Since then she has held teaching posts at various Canadian universities and spent one year, 1972–73, as writer in residence at the University of Toronto. As a writer she has shown remarkable flexibility; she has written film and television scripts, poetry, novels, short stories, literary criticism and even the libretto for an operatic masque. Among her collections of poetry are *The Circle Game* (1966), which won a Governor General's Award; *The Animals in That Country* (1968); *The Journals of Susanna Moodie* (1970); *Power Politics* (1971); and *Two-Headed Poems* (1978). Films have been made of her first two novels, *The Edible Woman* (1969) and *Surfacing* (1972); her critical work, *Survival: A Thematic Guide to Canadian Literature* (1972), has created more discussion than any comparable study. Her more recent novels, *Lady Oracle* (1976), *Life Before Man* (1979), and a collection of short stories, *Dancing Girls* (1977), have all been widely acclaimed.

Like many another Atwood character, Annette in "A Travel Piece" is coping with a love affair gone wrong. This one has dwindled to an "unbroken calm" that she wishes to have disturbed by "real events." The question that the reader is likely to ask is this: Are the events of the air crash the real ones she craves, or are they an hallucination induced by pills and alcohol?

Ernest Buckler (1908–)

After graduating from Dalhousie University in 1929, Ernest Buckler took an M.A. degree in philosophy at the University of Toronto,
and for the next five years worked in Toronto for an insurance
company. But in 1936 he returned to Nova Scotia and has spent his
life since then on the family farm near Bridgetown, combining
farming and writing. Like Sinclair Ross, with whom he has sometimes been compared, Buckler is not a prolific writer, although he is
a much admired one. His short stories have appeared in such magazines
as *Maclean's*, *Esquire*, *Saturday Night*, and *The Atlantic Advocate*.
His first novel, *The Mountain and the Valley* (1953), was acclaimed
as soon as it appeared and has come to be regarded as a classic in
Canadian literature. He has published a second novel, *The Cruelest
Month* (1963); a collection of sketches and stories, *Ox Bells and
Fireflies* (1968), which he calls a "fictive memoir"; a book on Nova
Scotia with photographer Hans Weber, *Window on the Sea* (1973);
and *Whirligig: Selected Prose and Poetry of Ernest Buckler* (1977).
A selection of his stories was published in 1975 under the title *The
Rebellion of Young David and Other Stories*.

"Penny in the Dust," the first story in that collection, treats a
theme common in Buckler's fiction, the painful subtleties of family
relationships and the anguish of unarticulated love. In an interview
Buckler once said, "I think heart is a big word, because it has the
same letters as earth. . . . Heart is what we live by; I don't think
we live by mind, I think we live by heart." This story is about a
heart that found its voice.

Morley Callaghan (1903–)

In the same year that he was admitted to the Ontario bar as a
lawyer, Morley Callaghan published the novel *Strange Fugitive*
(1928). From that time onward he has never practiced law but
continually practiced the craft of fiction. His fourteen novels include
Such Is My Beloved (1934), *They Shall Inherit the Earth* (1935),
More Joy in Heaven (1937), *Luke Baldwin's Vow* (1948), *The Loved
and the Lost* (1951), *A Passion in Rome* (1961), *A Fine and Private
Place* (1975), and *Close to the Sun Again* (1977). He has also
written plays, articles, and a memoir of his youthful experience in
Europe with Ernest Hemingway and F. Scott Fitzgerald, *That Summer in Paris* (1963); however, it is as a writer of short stories that he
is most widely admired. These he began writing in the 1920s while
working as a reporter with Hemingway on the *Toronto Star*, and in
the years since then he has had scores of them appear in such

magazines as *Maclean's*, *The New Yorker*, *Cosmopolitan*, *The Atlantic Monthly*, and *Esquire*. Fifty-seven of his best stories were published in 1959 under the title *Morley Callaghan's Stories*.

Because his style is spare and he portrays characters with unsentimental realism, Callaghan's work has often been compared with Hemingway's. But the differences between the two authors are more significant than the superficial similarities. In the existential conflicts that Hemmingway creates for his characters, their only resolution is to achieve a vestigial and mortal grace through stoical endurance or by following the warrior's code of honor. Morley Callaghan, on the other hand, creates a world that is infused with his own Roman Catholic convictions and background, a fallen world of sin and possible redemption. The critic Edmund Wilson said that Callaghan wrote parables that sometimes upset readers because their endings frustrated expectations and enforced thought. "The Snob" is that kind of story.

Roch Carrier (1937–)

The French-Canadian *conte*, as it is written by Roch Carrier, is shorter than most short stories in English and may seem to an English-speaking reader to be a cross between comic anecdote and parable. All of Carrier's fiction shows this mixture of lightheartedness and poignancy and has its roots in his childhood and adolescent experiences in the Quebec village of Sainte-Justine-de-Dorchester, where he was born. After leaving his village, Carrier was educated at the Université de Montréal and at the Sorbonne in Paris, where he took a doctoral degree in literature. He now lives in Montreal, where he is resident dramatist with the Théâtre du Nouveau Monde. His novels, which deal satirically with French-English tensions in Quebec during and after the Second World War, have all been translated into English. The first two, *La Guerre, Yes Sir!* (1968) and *Floralie, où est tu?* (1969), (or *Floralie, Where Are You?* [1970]), were adapted by Carrier for the Théâtre du Nouveau Monde.

His most recent collection of stories, *Les enfants du bon homme dans la lune*, has been published in English as *The Hockey Sweater and Other Stories* (1979). The twenty brief *contes* in the collection trace the coming-of-age experiences of the narrator (who is an apparent persona for Carrier himself) in the tiny Quebec village of Sainte-Justine, close to the Maine border. In "The Sorcerer" the narrator recalls an incident which shook the villagers with its black magic and which remains with him as a moment whose significance he may, or may not, understand.

Mavis Gallant (1922–)

For thirty years Mavis Gallant has lived as an expatriate in Europe and has written of North Americans and the English undergoing the subtle shocks of a European experience. She was born in Montreal and attended schools in Canada and the United States. For a time she worked for the National Film Board and for six years was a feature writer for the Montreal *Standard*. In 1951 she left North America for Paris, where she has resided ever since. Shortly before her departure from Canada, one of her stories was accepted for publication by *The New Yorker*, and most of her stories since then have appeared first in that magazine.

Mavis Gallant has written two novels, *Green Water, Green Sky* (1959) and *A Fairly Good Time* (1970). A selection of her short fiction appears in several collections, *The Other Paris* (1956), *My Heart Is Broken* (1964), *The Pegnitz Junction* (1973), *The End of the World and Other Stories* (1974), and *From the Fifteenth District* (1979).

In Gallant's novel *A Fairly Good Time*, the central character describes the letters that she and her mother write to each other as "an uninterrupted dialogue of the deaf." Gallant's exploration of the relationship between the son and his dying father in "The End of the World" also focuses on a failure in communication and on the father's psychological deafness, a deafness that persists right to the end.

Hugh Garner (1913–1979)

Hugh Garner wrote in his autobiography, *One Damn Thing After Another* (1973), "I was descended form a long line of Yorkshire woollen merchants, drunkards on the male side and temperance fanatics on the female." In 1919 his father brought the family from England to Toronto's Cabbagetown, then a slum area, and abandoned them. During the Depression years of the 1930s, Garner left Cabbagetown to become an itinerant harvest hand, a hobo, and a door-to-door salesman. Toward the end of the Depression, in 1936 and 1937, his first articles and stories appeared in *Canadian Forum*, a political and literary magazine with socialist sympathies. In 1937, like the main character in his novel *Cabbagetown* (1950), he fought for the Loyalist cause in the Spanish Civil War, and during World War II he saw action on a corvette in the Royal Canadian Navy, a sea experience that lent authenticity to his war novel, *Storm Below* (1949).

After the war he wrote widely as a journalist and television dramatist and continued to produce a flow of novels and short story collections, among which are *Present Reckoning* (1951); *The Yellow Sweater and Other Stories* (1952); *Silence on the Shore* (1962); *Hugh Garner's Best Stories* (1963), for which he won a Governor General's Award; *Men and Women* (1966); *The Sin Sniper* (1970); *Death in Don Mills* (1975); *The Intruders* (1976); and *A Hugh Garner Omnibus* (1978).

"The Moose and the Sparrow" is a good example of Garner's craftsmanship in the classical short story tradition. Every deftly placed detail prepares the reader to accept as plausible the violent ending and the narrator's explanation of it.

Phyllis Gotlieb (1926–)

The career of Phyllis Gotlieb shows an interesting balance between the conventional and the unusual. Conventionality marks her domestic life; she still resides in Toronto, where she was born and educated; she has borne three children; and she is the wife of a university professor. She is unusual only in what she writes. She has to her credit three volumes of poems, *Who Knows Me?* (1969), *Within the Zodiac* (1964), and *Ordinary Moving* (1969). In addition, she has written three novels, *Sunburst* (1963); *Why Should I Have All the Grief?* (1969); and *O Master Caliban!* (1975), as well as many short stories.

Of course, other poets have also written fiction, but what sets Phyllis Gotlieb apart from the rest is that she specializes in *science* fiction. Her short stories have appeared not just in academically respectable journals like *Tamarack Review* and *Queen's Quarterly*, but also in such racy magazines as *Amazing, If, Fantastic,* and *Galaxy.* Her first novel, *Sunburst,* set in the twenty-first century, is about a gang of psychopathically gifted children imprisoned by the rest of society in a technological ghetto after a thermonuclear accident has turned them into Frankensteins with monstrously destructive powers. Gotlieb plays a poignant variation on that theme in "Gingerbread Boy" in the conflict between the android children and their "parents."

Jack Hodgins (1939–)

The setting for most of Jack Hodgins' stories and his two novels is his birthplace, Vancouver Island. After working his way through the University of British Columbia with part-time jobs, he settled with his wife and children near Nanaimo, B.C., where he began his career as high school teacher of English and writer of fiction. In 1979 Jack Hodgins was writer-in-residence at the University of Ottawa. Since 1968 his stories have appeared in magazines in the

United States, Canada and Australia. Two of them were chosen for the annual *Best American Short Stories*. His first book, a selection of his stories under the title *Spit Delaney's Island* (1976), was followed by two novels, *The Invention of the World* (1977) and *The Resurrection of Joseph Bourne* (1979), which won a Governor General's Award.

Hodgins has said, "I guess I'm arrogant enough to think that my island can become a sort of mythical island, too, and maybe stand for people everywhere." With the characters in "Every Day of His Life" he achieves a curious blend of the ordinary and the mythical. The conversation between Big Glad and Mr. Swingler begins on a porch at the realistic level of conventional chitchat, but it mounts to a rooftop with talk of a painting, a mountain, and hints of supernatural communion. The two characters are comically of this world, yet also surreal, larger than life.

Harold Horwood (1923–)

The family roots of Harold Horwood have clung stubbornly to Newfoundland's rocky soil for the past three centuries, and his are planted firmly there, too. Although he travels the world, he always returns to the tiny settlement at Beachy Cove, where he has lived for many years and about which he has written so lovingly in his natural science essays, *The Foxes of Beachy Cove* (1968). A former columnist with the St. John's *Evening Telegram* and, for some years, representative of Labrador in the Newfoundland legislature, Horwood has written two novels, which are set in Newfoundland and Labrador, respectively. *Tomorrow Will Be Sunday* (1966) concerns a rebellious teenager's coming of age in a tiny outport village dominated by narrow religious beliefs; *The White Eskimo* (1972) narrates the struggles of the Innuit in the Labrador fur trade of the 1930s. In addition, he has written two historical studies and a biography. *Death on the Ice* (1972), written in collaboration with Cassie Brown, traces the events of a disastrous seal hunt in 1914, in which seventy-eight sealers perished. *The Colonial Dream* (1977) is a study of Newfoundland's past, and *Bartlett: The Great Canadian Explorer* (1977) is a biography of one of Newfoundland's greatest sea captains.

In 1979 Horwood published a collection of his short stories, *Only the Gods Speak*, which includes "Some of His Best Friends." In his foreword to the book Horwood writes, "All my life I have been committed to the idea of human liberation, but liberation that does not include a measure of personal growth and fulfillment is mere deliverance into some new form of bondage." The irony of this story is that the central character's personal growth has led him into a situation from which there is no exit but death.

W. P. Kinsella (1935–)

A native of Edmonton, Alberta, W. P. Kinsella currently teaches the writing of fiction in the English Department at the University of Calgary. He has a longstanding love affair with the subject, having taken a degree in it at the University of Victoria and an M.F.A. in English at the University of Iowa, Iowa Writers' Workshop. His short stories have appeared in such Canadian and American literary magazines as *Malahat Review, Story Quarterly, Descant, Wascana Review*, and *Fiddlehead*. In 1977 he published his first book, *Dance Me Outside*, a collection of comic stories all told by the same narrator, an eighteen-year-old Indian named Silas Ermineskin, who is taking a government course to qualify as a mechanic. This book and the one that followed it, *Scars* (1978), involve Silas and his friends from the reservation in a variety of encounters with white society. Taken together, the stories offer a satirical view of whites and Indians alike.

His third book, *Shoeless Joe Jackson Comes to Iowa* (1980), shifts the focus to stories with a wide range of characters and themes. All have a comic and satiric edge, but whereas some are realistic parables, others are excursions into fantasy, and still others take the reader into both realms. In "The Grecian Urn" the narrator's deadpan blending of the ordinary and the outrageous confirms a point made by another Kinsella character in another story: "There is a very thin line between fantasy and reality."

Margaret Laurence (1926–)

One of Canada's most celebrated novelists, Margaret Laurence was born in Neepawa, Manitoba. In the years following her departure from Neepawa, first to attend university in Winnipeg, then to accompany her husband to West Africa, where he worked as a civil engineer, Margaret Laurence thought that she had said a final goodbye to the small prairie town of her birth. Her first novel, *This Side Jordan* (1960), and her first collection of short stories, *The Tomorrow Tamer* (1963), were both based on her African experience. However, absence from Canada, further prolonged by several years spent in England, made remembered scenes and characters from the prairies rise to her mind with creative urgency, and her next four novels, *The Stone Angel* (1964); *A Jest of God* (1966), winner of a Governor General's Award; *The Fire Dwellers* (1969); and *The Diviners* (1974), also winner of a Governor General's Award, are all set in the Canadian West.

Like Sinclair Ross, whose early novel, *As for Me and My House*, she deeply admires, Margaret Laurence cannot escape from the need to write about the people and places that lie at the roots of her consciousness. Her major characters are all women from the same sun-blanched community, called Manawaka in her fiction, but clearly modelled on Neepawa. What strikes the reader about these women is the utter plausibility of their struggle to rise above the social and sexual bigotry that have marred their early youth. Hagar Shipley, the formidable old woman of *The Stone Angel*, has entered the imaginative life of almost every Canadian adult who reads the literature of his own country, and Rachel Cameron, the ironic spinster in *A Jest of God*, has had blood and fibre enough as a character to survive cinematic transplantation from the Canadian prairie to New England, the locale of the 1968 film version of the novel, re-entitled *Rachel, Rachel*.

Vanessa McLeod, whose viewpoint we share in "The Loons," is the narrator for all the related stories in *A Bird in the House* (1970). Margaret Laurence, who now writes from her home in Lakefield, Ontario, says that the Manawaka experiences of Vanessa are the closest she has come to writing autobiographical fiction. Of the birds in this particular story Laurence has written, "The loons seemed to symbolize in some way the despair, the uprootedness, the loss of the land that many Indians and Métis must feel. And so, by some mysterious process which I don't claim to understand, the story gradually grew in my mind until it found its own shape and form."

Stephen Leacock (1869–1944)

At the age of six Stephen Leacock accompanied his family from England to York County, Ontario, where they settled on a farm a few miles south of Lake Simcoe, near the town of Sutton. The father soon abandoned the family, but the mother managed to send her son to Upper Canada College where, upon graduation, he won an entrance scholarship to the University of Toronto. After receiving his degree, Leacock taught at Upper Canada College, and then, following graduate study in economics and political science at the University of Chicago, received an appointment to teach at McGill University in Montreal. From 1908 until his enforced retirement in 1936, he was head of the Department of Economics and Political Science at McGill. Although he is also the author of learned works related to his profession, Leacock is most famous for his humorous writings, of which the most popular are *Literary Lapses* (1910), *Nonsense Novels* (1911), *Sunshine Sketches of a Little Town* (1912), *Arcadian Adventures of the Idle Rich* (1914), and *My Remarkable Uncle* (1942).

In one of his last essays, "The Saving Grace of Humour," Leacock says of humour that "It helps supply for us, in its degree, such reconciliation as we can find for the mystery, the sorrows, the shortcomings of the world we live in . . . of life itself." "The Mariposa Bank Mystery," with its generous application of humour's healing balm, helps the reader forget real life's shortcomings, at least temporarily.

Alistair MacLeod

As a child, Alistair MacLeod moved with his parents from his native Alberta to live in the farming areas of Dunvegan and Inverness, Nova Scotia, where he grew up. He was educated at St. Francis Xavier University, the University of New Brunswick and Notre Dame University. At present he teaches creative writing and English literature at the University of Windsor. No narrow academic, he has worked as a logger and miner and, as his stories show, understands well the rigors endured by those workers and by the fishermen of the maritime provinces. He has been published in various literary magazines—*The Tamarack Review, The Atlantic Advocate, The Massachusetts Review*—and others. The first collection of his work appeared under the title *The Lost Salt Gift of Blood* (1976).

The title story, included in this collection, was also selected for the annual anthology *Best American Short Stories*. Few stories evoke more poignantly the sense of loss experienced by expatriate Newfoundlanders who have forsaken "the lonely gulls . . . the wind-whipped sea" for "the land of the Tastee Freeze" and an apartment on the sixteenth floor.

Susanna Moodie (1803–1885)

In 1832, just a year after she had married J. W. Dunbar Moodie, a British army officer retired on half pay, Susanna Moodie emigrated with him from England to the area near Peterborough in Upper Canada, which was then being cleared and settled by colonists. It was while her husband, a captain in the local militia, was away from their farm helping to quell the 1837 rebellion led by William Lyon Mackenzie that Mrs. Moodie began to write sketches for the Montreal magazine *The Literary Garland*. In 1852 some of these, along with other sketches and tales, were assembled into two volumes for publication in England under the title *Roughing It in the Bush*. It was followed, in 1853, by *Life in the Clearings*, an account of Mrs. Moodie's experiences in Belleville, where she and her family had moved in 1840 after her husband's appointment to the office of sheriff of Hastings County. After her husband's death in 1869, she moved to Toronto and lived there until her death in 1885.

"The Charivari" may illustrate the reason why no Canadian edition of *Roughing It in the Bush* appeared until 1871, although it had been popular in England for years. Mrs. Moodie's depiction of the hardships of life in the backwoods of upper Canada and of the uncouth customs of her neighbours created considerable local hostility. Nevertheless, the plain-speaking narrative style of "The Charivari" was a forerunner of the realism that was to dominate English Canadian fiction during much of the twentieth century.

Farley Mowat (1921–)

Farley Mowat was born in Belleville, Ontario, the son of a librarian father with wanderlust. As a result of the father's restlessness, the family was frequently on the move, living for short periods in various towns in Ontario and Saskatchewan. In 1935 young Mowat's uncle, an ornithologist, took him on a trip to the Arctic, an experience that awakened in him a protective love of nature and wildlife that was to endure into adult life and provide an important theme for many of his books. After graduating from the University of Toronto in 1949, Mowat began to submit articles and stories to magazines, and right from those early days he has earned his living as a full-time writer. Now in the prime of middle age, he has written twenty-three books that range from history and travel to ecology, fiction and autobiography. He is an internationally popular author whose work has been translated into twenty-two languages and is read in more than forty countries.

Despite his disclaimer, "I'm not a novelist," he has in fact written three novels for younger readers, *Lost in the Barrens* (1956), which won a Governor General's Award: *The Black Joke* (1962); and *The Curse of the Viking Grave* (1966). That he is also an accomplished writer of short fiction is borne out by *The Snow Walker* (1975), a much-praised collection of essays and stories about native peoples in the far north. His autobiographical books include two humorous accounts of his childhood years, *The Dog Who Wouldn't Be* (1957) and *Owls in the Family* (1961), and one serious memoir of his experiences in the Canadian Army during the Second World War, *And No Birds Sang* (1979). Among his other works are *Never Cry Wolf* (1963), *West Viking* (1965), *Sibir* (1970), and *A Whale for the Killing* (1972).

A theme that runs through much of Mowat's writing is unmistakably present in his story "The Iron Men." For aboriginal peoples the white man's technology is a dubious boon. After all, what lasting good did the Viking's crossbow bring to the Innuit? No

wonder Hekwaw cries at the end, "Take back your gift, Koonar . . .
its work here is done."

Alice Munro (1931–)

For more than twenty years Alice Munro lived in British Columbia with her husband and family, first in Vancouver and later in
Victoria, where she ran a bookstore. In 1976 she returned to western
Ontario to live with her second husband on a farm near Wingham,
the town in which she was born and grew up and which serves as the
prototype for her fictitious towns of Jubilee and West Hanratty, the
settings for many of her stories. In her student years at the University of Western Ontario she worked as a waitress, house servant,
tobacco picker and library clerk, all jobs that developed her writer's
skill in observing rural and small-town people and the ways they
impinged on each other's lives. Her stories examine these relationships from an intensely feminine point of view. Her central characters
are usually intelligent, highly sensitive, and troubled women.

Her published collections include *Dance of the Happy Shades*
(1968), which won a Governor General's Award for fiction; *Lives of
Girls and Women* (1971); *Something I've Been Meaning to Tell You*
(1974); and *Who Do You Think You Are?* (1978), which also won a
Governor General's Award. In his foreword to *Dance of the Happy
Shades*, Hugh Garner wrote, "Writers are a dime a dozen, even in
Canada, but artists are few and hard to find. Alice Munro belongs
among the real ones." "The Beggar Maid," with its painfully
truthful probing of a sexual misalliance, bears out Garner's judgment. The version printed in this anthology appeared originally in
The New Yorker and was elaborated by the author to integrate it into
the cycle of related stories, *Who Do You Think You Are?*

Yvette Naubert (1918–)

Like her fellow Quebeckers, Mavis Gallant and Mordecai Richler,
Yvette Naubert has lived in Paris, France. However, in 1979 she
returned to Canada in order to serve as writer-in-residence for the
1980 winter semester at the University of Ottawa and now gives
Ottawa as her address. Unlike either Gallant or Richler, she is a
Francophone and writes in French. So far her only book to be
translated into English is *Contes de la solitude* (1972), published in
English as *Tales of Solitude* (1978). Her other fiction includes the
novels, *La dormeuse éveillée* (1965) and *L'été de la cigale* (1968),
which won both the Prix du Cercle du Livre de France, and the Prix
du Concours Littéraire de la province de Québec. Her long serial
novel, *Les Pierrefendre*, traces the history of a French-Canadian
family through the nationalist movement in Quebec before and after

the Second World War. The first volume was published in 1972 under the title, *Prelude et fugue à tant d'échos*. She is currently working on the fifth volume, to be published in 1981.

One quality that Yvette Naubert shares with her English-speaking compatriot, Mavis Gallant, is a wry awareness of that perversity in human nature that so often bends human actions absurdly toward self-inflicted suffering. The reader may look into the mirror of Naubert's "murderer" and see the features of Everyman.

Alden Nowlan (1933–)

Alden Nowlan's childhood among the rural poor and his early apprenticeship to the craft of writing help explain his compassionate outlook on human problems and his concise, direct style in writing about them. Born near Windsor, Nova Scotia, to an impoverished family, he left school at the age of fifteen to work as a woodcutter. In 1952 he entered newspaper work, first as a reporter and editor for the Hartland, New Brunswick, *Observer*, and some years later as night news editor for the St. John *Telegraph-Journal*. Since 1968 he has been writer-in-residence at the University of New Brunswick.

Although he continues to work as a journalist, writing regular columns for the *Telegraph-Journal* and *The Atlantic Advocate*, he is known chiefly as a poet, with eleven volumes of poetry to his credit, one of which, *Bread, Wine and Salt* (1968), earned a Governor General's Award. His most recent books of poetry, *I'm a Stranger Here Myself* (1974) and *Smoked Glass* (1977), have won almost unanimous critical approval. A versatile writer, Nowlan has also published a collection of short stories, *Miracle at Indian River* (1968); a novel, *Various Persons Named Kevin O'Brien* (1973); a history, *Campobello: The Outer Island* (1975); and several plays in collaboration with Walter Learning. One of them, *Frankenstein* (1976), based on the novel by Mary Shelley, had great success on the stages of Halifax and Toronto. Some of the articles that he has written for various Canadian magazines were collected under the title *Double Exposure* (1978).

Many of his poems and stories portray the small-town and farm people of Nova Scotia and New Brunswick, whose lives have been constricted by a puritannical distrust of joy. "The Girl Who Went to Mexico" traces the brief history of one farmer who, at the story's end, is about to burst out of that iron cocoon.

Howard O'Hagan (1902–)

Howard O'Hagan's early plans were to become a lawyer. In 1919 he travelled east from his birthplace, Lethbridge, Alberta, to study law at McGill University in Montreal. After graduating in 1925 with a B.A. and LL.B., he came back west to practice his new profession. However, he soon tired of it and sought work as a guide in the Rockies—a job that he loved and at which he became an acknowledged expert. In between stints as a mountain guide he travelled widely to Australia, England, Italy, and Argentina, but in 1957 he returned to the Canadian west to stay. Today he lives in Victoria, British Columbia.

His output as a writer has been slender but highly regarded. *Tay John* (1939), his first novel, and his two collections of short stories, *Wilderness Men* (1958) and *The Woman Who Got On at Jasper Station and Other Stories* (1963), have all been reprinted; and *The School-Marm Tree*, a novel that he wrote in the 1950s but held back, was received with general praise when he published it in 1978. Most of his fiction is set in a mountain or forest wilderness and is distinguished by its power to evoke the mystery, menace and beauty of that wild terrain. In "The Bride's Crossing" the violence that usually characterizes O'Hagan's tales of "wilderness men" is muted to suit a comically romantic mood.

Mordecai Richler (1931–)

Mordecai Richler now lives in Westmount, an affluent suburb of Montreal, but when he was still an expatriate Canadian living in England he wrote, "No matter how long I live abroad, I do feel forever rooted in St. Urbain Street. That was my time, my place, and I have elected myself to get it right." The stories, essays, and novels that record his attempt "to get it right" have spread familiarity with Montreal's St. Urbain Street working-class microcosm far beyond Canada. Richler's books have been translated into French, German, Hebrew, Italian and Japanese.

When he left Sir George Williams University in Montreal without taking a degree, Richler travelled to Europe, living first in Paris, then London, where he worked as a freelance journalist and wrote scripts for radio and television, as well as for films such as *Life at the Top*. Although he was also turning out a stream of articles for Canadian, American, and British journals like *Maclean's*, *The Montrealer*, *Encounter and Spectator*, he still found time to work at his major craft, fiction. During the expatriate years he wrote a succession of novels, *The Acrobats* (1954), *Son of a Smaller Hero* (1955), *A Choice of Enemies* (1957), *The Apprenticeship of Duddy Kravitz* (1959), *The Incomparable Atuk* (1963), *Cocksure* (1968), and *St. Urbain's Horseman* (1971). The last two both won Governor General's Awards, and a novel written since his return to Canada in 1972, *Joshua Then and Now* (1979), has won nearly unanimous critical approval.

The Apprenticeship of Duddy Kravitz, which established Richler's reputation as a writer, was made into a movie in 1974 and has been exhibited successfully throughout North America and Europe. Its central character, Duddy, is the child of Jewish immigrants, a ruthless young hustler who uses his keen wits with manic energy and manages to scrabble out of the St. Urbain Street ghetto toward a place in the monied sun. Benny, the central character of the story in this anthology, is also a St. Urbain Street boy of the 1940s, but at that point all similarities end.

Charles G. D. Roberts (1860–1943)

When Charles G. D. Roberts was knighted in 1935 for his literary achievements, he had become one of Canada's most celebrated writers of prose and poetry. He is the author of more than forty books, among them novels, histories, many collections of poems, and twenty-one books of stories about animals and adventures in the wilderness. He was born in Douglas, near Fredericton, New Brunswick, and educated at the University of New Brunswick. After graduation he taught at a grammar school and published his first book, *Orion and Other Poems* (1880). For the next several years he worked first as an editor in Toronto, then as a teacher of literature at King's College in Windsor, Nova Scotia. By 1894 he had published seven volumes of poetry and his first book of short stories, *The Raid from Beauséjour* (1894). From 1897 to 1907 he lived in New York, working as a magazine editor and writing books like the novel *Barbara Ludd* (1902) and his first book of animal stories, *The Kindred of the Wild* (1902). In 1911, after a period of extensive travel, he settled in England, and during the First World War he served in both the British and Canadian armies. While in England he continued to write wilderness stories, which were collected in such books as *Hoof and Claw* (1921), but in 1926 he returned to Canada and for the rest of his life pursued his literary career in Toronto.

Although Roberts considered himself primarily a poet, he is remembered today chiefly as a writer of stories about animals and outdoor adventures. Most of his other works are out of print, but *Red Fox* (1905) is still popular, as are *Seven Bears* (1947) and *The Last Barrier and Other Stories* (1958), selections of his stories published under new titles. Roberts has been criticized for romanticizing his human characters and for endowing his animals with too great an ability to reason. Whether or not that criticism applies in "The Cabin Door" the reader may judge. One thing is sure: when Sissy Bembridge pushes against that cabin door the reader will be pushing with her.

Mazo de la Roche (1879–1961)

Not even Stephen Leacock or Farley Mowat has enjoyed a wider readership at home and abroad than Mazo de la Roche. In her own lifetime more then twelve million copies of her *Jalna* novels were printed in English and in many other languages. Today, whether in English or in translation, she continues to reach a host of readers. She was born in Toronto and educated there and in Galt, Ontario. In the 1920s, while living in a rural cottage a few miles west of Toronto, she conceived the idea of writing a novel about a wealthy landed family, modelled on people who occupied the estates near her cottage but heightened to romantic scale. The novel, entitled *Jalna* (1927) after the majestic house in which her fictional Whiteoak family lived, won the ten-thousand-dollar first prize in *The Atlantic Monthly* fiction contest and launched de la Roche on a career that was to produce fifteen more *Jalna* novels and create a family saga unique in Canadian literature. It ended in 1960 with *Morning at Jalna*, published a few months before the author's death.

Not all de la Roche's fiction was about an improbable Ontario gentry. Two earlier novels, *Possession* (1923) and *Delight* (1926), were in the tradition of realism, the second one portraying the problems of an immigrant girl working in a small-town hotel. In addition to novels, de la Roche published more than forty stories in Canadian, British, and American magazines. Some of these were collected in three books, *Explorers of the Dawn* (1922), *The Sacred Bullock and Other Stories* (1939), and *A Boy in the House and Other Stories* (1952). Many of the stories attest to her sharp powers of observation and her ironic sense of life's realities.

In 1929 Mazo de la Roche travelled to Italy, where she found the inspiration for "Quartet," published in *Harper's Bazaar* the next year. Its unblinking depiction of disillusionment is reminiscent of the pitiless irony of Guy de Maupassant.

Sinclair Ross (1908–)

Between 1941 and 1974 Sinclair Ross produced four novels and a collection of short stories: *As for Me and My House* (1941), *The Well* (1950), *The Lamp at Noon and Other Stories* (1968), *Whir of God* (1970), and *Sawbones Memorial* (1974). Although not a prolific writer, Ross has been an influential one. Margaret Laurence wrote in her introduction to *The Lamp at Noon and Other Stories*, "When I first read his extraordinary and moving novel, *As for Me and My House*, at about the age of eighteen, it had an enormous impact on me, for it seemed the only completely genuine one I had ever read about my own people, my own place, my own time." At one point in that novel Ross has his central woman character describe a June day on the prairies during one of the drought years of the 1930s: "The sun through the dust looks big and red and close. Bigger, redder, closer every day. You begin to glance at it with a doomed feeling that there's no escape."

The theme of no escape has dominated the vision of Sinclair Ross as a writer. Even though he worked in a Montreal bank from 1946 until 1968 and has for several years since then been living in Malaga, Spain, nearly all his fiction goes back to his formative years on the prairies. He cannot forget the care-worn men and women whose lives depended on the whim of weather and who for five years running could not harvest a crop from the parched soil. Born on a north Saskatchewan farm himself, he grew up among homesteaders and spent his young manhood as a bank clerk in a succession of prairie towns until his transfer to Montreal.

In "A Field of Wheat" Sinclair Ross explores not merely the ancient man-versus-nature conflict, but the resulting psychological tensions between a man and a woman who must share the ordeal and whose relationship has frayed under the constant friction of a struggle that they seem doomed to lose to their awesome antagonists—the land and the weather.

Gabrielle Roy (1903–   )

Born in St. Boniface, Manitoba, and educated there and in the Normal School in Winnipeg, Gabrielle Roy taught in rural schools in the province for several years. In 1947 she married and moved to Quebec City with her husband, where she still resides. Her first novel, *Bonheur d'occasion* (1945), translated into English as *The Tin Flute* (1947), was a realistic portrayal of life in a Montreal slum. It won the Prix Femina in France and a Governor General's Award for fiction in Canada. Her other novels include *The Cashier* (1954), *The Hidden Mountain* (1962), and *Windflower* (1970). Several of her other books are collections of autobiographical short stories or fictionalized memoirs of her early experiences in Manitoba. Among them are *Where Nests the Water Hen* (1951); *Street of Riches* (1957), which won a Governor General's Award; *The Road Past Altamont* (1966); *Enchanted Summer* (1976); and *Children of My Heart* (1978), which also won a Governor General's Award.

After her first novel, which dealt with the external reality of social conditions in an urban slum, Gabrielle Roy's writings have tended to focus on internal conflicts, on an individual's attempts to make real contact with other human beings or on his introspective search for some crucial truth to give his life significance. Although the young

teacher in "The Dead Child" fears that "human efforts are all
ultimately destined to a sort of failure," she and her class decide to
keep watch over the child's body, and in that otherwise futile ritual
of protection they experience communion.

Duncan Campbell Scott (1862–1947)

The short stories of Duncan Campbell Scott, deceptively simple
and sometimes starkly ironic, exemplify a realism that is typical of
Canadian fiction in the twentieth century. Scott was born in Ottawa,
Ontario, and was educated there and at Stanstead College, Quebec.
In 1879 he entered the federal government's Indian branch and in
1923 was appointed deputy superintendent of Indian affairs, a post
he held until his retirement in 1932. In 1887 Scott began to send his
stories to the United States to be published in *Scribner's Magazine*, and
in 1893 he published in Ottawa his first book of poems, *The Magic
House and Other Poems*. Before his death in 1947 he wrote six
books of poetry and three of short stories. His collected poetic
output, *The Poems of Duncan Campbell Scott*, appeared in 1926,
followed by one final collection, *The Circle of Affection* (1947). His
two best-known books of short stories are *In the Village of Viger*
(1896), and *The Witching of Elspie* (1923).

Many of Scott's narratives, both in prose and poetry, are about
Indians, halfbreeds, and white adventurers in the northland, a part of
Canada he came to know well during his journeys as an Indian
affairs official. Although the action of "Labrie's Wife" is set in the
historic past, the character and plight of the woman, seen only
through the fur trader's eyes, are common in much recent fiction
with a contemporary setting. Intelligent, strong-willed, defiant, she
must endure three masculine shortcomings distributed among three
different men: obtuseness, brutality, and romanticism.

W. D. Valgardson (1939–   )

Like many writers today, W. D. Valgardson lists teaching as his
bread-and-butter occupation. At present he teaches in the English
department at the University of Victoria, but he spent his childhood
and youth in Gimli, Manitoba, and in Winnipeg, where he attended
the University of Manitoba, taking a B.A. degree in 1961 and a
B.Ed. in 1966. Before moving to Victoria, B.C., he taught in
several high schools in his native province and at Cottey College in
Nevada.

W. D. Valgardson has contributed articles and poems to a variety
of magazines and journals and has written one novel, *Gentle Sinners*
(1980). But he is best known for his short stories, which have appeared

in *The Journal of Canadian Fiction, Tamarack Review, Dalhousie Review,* and *Queen's Quarterly* and have been collected in three volumes: *Bloodflowers* (1973), *God Is Not a Fish Inspector* (1975), and *Red Dust* (1978). "Bloodflowers," the title story for his first book, was chosen for inclusion in the 1971 edition of *Best American Short Stories*. Typical of Valgardson's work, this story portrays the responses of a central character who has become entrapped in conditions of physical and psychological isolation. The secondary characters and the setting, only suggestive at the outset of events, take on ever more ominous symbolic meaning as the story moves toward the climactic final image.

ABOUT THE EDITOR

JOHN STEVENS is a professor of English at the Faculty of Education, University of Toronto. He has written numerous articles on literature and the teaching of English and has edited or co-edited anthologies that are widely used in high schools and colleges across Canada. Among them are *Man and His World*, *In Search of Ourselves*, *Ten Canadian Short Plays*, *The Urban Experience*, *Canadian Stories of Action and Adventure*, and *Modern Canadian Stories*.

SEAL BOOKS

Offers you a list of outstanding fiction, non-fiction, and classics of Canadian literature in paperback by Canadian authors, available at all good bookstores throughout Canada.

The Mark of Canadian Bestsellers